A MIDNIGHT KISS
TO SEAL THE DEAL

SOPHIE PEMBROKE

HER TEXAS
NEW YEAR'S WISH

MICHELLE MAJOR

MILLS & BOON

First Published in Great Britain 2020
by Mills & Boon, an imprint of HarperCollinsPublishers,
1 London Bridge Street, London, SE1 9GF

A Midnight Kiss to Seal the Deal © 2020 Sophie Pembroke
Her Texas New Year's Wish © 2020 Harlequin Books S.A.

Special thanks and acknowledgement are given to Michelle Major for her contribution to the *The Fortunes of Texas: The Hotel Fortune* series.

ISBN:-978-0-263-29893-2

0121

MIX
Paper from
responsible sources
FSC® C007454

This book is produced from independently certified FSC™ paper to ensure responsible forest management.

For more information visit: www.harpercollins.co.uk/green

Printed and bound in Spain
by CPI, Barcelona

A MIDNIGHT KISS TO SEAL THE DEAL

SOPHIE PEMBROKE

To all the New Year's Resolution makers out there

Sophie Pembroke has been dreaming, reading and writing romance ever since she read her first Mills & Boon as part of her English Literature degree at Lancaster University, so getting to write romantic fiction for a living really is a dream come true! Born in Abu Dhabi, Sophie grew up in Wales and now lives in a little Hertfordshire market town with her scientist husband, her incredibly imaginative and creative daughter and her adventurous, adorable little boy. In Sophie's world, happy *is* for ever after, everything stops for tea and there's always time for one more page…

Michelle Major grew up in Ohio but dreamed of living in the mountains. Soon after graduating with a degree in journalism, she pointed her car west and settled in Colorado. Her life and house are filled with one great husband, two beautiful kids, a few furry pets and several well-behaved reptiles. She's grateful to have found her passion writing stories with happy endings. Michelle loves to hear from her readers at michellemajor.com

Discover more at millsandboon.co.uk

CHAPTER ONE

CELESTE HUNTER GRIPPED the phone in her hand a little tighter and whispered the words she'd never thought she'd say into it.

'What if I'm not good enough?'

On the other end of the line her agent, Richard, laughed. 'I don't believe it. Are you actually *nervous*?'

Celeste scowled, even though he obviously couldn't see her. 'Isn't that a perfectly natural response to appearing on television for the first time?'

'I didn't think you *had* natural responses, darling.' Richard sighed. She could just picture him shaking his head, his hand already hovering over his computer mouse as he moved on to more important things.

'I am human, you realise.'

'You're basically a walking encyclopaedia. Or history textbook, I guess.' She could hear his dismissive shrug. 'You're on a quiz show that is quite literally called the *Christmas Cracker Cranium Quiz*. I hardly think any of the questions are likely to stump you.'

'You're right.' Celeste knew she was intelligent. She'd had an excellent education and had a phenomenal memory for detail. Those were the things that had taken her as far as she'd gone in her academic career so far. She was a great historian.

That wasn't the part she was worried about.

'You're thinking about the new show,' Richard guessed, correctly.

'*Possible* new show,' she corrected him. The TV show they'd pitched for was very much still at the discussions stage, and Celeste just knew that the production company would be watching her appearance on the quiz to decide if she really had what it took to front a history show by herself. 'No counting chickens, remember?'

'Where does that saying come from, anyway?'

'Aesop,' Celeste answered absently.

'See! You know everything!' Richard yelled gleefully. 'Now stop worrying. I have to go deal with an actress with a secret lovechild with a politician. *That's* real problems.'

Celeste laughed. 'Good luck with that.'

'And you break a leg on that show, you hear me?' He paused, just for a second. 'But not literally. You know that, right? It's just a saying. Like the chickens.'

'I know that.' Poor Richard. He still hadn't quite adjusted to having an academic for a client, rather than actresses and pop stars. She'd never been entirely sure what had made him take her on in the first place—she didn't think he was, either. Curiosity, maybe. Or boredom.

Whatever, it seemed to be working out so far.

'Seriously, Celeste. Go sit in the green room with your laptop, and work on that book of yours. Not the academic treatise on whatever it was. The fun one. The popular one.'

'Two things I've never been in my life,' Celeste joked, but even she could hear the edge to it.

'That's what you're worrying about?' Richard sighed again. He was a big guy, in his late fifties, with a bushy beard that was more salt than pepper. When he sighed, his whole body moved, like a sad-faced dog. Even though she couldn't see him, just imagining it made Celeste feel a little better.

'If Tim and Fiona from the production company watch this…what if they decide I'm not enough? That I don't have…whatever it takes to be *good* at this.' That elusive X factor, she supposed.

'Have you ever *not* been good at something before?' Richard asked.

'Not really.' Apart from making friends and not boring people. Her best friend, Rachel, was the solitary exception to the rule. Even her brother, Damon, who she was pretty sure at least loved her, found her dull, she was sure. And her parents…well. They were pleased by her academic successes anyway. She hoped.

They certainly weren't pleased by any of her media successes. Apparently, she was *'dumbing down important research until all you have to say is derivative and reductive'*.

'Then have faith that you'll be good at this, too. Theo Montgomery's hosting, yeah? Follow his lead if you feel lost. He's good at charming a room, whatever the papers are saying about him at the moment.'

Celeste pulled a face. She didn't know what the papers were saying particularly, but she knew of Theo Montgomery. The sort of guy who got where he was because of his name, his face, and surface charm—but nothing underneath it. No substance.

Whereas she was nothing *but* substance.

Yeah, she really couldn't see Theo Montgomery being her new role model, whatever Richard thought.

Sighing, Celeste looked down at the Christmas jumper the wardrobe department had forced her into—worlds away from her usual, safe black outfits. Maybe that was the trick—to pretend this wasn't her here at all. She could be TV Celeste, instead of University Celeste.

Except she'd never really been very good at pretending to be something she wasn't.

Perhaps it was time to learn. If she wanted that show…

And she did. She couldn't explain why—especially not to her academic parents, who would be horrified she was contemplating something so…pedestrian. But she loved teaching history at the university, loved sharing her knowledge about her specialist area—women in classical literature and ancient history. And the idea of spreading that knowledge further, of getting people who might never have even thought about the subject before excited about those historical and mythical figures she loved, that excited her.

She just wasn't sure that she was the right person to do it.

'You're right. I'll go work on the book.' Working—whether it was researching or writing or teaching—always calmed her down. She knew what she was doing there.

It was only outside that safe world where she had all the answers that she struggled.

'Good. And, Celeste?' Richard said. 'Try to smile, yeah?'

Celeste scowled again, an automatic response to being asked to smile, honed after years of men telling her how much prettier she'd be if she did. And then she hung up, since her agent was clearly out of useful information.

She was just going to have to do this her own way. Starting with mentally preparing herself by focussing on something she *knew* she was good at. Writing her book.

And woe betide anyone who interrupted her.

Theo Montgomery was on a mission. Or a dare. A bet, perhaps. No, mission sounded better. More exciting, yes.

But also more…official. As if it gave him a reason for being there, sneaking around the green room instead of hanging out in his private dressing room as he normally would for a show like this.

And there had been a lot of shows like this. Well, not *exactly* the same—the *Christmas Cracker Cranium Quiz* was definitely a one-off. But he'd presented a lot of special occasion quiz shows, or entertainment specials. Apparently his was the face the network liked to trot out for this kind of thing.

He wasn't going to complain about that—especially right now. He knew that, after everything that had been published about him in the papers lately, he was lucky to still have the show. Even if it might be nice, every now and again, to be wanted for something other than his face, or his family name, Theo was under no illusions that the combination of both were what had got him where he was—TV darling, never short of work, or a date, or someone asking for his autograph.

Or where he'd been, before this mess of a break-up with Tania that was all anyone seemed to be talking about lately.

But overall, he had what he'd always wanted. What his family wanted for him, after a fashion. And he wasn't so bloody ungrateful as to complain about it now. Not when he had a lot of viewers to bring back on side, too. Viewers who'd listened to Tania's side of the story and jumped to the wrong conclusions.

The break-up had been amicable enough, Theo had thought. They hadn't even been together all that long. But the British press had loved the whole alliterative relationship, Tania and Theo, the reality TV star and the presenter, so they'd earned a lot of column inches.

And Tania had been a lot happier to tell her side of the break-up—with embellishments—than he had.

His agent, Cerys, had made it clear they were on a mission to salvage his career now. It was hard to be the nation's sweetheart when the same nation was tutting at him and saying 'that poor girl' behind his back.

Or, as Cerys put it, *'They want to be wooed, Theo. Charm them back onto your side again. Remind them why they love you.'*

So Theo would smile, and be charming, and ask the questions and laugh at the poor jokes attempted by the semi-famous contestants, and hint at the answers when they got stuck because it was *Christmas*, and nobody really took this sort of quiz seriously, right?

And talking of the contestants, that brought him right back to his current mission.

Because this was supposed to be a 'cranium quiz,' something a little harder than the usual *Who was Christmas number one in 1989?*—'Do They Know It's Christmas?' of course—the producers had also trotted out a higher intellectual calibre of celebrity guests.

There was the astrophysicist who did all the shows about the solar system, the kids' presenter who made Shakespeare accessible for primary school children, the morning TV doctor who treated the nation's bunions and STDs, the mathematician from that other quiz show, the guitarist from that band who also had a PhD in psychology and, last of all, the rising-star historian, an academic who was starting to make a name for herself, bringing the ancient world to life in guest slots on radio show interview and history podcasts.

Everyone except the historian he'd met on things like this before, or at some party or another after an awards ceremony. He'd actually been clubbing with the kids' TV presenter, David, while the guy was still in Shakespear-ean dress. And he and the mathematician, Lucy, had even had a bit of a thing, for a few nights, a couple of years ago.

No, his mission didn't involve any of them. It was cen-tred firmly on the historian.

Celeste Hunter.

Before the show started, he was going to find her, in-troduce himself, maybe even charm her a little. Because he was pretty sure that Celeste Hunter was someone he was going to want to get to know.

He might not have met her, but that didn't mean he wasn't aware of her. He'd heard her speaking on plenty of podcasts and radio shows over the last few months, in that way that often happened in the media. Rumour had it she was lined up for her own series, soon. Once a per-son got a little bit of attention from one show, suddenly they were everywhere.

Like him.

And in this case, Theo thought it was a good thing. Celeste Hunter was *interesting*. Engaging, even, when talking about subjects that mattered to her—like ancient history.

But she wasn't just a specialist, he knew. He'd heard her talk about periods of history throughout the ages. She was a *brilliant* addition to today's quiz, and he was a genius for suggesting her to the producers. They'd joke about history, riff off some of the questions, and she'd make him look really good again for the cameras. Because, although no one would guess from his public profile, Theo liked history. He even knew a bit about it—although nowhere near as much as Celeste. He was interested though and engaged—and, knowing there was a fair smattering of historical questions in the stack for Celeste, he was most excited about that part of the show.

Theo eased his way into the green room, past an assistant carrying a tray of coffees, and smiled at the various inhabitants. There was so much festive filming going on in the building today that all the contestants had been shoved together in one of the green rooms, after hair and make-up. Luckily they all seemed in good enough spirits about it.

He greeted all the celebrities he knew, exchanging quick pleasantries and jokes, and even a hug with Lucy the mathematician.

'It's so great that you could all be here for this today,' he said, filling the words with his trademark enthusiasm. 'I really think this is going to be a "cracker" of a show.'

There were good-humoured groans at that, and he flashed them all a smile before turning to find the one person in the room he didn't know already.

She was sitting at the other end of the green room, as far away from everyone else as it was possible to get. He'd only ever heard her on the radio, but Theo had to admit his first look at Celeste Hunter didn't quite match up to his imagination.

She'd sounded so self-assured, so confident on the radio, he'd assumed she'd be older—older than him, at least. But the slender, serious woman tapping away on her laptop in the corner looked younger than him, if anything. Her dark hair was artfully waved around her face, something he assumed Sandra in Hair and Make-up was responsible for, given the way Celeste kept pushing it out of her eyes in irritation. She was wearing black jeans and heeled boots, her ankles crossed in front of her as she stretched out her long legs, the laptop resting on her knees. The jeans were paired with a sparkly festive jumper that he thought might actually light up, given the dimmed bulbs dotted around the Christmas tree design.

It was so at odds with her serious, concentrated face, it made him smile as he approached, moving into her space and waiting for her to notice him there.

It took about a minute longer than it usually would.

Finally, Celeste Hunter tapped a last key on her laptop, looked up at him, and scowled. 'Can I help you?' She didn't sound as if she wanted to help him. Maybe he shouldn't have interrupted her work.

'Hi there! I'm Theo Montgomery, the host of today's show.' He gave her his most charming smile, and hoped for the best.

'Yes.' Her gaze flicked back to her computer screen, then up to him again.

Right. 'Since you're the only contestant today I haven't met before, I thought I'd come and introduce myself.' Like a normal, friendly person.

This usually worked a lot better than this.

She stared at him. 'Okay. Do you need me to introduce myself too?'

She sounded reluctant. Theo took a seat beside her anyway. 'You're Celeste Hunter. I liked your piece on the Roman Empire in Britain on the radio last week.'

That earned him a surprised look, but a scowl soon settled back across her face, as she looked back at her screen. 'Apparently it was derivative and reductive.'

He didn't contradict her, even though he hadn't thought that at all. His opinion wouldn't matter to her, he guessed, and even on five minutes' acquaintance he was sure she wouldn't hesitate to tell him so. He had enough experience of being told that his job was meaningless or didn't qualify him to talk on any subject except charming people. He suspected Celeste would say the same about him, and he couldn't imagine that tonight's quiz was going to change that.

Shame. This was one guest he'd actually been looking forward to meeting, had lobbied to have included because he'd assumed she'd be as fascinating and engaging in real life as she was when presenting on the radio. He'd hoped he'd be able to talk to her about his own interest in history, his own studies and hopes to move more into that sphere.

Apparently not. This was why people should never meet their heroes.

Theo got to his feet, fairly sure Celeste wouldn't notice or care if he just left now. Still, the good manners his mother had ingrained in him long before his agent had insisted on them meant that he couldn't just walk away. So he smiled, and said, 'Well, I'd better go and get ready—we'll be starting filming soon. I'll see you out there. Break a leg!'

Celeste winced at his words, then nodded at him in acknowledgment, before beginning to type again.

Right, then. Clearly not a people person—which was a shame, since apparently charming people was the only thing Theo was qualified to do. Celeste Hunter was uncharmable, though, it seemed.

Which was fine. After all, once they got through filming tonight's show, he'd never have to see her again anyway.

Whistling to himself, Theo waved goodbye to the other guests and headed back to his dressing room to perform his traditional pre-show routine.

This was going to be a great show, a great night, and Celeste Hunter wasn't going to ruin that for him.

Where the hell are Damon and Rachel?

Celeste paced the corridor outside the green room, waiting for her brother and best friend to *finally* show up. She'd tried working on her manuscript to distract her from her growing nerves and her mother's voice in her head, telling her that this show was an insult to her PhD, but then Theo Montgomery had interrupted her with that charming TV-star smile, and reminded her all over again that this sort of show was *not* what she'd studied all these years to do.

God, her parents were going to be so disappointed when they found out about this. A TV series of her own, she might have just about been able to swing. Well, probably not, but she could dream... The *Christmas Cracker Cranium Quiz*? No. She'd tried mentioning it before, in rather vague terms, but the look on her mother's face had stopped her even considering going into details.

Normal parents would be excited for her. Proud, even. But then Jacob and Diana Hunter had never pretended to be normal. Never wanted to be, either.

Which was why she needed Damon and Rachel to just *get here*. They were normal people. They'd remind her that, actually, this was fun and festive and a boost to her career. The chance to show that production company that she had what it took to front her own show. It was the kind of opportunity most people would be hugely grateful for, even if she had no idea who at the network had dredged her name out of the halls of academia to take part.

She had a feeling it wouldn't happen again, not after that moment in the green room.

She'd been rude to Theo Montgomery. She hadn't *meant* to be, exactly. She just didn't deal with interruptions well. And since she'd already been freaking out a little bit about the company she was keeping in there— people her *parents* would probably recognise, and they didn't even own a television—well, she'd sort of just reacted, without thinking about it. Damon had been trying to break her of that habit for most of his life, but it never seemed to take.

She should probably apologise. Later.

First, she needed to get through the filming.

Celeste had never done anything like this before. Radio, sure, where she just had to answer a few questions she definitely knew the answers to—that was why they asked her to come on the show, because she knew about it. They were always pre-recorded, and usually she had an idea of the questions the presenter was going to ask before she even showed up, so she could prepare.

She liked being prepared.

But this…as she'd looked around the green room it had been obvious that this was a general knowledge quiz, ranging from science and maths to literature and arts, and hopefully history somewhere in between. She would be expected to know things *outside* her area of expertise.

The exact opposite of what she'd been training for her whole life.

'You have to specialise, Celeste,' her parents had been telling her, ever since she was in her teens. *'If you don't know exactly what matters to you, then you won't matter at all. Generalists never get anywhere. You need to find a niche, squat in it, and defend it with your life.'*

Her parents were academics. She'd wanted to be an academic. Of course, she'd listened to them.

Her brother, Damon, meanwhile, had rebelled, gone completely the opposite way, and become the quintessential Jack of all trades. While she had settled into her niche—women in the ancient world—and only dabbled in other areas of historical research as a bit of a hobby.

A well-rounded view of world history was generally encouraged in the Hunter household. A well-rounded view of anything else was generally not.

And appearing on a Christmas quiz show that reduced human knowledge to questions about Christmas number ones was *definitely* frowned upon.

She'd swotted up on a lot of festive history, ready for the occasion, though. Just in case.

'We'll be starting soon, Ms Hunter,' a production assistant told her as she hurried past.

Celeste's heartbeat jumped, and she fumbled for her phone in her pocket. She needed to remember to switch it off. Or leave it in the green room, probably.

But first… She hit autodial for her last number and tapped her foot impatiently as it rang and rang.

'Where are you?' Celeste asked, as soon as her best friend, Rachel, answered. 'We're starting filming any minute!'

'We're here, we're here,' Rachel replied soothingly. But Celeste could hear a car door opening, which suggested they weren't, actually, inside the building or anything. 'We'll be there any second now, I promise.'

'Okay. Hurry!' She hung up. Hopefully that was Rachel getting *out* of the car, rather than into it, or they'd never make it. And Celeste wasn't at all sure she could do this without them. Actually, she wasn't sure she could do it *with* them there, either, but the odds seemed slightly better, so she was going with it.

Three endless minutes later, Damon and Rachel tumbled through the doors into the lobby, and Celeste's whole body seemed to sway with relief. Only for a moment, though, because really they were very late.

'What took you so long?' she asked, grabbing Rachel's arm and pulling her into step with her. 'Let me guess, Damon was flirting with your stepsisters?' She should have predicted that. Allowed time for it. Historically, adding extra time to any schedule to compensate for Damon flirting was never a bad idea.

'Actually, it was my fault. I had to fix a window display before we left.' Rachel sounded apologetic, and Celeste felt briefly guilty for being so cross. She was sure that Rachel's stepmother would have been the one nagging her to fix it. For reasons Celeste only kind of understood, Rachel was reluctant to break the fragile peace that existed in her family, so of course she'd have risked being late to make her stepmother happy.

She still reckoned that Damon would have been flirting with Rachel's stepsisters in the meantime.

'Are you ready?' Damon asked, all charm and confidence and totally at ease with himself, as usual. How her little brother had got *all* the charm in the family, Celeste wasn't sure, but it did seem rather unfair. He always joked that it was because she got all the brains, but his highly successful business argued otherwise.

'Not really,' she admitted.

But it was too late. It was showtime, and there was already a production assistant hurrying down the corridor towards them ready to usher Celeste onto the set, while Damon and Rachel slipped into the audience.

'Break a leg,' Rachel whispered to her as they headed for their seats.

'Hopefully not,' Celeste muttered to herself. But she felt better for knowing that Damon and Rachel were out there anyway.

This would be fine.

CHAPTER TWO

THIS WAS HORRENDOUS.

Maybe if Theo broke some sort of minor bone he could get out of doing the rest of the show. There was bound to be someone else in the building who'd be happy to take over from him. Let *them* deal with the quiz show guest from hell. Because he was pretty sure this festive televisual outing was going to do nothing to repair his fractured reputation.

As Celeste explained—not for the first time—why the answer card he'd been given was actually inaccurate, Theo could see the producer, Derek, glaring at him from just off set. Damn. Apparently, Derek remembered exactly whose idea it had been to invite Celeste on the show in the first place. He'd been kind of hoping everyone would have forgotten about that.

The worst part was, under other circumstances, the stuff she was saying would be interesting. And she was passionate and engaged as she talked about it—far more than she had been during that awkward meeting in the green room. Theo found he genuinely wanted to know more about why the story about Prince Albert bringing Christmas trees to Britain from Germany was wrong. Just…not right now. Not in front of a studio audience that was clearly getting more uncomfortable by the second. Not when they had to finish another three rounds of this damn quiz, and the other celebrity contestants were getting restless.

Had she finished? He thought she might have done. To be honest, he'd stopped listening, and focussed instead on his inner panic about his career circling the drain.

Theo grabbed the next card from the pile and prayed that it would be about anything other than history. Thank God, children's literature. That should buy him a minute or two. He was sure there was a question in the stack somewhere about who sent the first ever Christmas card, and he had a feeling the answer was going to be wrong.

Had she been reading up about festive history, ready for tonight? She must have been.

'*Move it along, Theo,*' the impatient voice came in his ear, and he tried to focus on the words on the card.

'In your teams now, can you name all eight of the reindeer that feature in the classic Christmas story, *The Night Before Christmas*?' That should be safe enough, right? For starters, Celeste wasn't a team captain. David would have to give the answer to this one. And then it was the end of the round, and Theo was pretty sure they would call a break after that. They'd been at this for hours longer than they should have been already.

David buzzed and gave the correct answer, while Celeste sat silent beside him. Had she even weighed in on that question? Theo didn't think so. Obviously, she didn't know *absolutely* everything, then. That was kind of reassuring.

A break was called, and Theo jumped out from behind the presenter's desk, desperate to move. He'd never been good at staying still, one of the reasons he'd rejected any kind of office job as a career option. He needed variety, and the ability to wander about and chat to people.

He veered left, away from the production team, though, when he realised they were in a serious-looking huddle, presumably discussing this disaster of a show. The rest of the contestants similarly had gathered around the red team's side, leaving Celeste sitting alone behind her team's desk.

Theo sighed. This kind of was his fault. He'd suggested bringing her in when, clearly, this wasn't a good fit for her. She must be hating every minute.

He'd never been any good at letting a situation fester—not at work, anyway—so he moved towards her, ignoring the part of his brain that told him that, on past evidence, this was a stupid idea. She looked up as he approached, and Theo could see the resignation settle on her face.

'Hey, how are you doing? Do you need more water?' The jug in front of her was full, and Celeste just gave it a pointed look before returning her gaze to meet his, with a slight smile.

It was a disturbingly direct gaze, and Theo shifted uncomfortably under it. There was none of the charmed expression and delightedness he usually tried to inspire in people in that smile.

Celeste Hunter's eyes said, *I am here, you are here, why is this?* And nothing more.

Theo bit the inside of his cheek to stop himself automatically confessing all the reasons for his existence and—more pertinently—her presence on his quiz show.

'Did you need something?' Celeste asked, eventually, having obviously concluded that he was too stupid to continue this conversation on his own after his ridiculous water statement.

'I just wanted to see how…how you thought this was going.' Over Celeste's shoulder, he could see the production team watching him. He was pretty sure the other contestants would be doing the same behind him. All waiting to see if she was about to tear him to shreds again.

'I think your question team need to be a little more thorough in their research,' she said, folding her hands neatly on the table in front of her. 'But otherwise, fine.'

Fine. She thought this was fine. 'Have you ever actually seen a TV quiz show?' The words were out of his mouth before he could stop them, and he heard an audible gasp from Lucy the mathematician.

Celeste's expression didn't change. Her hands didn't move. She was completely and utterly still and in control.

'Of course, I have. Well, once or twice. Maybe just once, start to finish. They weren't exactly required viewing for my PhD. But I did my research and watched *you* on some of those shows. Clips of you anyway.' She tilted her head to study him. 'Your face is less shiny on TV.'

His face was less shiny when he wasn't so stressed.

'Why did you agree to do this show?' he asked desperately. He couldn't be the only one to blame here, right? Yes, he'd suggested she take part. But *she'd* agreed.

'I wanted to…' For the first time, she flinched, and looked away. 'My agent thought it was a good idea. He said it would build my profile.'

Of course. Even if Celeste clearly had no showbiz instincts, her agent would. He wondered if the poor guy was sitting out there watching, seeing all his dreams of discovering the next big docu-star going up in the smoke coming out of Celeste's ears as she argued with the answer card.

Come to that, he hoped his own agent wasn't out there tonight. She hadn't said she'd be coming, had she? He'd rather delay the inevitable tongue-lashing until after the thing had been aired.

He glanced out towards the audience and frowned. Was it less full out there than it had been before? He turned to the door and saw a queue of people leaving the studio. Surely it hadn't been that bad?

'Hang on a minute,' he said to Celeste, and crossed the set in a few long steps, collaring a young production assistant called Amy, who coloured prettily when he asked what was going on.

'They're needed in another studio,' she replied.

'There's another show *stealing* my audience?' He tried to sound outraged, but it came out rather more petulant, he thought. Damn, he was tired.

Amy glanced towards where Celeste was now disagreeing with David, her team captain, about something. 'To be honest, I'm pretty sure they all went willingly.'

Theo sighed as the studio doors closed and the call went up to resume filming. 'I don't blame them. Come on, let's get this over with.'

Oh, that had been horrible. Whose idea had this been anyway? Why on earth had she ever thought that she could do a show like this anyway? She wasn't built for it. She couldn't smile prettily or charm people as Theo could. She could educate them, correct them. But make them like her? No.

She was never going to get her TV show after this. But what else was she supposed to do? This was who she was.

Okay, maybe she hadn't needed to get into that argument with Theo about who sent the first Christmas card. And she probably shouldn't have told him his face was shiny; TV guys were sensitive about that sort of thing, right? But in truth, she'd been flustered. And nervous. And lots of other things she wasn't used to being.

In her confined, academic world, she was in control. She could be calm, collected and sure, safe in her knowledge and her education. Out here in the showbiz world… not so much.

There had just been so much she *didn't* know. Oh, not so much the specialist stuff, where the questions had clearly been put in to cater to individual contestants' knowledge base. She didn't care about them; they weren't her speciality, why should she know the answers?

It was the general, everyday Christmas knowledge that got to her. Like the quick-fire round at the end, all about silly Christmas traditions that everyone was clamouring to answer because they were so easy.

She'd hardly known any of them. And the ones she did, she'd only learned from watching TV with Rachel.

Her family had their own, unique traditions, she supposed. Just another way that they weren't like everyone else. Her parents had always implied it made them superior, in some way. But right now, Celeste wasn't so sure.

The other contestants had all left by now—she'd heard them talking about going to a bar together afterwards, but she hadn't been invited. Not that she'd have gone if she had. The crew were clearing up and the audience filing out—a lot fewer of them than there had been, Celeste admitted. The filming had gone on much longer than planned.

She supposed that was probably her fault.

No, not just her fault. Theo Montgomery's fault, too. He was the one who had kept arguing back at her, who couldn't accept that she was *right*. She knew history. It was the one thing she *did* know. So why wouldn't he let her tell him he was wrong?

Maybe he was just one of those men who had to be right all the time. Like her father.

There was no sign of Damon and Rachel in the thinning audience so, figuring that the coast was probably clear by now, Celeste headed back to the green room to gather her things, changed out of the miserably sparkly light-up Christmas jumper and handed it back to the wardrobe people. Then, resigned to chalking the whole TV thing up to experience and never trying it again, she headed out to find her missing brother and best friend.

The first half of that proved to be easier than she'd expected: Damon was waiting for her in the corridor outside the green room. Celeste tried not to show how relieved she felt to see a friendly face.

She and Damon might be as different as siblings could be, but he *knew* her. Understood her, at least more than most people.

Celeste didn't have many people in her life who mattered to her, but Damon and Rachel were the heart of them.

She showed her love by scowling at her brother and stomping towards him.

'Where on earth did you go? And where's Rachel?'

Damon's easy smile made her feel a little less stressed, at least. 'We got dragged in to film this New Year party show. They didn't have enough partygoers because of some issue on the Tube, and your filming had already gone on longer than it was supposed to anyway.' Of course they had. Because wherever Damon went, he always found the coolest room to be in, the best party to attend. And it was never the same one that Celeste was in.

Celeste rolled her eyes as she pushed past him to continue stomping down the corridor and decided to focus on the second part of his statement. Yes, the filming had run long. But it wasn't *her* fault. 'Only because *that man* kept getting things wrong.'

She didn't need to look back to know that Damon was laughing at her. Silently, but still laughing. 'In fairness, Theo Montgomery was only reading out the answers on the cards.'

'Because he's not bright enough to actually know anything himself,' Celeste shot back over her shoulder. Then she winced and felt the colour flooding to her cheeks as she saw the man emerging from the room behind Damon into the corridor.

Theo Montgomery, of course. And from his raised eyebrows, he'd heard everything Celeste said.

She hadn't meant it, not really. She was just off kilter, and that made her defensive. Damon knew that, because he knew her. Theo didn't.

Damon stepped towards him, hand out for Theo to shake, which he did. Because he was a nice guy, like her brother, who knew how to be polite and charming in a way Celeste was never going to manage.

'Mr Montgomery. I'm Damon Hunter, Celeste's brother—we met earlier? I just wanted to take this opportunity to apologise for my sister.'

Great. Rub it in. Yes, I'm rubbish with people and you're not.

Why did she like her brother, again?

'No need,' Theo said, just as jovially. 'Trust me, I've heard worse. You stayed for the whole filming?' He sounded amazed at the prospect. Celeste didn't blame him.

Damon shook his head. 'No, I just follow my sister around to make the necessary apologies. And now that's done, I'm heading home.'

Wait. They couldn't go home. Because they were still

missing someone. Celeste might not have the interpersonal skills of her brother, but at least she kept track of her best friend. The people that mattered to her, Celeste understood and cared for.

Everyone else…not so much.

'Where's Rachel?' Celeste asked again, ignoring Theo. 'I said we'd give her a lift home.'

'She, uh…she left early,' Damon said.

Okay, that was a lie. If her brother knew her, she knew him too, and she knew when he was lying. Besides, he sounded guilty as hell.

Celeste narrowed her eyes. 'What did you do?'

'What makes you think I did anything?' He turned to Theo. 'Does it make you feel any better that she treats *everyone* this way?' he asked, as if she weren't there at all.

'A little,' Theo admitted. Celeste continued ignoring him.

'You always do something,' she said to Damon, instead. 'Let me guess, you were flirting with some other woman at the bar and leaving her all on her own?'

'I can promise you that absolutely was not the case. I was attentive, friendly, we even danced together.'

'Rachel *danced*?' Well, that was a red flag if anything was. 'I have never once, in ten full years, seen my best friend dance. There is something else going on here, and you are going to tell me all about it on the way home. Come on, let's get to the car.' Then, suddenly remembering his existence, she turned to Theo. 'Thank you for having me on your show, Mr Montgomery. I'm very sorry that the question team screwed up so many of your answer cards.' Okay, it probably wasn't exactly what the etiquette guides would recommend, but she'd made an effort. That counted for something, right?

'Once again, apologies for my sister's attempt at an apology,' she heard Damon saying as she walked away.

She was out of earshot before Theo replied, which she decided was probably for the best.

'Did you skip the year at school where everyone else learned how to make friends?' Damon asked as Celeste settled into the heated front seat of his overly fancy car.

'Actually, yes.' Her parents had insisted that she be put up a year, since her birthday was so early in the year anyway, and she'd already known everything they'd be teaching her in reception. Until recently, that had always been a point of pride for her.

Suddenly, she wasn't quite so sure it should be.

Damon rolled his eyes and started the engine. 'Right, of course you did. Well, maybe it's time for some sort of catch-up lesson. Starting with, if you want to make friends you have to actually let people in, rather than automatically pushing them away.'

'I don't know what you're talking about.' She crossed her arms over her chest, happy to be back in her own plain black V-neck sweater again. Sparkly festive-wear was really not her thing.

'Did Theo Montgomery try to be nice to you?' Damon asked patiently.

'Maybe.' She supposed that was what he'd been doing when he'd interrupted her in the green room. At the time, she'd only registered that he'd disturbed her work and heightened her nervousness, not why he'd been doing it.

'Was he, in fact, friendly?' Damon pushed. 'Because he seemed like a friendly guy to me.'

'I suppose.' Celeste scowled out of the car window. 'What does it matter now? I never have to see the guy again.'

Damon sighed. 'Call it a lesson for next time. When someone is pleasant to you, try being pleasant back. You might actually make a friend. Or something more.'

'You're assuming that I want more friends,' Celeste pointed out, ignoring the pang inside her chest at the idea. Yes, maybe she sometimes wished she were better with people, as Damon was. And yes, it would be nice to meet someone. Someone special. But that wasn't how her life went. She'd accepted that long before now. 'I have too much research to do—and a whole book to write—to have time to spend with new friends. Besides, I have Rachel.'

'Yes, you do,' Damon said, his voice suddenly soft as he spoke about her best friend.

Celeste turned to study his face in the glow of the streetlights they passed. Yep, there was definitely something going on there.

'What really happened with Rachel tonight?'

'I told you.' Damon reached out and pressed the button to turn on the radio, and a Christmas number one from before she was born filled the car. 'Nothing happened.'

He was lying. But then, so was she.

So Celeste let it go. For now.

Four days later, Theo woke up too early on Saturday morning to his phone buzzing. And buzzing. And buzzing, until it buzzed its way off the bedside table and crashed onto the floor.

He lay back, buried in the pillow, listening to it vibrate against the hardwood floor of his London flat, and weighed up the merits of ignoring it against answering it.

On the one hand, his phone lighting up the moment his do-not-disturb ended at—he squinted at the clock—sixthirty in the morning had never yet turned out to mean anything good. On the other, he wasn't going to get any more sleep with this racket going on, and his downstairs neighbours would be banging on the ceiling soon if he didn't stop it. His apartment building might be in one of the most expensive areas of London, and security was excellent, but someone had definitely skimped on the soundproofing.

The phone stopped. Theo held his breath.

Buzz.

He sighed as the device began its journey across the floor again, powered only by its own vibrations. Then he swung his legs out of bed, swooped down and picked it up.

'Hello?' He suspected that there were a hundred notifications waiting for him, from the way it had been behaving, but right now the immediate call was his priority. Especially as the caller ID read Lord And Master, after the caller had nabbed his phone in the pub one night and changed it. He really should change that back some time.

'Where the hell have you been?' Cerys, his long-term agent, snapped the moment he answered.

'Sleeping. Like normal people. It's the weekend, Cerys.' He forced a loud yawn, just to prove the point.

'Theo, you forget that I know you're not actually the lazy, artless aristocrat you pretend to be. So quit acting with me and pay attention.'

Damn. With anyone else he would have got away with that. People saw what they expected to see, in Theo's experience. And when they looked at him they saw someone who had all the advantages of life, all the education, money, looks and privilege it was possible to have, and used it to entertain people on telly on a Saturday night. So they expected him to be equally frivolous with his brain, his time, his money, his life.

In a lot of ways, they weren't wrong.

In others…well. Theo hoped he'd prove them at least premature in their judgement, eventually.

But not Cerys. Cerys knew exactly who he was, what his ambitions were and how damn hard he worked to get there. Which meant there was no fooling Cerys.

And since he was already in her bad books for the whole Tania mess, he'd better play nice.

'What's happened?' he asked, sitting up a little straighter, and reaching for the tablet on his bedside table. Despite being in silent mode, it was managing to convey a sense of dramatic urgency through constantly flashing notifications from every social media or news site he'd ever signed up to.

'Did you watch the show when it aired last night?' Cerys asked, sounding calmer, at least.

'The *Christmas Cracker Cranium Quiz*?' Theo enunciated carefully; that name was a total tongue-twister, one he almost suspected the producers of coming up with as punishment for him for something, as he'd had to say it repeatedly through the show. Maybe one of them was friends with Tania. That would explain a lot.

'I don't know, Theo, did you spend twenty minutes mansplaining festive history to an actual *historian* on any other show this week?' Cerys snapped.

'What?' That wasn't what had happened. Was it? Theo ran through the filming again in his head. Celeste had argued with all of the history questions, of course, but that was just a small segment of the show. And he'd just explained what he'd had written on the answer cards…

Or *mansplained*. Apparently.

'I didn't—' he started, searching for a defence, but Cerys cut him off before he had time to find one anyway.

'I've seen the show, genius. Whatever you think happened isn't what the great British public watched last night, and that's all that really matters. *As you already know!*'

Theo winced. 'I need to watch it.'

'Yes. And while you're watching it, you need to read what everyone else who watched it is saying about it. About you.'

'I'm not going to like that part at all, am I?'

'Not even a little bit.' Cerys was a great agent, but she didn't believe in all that 'babying the client along' nonsense. They'd known each other too long anyway, Theo reasoned. If she suddenly started being nice to him, he'd know his career was over. 'You thought the Tania stuff was bad? This is worse. That was just you being an arsehole over a personal break-up—'

'I told you, it was amicable!' he interrupted.

Cerys ignored him. 'This is you being a patronising, superior arse on prime-time television.'

He hadn't been. Had he?

Theo shook his head. Cerys was right: it didn't matter what had actually happened. It mattered what the viewers *thought* had happened. He'd definitely learned that since the split with Tania.

Since Cerys was still being blunt and shouting at him, there must be a way out of this mess.

Travel back in time and not suggest Celeste Hunter as a guest on the quiz? Or just erase all knowledge of Celeste Hunter from my brain?

Hopefully a more practical way than anything he could come up with right now.

'Okay. I'll watch the show. I'll read the comments. And then what do I do?' he asked plaintively.

Cerys paused. Oh, that wasn't a good sign. Not at all.

'Cerys?'

'Shh. I'm thinking.'

Theo sat in anxious silence, willing his own brain to give him the answers. But then, he'd never been employed for his brain, had he? And even if he had, this kind of problem required the sort of strategic thinking that he'd never been good at.

That was why he'd hired Cerys.

As the silence stretched on Theo allowed himself to glance at the notifications on his tablet, taking in just the first lines of the many, many comments about him as they filled the screen.

Nation's sweetheart or nation's misogynist?

God, typical man. Has to be right about everything.

Privilege on show.

Well, of course he went to Eton, didn't he? So he thinks he knows everything.

It wasn't worth pointing out that he'd actually gone to Winchester, Theo knew. He put the tablet aside, although he was itching to read more—and to watch the actual show. Because as far as he remembered, he *hadn't* pretended to know better than Celeste. Because he didn't. Obviously. At least, not when it came to history.

He'd just had to give her the actual answer that was written on the card, as the director had been telling him to through his earpiece.

Had something happened in the editing room to make him appear a total arse? Or had he been more arsey in the first place than he'd ever realised? He wouldn't know until he watched it back.

God, he hated watching himself on television.

'Okay, here's what we're going to do,' Cerys said suddenly, and he tuned back into the phone call. 'We need to fix this—and quickly. Your reputation was battered enough before now; this really won't have helped. I don't think the Powers That Be will be planning on making any panicked changes before New Year, but we don't want to take that chance.'

'You mean, before I present the *New Year's Eve Spectacular*.' Live, in Central London, the biggest event of his career so far. The last thing he needed was protestors showing up to shout insults up at him or throw tomatoes or whatever. Or even just fewer people tuning in than normal to watch it in the first place, because he was presenting.

Or the Powers That Be deciding not to take the risk and instructing him to come down with a strategic case of laryngitis before December the thirty-first, so someone else could take his place.

Television was a precarious career, he'd always known that. But until now, he'd never realised quite how easy it was to slip and tumble down the slope from the top.

Cerys had always assumed it would be a sex scandal that would bring him down. So far, he was in trouble for *not* wanting to have sex with Tania any more, and for arguing about history. She must be so disappointed.

'Exactly,' was all she said. 'We need to fix this before anyone starts talking about making any changes. So right now, I'm going to make some phone calls, and get a number for you. While I'm doing that, you watch the show.'

'And then?'

'Then I'm going to call you back, give you that phone

number, and you are going to follow my instructions *to the letter*. Okay?'

'Yes, ma'am,' Theo answered. Because although he already knew he wasn't going to like whatever Cerys's plan was, he liked the idea of losing his career even less.

CHAPTER THREE

Have you watched this yet? Call me when you have.

THE INNOCUOUS EMAIL had come through from her agent, Richard, that morning, but Celeste had been buried deep in the research for her next chapter, so had put it off until she was ready for her scheduled mid-morning break. Now, as the final credits on the *Christmas Cracker Cranium Quiz* rolled, she smiled to herself.

That hadn't actually been nearly as bad as she'd expected. She'd avoided watching the show when it had aired the night before, partly because she was nervous about how it would turn out, and partly because she'd been having dinner with her parents and some of their department colleagues, and there was no television in the Hunter family home.

She clearly had a friend in the editing suite. Celeste remembered the actual filming as being more confrontational on her side—the way she always got when she was nervous or feeling intimidated. But in the final cut, Theo came across as far more superior, more patronising, than in real life.

Which, she supposed, wasn't entirely inaccurate, as he hadn't given her *any* points for all the questions she'd answered far more correctly than his bloody answer cards had.

Finishing the last gulp of her cup of tea, Celeste turned to her other breaktime indulgence—checking her social media accounts. While she didn't tend to post much, she kept up with the world outside her office through them—they were sort of her guilty pleasure. She mostly followed other historians, archaeologists, researchers and writers—as well as a few university and academic accounts, plus the odd political or news website or reporter. She'd actually had to turn off the notifications on her phone and computer, to stop herself getting distracted when she was working. And she *never* let herself check them first thing in the morning. That was a slippery slope she didn't want to fall down.

Which was why she had no idea she'd become an overnight Internet sensation until she checked her phone.

She blinked at the number of notifications showing, and tapped through to them, scrolling slowly as she took in the words.

Celeste Hunter doesn't need Theo-bloody-Montgomery mansplaining history to her.

There were screenshots, too. Oh, God, she'd become a meme.

Celeste: I have a PhD in this.

Theo: I have an answer card written by an inadequate researcher. So I must be right!

Celeste: I'm an actual professor of history.

Theo: Yeah, but I have generations of white male

*privilege on my side. Who do you think they're
going to listen to?*

There were more. So many more.

Then she remembered the second part of her agent's
email. *Call me.*

'So are we thinking the show went well?' she asked,
weakly, when Richard picked up.

'For us? Very well.' She could practically hear his
grin down the phone line. 'For Theo Montgomery, not
so much. Not that that's our problem.'

'I feel kind of bad about that,' Celeste admitted. 'The
way the show was edited… I mean, yes, I *was* right. But
he wasn't actually so patronising about it in person.'

'Nobody cares what *really* happened, Celeste. You
know that.'

'Yeah.' She'd learned, a little, over the past year. After
the first radio slot she'd done, as a favour for a friend
who'd had to drop out at the last minute, it seemed as if
she'd got her name on some sort of list. Suddenly she was
every producer's pet historian, trotted out to offer an historical perspective on current events, on school history
exams, on latest discoveries and research. No matter that
her official area of expertise was ancient history, she'd
become a knowledgeable semi-pro on the whole span of
human existence. At least it was the one thing her childhood had prepared her for.

And it had led to the talks about her own TV show,
looking at women through history—starting with
Ancient Greece.

She supposed something like this could only be good
publicity, and production companies definitely loved
good publicity. No wonder Richard was sounding so
thrilled.

'So, we need to capitalise on this,' he went on. 'We need to show that production company that your series is a sure bet. We could have it commissioned by January! Get you on display a bit more, now you've stepped out from behind the radio mic and people know what you look like.'

Celeste pulled a face at that last bit, glad that Richard couldn't see it. On display wasn't exactly her favourite place to be, she'd learned. Especially when it wasn't on her terms.

'What's your calendar like between now and the new year?' Richard asked.

She looked at the stack of research materials, liberally spotted with sticky notes, that were supposed to form the basis of her book. Not even the popular history book she was supposed to be writing to support the case for the TV show, but the *other* one. The proper, serious, academic text that would cement her career at the university—the one her parents would approve of.

The one that was going nowhere at all.

'I have some time,' she told Richard. 'Term ended yesterday, so I don't have any more lectures or seminars to give until January.'

'Great! I'll see if I can get some appearances set up for you, then. Keep in touch!'

And he was gone. Celeste sighed, and put down her phone—until she noticed the new message notification, the one notification she allowed herself, since hardly anyone ever messaged her, was flashing.

Fancy lunch? My treat. Seems like I owe you. Theo Montgomery.

Cerys had been right. He *hated* this idea.

He especially hated the part where he was sitting in

a restaurant, alone, with people staring at him, whispering behind his back. He didn't need to be able to make out the individual words to guess what they were saying. Exactly the same things as everyone on social media—and the morning TV shows, apparently—had been saying since the *Christmas Cracker Cranium Quiz* aired. Plus, all the older gossip about Tania and the break-up, probably, just for good measure.

He'd watched the show. He'd read the comments. He'd watched the show *again*.

Then Cerys had called back, given him Celeste's phone number, and told him exactly what he needed to do.

'Make it right, Theo. And quickly.'

He hadn't honestly been sure that Celeste would respond when he texted her. He should have called, probably—Cerys had told him to—but Theo remembered what had happened last time he'd interrupted Celeste, in the green room, and decided that it might go better if he allowed her to respond in her own time, rather than ambushing her with a phone call.

Perhaps it was the right move, because she *had* texted back. And she'd agreed to meet him, here, in a neutral restaurant, ten minutes ago. He checked his watch; no, fifteen now.

Celeste didn't seem like a habitually late person to Theo, but, apparently, he was wrong. That happened a lot. Just ask his parents. *They* still hadn't forgiven him for 'losing' Tania—a rich, beautiful, famous prospective daughter-in-law they would have embraced willingly, despite her 'unfortunate start' on reality TV. His parents always claimed to have incredibly high standards for their social circle, but as far as Theo could tell they mostly all came down to 'money' and 'fame'.

God, what if this debacle lost him both of those? Infamy, he knew, was not the same thing.

Maybe his father would take some comfort in the fact that he'd been right all along, and Theo really would never amount to anything worthwhile. If Celeste didn't show up for this lunch, it might be the best he was going to get.

Finally, after another five minutes, the restaurant door flew open and Celeste Hunter strode in, wrapped in an elegant white wool coat, black boots clicking on the tiled floor as she crossed towards him. Her dark hair was twisted up on the back of her head, her lips painted a bright Christmas red, and she seemed completely unaware of the way every person in the restaurant turned to look at her as she approached him.

Theo was not unaware. He could hear the whispering, the *'Isn't that her?'* that hung in the air behind her.

'I'm sorry I'm late,' she said, stripping off her coat and hanging it on the back of one of the empty chairs. Underneath it, her black jumper matched her black jeans. Her lipstick, Theo realised, was the only colour about her. 'There were all these…people waiting outside my office at the university. Apparently last night's show was a bit of a thing.'

A bit of a thing? Did she really just describe my career-crippling disaster as 'a bit of a thing'?

She had. Because, of course, that was all it was—to her. *Her* career was the university, her academic life. TV was merely a bit on the side.

Whereas it was all he had.

'Apparently so,' he said drily, although she didn't seem to pick up on the faint hint of sarcasm in his voice. 'In fact, some of the rumours online are starting to get a little outlandish. And nasty.'

She had the good grace to wince at that, at least. 'If only you'd just admitted I was right at the time, huh?'

Theo honestly couldn't tell if she was joking or not. Why was this woman so hard to read? He was *good* at people, usually—it was what had got him as far as he'd come. But this woman? He had no idea what was going on inside her head—or how she was going to react when he put Cerys's plan to her.

She might go along with it. Or she might verbally eviscerate him while pouring hot oil onto his chest on the restaurant table while the crowd cheered her on. It was hard to tell.

He was just going to have to take his chances. But he could at least improve them by softening her up first.

'Thank you for coming, despite everything.' He flashed her his best 'love me' smile, and she looked a little taken aback. Fortunately, the waiter arrived at that moment with the wine he'd ordered, and poured them both a glass.

God, he hoped she liked Viognier, or this would be off to a worse start than ever.

He held his breath as she took a sip, then started to let it out when she smiled at the waiter, only to have it catch in his chest again.

That smile, he thought, as he half choked on his own breath.

She hadn't smiled like that when they were recording the show. And she definitely hadn't smiled at him like that ever—not even when he'd done nothing beyond politely introduce himself. Yet the waiter got that smile—all bone-deep pleasure and gratitude.

He supposed it was reassuring to know that she *could* smile like that. It might make the next phase of Cerys's plan easier.

Theo took a sip of the wine to soothe his throat after the coughing fit Celeste had totally ignored. It was nice enough wine. But not worthy of that smile.

'This is delicious, thank you,' Celeste said to the waiter. 'Did you suggest it?'

The waiter—young, spotty and obviously impressionable—blushed. 'Um, actually your, uh, companion chose it.'

The smile disappeared as she turned back to Theo. 'Oh, well. It's still nice wine.'

Theo decided to let that one pass while they ordered—Celeste asking the poor waiter what most people ordered, then going with that.

'So.' Celeste folded her hands on her lap, over the napkin the anxious waiter had placed there, and looked Theo dead in the eye. 'I imagine you invited me here to apologise?'

He had, of course. That was step one of Cerys's master plan. But being asked to do so outright like that…it made him want to, well, not.

Theo lifted an eyebrow. 'You don't think there's any reason you should need to apologise to me?'

That earned him a flash of a grin. Nothing like the smile she'd given the waiter for the wine, but still. Better than anything he'd managed from her so far.

'Of course,' she said, her tone heavy with sarcasm. 'I'm so sorry that your mansplaining and patronising behaviour got you into trouble with your adoring fans.'

Theo rolled his eyes. 'Come on, I was actually there too, remember? I haven't just watched the edited footage. I know what really happened.'

She raised both eyebrows, and sat back in her chair. 'Enlighten me, then.'

He wanted to. He wanted to fight his corner, wanted

to stand up for what he felt had really happened. But he also wanted all the other people sitting in the restaurant to stop listening to their conversation.

This was never going to work. Cerys hadn't met Celeste, or she'd never have imagined for a moment that it *could* work.

But what other option did he have?

Theo took a deep breath, and started again.

'You're right. I *did* ask you here to apologise. Let's start over, shall we?'

One step at a time, that was all he had to focus on. If this went well, he might not need all the other steps of Cerys's absurd plan.

He just had to keep the conversation civil for one lunch.

How hard could that be?

Why on earth had she agreed to this lunch? Curiosity, Celeste supposed. The curse of the academic. She just couldn't help but want to know what happened next, and why.

Plus Richard had been pretty insistent, when she'd called him back to ask what to do. Apparently, being seen with Theo Montgomery again, even if she wasn't sure why he wanted to see her at all, was a Good Thing, publicity-wise.

'Keep them talking,' as Richard put it. *'Doesn't matter what they're saying, as long as they're talking about you.'*

But Celeste was pretty sure Theo *did* care what people were saying. Was it just that he was so used to being the Nice Guy he couldn't handle people thinking otherwise? Or was he concerned about the effect on his career?

Or—and this seemed the least likely—was he genuinely sorry about how things had gone down at the filming?

That last went out of the window as he asked if perhaps she should be apologising to *him*, of all things. But then he pulled himself together and she saw something she hadn't expected to see from Theo Montgomery.

Authenticity.

He immediately hid it again, behind that charming smile and smooth words, suggesting they start over. But for a second there, Celeste almost believed she saw the real human behind the TV persona.

And he looked just as baffled and annoyed about this lunch as she was.

Interesting.

She'd pegged him as a faker straight off—she'd had enough students who tried to pretend they'd done the work to know how to spot a faker at a hundred paces. Besides, wasn't that the whole point of TV? To show a faked-up version of reality? Even her own appearance on the quiz show hadn't been authentic—she'd never be caught dead in a Christmas jumper outside that studio.

Some people, she knew, had been faking so long they'd forgotten how to be real. She'd assumed Theo would be one of them.

Apparently, there was still some hope for him after all.

'I'm sorry that the research on our show wasn't up to your own standards,' Theo said, which she noticed wasn't actually a real apology on his own behalf. 'I could tell that you'd prepared well for the show, and to a level that our researchers clearly weren't expecting.' A flash of that charming smile. 'And I'm sorry that I couldn't accept your—obviously correct—answers. I hope you didn't feel that I was mansplaining to you. On the contrary, I had the producer in my ear telling me to read out the official answer—but *I* was far more interested in the answers you were giving.'

Did she believe him? Celeste wasn't sure. But then he went on, 'Is it really true that Prince Albert wasn't responsible for bringing Christmas trees to Britain?'

So, he'd been paying attention. Or he'd just watched the show again in preparation for this lunch.

'Are you questioning me now?'

He held up his hands in surrender. 'I swear to you I'm not. Is it so hard to believe that I might be interested in the answer?'

Yes. Not just because he hadn't been the other night—she could understand that, under the constraints of filming and with his producer talking in his ear, hurrying him along, he might not have had the time or mental space to care about the real answer then. But in her experience, even when she stripped away those problems, most people weren't all that interested in the real answers anyway.

The simple, familiar stories were more interesting. Prince Albert had brought the Christmas tree. Thomas Crapper invented the toilet—except he didn't. Santa Claus was designed by a popular drinks company in the thirties—also not true.

People didn't want the complicated, multi-layered truth—the same way that people didn't want to bother with her, and her difficult to understand nature. They wanted the straightforward historical anecdotes that made sense and that people nodded along with—exactly how they wanted Theo Montgomery and his bland smiles, rather than her, on their TVs every night.

Except…the people who'd posted on social media about the show *had* been interested in her answers. They were cross that Theo had cut her off before she'd fully explained them.

They hadn't said she was boring, unlike most other people outside her family. They'd been *interested*. In her. And maybe it was because it was Christmas, and lots of people were interested in Christmas, right? But if she could get them interested in that—if she could get *Theo freaking Montgomery* interested in that—maybe she could get people interested in the lives of women in the ancient world, too. Maybe she really could pull off her own show.

It had to be worth a try, right?

'Queen Charlotte, the wife of George III, put up the first one in 1800,' she said, watching to see if his eyes glazed over. They didn't. 'Where she grew up, in the duchy of Mecklenburg-Strelitz, Germany, the tradition was to decorate a single yew branch. She brought the tradition over with her in 1761, and the whole palace started getting involved in it. Then in 1800 she was planning a children's party at Windsor and decided to pot up a whole yew tree and decorate it with sweets and baubles and load it with presents. The kids were enchanted, of course, and Christmas trees became all the rage in English high society.'

Theo smiled, looking genuinely charmed at the information. 'I did not know that. Thank you.'

'You're welcome,' she replied, suddenly awkwardly aware that she was basically lecturing her lunch date on British history.

Well, it wasn't as if she had much else in the way of small talk, was it? That was always the problem with her dates, or interactions with people outside the history department. She bored them quickly. Hell, sometimes she even bored herself. She wished that she could just let things go, not feel she had to correct people all the time. But it was as if there were an itch inside her, whenever things were factually lacking. And the only way to scratch it was to present the true facts.

No wonder it had been so long since she'd had an actual date.

The rest of the meal passed pleasantly enough. The waiter brought their meals, which were fine, although Theo questioned her choice of the chicken Caesar salad in the depths of winter.

She shrugged. 'The waiter said it was their most popular dish.' She always ordered the most popular dish. She knew nothing about food, really, and, beyond it being the fuel her body needed to keep functioning, she'd never really thought about it much. So it seemed much more sensible to her to let the consensus of others decide what she should eat.

Theo obviously didn't agree. 'What if the most popular dish was something you didn't like?'

'Then I'd order the second most popular dish. Obviously.'

It was only by the time they'd reached dessert—which she'd declined in favour of coffee, as had Theo—that she got the feeling that there was more to this meal than just a simple apology.

'I have to admit, I had a secondary reason for inviting you to lunch today,' Theo said, as he toyed with the foil wrapper of the mint that came with his coffee.

Wow. Her intuition was actually correct, for once. Delayed, of course, but right. That didn't happen often. At least, not with people she didn't know. Damon and Rachel she could read in an instant—she'd been studying them both for years. She'd *learned* them, the same way she learned everything else. Strangers, not so much.

'I suspected as much,' she said.

Theo smiled. 'I imagined you would. You're an intelligent woman.'

She liked the way he said that. She shouldn't, because she was sure he was just buttering her up for the next part. But when Theo said, 'You're an intelligent woman,' she didn't hear it as an insult. He wasn't saying: 'You have brains, why can't you understand people?' Or: 'You're smart, but don't think you're smarter than me.' Or even: 'You're intelligent, why won't you just agree with me, when I'm obviously right?'

He was just saying that she was intelligent, and that it was a good thing.

She liked that.

'So? Why am I here?' Celeste asked.

Theo drew in a breath, then looked up and met her gaze with his own. She made herself hold it, look for the truth, even though she wanted to look away with every fibre of her being. She didn't look people in the eye like this, not unless she had a point she needed to hammer home and wanted to be sure they had it.

But now she was just…listening. And looking for the truth in Theo's eyes.

'Because the show that aired last night was edited to show me in a bad light. I don't know why, or by who. And I need you to believe that I didn't intend to dismiss you or disregard the points you were making about historical accuracy.'

'Why?' That was the part she didn't understand. Why did he care what *she* thought?

'Because I'm going to need your help to fix it.'

CHAPTER FOUR

CELESTE DREW BACK a little at that. 'What do you need me to do?'

'Exactly what you are doing,' Theo replied, as reassuringly as he could. 'Just being seen with me today, showing that you don't actually hate me, that will help.'

She looked around her. 'You mean, you've got someone here to photograph us together? This was all a trick to get me to pretend to like you?'

Ow. 'I was kind of hoping that if we had lunch together you would *actually* like me. Most people do, you know.'

'I'm not most people.' As if he didn't know that. 'So, where is he? The photographer, I mean? I haven't seen anyone taking photos of us. Does he have one of those long lenses?'

'I didn't hire a paparazzi with a tele-focus lens,' Theo said patiently. 'I didn't hire anybody. I didn't need to.'

Celeste's eyes narrowed. 'Explain.'

'Celeste, people have been taking photos of us on their phones since the moment you walked in. They've been talking about us, while we've been sitting here eating. There's hardly a table in this restaurant where at least one person hasn't turned to watch us, to try to listen to what we're saying.' He was used to it, after years in the TV spotlight. Normally when he dined with someone from outside the industry they found it distracting, disturbing to be watched all the time.

But Celeste hadn't noticed it at all.

'Why? Because you're so damn famous and popular?' She was glancing around now, furtively, obviously trying to catch someone with their phone out. It was kind of almost cute—if anything about Celeste Hunter could be called cute.

And she obviously didn't realise how unpopular he was right now. He supposed she didn't really follow celebrity gossip online.

'Because our faces were all over their social media feeds this morning,' he said, with a sigh. 'Because if other people are talking about us, they want to be able to talk about us, too. And if they can say something new, something their friends haven't heard yet, all the better.'

'So this morning the story was that we were mortal enemies after a stupid quiz show,' Celeste said slowly. 'And you're trying to change that narrative. Show people that actually we're friends.'

'Exactly.' He'd known she'd get it, once she got past the part where people she'd never met cared about her life. As he'd said, she was an intelligent woman.

'I probably shouldn't tip my cup of coffee into your lap for manipulating me into lunch, then, should I?' she asked sweetly.

Theo winced. 'Ideally not, no. And I didn't intend to manipulate you. I kind of thought it would be obvious.'

'Yeah, well. You might have noticed I'm not entirely up to speed on things that happen outside my field of expertise.'

It was the first admission of anything approaching a fault or weakness that she'd given, and it made Theo like her all the more.

That was the strangest part about this lunch, he realised. He was actually enjoying it. Even when they were bickering or she was threatening his lap with coffee, he was having *fun*.

Huh. He really hadn't expected that.

'So, what do you say?' he asked. 'Do you want to pretend to be my friend and help rehabilitate my reputation, so the Great British Public can stop calling me a patronising, mansplaining bastard?' Amongst all the things they'd already been saying about him before, about him being a careless, unfeeling abandoner of women.

She looked at him thoughtfully. 'You realise there's also a cohort of your defenders calling me an uppity bitch who thinks she knows better than everyone?'

'Yeah, but you *do* know better than everyone—when it comes to history anyway.'

'Not everyone. Just most people.'

'And you're not an uppity bitch. In fact, I think I might actually like you if you'll let me get to know you.' She looked surprised at that, and he laughed. 'Yeah. I wasn't expecting that, either.'

Although he *had* been—until he'd met her. When she was just a voice on the radio, he'd thought he would like to get to know her. He'd been drawn to the passion in her voice when she'd talked about subjects she cared about— that he cared about, too. So yeah, he'd wanted to get to know her. He just hadn't expected it to be under these circumstances.

'Maybe we can prove them all wrong, then,' she said slowly. 'Or at least teach them not to judge people or their motives on first appearances.'

Theo rather thought she was crediting them with too much power over social media in general, and the Great

British Public in particular. But if that was what it took
to get her to agree…

'I say we could give it a damn good go.'

Celeste looked up at him and smiled. 'Then it's a deal.'

She stood up, holding out a hand for him to shake, and
the movement jogged the table. The tablecloth caught between her and the surface, twisting as she moved, tugging it up, off balance and…

Tipping Theo's coffee right into his lap.

A gasp went up through the restaurant, and Theo heard
the click of a dozen fake camera shutters on phones.

He looked up to find Celeste with one hand over her
mouth, looking as though she was trying to stop herself
from laughing.

'At least it wasn't *my* coffee,' she said as she handed
him her napkin.

'That makes it all better,' Theo grumbled.

Apparently, making people believe they were actually
friends was going to be even harder than he'd anticipated.

It looked like Theo and Celeste were a story that wasn't
going away.

On Sunday morning, Celeste woke up to a lot of social
media notifications, and a sense of impending doom. The
doom part was easy enough to fathom—it was the first
Sunday of the month, which meant it was Hunter family
dinner day. Which was cause enough for doomy feelings in itself, but made worse by the fact that she wasn't
properly prepared for it.

It wasn't enough for her parents to get the four of them
around the dining table once a month for a nice catch-
up and a roast. Diana and Jacob Hunter had to make it a
competition. One with themes and decorations and com-

plex menus—and one that Celeste always tried hard at but seldom ever won.

She definitely wasn't going to win anything today, having spent all her prep time yesterday either having lunch with Theo or on the phone with Rachel, who'd sounded very peculiar when she'd called. Celeste might not be the best at reading people normally, but *Rachel* she understood. They'd been best friends since university and she was, as Damon put it, Celeste's social proof that she could actually manage human interaction outside the lecture theatre.

She had a strong suspicion that her brother might be behind her best friend's strange mood. Damon, unlike her, was excellent with people—all people. Often too excellent. Women, in particular, tended to fall fast and hard for him—only to be heartbroken when he let them down, however gently he tried to do it.

Rachel had known Damon for almost a decade, so Celeste had hoped she was immune. But after her disappearance from the TV studios, plus that call last night… Celeste was starting to have suspicions.

Which were definitely still on her mind as she went shopping for ingredients for an emergency starter she could whip up in a hurry in time for lunch. Salmon, perhaps. Damon hated salmon.

Queueing at the supermarket checkout, she scrolled through the notifications on her phone. Gone were the usual links to journals or news items about archaeological digs she had come to expect. Instead, there were at least four different photo angles of Theo getting covered in coffee, plus a few other shots of them just eating lunch together. Opinion seemed to be divided over whether they were arguing or having a nice time.

Both. Which she supposed was why people were so confused. It was baffling the hell out of her.

Normally, when she argued with a person, they got annoyed and left her alone. But Theo seemed to want to spend *more* time together. Which was definitely not normal.

It's only because he's trying to save face, improve his image, that sort of thing.

She needed to keep reminding herself of that. He was a faker, and he'd fake liking her for as long as it served his purpose—then drop her. In some ways, Theo was like Damon—too charming for his own good. Luckily Celeste, unlike Rachel, *was* immune to that sort of charm.

And it wasn't only Theo's career and image that stood to gain from this association, it turned out. Richard was thrilled that their continued association was only drawing more attention to her—and increasing the odds of the production company they were talking to taking a chance on her. As a cloistered academic, she knew he'd been at a bit of a loss on how to market her—especially since her love of *reading* social media didn't extend to remembering to post regularly, or even having any idea what to post. Rachel kept offering her tips. Maybe she should just hire her best friend to pretend to be her on social media. She had no doubt that people would like her better if she wasn't, well, actually her.

'Excuse me. Are you… Oh, what's your name? The one from that quiz show. The Christmas Cracker one.' The woman behind her in the queue, gripping a TV listing magazine with Theo Montgomery on the front, smiled up at Celeste.

'The *Christmas Cracker Cranium Quiz*? Yes, that was me.' Celeste waited to see if that was a good thing or a bad thing.

The woman's beaming smile grew wider. 'I thought it was you! I said to my husband—where's he gone? Fred? Honestly, men. Anyway, I said it was you!'

'And it is, actually, me,' Celeste confirmed, just in case that had got missed somehow.

'Can you sign my magazine for me?' The woman brandished a pen towards Celeste, and she took it, mostly because she was at a loss as to what else to do with it. As she signed her name just to the left of Theo's sharp cheekbone, the woman kept talking. 'I love Theo Montgomery as much as anybody, and I never really believed all that rubbish his ex put about, but, I have to say, it was quite nice to see him put in his place for once! He always has all the answers, doesn't he? Such a charmer. My Fred says he's *too* smooth, but, really, what would we watch if he wasn't on? He hosts all the best shows these days, doesn't he?'

'I suppose he does.' Celeste handed the signed magazine back.

'And he *is* lovely, don't you think?' the woman said wistfully.

'I'm sure I wouldn't know.' Celeste turned away, relieved to see it was her turn at the checkout at last.

All this thinking about Theo Montgomery couldn't possibly be good for her.

She managed to forget about him, more or less, over lunch with the family.

The Hunter Family Monthly Lunch was, as most things were in her family, deeply competitive. Each month, she, her mother and her father were assigned a course of the meal to prepare and serve. Whoever was in charge of starters was also in charge of decorating the dining room in a suitable historical theme. Damon was only ever in charge of bringing the wine, because he refused to compete.

The aim of the dinner was to produce the most interesting dish. Not necessarily the most delicious—Celeste had once won almost a full score from everyone for an authentic Greek dish with a great historical backstory that had unfortunately tasted like rotten fish. Mostly because it almost *was* rotten fish.

On that basis, she knew she'd have failed today. The only saving grace her salmon terrine possessed was that it would annoy her brother, and her decorations were decidedly sub-par.

And sadly, none of that distracted her mother from more important matters at hand.

'I saw some of that festive TV show you were associated with, Celeste,' Diana said, her frown disapproving over the fluttering of her authentic replica regency fan, to match her dress. The Hunters always believed in dressing for dinner, even if they weren't always from the same era.

'Uh…really? Where did you see that?' Stalling for time, Celeste reached across the table for the wine bottle and refilled her mother's glass, as well as her own. At least her father was out of the room, fetching his main course from the kitchen. She'd hoped against hope that her parents' TV ban would mean they'd have missed the whole debacle, but apparently she wasn't that lucky.

'A colleague sent me a web link to a clip from it.' Diana's fan fluttered a little faster. Across the table, a wicked smile spread over Damon's face.

Celeste knew exactly what he was thinking. Discovering that Celeste was taking part in a lowbrow, populist TV quiz was one thing. Being told so by a colleague was far worse, because that meant that Other People knew. People that mattered to their parents.

She wondered who had sent it to them. Someone who thought it was a bit of festive fun? Or a colleague with a grudge? It didn't really matter which, she supposed. The Professors Hunter didn't *do* fun—at least, not when it came to things that mattered, like history or archaeology, their respective specialist subjects.

'Um, which part?' Celeste asked, desperately hoping that the clip would be one of the tamer ones she'd seen around the Internet. Maybe the introductions, or something.

'You, arguing with some gameshow host about how Christmas trees came to be a British tradition.'

So, not a nice tame bit. That was the part that had the Internet most riled up. Of course.

Damon was apparently unable to hold his laughter in a moment longer.

'That link is everywhere, Mum,' he said as Celeste glared at him. 'Have you seen what they're saying about it on Twitter?' He leaned across the table towards Celeste. 'Did you *really* have a make-up lunch with Theo yesterday? The whole of social media is aflame, wondering what's going on between you two.'

Celeste felt the heat flood to her cheeks as she remembered the lunch—and how it had ended. Then she remembered why she was cross with Damon in the first place, and turned the tables.

'Never mind my lunch. Did you *really* take Rachel for afternoon tea at the Ritz?'

'It was for work!' Damon protested, far too quickly for Celeste's liking. 'She's helping out on my latest project.'

'Isn't Rachel an English graduate?' Diana asked. 'How is she going to help with your...what was it? Cinema project?'

'The cinema project was two years ago,' Damon said. 'This is a new one.'

Of course, it was. It was always a new project with Damon. Always the next shiny thing.

Celeste didn't want him treating Rachel that way. And while she was pretty sure he wouldn't, pretty sure wasn't enough when it came to her best friend. 'Just…be careful with Rachel, please? I'd hate for you to, well, give her any ideas.'

'It's work,' he repeated, his voice flat. 'That's all.'

Work was good. Rachel had been stuck in her job, working for her stepmother, for too long. Doing something new and fun with Damon could be good for her. As long as it really was just work.

Rachel didn't date much, and, after a nasty experience with one of her stepsisters' friends the summer before, Celeste couldn't see her jumping into anything new. But it *was* Damon. And Rachel had always been just a little bit misty-eyed when it came to Celeste's brother.

She had to warn him about that. He'd be careful if he thought he might hurt her. He wasn't a bad guy, just… not the settling-down type. With anything.

'Good,' Celeste said, looking away as she spilled her best friend's secrets for her own good. 'Because, to be honest, I think she's always had a bit of a crush on you. I'd hate for you to lead her on, even accidentally.' Urgh, she hated doing this. 'Just don't break her heart, okay? I know what you're like.'

The double doors to the dining room swung open and their father appeared, the white of his Roman-style toga backlit by the hallway bulbs against the dim candlelight on the table. In his arms was a large platter with what looked like an entire pig on it, apple in mouth and all, surrounded by jellies with apple slices and spices inside.

'Dinner is served!' Jacob announced, holding the platter high, a smug smile on his face.

Celeste laughed, and turned her attention back to lunch, happy to forget all about Damon's love life—and her own fake one—for the afternoon.

Having hot coffee dumped in his lap wasn't, in Theo's opinion, the best way to spend a date. But by Monday morning, his lunch with Celeste seemed to be having the desired effect, at least.

'She's good for you,' Cerys announced, when she'd finished cackling at the photo of Celeste trying to hide her own laughter as he mopped up the coffee with a napkin, which was doing the rounds on social media that morning. 'If you can convince people she actually likes you—or, even better, wants you—it'll help give the impression that there's more to you than just a pretty face.'

Theo didn't ask if *Cerys* believed that there was more to him than his looks. He wasn't sure he wanted to hear the answer.

But the ultimate confirmation came as he walked into a meeting late on Monday morning with all the bigwigs involved in the *New Year's Eve Spectacular* he'd hopefully still be hosting in just a few weeks.

It might have been hard to think about the new year with Christmas still around the corner, but after the debacle of the *Christmas Cracker Cranium Quiz* Theo was more than happy to just skip the festive period altogether and start fresh on January the first.

'Good to see you keeping your face in the spotlight ahead of the big show,' one of them told Theo as he took his seat.

'I heard it wasn't his face, so much,' another murmured, loud enough to be heard around the table. Theo ignored them and reached for the coffee pot. 'Careful with that, old boy. Heard coffee's a bit of a sensitive issue for you right now.'

That caused a wave of laughter that cascaded through the room. It irritated him, but Theo had learned many years ago not to let that show. His father loved to see the effect of his jibes and would keep needling if he thought he was close to getting a reaction. Making Theo blow up had been easy when he was a boy, harder as he became a teenager and learned not to play the game.

These days, one of his bestselling points was his easy-going nature, his ability to take a joke at his own expense and keep smiling. Something to thank his father for, he supposed.

Always smiling. That was the job.

'Well, at least I got lunch with a beautiful woman first,' he joked, pouring his coffee without spilling a drop.

That, of course, just opened up a new flood of questions.

'What really is going on with you two?' Matthew, from Finance, asked. 'I read online that you've been secretly dating for months. And Fran said it was you who suggested getting Celeste on the show, so...' He left it hanging, an open question.

Theo considered how best to answer, Cerys's words still echoing around his head.

'If you can convince people she actually likes you—or, even better, wants you—it'll help give the impression that there's more to you than just a pretty face.'

Wasn't that what he wanted people to believe? He'd asked Celeste to help him rehabilitate his reputation—but now he wondered if she could do more. Could being seen with her help him persuade his bosses, and maybe even the Great British Public, that there was more to him than just the ability to smile on cue?

Maybe that was asking too much. But it could be a start...

'You know me, Matthew,' he replied, with that smile he was so famous for. 'I don't kiss and tell. Now, what's on the agenda for today?'

There was still plenty to discuss before the filming date, so he managed to keep the group around the table more or less on topic for the rest of the meeting. But as they all filed out, Mr Erland, one of the real bigwigs, held Theo back.

'I just wanted to say—I was worried, after Friday night. I thought we might have to look at replacing you for New Year, if the country was against you. But you seem to be turning it around.'

Theo's heart thumped in his chest. 'I'm certainly try-ing, sir.'

Mr Erland slapped him on the back. 'And I always back a trier. Keep it up, Theo, and we'll see you right.'

Hands in his suit pockets, he headed out after the others, whistling a Christmas carol Theo remembered singing in school.

Once he was sure he was gone, he reached for his phone, and scrolled through for the latest name added to its memory.

Celeste answered promptly, but, from the click-clacking he could hear in the background, she didn't stop typing while she spoke to him.

'Yes?' No messing around with unnecessary words for Celeste. It was kind of refreshing, after a meeting that had seemed to be seventy per cent waffle.

'Are you free this afternoon? Well, this evening, really, I suppose.' It was already almost two, and he needed to eat lunch and deal with some emails before anything else.

'Which is it, Theo? Afternoon or evening?' The typing sounds paused for a second, while she waited for his answer. Theo smiled.

'Is your answer different depending on which one I pick?' Dropping into one of the abandoned chairs, he kicked his feet up onto the meeting table and leaned back on two chair legs.

'No. I just like a little precision in my scheduling.' Of course, she did.

'Four-thirty, then. At Hyde Park.' He grinned as the plan came together in his head. 'I want to show you a Winter Wonderland.'

'You mean *the* Winter Wonderland, I assume?' she corrected him. 'Fairground rides and stalls and such? For kids?'

'Not just kids,' Theo countered. 'It's actually one of my favourite things about London at Christmas.'

'Of course, it is.' She sighed. 'Fine, I'll meet you there at four-thirty. Which gate?'

Theo considered, mentally reviewing the map of the place in his head. He'd been there often enough to know the basic layout. 'The Green Gate,' he decided. It was closest to the Bavarian village, and he had a feeling he'd need a glühwein by then. 'I'll see you there.'

He was about to hang up, when he realised that Celeste hadn't. He waited and, after a moment, she spoke again.

'So…we're really doing this? Pretending to be friends?'

Theo thought back to what he'd told his colleagues earlier. At some point, he'd have to break it to Celeste that he was hoping they could pretend to be *more* than friends. At that point, he figured he'd either get a glühwein to the face, or maybe, just maybe, a kiss for the cameras that were bound to be hanging around the Hyde Park winter attraction.

He'd much, much rather the kiss, he decided. And not just because he'd had enough drinks thrown over him lately.

'I told you,' he said, after too long a beat. 'Most people end up *actually* liking me, once they get to know me.' Silence from the other end of the line. 'But if you have to pretend, yeah, I'll take that, too.' He knew when to admit defeat.

'Then I'll see you at four-thirty,' Celeste said, and hung up.

CHAPTER FIVE

'MOST PEOPLE END up actually *liking me, once they get to know me.*'

Theo's words were still fresh in Celeste's mind as she hopped off the Tube at Hyde Park Corner, wound her scarf a little tighter around her neck, and headed in the direction of noise, lights and Christmas music.

She hadn't wanted to tell him that actually liking him was exactly what she was afraid of.

Lunch with him had been fun, apart from the coffee incident. And even that had been kind of funny, if she thought about it. Most people she knew would have been furious to find themselves suddenly doused in hot coffee, but Theo had merely rolled his eyes and mopped up the mess. At least it hadn't been boiling, she supposed.

And yes, they'd bickered for most of the lunch, but even *that* had been fun. It turned out she didn't mind people disagreeing with her quite so much when they actually listened to her reasoned arguments and, sometimes at least, changed their mind off the back of them. She was so used to arguing with people who held such deeply entrenched opinions they'd never change them, whatever evidence she presented, that Theo was a lovely change.

He even seemed genuinely interested in her historical

knowledge—something she definitely hadn't expected after the *Christmas Cracker Cranium Quiz* debacle.

But none of that meant that she should start liking him, for one, very good reason.

He didn't like her.

He was pretending to, obviously, to convince the Great British Public that he wasn't a mansplaining, patronising, patriarchal idiot. He was a faker. Pretending was what he did. But he didn't actually *like* her. Very few people did. Rachel, possibly Damon. Maybe one or two of her colleagues or students, from time to time. She wasn't honestly sure about her parents. She'd always worked more on winning their respect, professionally, than worrying about whether they *liked* her.

It had never bothered her before. She had the people that mattered to her, and she had her work. Everything else was basically surplus to requirements. She knew she wasn't always easy to get along with, that her priorities weren't always the same as other people's. But she had the respect of the people who mattered, who made decisions about her career and her future.

What else could she want?

Except suddenly, ridiculously, she wanted Theo Montgomery to like her, the way she liked spending time with him. And that was stupid, so she was going to push it aside and focus on the fact that they were *pretending* to like each other for reasons entirely to do with their careers and nothing to do with them as people.

'Easy,' she said, out loud, gaining an odd look from a small girl in a princess costume who was walking along the path towards the Winter Wonderland with her parents.

Celeste ignored that, too.

Hyde Park's Winter Wonderland was quite the spectacle. Celeste had never been before, although she knew groups of colleagues from the university had organised trips in past years. It would be easy to get lost, especially with only the poorly drawn and not-to-scale map she'd printed out before leaving the university to guide her. She was glad that she'd insisted that Theo specify which gate they should meet at, as there were four, all leading to different areas of the fair in which to start their exploration. She was relieved to see that Theo had chosen the one nearest the Bavarian village, rather than the ice-skating rink. She'd never actually been skating, but she was willing to bet she'd fall over a lot. She wasn't clumsy, usually. But she made a point of sticking to what she was good at, rather than risking being bad at something new.

Another reason not to try and be friends with Theo. Making friends was most certainly something she wasn't good at.

She spotted Theo almost instantly, leaning against a lamppost, his expensive-looking wool coat and what had to be a cashmere scarf lit by the soft glow. His face was as ridiculously perfect as on the telly, and for a moment Celeste was thrown back to that moment in the green room when he'd interrupted her work. She'd looked up and seen the most attractive man she'd ever met in real life smiling down at her, and panicked.

So she'd done what she always did, and gone into what Damon called her 'superior professor' mode.

Apparently, it took more than abject rudeness to drive Theo Montgomery away when his career was on the line, though. As she approached, he looked up and smiled as he saw her. Pushing away from the lamppost, he headed straight for her.

'You came!'

'You thought I wouldn't?' Maybe she shouldn't have.

Maybe she should have stayed safe in her small office, her small, contained and organised life.

No. She was overthinking this. Hadn't she spent yesterday reminding herself that she was immune to charm, and all that stuff? This was a career decision, pure and simple.

She pasted on a smile, and Theo recoiled.

'What?' She let the smile drop.

'That's better,' he said, looking relieved. 'I was afraid you were going to throw glühwein over me before we even got inside.'

Celeste held up her empty hands. 'No glühwein.'

Grinning, Theo grabbed one hand and held it in his own. 'Well, that will never do. Let's go find you some. You can drink while we explore, and then we can talk.'

'Talk?' Everything was moving so fast. Theo's words, his long stride, the spinning lights of the Ferris wheel in the distance. 'We need to talk?'

'Absolutely. And I'd definitely like to do it once we've both *finished* our drinks this time.'

She couldn't help but laugh at that.

Theo slid her a sideways look as they strolled into the Winter Wonderland. 'That's better.'

'What's better?'

'That smile,' Theo replied. 'That's a real smile—not whatever that terrifying thing at the gate was.'

'Yes, I suppose it was.' A real smile. A real laugh. How long had it been since she'd had those things with anyone who wasn't Rachel or Damon? Too long. Way too long.

Still gripping her hand in his, Theo led her towards the Bavarian village, with its cosy wooden chalets and strings of lights illuminating the crowds.

'Come on,' he said. 'Glühwein waits for no one.'

Maybe this wasn't such a terrible idea, Celeste thought as they approached the nearest stall. Maybe this was just what she needed.

Maybe it was the glühwein, or maybe the intrinsic excitement of the Winter Wonderland experience, but Celeste seemed charmed by the evening. Even Theo's ego wasn't big enough to assume that was due to his company. But she'd laughed at his jokes and hardly complained about the accuracy of the Bavarian-ness of the village—low—at all.

Okay, it had to be the glühwein, because Theo was actually having fun.

'How do you feel about ice skating?' he asked as they passed by the outdoor rink.

'Faintly panicky,' Celeste admitted, a show of weakness he hadn't expected from her.

It seemed the more time they spent together, the more she relaxed and showed him the woman behind the prickly, know-it-all exterior.

'We'll save that for another day, then. Ferris wheel?' She gave him a doubtful look. 'Want to just drink more glühwein and maybe find some roasted chestnuts?' he tried again.

Celeste looked relieved. 'That sounds good.'

'You're not much for doing things outside your comfort zone, are you?' Theo asked, as they found a table outside one of the pseudo-Bavarian chalets to enjoy the glühwein.

'I went on your stupid gameshow, didn't I?' she countered. 'Although who possibly thought that I'd be a good guest, I can't imagine.'

Theo winced. 'That…that might have been me, actually.'

'Oh.' Celeste blinked a few times, her eyes round in

the glow of the fairy lights. 'I...wait. How did you even know I existed?'

He shrugged. 'I'd heard you on the radio a few times. You know how it goes, you've never heard of a person before but suddenly, once you've heard them once, they seem to pop up all over the place.' It was all down to the Baader-Meinhof Phenomenon, Theo knew. A frequency illusion, that owed everything to the brain's predisposition to patterns and nothing to fate.

See? He knew stuff, too.

'I've only been on the radio half a dozen times,' Celeste said slowly. 'And only on historical or political programmes. I wouldn't have thought they'd be your cup of tea.'

'I'm interested in lots of things,' Theo replied vaguely.

He wasn't about to tell her about the part-time history degree he'd been studying long distance for the last couple of years. His first attempt at university had ended in failure when he'd dropped out in his second year, and lucked into a TV gig through a random acquaintance. He hadn't been prepared to study then, at eighteen and nineteen, and he hadn't been at all interested in his course—it had ultimately been the subject with the least competition to get into his chosen university. Or rather, the university his parents had expected him to attend, all while telling him he wasn't really bright enough to be there. Looking back, *of course* he'd dropped out—and his father would never let him forget it.

Now he was older, well, he had more respect for and interest in learning. It was fascinating to be studying again, something that really held his attention this time. And he *definitely* hadn't told his parents—or anyone else—that he was doing it.

But he knew his tinkering around the edges of academic study was nothing compared to Celeste's career, so he didn't mention it.

She still looked suspicious, though. Time to change the subject.

'What do you think of the Winter Wonderland?' he asked.

Celeste studied their surroundings thoroughly before answering the question, so Theo found himself doing the same. He took in the busyness, the noise, the lights, the music, the kids, the stalls, the rides… He had always loved the chaos of it all, but, seeing it through Celeste's eyes, he found he could only see the things he knew people complained about in reviews.

Still, when he turned back to Celeste, she was smiling. 'I like it,' she said simply, and Theo felt something inside his chest relax. Then she turned that studious, assessing gaze onto him, and he tensed up again. 'Now. You said we needed to talk?'

He had said that, yes. He was regretting it now, though. It was one thing to *imagine* that Celeste might toss another drink over him when he confessed that he'd hinted to his colleagues that they were actually dating. It was another entirely to facilitate it by confessing.

But it was the right thing to do. Well, the right thing was probably not to lie about it in the first place, but since that ship had sailed…

Theo took a long gulp of his glühwein and tried to think about the best way to broach the subject.

Celeste got there first.

'Is this about all the theories about us online?' she asked. 'My brother tells me that his favourite is the one where we've secretly been dating for months, and were having a lovers' tiff the day of the filming. And, I suppose, when we had lunch. Given the coffee incident,' she added thoughtfully.

He watched as she finished off her glühwein. Perfect. He'd buy her another, if she wanted, after this. But first…

'Is it so bad if people think we're dating?' he asked innocently.

Her gaze turned sharp, apparently totally unaffected by the alcohol. 'Who did you tell that we're dating?'

How did she know? 'I didn't *tell* anyone. I just…might not have corrected people when they assumed.'

Celeste tilted her head to the side as she studied him. Theo shifted uncomfortably, feeling like an artefact in a museum that she was trying to puzzle out. The Rosetta Stone, perhaps. Or one of those carvings that made no sense until you looked at them upside down.

'Why?' she asked finally. Apparently, she couldn't read everything about him, after all. That was strangely reassuring. 'I mean, I know you wanted people to think you were a nice guy again and everything, but that doesn't mean you have to let people think you're actually interested in me. It's not like anyone is genuinely going to believe that I'm your type.'

Theo blinked at that. 'Why wouldn't they believe that? I mean, I'm not sure I really have a type. But you're beautiful, intelligent, funny—'

'I am not funny.'

Of course, *that* was the one she objected to. Theo grinned. 'Yes, you are. You might not always mean to be, but I find you hilarious.'

It was just as well her glass was empty, he decided as she gave it a meaningful look.

'The point is,' he went on, reaching over to take her hand—partly for comfort, partly so she couldn't make a grab for his still-half-full glass, 'anyone would believe I'd want to date you.'

'Even after that show?'

'Especially after that. Did you watch it back? You positively sparkled that night. You were fiery and authentic—and you were right.'

'I was wearing a Christmas jumper.'

'That didn't make you any less right. Or less passionate.' He stroked his finger across the back of her hand, absently. As if it was the most natural thing in the world. And she was watching him do it, he realised. Not stopping him, just watching. 'You had confidence in your knowledge, and in yourself. Trust me, that's very sexy.'

Her gaze shot up to meet his at that, and he saw the astonishment in her eyes. He got the impression people didn't call Celeste Hunter sexy very often. Probably through fear. Because whatever else she was, with those long legs and heeled boots, that dark hair pinned back to reveal her bright, smart eyes…she was definitely sexy. Or maybe Theo had some sort of academic fetish. That wasn't impossible.

'You think I'm sexy?' she asked, in disbelief.

'Who wouldn't?' he countered. 'In fact, the much bigger problem is going to be convincing the Great British Public that you're interested in *me*.'

She smiled at that. Then, without looking down, she turned her hand over under his, so their palms touched. 'We're really doing this, then? Pretending to date, just to improve our professional reputations?'

Theo lifted her hand to his lips and kissed it. 'You know, I think we are.'

Sitting in her office on Tuesday morning, Celeste stared at the photograph on her phone screen. Apparently, they'd been observed together at the Winter Wonderland, and by more than one person if all the different camera angles she'd seen on social media were anything to go by.

She wasn't surprised they'd been photographed, not any more. Theo was a big name in the country, a national boyfriend, almost. People were interested in what he was up to—and, after their fight on TV, together they were a curiosity.

What surprised her was herself. Or rather, her image in the photograph.

She looked happy. Not in an 'all her students turned in their essays on time' way. Not even in a 'knowing exactly how to end this next chapter' or a 'finding the primary source evidence to solidify her case' way. But in an unguarded, relaxed, 'having fun' way.

It was weird.

Oh, she had fun, of course—but only with people she knew well. Which basically meant Rachel, Damon, and a few acquaintances from the university. She'd expect to see herself looking that way at a conference dinner, perhaps, where she was surrounded by people who cared about the same things she did, who were interested in what she had to say because of her reputation, her academic successes.

This wasn't that.

The photo in question showed them sitting outside one of the Bavarian village chalets, drinking glühwein and chatting. But Theo's hand was resting on hers, and he was leaning towards her as if what she had to say were the most interesting thing he'd ever heard.

It's all an act, she reminded herself. He's an actor. A faker.

But she wasn't. And she knew the joy on her face was real.

She liked spending time with Theo, in a way she hadn't enjoyed a new acquaintance's company since…she couldn't remember when. And that could get dangerous.

Celeste shook her head. She'd be careful. Besides, almost everyone in the world started to irritate her after a while; Theo would be no different, she was sure. Right now it was fun, but they didn't actually have anything in common, beyond the fact they both wanted their TV projects to be a success. That was all.

And so, when her phone rang again, and Theo's name flashed across the screen replacing the photo of them together, she took a breath, answered, and said, 'So, what's our next move?'

Of course, Celeste reflected a few days later, she hadn't expected the next move to include wearing a swimming costume, outside, in mid December.

'Are you sure about this?' she asked, pulling the fluffy bathrobe she'd been given at the entrance tighter around her.

'Absolutely!' Theo's own bathrobe was tossed over his shoulder, as if the cold didn't bother him anyway. His surf shorts couldn't be much warmer than her one-piece, but they did show off his lightly muscled chest and broad shoulders nicely.

Not that she was looking.

Or was she supposed to be looking? If she was really dating him, she'd be looking, right?

She peeked over at him.

Yeah, she'd definitely be looking. There was a reason Theo was such a favourite on Saturday night TV, and it wasn't all to do with his smile.

He wasn't looking at her, though. He was striding ahead, along the deck of the boat he'd brought her to. It was more of a floating platform, really, Celeste decided. With a bar in the middle, some high cocktail tables, a sturdy rail around the outside, and, of course, the hot tubs at either end.

Celeste followed Theo as he stopped and spoke to people he passed, even posing for a selfie with a group on girls on a hen night. Then, as he reached the far end, he turned back to take her hand, his gaze not leaving her face for a moment.

Good. That was good. She didn't want him ogling her anyway, even if she was mostly covered by her bathrobe.

Although it probably meant she should stop ogling him. Damn.

'Ready?' Theo asked.

'As I'll ever be.' She paused by the edge of the hot tub.

'You realise you have to take the robe off, right?'

'Unfortunately.'

It wasn't that Celeste was insecure about her body. It was just that it wasn't something she often flaunted like this. Usually she was safely tucked up in her personal uniform of black jeans and boots, with a black top. She went a little different with her winter coat—that was white. But otherwise, her only colour tended to come from her bright lipstick. She wanted people looking at her lips and the words she was saying, after all, not her clothes. Plus, it made getting dressed in the morning a whole lot simpler when she didn't have to worry about things going together.

She swallowed. It wasn't as if anyone would be looking at her anyway. And her swimming costume was basically an extension of her normal wardrobe—boring and black. Nobody would even notice it next to the highly coloured and patterned bikinis on show.

Celeste let the robe fall from her shoulders and turned

to place it over one of the loungers beside the hot tub. When she turned back, Theo's gaze remained focussed firmly on her face, although she couldn't help but notice that his jaw was clenched. Was that with the effort of not looking at her swimsuit-clad body?

God, I hope so. The thought caught her by surprise, and she slipped into the water quickly to try and wash it away.

She didn't want Theo looking at her that way—unless it was to make her feel less bad about looking at *him* that way.

'So, what on earth made you think that an outdoor hot tub on the Thames in December was a good idea for our next "date"?' she asked as Theo handed her a glass of champagne.

Settling into the ledge seat around the edge of the hot tub, Celeste let the bubbles pop against her body, the warmth of the water welcome after the chilly winter air, and took a sip of the champagne, letting *those* bubbles pop against her tongue. Somehow, her shoulders already seemed less tense, as if the stress of hunching over her computer all day getting nowhere were seeping out of her into the water.

'That.' Theo sounded smug as he spoke. 'That's what gave me the idea. Wanting to put that look on your face.'

'What look?' Celeste scowled, but it only made him laugh.

'Not that one. The one you had before, when you took your first sip of champagne. You looked like the worries of the world were lifting from your shoulders.' He smirked at her. 'You're too tense, Celeste. I knew that the first moment you snapped at me in the green room.'

'You interrupted me while I was working,' she pointed out. 'So what, now it's your mission to destress me?'

'Perhaps.' Something changed in his smile. She couldn't figure out what exactly, since she wasn't even sure that his lips had moved at all. But suddenly it felt more secret, more private—and warmer, somehow. Maybe it was his eyes, or the lighting on the boat. That was it, just the lighting. Nothing to do with him, or her, at all.

Faker, she reminded herself, silently. *He's a faker*.

She looked away—and in doing so, noticed that they were being watched.

It was hard to whisper to Theo without getting closer; making herself heard over the bubbles was a challenge, and doing so without the guy sitting on her other side hearing even harder. So she shifted a little under the water until she could feel Theo's thigh pressed up against her own.

Glancing up, she saw him swallow, and his gaze flashed down, just for a moment, in the direction of her cleavage before it found its way back to her face.

'Don't look now,' she murmured, 'but there's someone over by the railing with their camera out. I think they're taking a photo of us.'

Of course, he looked. And then he waved. Because that was the sort of irritating man he was.

'I said don't look,' she grumbled.

'Ah, but if I don't look, how can I be sure they've caught my best side?' Theo asked. 'Besides, they're probably the fifth or sixth person to take photos of us since we got here. I've seen at least three.'

'Is that including the hen-party selfie you posed for?'

'Ooh, no, add that one in.'

Celeste shook her head. 'You love this, don't you?'

Theo shrugged. 'It's just part of the deal. It's not why I got into it, if that's what you mean.'

'Why did you, then?' she asked, suddenly curious. 'Did you always want to be a TV star?'

He laughed at that. 'Not a star, no. I suppose…maybe I did do it for the attention, a bit. I just wanted to do something that made people smile, made them stop in their busy lives and have a laugh, perhaps. Plus it was basically the only thing I was qualified for. Smiling and asking people questions like, "Where do you come from?" It's an aristocratic thing.'

His smile was self-deprecating, but somehow Celeste got the impression that he wasn't actually joking.

She wanted to ask him more about that, but she didn't know how. Damon would have; he was the sibling with all the conversational ability. She'd never needed it before.

But now, she wished she'd spent a little more time on it.

Before she'd found a way to phrase her question, Theo had already moved on.

'So. What are we doing this weekend?'

'Together?' Celeste furrowed her brow as she looked at him. 'I'd sort of planned on staying in and working on my book…'

'As fun as that sounds, it's not going to get us seen.' Theo shifted closer still, a conspiratorial smile on his lips. 'Have you seen the press this thing is getting us both? My agent is over the moon.'

'So is mine,' Celeste admitted reluctantly. 'Apparently raising my profile before the producers make a decision about my new show next year is vital, and *this*—' she waved her hand in the tiny space between them, being very careful not to touch any of those wet, firm abs he was showing off '—is doing that nicely.'

'There are still a few people on social media claiming we're faking the whole thing, though.'

'Which we are.'

'Which is why we need a plan to convince people. Starting tonight, and continuing this week.' Theo settled back against the edge of the hot tub, resting one long arm around her shoulder. He was only touching her ever so lightly, but Celeste still had to force her body not to shiver in response. To the rest of the boat—and the all-important cameras—he probably looked as if he were whispering sweet nothings in her ear.

He wasn't.

'I'm filming Monday and Wednesday evenings, and there's a few meetings I need to attend during the week-days, but there should still be plenty of scope for us to get together and be seen. I'll send you some calendar in-vitations once I don't need to worry about submerging my smartphone in bubbly water. What have you got on this week?'

Celeste shook her head as she tried to remember. It was hard to focus when Theo's warm voice was rumbling so close to her ear. 'I have to take my brother Christmas shopping on Thursday,' she replied. 'Other than that… I'm mostly just working on my own. Term is over, you see.'

'Ah, your brother. Maybe it's time to meet the fam-ily—properly this time. What do you think? Lunch?'

CHAPTER SIX

THEO WAS STARTING to regret his suggestion of lunch with Celeste's brother.

It wasn't just that he was, yet again, sitting alone in a restaurant, being watched by people with camera phones, waiting for Celeste—who was late. Again.

It wasn't even that he'd belatedly realised that an over-protective brother might not be all that keen on his plan to pretend to date Celeste for publicity—although that wasn't making him feel any better about the lunch ahead, he had to admit.

No, his biggest problem was his own motives.

Yes, being seen with Celeste had gone a long way to rehabilitating his reputation: if *she* didn't hate him, it made it slightly harder for everyone else to. There'd even been a couple of pieces about how Tania had moved on very quickly with her new fiancé for someone who'd been supposedly heartbroken and torn up by his abandonment. Oh, there remained a vocal minority complaining about him on social media, but those following his supposed romance with Celeste were happily drowning them out.

And yes, Cerys was thrilled. So thrilled, in fact, she'd told him he could ease up now. Let something else over-take them in the news cycle, until their romance was forgotten and nobody really noticed they hadn't been seen together in months.

Except he'd done the opposite. He'd invited himself to lunch with her brother. Because he'd seen her in that plain, boring swimsuit and known he'd wanted to see more. Not just that; he'd had fun. Real fun, on a fake hot-tub date.

What was it about her that drew him in? Part of it had to be the passion she showed when she talked about history, or anything she was knowledgeable about. But it was more than that. The way she let him see under that prickly exterior sometimes. Or how much fun it was to ease her out of that comfort zone she loved so much. Or even just the simple way she made a decision about how she felt about things based on what she thought, not on what anyone else said.

Whatever it was, Theo was too far into this, and he knew it. He just didn't seem to have any inclination to get out again.

And then there was the text message he'd received from his mother that morning.

Looking forward to seeing you for dinner on Sunday. We understand—from social media, I might add—that there's a new woman in your life. Your father says you should bring her along to see the old pile. Let her know what she's getting into.

He wasn't entirely sure how he was going to persuade Celeste to have Sunday lunch with his parents—or how he'd explain it to them if she didn't come. Or which was the worst of the two outcomes, to be honest.

But he was going to have to worry about it later. The restaurant door swung open and Celeste strode in, flanked by a tall, handsome guy in a dark coat, and a woman Theo hadn't seen before. She had her dark hair clipped back from her face, and wore a sweater dress under her coat. She was pretty, in a curvy, petite way— but his gaze was quickly drawn back to Celeste, slipping out of her white coat to reveal her customary black clothing underneath.

God, she was beautiful.

Her companions paused just inside the door, looking faintly astonished. Apparently, they hadn't been following Celeste's social media mentions lately, then.

Celeste said something to them both that he couldn't make out, then smiled—her painted red lips wide, although Theo could tell even from the distance between them that it wasn't one of her *real* smiles—and headed towards him.

This was it.

Theo stumbled to his feet as they approached, trying to return Celeste's smile. As she reached him, he did what he always did on dates: he embraced her, then pressed a kiss against her mouth.

Oh. Ohhh.

It was only meant to be a quick brush of the lips, maybe only at the corner of her mouth, even. But somehow it was suddenly more. Nothing deep—no tongue, as Cerys always warned him about kisses in public. But still.

Their first kiss.

And suddenly Theo was very sure that there needed to be another. And another. And…

Celeste pulled away after a moment, colour high on her cheeks. Good. At least he wasn't the only one affected by that kiss.

She pulled herself together more quickly than he could though.

'Sweetheart, you remember my brother, Damon? And my best friend, Rachel?' Celeste said, looking meaningfully towards their lunch guests.

Rachel. Celeste's best friend, Rachel. So he was doing lunch with the brother *and* the best friend.

He really hoped they were both in a good mood.

Switching into TV-host mode, Theo turned on his smile and reached out to welcome Rachel with a hug—*without* kiss—and shake Damon's hand. Neither of them looked as if they were about to bite his head off, but they did both look a little baffled by the whole situation.

Theo knew how they felt.

Pulling out Celeste's chair for her, he ensured she was comfortably seated before taking his own place at the table. Across the way, Damon was doing the same for Rachel.

Theo frowned. Had Celeste mentioned that her brother was dating her best friend? He was pretty sure she hadn't. That was weird, right?

But he couldn't worry about that now. He'd already clocked the paparazzi stalker at a table in the corner, thinking he was being surreptitious as he snapped away, taking photos of the four of them destined to be on the front page of every gossip site tomorrow.

The important thing was to make this seem like a perfectly normal lunch. That was all. So he smiled, and he laughed, and he made small talk. He let Damon pick the wine—who, in turn, got Rachel to choose—and shared mouthfuls of his main course with Celeste from his own fork. The latter prompted an odd look from his lunch date, and frankly astonished ones from their companions. But it looked like a real date, and that was all that mattered.

The only concerning part, really, was the feeling in

his stomach that it *was* a real date. Because that was how it felt.

And a big part of him wished that it were.

Huh. That was definitely new. And worrying.

Finally, as they polished off the puddings, Theo glanced casually over at that table in the corner, not for the first time since they'd started eating, and realised that the photographer had left at last.

Leaning around Celeste to peer out of the window, Theo watched the guy wandering off down the London street, waiting until he was around the corner before he collapsed back into his seat with relief.

'He's gone?' Celeste asked, shifting her chair away from Theo's to a more normal distance. Ridiculously, he missed her immediately.

Theo nodded. 'Finally.'

Across the table, Rachel frowned. 'Who's gone?'

'Our reporter-stalker,' Theo said tiredly. 'Come on, let's grab after-dinner drinks in the back bar, where it's more private. Then we can explain.'

The back bar was cosy, warm and empty. Theo spoke briefly to the head waiter on their way in, and he nodded, then shut the door behind them, returning moments later to enter, after knocking, with a tray of coffees and liquors. Then he departed again, leaving them in peace.

Finally.

Celeste sank into a chair a strategic distance away from Theo, and tried to think.

She needed to get things straight in her head again because that lunch had felt uncomfortably like a real date. Not just lunch; hugging Theo hello—*kissing* him even— had felt normal. Natural. Even eating his food from his fork had been fine, despite the fact it was something she'd never even done with her last boyfriend, and they'd been together for almost a year.

She knew it was all fake, of course—intellectually. Knowing things intellectually had never been a problem for her.

It was the emotional side that stymied her, every time. And after a week and a half of pretending to date Theo Montgomery…her emotions were starting to scream at her.

Maybe it wasn't her emotions. Maybe it was just her libido. *That* at least would make sense. He was an attractive guy. She was a sexual being. Didn't everything in history always come down to sex, one way or another?

Glancing up, she found her little brother glaring at her, and promptly decided to stop thinking about sex.

'What the hell is going on here?' Damon demanded.

Wish I knew, brother.

Rachel sat down beside her, and Celeste heard the unspoken message her best friend was sending.

I might have come here with him, but I'm on your side. Always.

That was something. She'd been…worried, to say the least, talking to Damon about Rachel as they'd shopped for Christmas presents for their parents that morning. And seeing them together at the Cressingham Arcade where they were both currently working hadn't made her concern lessen any.

She'd tried to talk to Rachel about Theo that week, but her friend had ducked her calls—probably, Celeste suspected, because she was in bed with Damon. In a way, she'd almost been glad when Rachel hadn't answered because, really, what was she going to say?

At least she'd shamed Damon into inviting Rachel to

their parents' Christmas Eve party. That was the least he could do.

And he was still waiting for an answer to his question.

'Do you want to explain, or shall I?' Theo asked Celeste, his upper-class tone lazy. That had irritated her a few days ago—the laziness, more than anything. It should irritate her now.

'I'll do it,' Celeste replied, sharply, pushing the thought aside. 'You'll get it wrong.'

'Probably,' Theo agreed easily. He was just *so* laid-back. That was annoying, wasn't it? She was sure it used to be annoying. 'I'll pour the coffees, then.'

She tried to focus on the matter at hand: explaining her relationship with Theo. Maybe it would even start to make sense to her, too.

'So. Damon, I know you watched the car crash that was our festive TV quiz. Rachel, I assume you did too?'

Rachel nodded.

'It didn't go down particularly well with the Internet fans. Or my agent,' Theo said.

Celeste shot him a look to say, *Who is telling this story, you or me?* Theo shut up and let her continue. *One point in his favour. Still so many against.*

Except it was getting harder to remember those points against, when everything felt so natural when she was with him. So easy, in a way personal interactions rarely were for her.

'So Theo called me and asked me to help him rehabilitate his reputation,' she said.

'And yours,' Theo interjected.

Celeste rolled her eyes. 'My reputation is based on my research, my publications, my education and my brain, not my ability to be pleasant on television. Unlike yours.'

'Your reputation with TV companies, however, is

based *entirely* on that,' Theo pointed out, apparently un-ruffled by the accusation that he was just a pretty face.

Celeste ignored him. Mostly because he was right.

'So what happened next?' Rachel asked, obviously well aware of how Damon was glowering at them both.

'We agreed to a few public appearances together, as friends,' Celeste said, trying her hardest to make it sound as if it were the most normal thing in the world.

'It got a little bit out of hand from there,' Theo admit-ted. 'There were these stories online...'

'People thought we were faking it,' Celeste explained.

'Which you were.' Damon was still glowering as he spoke.

'So we had to prove that we really *were* okay with each other,' Celeste went on, ignoring her brother. 'By pretending we were in love.'

'So you're mortal enemies pretending to sleep together for the cameras,' Damon said drily. 'The miracle of mod-ern love, huh?'

'Like you can talk,' Celeste scoffed, then turned to Theo. 'This one spent all morning telling me how he and Rachel are just colleagues who sleep together. Ap-parently, they're having a "festive fling".'

She regretted the words the moment they left her mouth. Of course, that was *exactly* what Damon had said, but, watching Rachel's face as her smile stiffened and the light in her eyes seemed to dim, she knew it was a mistake.

'Sorry, Rachel, that came out wrong,' she said, wincing.

'No, it's true.' Rachel reached for her liquor. Never a good sign. 'He's my festive fling. Right, Damon?'

'Right,' Damon said, although he sounded just as du-bious as he had that morning when he'd said it.

Oh, Damon. Oh, Rachel.

She couldn't get her best friend out of this one, or her brother, either. They'd have to figure it out themselves. *She* couldn't even figure out what the hell *she* was doing, pretending to be in love with Theo Montgomery until it almost felt real.

But Celeste had a feeling there were going to be a lot of broken hearts, come the new year.

Theo didn't know what was going on with Damon and Rachel but, to be honest, he wasn't totally sure he *wanted* to know, either. Things were confusing enough to deal with just pretending to date Celeste.

'What do you want to do now?' he asked her as they strolled out of the restaurant together. Damon and Rachel had left, their stalker cameraman had got all he needed, and, really, it was the perfect time for them both to get back to their regularly scheduled lives.

Except he didn't want to. He wanted to spend more time with Celeste. And Theo was almost certain that was going to become a problem, sooner or later.

'Isn't there somewhere we need to be seen together?' Celeste asked.

Every other night, he'd managed to find some sort of event or place he'd been invited to, and convinced her to make an appearance with him for the publicity. Today, for the first time, he had nowhere he was supposed to be, and no ideas.

Celeste rested her head against his shoulder for a second, as if the rigmarole of the lunch had exhausted her. She had her arm looped through his, close against his side, and Theo had an overwhelming need to keep her there.

It was that thought that sparked the idea.

'Ice skating.' It was perfect; he could hold onto her, in public, with perfect justification.

Celeste, however, looked sceptical. 'We're going back to Winter Wonderland?'

Theo shook his head. 'There's a rink at the Tower of London—well, in the dry moat anyway. Come on. It'll be fun!'

'I do like the Tower,' Celeste said tentatively, and he knew he'd got her. History always was the way to her heart.

Not that he was trying to get there. That was absolutely not what this was about.

He just…needed to hold her close. Was that so bad?

There was a queue at the box office when they arrived. He probably could have used his smile and his face to get to the front of it, but he didn't. Whatever Celeste thought, this wasn't actually another publicity date. This was about spending time with her, like a normal couple.

Even if they categorically weren't.

Did she even *like* spending time with him? He had no way of telling. She was the one person in his life he couldn't read. Everyone else was easy—even Damon and Rachel had been obvious in their own way. He wondered if Celeste realised how much trouble there was going to be there, very soon…

But he wasn't thinking about them. He was thinking about Celeste—which seemed to be one of the few non-work things he *did* think about these days.

He'd never imagined, after their first meeting, that he'd enjoy her company so much. And, in fairness, she was still blunt and impatient, and had given him a real earful the one time he'd called and interrupted her train of thought *just* when she was getting a handle on the chapter she was writing.

But she was also fascinating, full of facts and observations he'd never have imagined if he hadn't met her. There was a passion there he so rarely saw in anybody—

one he suspected she only showed when she was talking about history, or perhaps about the things that mattered to her most. He loved listening to her talk—when she wasn't snapping at him. And he loved to watch her think.

Like now, standing in the queue at the Tower of London ice rink, as she stared up at the majestic castle. Her dark hair was swept back from her face as usual, giving him the perfect view of her porcelain skin and the thoughtful look in her eyes.

He couldn't resist. 'What are you thinking about?'

'Do you know, there's been a fortress here since just after the Norman conquest?'

'I did, actually.' She looked at him in surprise, and he shrugged. 'School trip.' It was a lie. He'd come here on his own, as an adult, and read the guidebook cover to cover. Why didn't he just tell her that?

He knew the answer to that too, deep down. Because he was afraid. Afraid that this highly educated woman would laugh at his pretensions to knowledge. What did he know, really? He'd flunked out of university and made his career in a field that just required him to smile and look pretty.

Theo shook the thought away. 'It was a prison too, right? Weren't the Kray twins held here?'

'They were, actually. The last execution here was during the war though—a German spy.' Her smile turned mischievous, and Theo felt his heart skip a beat at the sight. Oh, he was in trouble.

'They say the place is haunted, you know,' she said, and Theo laughed with surprise.

'You believe in ghosts?' he asked incredulously. She was so logical, so academic—so determined to see the evidence and the proof that she'd required dozens of social media screenshots from him to even believe that people were interested in their relationship.

Celeste shrugged. 'Not really. But the stories are always interesting—and the people who claim to have seen them sound terrified. One of them is said to be a grizzly bear, from when the Tower was a zoo.'

'Well, if we see a bear out on the ice, I promise we'll skate in the opposite direction,' Theo said. 'Come on, we're up.'

Celeste bit down on her lip, obviously nervous, as Theo stepped out onto the ice a short while later. He held out a hand to her and she took it, gingerly.

'You've not done this before,' he remembered.

Celeste shook her head. 'Never.'

'Because you didn't want to, or...' He trailed off. If she genuinely hated the idea of ice skating she'd have said, right? He didn't want to be that jerk who dragged her into doing something she didn't want to, just because he thought it would be romantic. Especially since any romance between them was all for show anyway.

'It just...never really came up as an option.' She shrugged. 'My parents weren't big on non-academic activities. And by the time I left home and went to university, well, I was usually busy studying anyway.'

There was something in her voice, a loneliness Theo hadn't heard from her before, and it made his heart ache. She'd been locked away in her ivory tower, learning every dry fact and opinion she could. But when had she actually experienced the world she was learning the history of? He got the impression, not nearly as much as she should have.

'Come on.' He squeezed her hand and led her slowly out onto the ice. 'Don't worry. I won't let go.'

He could have got her one of the plastic penguins kids

used when they were learning to skate, he supposed, but he got the feeling that Celeste hated looking incompetent or unknowledgeable as much as he did. But where he laughed his inferiority off and pretended not to care, she got prickly and defensive. He didn't want that. So instead, he kept her close against him and held her up when she started to lose her balance.

They made their wobbly way around the outside of the rink, ignoring the people watching from the cafe and bar at the end, hot chocolates in hand.

'See?' Theo said. 'I told you you could do it.'

Celeste beamed up at him. Unfortunately, she also stopped focussing on her feet, and her skates slid away underneath her. Theo grabbed her and tried to keep her upright. His stomach lurched as he felt his blades sliding, too. He could grab for the edge, but that would mean letting go of Celeste—

They both crashed to the ice with a jarring crunch.

'I knew I should have used a penguin,' Celeste said, staring up at the night sky above them.

'I reckon it would have been harder to land on than I am,' Theo pointed out from underneath her.

'True.' She looked over at him and he was amazed to realise she was still smiling.

'You don't mind that you fell?'

She blinked. 'I…guess not. I mean, it was fun, even if I wasn't very good at it.'

'It was fun,' he agreed, looking into her eyes and wondering at their depths.

For a long moment, Celeste stared back. Then she blinked and said, 'Come on. I think we deserve a hot chocolate.'

'I reckon they agree.' Theo nodded towards the crowd

that had gathered at the side of the rink nearby, all clapping and cheering.

Celeste froze for a moment, then relaxed as she said, 'They recognise you.'

'And probably you.' Theo levered himself out from under Celeste, and back to a standing position. Then he reached down to pull her up beside him, bracing himself against the side of the rink.

One arm wrapped around her waist, he bowed to their audience, pulling Celeste down with him, laughing as she did the same. He liked her like this. Close and carefree. Not caring that she looked like an idiot.

He cared, of course he did. But he knew that the best way to deal with it was to pretend that he *didn't* care. That, and a little bit of distraction...

Swooping around, he swept Celeste into his arms, so her breasts were pressed against his chest, and her skates were barely touching the ice. God, he hoped he didn't fall again now. That really *would* be humiliating.

'What are you doing?' she asked, her voice a low murmur.

'Giving our audience what they really want,' he replied.

Lowering his lips to hers, Theo finally did what he'd been wanting to do since the moment they met at the restaurant, and kissed her. Properly, this time. With tongue.

Somewhere, Theo decided, as whoops went up from the crowd and cameras flashed, Cerys would be having an apoplexy.

Then he lost the ability to think about anything at all except kissing Celeste.

He didn't miss it.

CHAPTER SEVEN

THEO MONTGOMERY WAS kissing her.

Not like that perfunctory hello kiss at the restaurant; this was a real, no-holds-barred kiss. The sort that would *definitely* send her sprawling over the ice again if he weren't holding her up. Since that brief, hello kiss at the restaurant had scrambled her brains for a good half an hour, she dreaded to think what this one would do.

It's all for show. Remember that. He's just playing up to his audience.

But it *felt* real. That was the problem.

The aches and bruises that covered her body from her fall were rapidly being replaced by other, far more pleasant, sensations. Tingly ones, that reminded her it had been far, far too long since she'd had anyone but herself to keep her company at night. Warm ones, that drove away the chill of a winter night. Hopeful ones, that never wanted these other feelings to end…

Theo pulled away, and Celeste just about resisted the urge to grab his head and pull his mouth back to hers. Mostly because if she let go of his body even for a moment she was pretty sure she was going to fall over again.

The crowd gave up one last, loud cheer, and then dispersed.

'Hot chocolate?' Theo asked, as if nothing had happened at all. As if he hadn't just rocked the foundations of her happy, solitary life by reminding her of all the good things that happened in pairs.

And no, she wasn't talking about the ice skating.

'That would be great,' she managed. 'And I think I'd like my real shoes back, please.'

She needed solid ground under her feet again. Literally *and* metaphorically.

The bar and cafe at the end of the rink were packed with people, but Theo managed to smile their way to a window seat just as another couple were leaving. He disappeared, leaving her looking out over the ice and the castle alone, until he returned with their hot chocolates. It was enough time, at least, for Celeste to bring her brain back down to earth, which she appreciated.

'So, how did you like your first ice-skating experience?' Theo placed her steaming mug, topped with whipped cream, a flake, *and* mini marshmallows, on the counter in front of her.

Celeste beamed at the sickly sweet concoction. Hot chocolate was, in her opinion, the best part of the festive season.

'Worth it for this,' she answered, because she wasn't about to tell him that the *other* best part of this particular festive season was kissing him.

All a show, she reminded herself. She really couldn't afford to forget that.

They drank their hot chocolates in companionable silence as, outside, visitors spun around the rink on their skates, all in the shadow of the ancient castle looming above them. Even Celeste had to admit it was pretty magical.

'You're thinking again,' Theo said, his voice low and

rumbly and incredibly distracting. 'More ghost stories about the tower?'

Celeste shook her head. 'I was just thinking how nice it is to see the modern world interacting with history this way. I didn't think it would be, somehow.' She'd assumed that using historical places this way would diminish them, somehow. Probably because of a lifetime of her parents stressing the value and importance of historic and archaeological sites in their own right, for research and learning, for academics who would publish long, often boring papers on them.

And they *were* important, of course. Those historical sources and places were how she'd built her career. She wanted them to be treasured and looked after.

But she wondered now if they couldn't be used, too. Tourists traipsing over the Acropolis in Greece might not do much to preserve it or improve the experts' knowledge of the ancient world. But they *would* increase those tourists' knowledge. And they'd share that knowledge with their kids, their families.

Her father might grumble as another historic site opened its doors to people who hadn't studied the period as he had, didn't understand what they were seeing. He might claim it was all for the money, but the money was what paid for the research to happen.

More importantly, the interest had to be there. If people didn't care about the history of a place, why would they pay for it to be preserved and studied?

All stuff she'd known academically. But here, watching history meld happily with the modern world, she felt that she understood it, rather than just knowing.

There was the world of difference.

This is what I want to do with my TV show. Bring history to life.

'I like it,' Theo said, simply. 'I like that our city has such a fascinating past, and I like most that it's not locked away there. That we can see it, experience it every day, just living here.'

She'd lived in London her whole life, but she wasn't sure she'd ever just enjoyed the place. She'd either been studying *or* living. Never both at the same time.

She thought she might want to, though. With Theo.

'I think…this is what I want my new show to be,' she said, slowly. 'A way of bringing history beside the modern day. Of making it real to people, not abstract.'

That was the part her parents didn't, couldn't understand. For them, it was another world—one they'd rather live in than this one.

But Celeste wanted both. She just hadn't realised it until now.

'I think that sounds brilliant,' Theo said. 'I can't wait to watch it.'

'If they commission it,' Celeste replied. 'It's still not a sure thing.'

'Ah, Aesop's chickens, huh?' Theo grinned. 'Not counting them before they hatch.'

'That's right.' She tilted her head as she studied him, a surprising thought coalescing in her brain.

'What?' he asked, his expression suddenly nervous.

'Tell me the truth. You're a bit of a history buff, aren't you?'

His gaze slid away from hers. 'It's an interesting topic. I'm interested in lots of things.'

Celeste knew she couldn't read Theo the way she read Rachel, or even Damon. But she was starting to get a feel for him—and not just in the kissing way. There was something more here. He couldn't fake his way out of this, not with her.

'You'd heard me on history shows on the radio often enough to ask me onto that quiz show.'

'I thought you'd be an interesting addition.' He tossed her a smirk. 'Look how right I was.'

'Did you really come on a school trip to the Tower of London?'

Theo paused for a second, then shook his head. 'No. I came as a tourist last summer.'

'Because you're a history buff.'

'Because I was writing an essay about it for my history degree.'

Celeste blinked. Okay, maybe she couldn't read him at all, because she definitely hadn't seen that one coming.

'You're studying history?' she asked.

'Part-time.' He shrugged. 'It's no big deal.'

But it was, she could see that in the tension of his shoulders, the way he wouldn't look at her.

This was Theo behind the smile, behind the fakery.

'Does anyone else know you're doing it?'

His gaze shot up to meet hers at that. 'No. And…I'd appreciate it…'

'I won't tell anyone.' She smiled. 'But I think it's wonderful.'

'You do? For all you know I could be rubbish at it.'

Celeste had had rubbish students before. Ones who didn't show up for lectures, or never turned in essays. Ones who only cared about the university experience, not the studying.

If Theo was doing this in his own time, on top of a full-time job, when he really didn't have to…he was doing it for the love of the subject.

And *that* she most definitely understood.

She smiled at him, and lifted her half-empty mug for him to toast with his own.

'What are we toasting to?' he asked.

'To you, and your studies.'

'How about to you, and your new show?' he countered.

'Fine. To bringing history to life, and into the present.'

'Works for me.' He drank, leaving a hot chocolate moustache on his upper lip, which he licked off. Celeste tried to pretend that the action didn't make her heat up again.

'Now,' he said, when he'd finished. 'Important question for you. How do you feel about Sunday lunch with my parents?'

It was hard for Theo to express quite how much he didn't want to be here. From the way Celeste was watching him, though, her bottom lip caught between her teeth, he had a feeling she understood, at least a little.

Taking a breath, he opened the door of the car. 'Ready?'

'As I'll ever be,' she joked, but he could barely bring himself to smile in return.

Why had he done this? The only thing he could think was that the kiss on the rink had addled his brain to the point where he'd not only told her he was studying history, for heaven's sake, but also forgotten all the perfectly good reasons why he *shouldn't* take Celeste to meet his parents.

Starting with, if *he* didn't want to be there, why should she?

But it was more than that, of course. While he had no doubt his parents would be nice enough to Celeste, he couldn't hope to say the same about how they'd be towards him.

Still, he forced himself not to actively grimace as he helped Celeste out of the car and took her arm. Her dark hair was down today, for once, and it moved in the winter breeze before settling on her white coat.

Any other woman of his acquaintance, coming to meet his parents for the first time, would have asked him what to wear. Not Celeste. He had no doubt that under that coat was an all-black outfit—although a dress or skirt rather than jeans, given the tights she was wearing with her boots today. Her lips were bright red, like Snow White's, and he wanted to kiss them. For courage, perhaps.

Or just because he'd been dreaming of them since he last touched them with his own.

Celeste stared up at Sorrelton House, its many chimneys jutting up into the grey winter sky. 'This is where you grew up?'

Theo tried to imagine seeing the place for the first time. He couldn't remember when he had, of course. He'd been born within its walls, and some days it felt as if he'd never left.

It was a large house. No, that was an understatement. It was unnecessarily huge, for the three of them living there when he was a child, and for his two parents now. Even if he added the live-in staff, which was down to only a few long-standing employees, it was too big. He remembered them closing up the East Wing when he was a child; he didn't think it had ever been opened up again since.

'Yep,' he said, succinctly. 'Come on.'

It was because they didn't have a real title, he supposed, that his parents insisted on all the grandeur. They were minor, minor aristocracy, but even that small amount made a difference. They couldn't live like *ordinary* people, could they? But they didn't have the land or inheritances to live like lords, either.

Theo wasn't sure anyone could afford to live at Sorrelton House these days, the way it had been designed to be lived in. After so many years, the place was a complete money pit.

He didn't bother ringing the doorbell; it would only risk giving Jenkins a heart attack, and it took him forever to get up to the main door from the kitchen, where he spent most of his time gossiping with Mrs Harrow. So instead, he led Celeste around to the side entrance, the one nearest the stables, and slipped in that way. At least he knew that Celeste wouldn't be the least bit interested in the pomp and circumstance of the main entrance hall anyway.

Except in her very own Celeste-like way, of course.

'It's Georgian, right?' she asked, pausing to examine the brickwork as they rounded the corner to the side entrance.

'I believe so.' His voice sounded tight, even to his own ears. Celeste didn't seem to hear it, though.

'Do you know much about the history of the place? Before your family came here, I mean?' She paused. 'Unless it's *always* been in the family? Are you one of those families?'

'No. My great-grandfather bought it, I believe. Before that, I'm not sure. I imagine my father could tell you, if you really want to know.'

He didn't—want to know, that was. He never had—not since he was a child. His father had made clear that the house was a responsibility, and obligation—one he never expected Theo to be capable of fulfilling to his satisfaction.

So, no. He didn't want to know about the history of Sorrelton House. He wanted to get through this lunch and get back out again, as smoothly and as quickly as possible. That was all.

Celeste was watching him now, curiosity and maybe even concern in her eyes. Theo turned away, fumbled open the door and strode into the house proper. If he moved fast enough, maybe the memories wouldn't hit him so hard.

'Theo? Is that you?' His mother's voice echoed down the empty hallways; she might be getting older, but her hearing was still as sharp as it had ever been. Maria Montgomery had always been able to hear a whispered insult or a secret from a good hundred yards. Apparently, it was still her super power.

'Yes, we're here, Mother.'

Reaching out blindly behind him, he somehow found Celeste's hand and gripped it firmly in his own. They'd agreed on the drive out of London how they'd play this. A new couple, yes, but nothing serious. He didn't want his parents getting any ideas about marriage or anything— not least, because he knew that Celeste wouldn't be their first choice for him. Or second or third, come to that.

After all, she was only beautiful, intelligent, funny and, against the odds, mostly a nice person.

'Where's the money, Theo? Or at least a title? Come on, boy, try harder. That was always your problem—you just never tried hard enough.'

He could almost hear his father saying the words in his head.

Really, what was the point of coming home to be berated by him, when he could do it perfectly well for himself?

'There you are!' Maria burst into the main hall at the same time Theo and Celeste reached it. 'We were starting to think you'd got lost. Or forgotten.'

'Are we late?' Celeste asked, confused. 'I thought you

said one, Theo?' He saw her glance at the grandfather clock, as it chimed quarter to one.

Theo didn't answer. Maria didn't bother either as, of course, they were actually early. Five years ago, maybe he'd have second-guessed himself, thought he'd got the time wrong. He knew better now. But how could Theo explain to Celeste that his mother just liked to start with them at a disadvantage, any way she could?

He should have warned her in the car. Shouldn't have brought her at all. But somehow, when he was away from this place, he always believed that it couldn't be as bad as he remembered. That he was building it up in his head, somehow.

It was only once he returned that he realised the truth of it all.

'Come, come. Your father is already in the dining room, Theo, and you know he doesn't like to be kept waiting.' Maria turned away and bustled down the passageway to the dining room at the back of the house.

'I'm sorry,' Theo whispered as they followed.

'What for?' Celeste asked.

'Everything that happens in this house.' That should probably just about cover it.

He braced himself, and headed for lunch.

Forty minutes later, Celeste had a new respect for Theo Montgomery, and his ability to keep smiling and stay polite in the face of abject rudeness. She'd thought he'd done a good job at being pleasant to her, even after she'd spent their first meetings arguing about everything.

Now she knew his secret. He'd been training for this his whole life.

His father, Francis Montgomery, was easy enough to figure out. Perpetually disappointed by life, as far as she could see, and passing that disappointment onto Theo. He was every historical figure who'd ever lost a kingdom, or power, or influence, and blamed everyone but himself. Even the way Theo passed him the gravy wasn't satisfactory.

It was much easier to understand people when you thought of them as historical figures, she decided. Maybe that was the trick she needed, and hadn't realised until now. Something else Theo had given her.

'*He* dropped out of university, you know,' Francis told Celeste, apropos of nothing, over dessert.

She hadn't known. It had never come up. She wasn't entirely sure why it had come up now. And Theo clearly had no intention of telling them about his current studies, so she wouldn't. 'Well, it doesn't seem to have stopped him,' she said cheerfully.

Really, a dinner at which *she* was the cheerful, pleasant, upbeat one was a definite first. And not a good sign.

She glanced across at Theo, who sat staring sullenly at his syrup sponge pudding and custard. She'd never known him go so long without smiling before.

'I think it was the expectation,' Maria, his mother, said, almost as a secret aside, as if Theo couldn't hear them.

'*I* think he was too stupid,' Francis interjected. Maria ignored him.

'Oxford does come with certain expectations, don't you think?' Maria went on. 'And really, all that pressure on young minds. Some people just aren't cut out for that kind of life, are they? But he so wanted to go... *I* always knew my Theo wasn't really going to set the world aflame. It takes a special something for that, don't you think? And we knew early on that Theo didn't have it. But he's found his niche, and that's something,' she added, sounding doubtful.

'He never wanted to work hard, that was the problem,' Francis opined, leaning back in his chair, wine glass in hand. 'That's what happens when people get everything handed to them on a plate, like Theo has. They don't know how to work for it. Born lazy.'

'Well, Theo does actually have a job,' Celeste pointed out. She stared at Theo, waiting for him to say something, to defend himself, but he barely even looked up from his pudding. 'I've seen him do it—that's how we met, in fact. He works hard.' She thought of all the meetings and filming he'd had scheduled at odd times that week, all the time spent making sure everything was in place for the *New Year's Eve Spectacular*. All the emails and calls. Theo was properly involved in the projects he took on; he did a lot more than show up and smile, whatever people thought.

Whatever *she'd* thought, before she got to know him.

When you added in his studies, plus his fake dating her, Theo was anything but lazy.

But his parents didn't look convinced.

'And now, of course, he associates with all these women who are only interested in his name, or his money—no offence, of course,' Maria went on.

'None taken,' Celeste lied, her voice mild. *That*, at least, made Theo look up and give her a tight smile. She wondered when he'd learned to read her so well.

Maybe around the time she'd learned to read him.

His mother was a harder read—but Celeste was pretty sure she was toxic, one way or another. She reminded her of Rachel's stepmother, the few times they'd met, and that was *definitely* not a good thing. Maybe it was just living with Francis that had soured her, until she couldn't find a good thing to say about her own son.

'I always tell him to bring them home to see the old place,' Francis said, with a wheezy laugh. 'That'll put them off! He can't afford to marry a poor girl, not unless she's at least got a decent title they can trade on.'

There was an awkward pause. Were they really waiting for her to tell them if she had money and/or an aristocratic family?

'Of course, he never does bring anybody home,' Maria said, looking wistfully at Theo. 'I would like to see him settled—with the *right* girl, of course.'

Celeste didn't need the sharp look Theo's mother sent in her direction to get the message there. She might not always be great at reading the subtleties of human nature, mostly through lack of experience, but really, there was no subtlety here.

And Celeste didn't have the patience for death by a thousand insults.

'Well, I think we can all agree that's not going to be me!' Smiling cheerfully, she placed her spoon in her bowl, pushed away the stodgy pudding, and got to her feet, smoothing down her plain black dress. 'And now, I'm afraid, Theo and I really need to get back to London. Don't we, sweetheart?'

'Afraid so.' Were those the first words Theo had spoken since they sat down at the table? 'Sorry, Mum, Father.' He didn't hug them goodbye. She wasn't surprised. The Montgomerys were even less affectionate than her own family, which she hadn't really thought was possible.

'Thanks so much for having me,' Celeste said, as she backed out of the room, because if nothing else she'd managed to learn *some* manners over the last twenty eight years of her life. Even if she wasn't sure these people were really worthy of them.

Neither she nor Theo said anything else until they were in the car, down the driveway and back on the main road again, speeding away from Theo's childhood home.

'Well,' Celeste said, finally.

'I'm sorry.' He sounded so miserable, so tense, that she almost wanted to tell him to pull over so she could kiss him again, just to try and cheer him up.

'It's okay,' she said. 'I mean, it's not. They're awful. But honestly, I'm used to dreadful family dinners, so it was almost nice to sit through someone else's for a change. It's a good job I got to know you first, though.'

'Why's that?'

'Because otherwise I might believe some of the things your parents said about you.' She looked over at him and wished he weren't driving, so he could see the truth of her words in her eyes. 'As it is, I know you're nothing like the man they seem to think you are. So that's good.'

Was that the start of a smile, curving around his lips? She hoped so.

'Nothing like, huh?'

He was fishing for compliments now, but, after meeting his parents, she decided he probably deserved a few. 'Nothing at all. You're definitely not lazy, and you're proving with every essay you submit, every online seminar you attend, that you're capable of studying when you want to.' She'd talked him into showing her some of his modules and marks after a few more drinks after the ice skating. From his online tutor's comments, she could see that he was a conscientious and dedicated student, with interesting opinions and interpretations of events and sources that weren't just a repetition of someone else's analysis.

She almost wished he were one of her students. Except then she definitely wouldn't be able to think about kissing him, so it was probably best for all of them that he wasn't.

He was smiling now. She'd made him smile, just by telling the truth as she saw it. She liked that.

'I'm still sorry you had to sit through that lunch,' Theo said.

'That's okay,' Celeste said cheerfully. 'I know exactly how you can make it up to me.'

He raised an eyebrow at that. 'Oh? How's that?'

'You can come to *my* parents' Christmas Eve party with me.'

CHAPTER EIGHT

SPENDING CHRISTMAS EVE in a room full of people who were categorically proven to be brighter and better educated than him wasn't exactly in Theo's plans when December started. But then, nothing in his life seemed to have gone to plan since he'd met Celeste, so maybe it was all par for the course.

The Hunters' town house in central London was worlds away from his own family seat in most ways, but from the moment they'd arrived Theo had sensed something familiar. Something he didn't like. Celeste, however, seemed perfectly comfortable, so he'd pushed the feeling aside and tried to enjoy the party. She'd been there most of the day, helping prepare for the party, and by the time he arrived—with the obligatory bottle of wine for the hosts, or for himself, in case he got really desperate—there were already half a dozen people milling around the living spaces of the house, including her brother, Damon.

'You okay?' Celeste asked as she drifted past holding a tray of interesting-looking hors d'oeuvres. She was wearing a different dress from the one she'd worn for lunch with his parents a few days before, although it was, obviously, still black. This was cut high in the front but fell low on her back, then swished all the way to the floor, only just revealing that her usual boots had been replaced with high heels.

Theo wanted to pull down the shoulder straps and watch it fall to the floor. Although probably not in the middle of her parents' party, he supposed.

'Fine.' He looked around the room. From the few introductions he'd made, everyone here had several more degrees than him, and mostly wanted to talk about their research with other people who would understand how impressive it was.

He was not that person.

Celeste rested a hand against his arm for a moment. 'Sure?'

She'd been like this since she'd met his parents—more sensitive, more concerned. Less Celeste-like. As if seeing inside his secrets allowed her to drop a little of her own armour. And she was letting him in here, too. Showing him her world.

As if this thing between them *meant* something to her.

Or as if she wanted company at a boring family party. That was the more likely answer.

'I'm feeling...a little out of my depth here,' he admitted reluctantly. He'd worked so hard over the years to fit in anywhere, to win people over, to make them smile in a way he'd never been able to achieve with his own parents. But here...he felt inferior again, just like at home.

He didn't like it.

Celeste reached up and pressed a soft kiss to his cheek. 'Just stay away from my mother and you'll be fine,' she told him.

Well, that was encouraging.

'Keep me company for a few minutes?' he asked, trying not to sound desperate. 'I've barely seen you tonight.'

She flashed him an amused smile. 'You know the people here aren't likely to be posting photos of us on social media, right? Some of them might not even know who you are…'

Theo faked horror at that idea, although actually, right then, it seemed like the better option. He didn't want to be singled out and identified here. Didn't want to be highlighted as the know-nothing TV star.

He wanted to be here as Celeste's date. Nothing more, nothing less.

'That's not why I want to spend time with you.'

'I know! You want my feedback on your latest essay, right?' she guessed. 'I've told you, I'll do it, but only if you give me tips about not appearing scary on television.'

'You don't need them, but I'll give them to you, sure. But not tonight.'

She gave him a speculative look. 'Is it because I've already lectured you on my research and books and you figure I'm the only person in the room who won't bore you again?'

'I'm never bored listening to you.'

'Ah, so it is that,' she said, with a grin. 'In that case, try and avoid my dad, too.'

'Celeste…' She started to move away, and he snaked an arm around her waist to keep her closer. 'Is it so hard to believe I might just want to spend time with you? Because I like doing that?'

The surprise in her eyes hurt, a little. It so obviously hadn't occurred to her that he *might* want to do that—which suggested that she didn't want it.

Then he looked a little closer, as she bit down on her lower lip and met his gaze. '*Do* you? Because generally most people don't.'

'I'm not most people,' he told her. 'And yes. I do.'

A small smile spread across her face, a real one, one

he believed. She opened her mouth to respond—until someone called her name from across the room and, with an apologetic look, she slipped away.

Theo sighed, and reached for another drink. He had a feeling that the evening was going to be a very long one.

An hour later and Theo was still looking pretty miserable. Celeste wished she could stop and stay with him for a while—especially since it seemed he actually *wanted* her company, and not just for appearances—but she had bigger concerns tonight. Mostly around her brother and her best friend. She couldn't afford to be distracted by the thought of kissing Theo again.

However tempting that was.

Her conversations with Damon during the day hadn't made her feel any better about whatever was happening between him and Rachel, although she suspected they couldn't keep pretending it wasn't an issue for very much longer. And Rachel still wasn't here…

Celeste's phone buzzed in her pocket. God, she loved a dress with pockets.

I'm outside. Come meet me?

It was Rachel, of course. Dumping her tray on the nearest flat surface, Celeste headed for the door—wincing as she realised that her father had cornered Theo and looked to be practising his latest lecture on him. At least Theo was still managing that polite, TV-star smile. When that started to slip, that was when she'd worry.

'Why didn't you come in? It's freezing out here,' she said as she opened the door, looking around for her friend. Then she spotted her, at the bottom of the steps that led to the town house's front door.

One look, and she knew. She stared, speechless for a moment.

Then, 'Oh, my God, you're in love with my brother,' she blurted.

'I wanted to speak to you first,' Rachel said, with a small smile. 'Before I talk to him.'

Oh. Oh, she'd been right. Everything *was* coming to a head tonight.

Celeste shut the front door behind her and stepped out into the biting cold of the December night. Descending the steps carefully in her heels, she sat on the second from the bottom one in the freezing cold with her best friend.

'Tell me everything,' she said.

And Rachel did.

Some of it she already knew from her conversations with Damon, or the double-fake-date lunch they'd shared. Some of it was new.

And all of it boiled down to one thing—the same thing Celeste had known from the moment she saw her.

Celeste waited until Rachel had run out of steam and words before she spoke.

'So like I said, you're in love with my brother? Is that right?'

Rachel nodded. 'And I'm hoping he feels the same about me.'

Celeste thought back to her last conversation with Damon, in the kitchen before the party started. He'd seemed…conflicted.

'I think he does,' she said slowly. 'The thing will be getting him to admit it.'

She didn't want to give her friend false hope, because her brother was basically a lost cause when it came to love. But on the other hand…

'If anyone can do it, I reckon you can,' she said.

Rachel flashed her a quick grin. 'Do you know, apart from my mother before she died, you were the first person in my life who ever listened to what I had to say without talking over me, or telling me what I should feel. Damon was the second.'

No wonder she'd fallen for him. Celeste knew what a rarity that was in Rachel's life; she'd often assumed that her listening skills were the only reason her best friend put up with her at all. She might not agree with her all the time, and she'd most definitely tell her when she'd got something factually wrong, but she would at least listen first.

'It's one of the most useful things our parents ever taught us,' Celeste said lightly. 'You see, you can't brutally demolish another person's argument or theory without listening to it properly in the first place.'

Rachel laughed, but it sounded more desperate than amused.

'What's he going to say when I tell him?' she asked quietly.

Celeste had no idea. But her friend needed to know the answer, one way or another. 'Let's go and find out.'

Rachel stood up, smoothed down the beautiful wine-red dress Celeste had helped her pick out at the Cressingham Arcade, and nodded.

Inside, the party was still…well, mildly happening, rather than raging. Across the room, Damon stood with their mother, but he turned away from her as Rachel entered, and Celeste almost *felt* the moment his gaze met her friend's.

Whatever Damon told her tonight, it was clear to her that this thing between him and Rachel was no festive fling.

Rachel's heel skidded on the parquet flooring, and

Celeste gripped her arm a little tighter, as Theo had hers on the ice rink.

'You okay?' Celeste murmured.

'No.' Rachel held onto Celeste while she found her balance. 'But I will be.'

'Do you want me to come with you to talk to him?' Not that she was sure what she could do, but she could tell her best friend was scared. Rachel was the one person in the world she'd *always* been able to read right. She'd learned her, the same way she learned dates and names and sources. Because from the moment Rachel had become her friend, she'd known she had to work as hard to keep her as she did her grade average.

'No,' Rachel said. 'I need to do this alone.'

'You're sure?'

Rachel's gaze skittered towards Damon, and Celeste's followed. He looked as if he was bracing himself for Sunday lunch with the parents—or, worse, Christmas Day. Maybe he was.

Oh, she had a feeling this was going to go very badly.

'Sure,' Rachel said, sounding more certain than Celeste felt. 'Besides, I need you to do something else for me.'

'Anything,' Celeste said. She couldn't fix this for her friend, but she could help her through it.

'Distract the rest of the room?'

Huh. She hadn't been expecting that, but she supposed it made sense. There weren't so many people at the gathering that any argument between Rachel and Damon would go unnoticed. In fact, it would probably be the most exciting thing that had happened at one of the Hunters' Christmas Eve parties in years. Of course, Rachel wouldn't want a gaping audience—unlike every time she and Theo went out in public.

'Just while I get Damon out of here. I don't want an audience for this,' Rachel went on.

Celeste tried to smile, although she wasn't sure she managed it very well. 'On it.'

She didn't look back as she crossed the room; Rachel had to do this alone now. And she had a job to do.

Unfortunately, the only way she knew to draw the attention of the masses was by kissing Theo Montgomery.

The things she did for her friends...

Celeste's father was obviously a very intelligent man, Theo decided, but he was no storyteller. He'd been talking— at length—about his research and discoveries for the last fifteen minutes, and Theo was still no clearer what he'd actually been doing.

Celeste would have made the story exciting. He'd have listened to her explain anything. Partly because he was stupidly in thrall to her, but mostly because, despite what she believed about herself, she was actually good at making history interesting. At telling the stories that made the past come to life.

He'd known that about her before he'd even met her, from listening to her on the radio. It was how he knew her new TV show would not only be picked up, but be a success. And it was, now he thought about it, probably why there'd been such uproar after the *Christmas Cracker Cranium Quiz* had aired. People weren't just cross because he'd been mansplaining to her, but because they'd wanted to hear what she had to say, and he'd been following the producer's orders to cut her off.

She'd asked for tips on being on TV but, in truth, she just needed to be herself. She needed to see herself the way *he* saw her—as a passionate, engaged, fascinating historian who made stories of the past feel real and immediate.

He didn't know what her history with men, or other people generally, was like—he hadn't asked and he wouldn't—but he got the impression that others might not have always taken the time to see her that way. Maybe they'd been put off by her sometimes prickly nature—something he suspected now was more down to social nerves than anything else. Or perhaps the people she met simply didn't like being told they were wrong, even when they were.

But she'd let him see beyond the prickles. And he'd been told he was wrong his whole life. It was actually a relief to be told it when it was true. At least Celeste also acknowledged when he was *right*.

She hadn't laughed at the idea of him studying for a degree; she'd encouraged him. And she'd put up with lunch with his parents without flinching, then told him they were wrong about him.

Something he'd been waiting to hear his whole life. Not from fakers like him, who lied for a living.

From someone who told the truth no matter how inconvenient. From Celeste.

And that was why he'd been politely listening to her father drone on for the last thirty minutes, without excusing himself and leaving this travesty of a party. Because if he left, he wouldn't see her again tonight—and, God help him, he wanted to see her again.

He tuned out Jacob Hunter completely as Celeste returned to the room, arm in arm with Rachel—looking stunning in a wine-red gown that had Damon, across the room, standing gawping at her like an idiot. Huh. Obviously things were afoot there.

Suddenly, Celeste broke away from her friend and

headed towards him, a determined glint in her eye. Her father didn't seem to have noticed, as he was still continuing a run-on sentence that had been going on for half a glass of wine now. Theo put his glass down on the nearest table, and braced himself for whatever was about to happen.

Celeste grinned. Oh, but he had a bad feeling about this...

She ignored her father as much as Mr Hunter was ignoring her, her gaze not leaving Theo's as she approached. And then she was in front of him, almost pressed up against him, in fact, that slippery black fabric sliding against the front of his freshly pressed shirt.

'Just follow my lead on this one, okay?' she murmured.

And then she kissed him.

It was like the ice rink all over again, with a similar chance of him falling over, just out of shock. Theo froze for less than a second, before the feel of Celeste's mouth on his let his instincts take over, pushing his brain to the back of the queue.

He knew how to do this, whatever her reasons. Hell, he wanted to do this, had been dreaming of doing this, ever since the last time. His baser instincts weren't going to let his brain ruin this for him now.

Around them, there were murmurs, comments, and he happily ignored all of them. If Celeste didn't care what her family and friends were saying about their public display of affection, he sure as hell didn't. Instead, he sank into the kiss, holding her close and wrapping his arms tight around her as if he never intended to let go.

Maybe he didn't.

Celeste, however, had other ideas. Apparently oblivious to the way her kiss was changing his whole world around him, she pulled away, and glanced over her shoulder.

'Okay, they're gone.' She let him go, flashed a smile at her father, and headed out into the hallway.

Theo blinked, then followed.

'What was that about?' he asked as the door to the living space swung shut behind him, and they were alone at last.

'Rachel needed to talk to Damon, without an audience.'

'So you drew the audience's attention our way instead,' Theo surmised.

She smiled. 'Exactly.'

Theo watched her, watched as her smile started to waver. 'Did I do it wrong?'

He laughed, not at her but at himself. 'Sweetheart, trust me. I don't think you know *how* to do it wrong.'

Celeste gave a one-shouldered shrug. 'Oh, you'd be surprised. Guys are generally with me for my brain, or my university connections, rather than my lips or my body. Which, you know, is a good thing, I suppose.' He'd sworn to himself he wouldn't ask about her past romances. It was none of his business—especially since this wasn't even a real relationship. But if she was just telling him, that was okay, right?

'Not if they're just using those parts of you.' He frowned at her. 'Wouldn't you rather have someone who wanted *all* of you? Brains and body, your soul *and* your sexuality?'

Tossing her hair back over her shoulder, Celeste barked her own laugh this time, too sharp and short to contain any actual humour. 'You can talk. You only want me for my publicity.'

God, if only she knew the truth. How much he *did*

want her, just as she was. Except for her, this was still about her career, and his. She'd never hinted at wanting anything more. And he could only imagine how people would laugh if he even pretended to be smart enough to have anything more with her. Half a distance-learning degree wasn't going to match up to her PhD and academic credentials any time soon.

But if she honestly thought he wasn't attracted to her, that he didn't dream about her lips, her body under his... then she really hadn't been paying attention.

The question wasn't whether he wanted her. It was whether *she* wanted *him*.

He waited, just a moment, until her gaze settled back on his again. He didn't laugh off her comment the way he would have done before that kiss. Didn't make a joke, and let the moment pass. Didn't hide anything, for once.

He let her see the heat in his eyes. And, because he was watching oh-so-carefully, he saw the answering flare in her own, before she blinked and tried to bury it.

'Celeste.' Theo stepped closer, relieved when she didn't move away. 'Do you really think this is still all about the publicity?'

'Isn't it?' Her tone was defiant, but he heard the hope behind it. 'What else could it be? We had an agreement...'

'And then I kissed you on that ice rink and nearly lost my mind with wanting you.'

A sharp intake of breath was the only response she gave him.

He stepped closer. Her back was already up against the bannister, and he was so close now he could reach past and rest one arm on the wood right beside her head. If she gave him the slightest hint, he'd back away.

But she didn't. That heat was back in her eyes, and he could feel it growing between their bodies, too.

'Celeste, I don't know what this is between us. But it's sure as hell not about the publicity right now, okay? There's no one watching. No cameras. And I still need to do this.'

He ducked his head to capture her mouth with his own, loving the small sigh she gave as their lips touched. She wanted this as much as he did. Needed it, even.

He'd worry about what the hell that meant tomorrow.

It was long moments before he pulled away, panting slightly, and rested his forehead against hers. 'How long do we have to stay at this thing?'

Celeste shook her head, as if she was trying to clear it. 'I told my parents I'd stay here tonight. It's Christmas Eve, Theo.'

He swore. Christmas Eve meant he needed to drive back to Sorrelton House tomorrow morning, to brave the festivities with the family. Christmas Eve meant Celeste would have her own family stuff to do.

'That means I have a bed upstairs,' she pointed out, and all the blood in his body rushed in one direction.

But before he could sweep her into his arms and carry her up the narrow town-house staircase, Rachel came barrelling through from the kitchen, her face blotchy with tears.

Celeste broke away from him instantly, taking her best friend into her arms and whispering with her. Then she turned back to Theo, her face thunderous.

'Can you get Rachel a taxi, please? I need to go and speak with my brother.'

CHAPTER NINE

HER HEAD STILL swirling from that kiss, Celeste stormed out into the back garden to find Damon.

'I warned him,' she muttered to herself. 'I *told* him to be careful with her heart, and now look. Honestly. *Men.*'

The fact wasn't completely lost on her that she was avoiding thinking about the man she'd just walked away from inside. Had she really been just about to lead Theo Montgomery up to her childhood bedroom and let him seduce her? Or seduce *him* if it came to it?

Yes, her mind replied. And her treacherous body added, *And you still might.*

Focus, Celeste.

She needed to deal with Damon first. Then she could figure out what the hell was going on with Theo.

She found him, eventually, sitting forlornly on the swing at the end of the garden. Her steps faltered for a moment, when she saw how heartbroken he looked.

This is what love does to you. Where lust can lead.

She shook her head. This wasn't about her. And she wasn't Rachel, and Theo wasn't Damon. They both knew what they had was fake. They lived different lives in different worlds that had only intersected for this brief, wonderful time. In the new year, it would all be over, and as long as she remembered that she'd be fine.

'You are the biggest idiot known to man,' she said, sitting down beside him.

'I know.' God, he sounded miserable.

'Let me guess.' Celeste kicked off the floor with one foot, making the old swing seat sway forward and back. 'She asked you to commit and you said no.'

'Basically.'

'Why? Because you wanted to be free to sleep with as many other women as possible?' If that was the case, she was walking out of here right now and leaving him to be miserable on his own.

'No!' The horror in his voice surprised her into silence. 'Because I'm not that guy. I'd let her down, in the end, when she realised that.'

Oh. *Oh, Damon.*

His head was bowed, his hands clasped between his knees, so she saw clearly the moment his spine stiffened, as if someone had walked over his grave.

'Damon?' she asked, concerned.

'I'm okay.' A lie, but she let him have it. If he was having a come-to-Jesus revelation moment, she didn't want to ruin it. Especially if it might just set him on the right path again.

'For what it's worth? I don't think you'd let her down, little brother.' Standing up, she pressed a quick kiss to his hair, something she couldn't remember doing since he was a child. 'In fact, I think you've got a better handle on this love thing than most of us. You just need to be brave enough to go after it.'

She was as surprised by her words as he obviously was, but she knew they were right, deep down. Damon was a good guy, and if he loved Rachel then he'd do everything in his power to make it right.

Celeste headed back up to the house, her head still

whirling. The whole thing was just a reminder how distracting and distressing love could be. She'd never been sure if her parents really loved each other, or if their academic goals were just so neatly aligned that they'd decided they might as well team up. Either way, they'd made a good enough go of it, but they weren't exactly role models for affection and romance. Or parenting, come to that.

It seemed she'd spent her whole life trying to prove to them that she was as good as they were, earning their love through academic achievements—while Damon had gone the opposite way entirely and followed his own path, never trying to impress anyone at all, never committing to anything.

Celeste had already heard her mother's opinion about her choice of date for the evening; she imagined that it was probably about as favourable as Theo's parents on her. She didn't have a title or money. And Theo didn't have a PhD or a research grant or publishing history. He didn't even have an Oxbridge degree, it turned out.

She reached the back door and stared through the kitchen to where Theo was standing in the hallway, alone. He leaned against the bannister where he'd kissed her, running his hand through his hair. Was he having the same second and third thoughts as she was? Probably.

They weren't a match, that much was clear. But did they need to be, really?

Only if it's for ever.

And it wasn't. It was just for now. And right now... Celeste's body knew what she wanted, even if her mind was still spinning.

She let the door slam shut behind her, and Theo looked up instantly, his gaze locking with her own.

'I put Rachel in a cab,' he told her as he moved closer. 'She was heading to the Cressingham Arcade.'

'Good.' If Damon wanted to go after her, he'd find her easily enough there, right? Those two could figure things out on their own from here.

She had her own love life to sort out.

No, not love life.

Her *sex* life. Something that had been dormant for far too long—not a problem that she imagined Theo having. Which meant maybe he could help her get over her drought, with both of them clear that was all this was.

She stepped towards him, closing the gap. 'In that case, where were we?'

Theo's eyes were dark. 'You were telling me about the bedroom you have upstairs. And how it's Christmas Eve.'

The way he looked at her, she felt like his Christmas gift, waiting to be unwrapped.

Maybe she was.

Do I really know what I'm doing here?

No, she admitted to herself. She hadn't got a clue. But she'd lived her whole life so far knowing exactly where she was going—which degree, which research project, which professor she wanted to study under.

Perhaps it was time to take a leap into the unknown, for a change.

In the other room, she heard her mother laugh, and her father clink some silverware against a glass, ready to make his customary Christmas Eve speech. She didn't need to hear it to know it would be the same as the year before, and the year before that.

She was ready for something new.

'Come upstairs with me?' she asked softly.

Theo hesitated, and she almost took back the whole thing. 'Why?' he asked.

Celeste swallowed. But she'd come this far, she wasn't going to stop now. And besides, having a clear overview of her objectives was a positive thing, right? That was what her PhD supervisor had always said anyway.

'Because I want you, and I think you want me. Not just for the publicity, but for the fun of it, too. So I think you should make love to me tonight, because I can't imagine going another minute without kissing you again.'

Theo surged forward at her words, sweeping her into his arms and kissing her the way he'd wanted to all night. She kissed him back, with all the passion she put into the things that mattered to her: history, proving people wrong, and kissing him.

God, he loved a woman who had her priorities in order.

'Upstairs,' he murmured against her lips.

He could hear Celeste's father droning on in the other room, but there was no way his guests were going to put up with that for very long, and he wanted to be secluded away in her bedroom before any of them escaped out to the kitchen and found them half naked.

Because he was going to have Celeste half naked—no, totally naked—very soon, wherever they happened to be at the time.

'Yes,' she gasped back. 'Upstairs.' She looked back through the door into the garden. He followed her gaze, and saw a figure approaching in the darkness. 'And fast, before my brother gets here.'

They ascended the narrow staircase together, still touching and kissing at every step, hiding their ebullient laughter as Damon stormed through the hallway below and straight out of the front door. And then they were at a dark wooden door, and it was opening, and all Theo could see was a bed and Celeste, and suddenly the laughter faded.

'You're sure about this?' he asked softly, wanting her to know she could change her mind, at any point.

But she nodded, firmly. 'Very.' She bit down on her lower lip for a moment, the telephone-box-red lipstick she'd been wearing almost all gone now, probably smeared across his face.

He kicked the door shut behind him and swept her up into his arms.

Theo wanted to take it slow, to make it worth the wait, to make it better than she could imagine. But as with all things, Celeste had her own ideas, too. Not that he was complaining about them.

In no time, his jacket, shirt and tie had been stripped away, and her hands roamed across his chest, followed by her lips. Swallowing the lust that coursed through him at her touch, he pushed the straps of her dress down her arms, kissing every inch of creamy skin as it was revealed. Her shoulders, her collarbone, the curve of her breasts...

She arched against him, pressing her softness up against all the parts of his body that were anything *but* soft right now, and Theo almost lost his mind.

'On the bed,' he said, his voice desperate and rasping, even to his own ears.

'Yes,' she replied. Then she grabbed his shoulders and, twisting them around, pushed him down onto the mattress so she landed on top of him.

Theo gazed up at her. Her dark hair was loose around her bare shoulders, tousled and wild. Her eyes were huge in the moonlight, her creamy skin almost glowing as he ran his hands over it, from her shoulders, down her arms, skirting her bare breasts, to where her black dress was pooled around her full hips.

She looked like an ancient goddess—Aphrodite or

Venus—come to enchant him. Or a queen, perhaps. Anne Boleyn, seducing her Henry and changing history.

All Theo knew, in that moment, was that whatever she asked for, he would give.

Another time, another place, the thought would terrify him. But right now...

'Are you going to have your wicked way with me?' he asked, the familiar smirk on his lips giving him courage.

This could be just like every other meaningless encounter in his life. Just because it was *Celeste*, didn't mean it had to, well, mean anything.

She grinned down at him, her hair brushing against his chest as she dipped her head to kiss him. 'Definitely.'

'Good.' He grabbed her around the waist and pulled her flush against him as he kissed her again.

He'd worry about everything else in the morning. Right now, he intended to enjoy every minute.

Celeste awoke on Christmas morning in her childhood bed, with Theo's arm resting heavily on her waist, his breath almost a snore in her ear—and her bedroom door crashing into the wall behind it as Damon and Rachel burst in.

'We're getting married!' they announced, in gleeful unison. Celeste blinked at them. Their eyes seemed feverishly bright with happiness or lack of sleep, their cheeks pink from the cold, and their hands clasped tight together.

Grabbing the sheet to her chest, Celeste struggled to a sitting position, which was harder than it should be since apparently Theo slept like the dead.

She should probably cut the guy some slack. She couldn't exactly blame him for being tired after all their... exertions, the night before. Heat rose to her cheeks at the memory of him declaring it was his turn, after she'd, well, had her wicked way with him, as he put it.

They'd stopped keeping track of whose turn it was, after that, but suffice to say the night had not been exactly *restful*. Thank goodness for solid Victorian walls, and the fact that her parents' bedroom was on the next floor up.

She forced her mind back to the present. The room was still mostly in darkness. If she was lucky, maybe they wouldn't notice that she was naked. Or that she wasn't alone in the bed. It could happen.

Then their words caught up with her.

'Wait. Married?'

She'd hoped her brother and her best friend would be able to sort things out. But *married*? How had Damon gone from a confirmed commitment-phobe to a husband-to-be in just one night? That seemed a lot to chalk up to Christmas magic.

But perhaps that same magic was responsible for what had happened with Theo, too. Because in the cold morning light it seemed more like an impossibility than ever. Apart from the bit where he was still snoring in her bed beside her.

Damon shrugged. 'We just figured…once you know you want to spend your life with another person, why wait?'

'Plus, you had to come up with something really good to make up for being such an arsehole,' Celeste said, reading between the lines.

Rachel thrust her left hand towards her, showcasing a glittering diamond. 'You get to be maid of honour, of course. And you can't wear black.'

'Black is very chic for bridesmaids these days,' Celeste said automatically, with no idea at all if it was true.

'I'm more worried about the "maid" part,' Damon said,

a small frown appearing between his eyebrows—yet still utterly failing to completely hide his happy glow—as he gazed past her to the lump under the sheets beside her.

Celeste rolled her eyes. 'Little brother, my sex life is none of your business.'

Of course, Theo chose that moment to wake up, rolling over languidly onto his back before sitting up, his chest bare as he rested against the headboard.

'Merry Christmas, everybody. What did I miss?'

'Damon and Rachel are getting married, and you and I are having the most awkward morning after known to history.'

'And you know history,' Theo replied. 'Congratulations, guys. Damon, I'd shake your hand, but I'm not entirely sure where my trousers are.'

'I think they're over by the window.' Rachel squinted in the semi-darkness of the room. 'I can see the belt buckle shining in the moonlight.'

'How romantic,' Damon said drily. 'So, you've heard our news. Care to fill us in on yours?'

'No news!' Celeste said brightly. 'Just, you know, carrying on the charade that Theo and I are madly in love and together. All for show.'

'Except you're both naked under there.' Damon did not look entirely pleased at the idea. She supposed she didn't blame him. She had made it very clear that there was nothing real between her and Theo, and the guy did have a bit of a reputation. Celeste frowned. Except so did Damon, and his relationship with Rachel had been equally iffy to start with. Her brother had literally no moral high ground to stand on.

Plus, as she'd already pointed out, her sex life was none of his business.

Rachel, thankfully, was slightly more subtle than

her new fiancé. 'Anyway, we just wanted to share our news…'

'You don't know that we're naked. We could have clothes on,' Celeste said, because apparently she just didn't know when to stop digging. Beside her, Theo was smirking. She could feel it.

'I can see your underwear hanging from the wardrobe door handle,' Damon replied.

'And now we'd better go and tell the rest of our families,' Rachel said, bundling Damon towards the door again. 'Happy Christmas, you two! See you both later.'

'Merry Christmas,' Celeste called after them. 'And, uh, congratulations!'

The door crashed shut behind them, and then it was just her and Theo.

Naked.

In her bed.

'So, that was an exhilarating way to start the day,' Theo said. 'What do you say we take another nap to get over it? Or something.' His hand crept up her bare side at the 'or something', leaving her in no doubt what he was hoping that something might be.

And she wanted that, too. She could feel her body already starting to respond to his touch, her nipples tightening under the thin sheet that covered them, the ache that pulsed through her. How could she want him this much when, to be fair, she'd already had quite a lot of him last night?

Christmas Eve magic, that was what it had been. And, oh, it had been magical.

But in the cold light of day, this desperate need to touch him left her with more questions than she liked.

Hang on. Cold light of day. Cold, yes, but there still wasn't much light pushing its way around the curtains.

'What time is it?' she asked, pushing his hand away.

Theo grabbed his watch from the nightstand. 'Urgh. Four-thirty. No wonder it still feels like the middle of the night. We should definitely get some more sleep.'

Celeste wriggled back down under the covers. Maybe if it was still last night, she could enjoy this—enjoy him—a little longer.

Because she knew this couldn't, wouldn't last—that had never been the plan. But maybe it didn't have to be over just yet.

She reached out and ran her hand up *his* side, just as he'd done to her, from thigh to chest, before bringing it back down his front instead. 'Sure about the sleeping part?' she asked.

'Not in the slightest,' Theo replied, and kissed her.

CHAPTER TEN

HE'D DEFINITELY HAD worse Christmas mornings, Theo
decided, as he left the Hunter town house a little later
that morning, whistling to himself in the cold, still dark
air. Yes, he was knackered, and slightly hungover, and
certain muscles ached in pleasurable ways after the kind
of workout they'd only dreamed of for the last few years,
but still. *Definitely* worse mornings.

Celeste had tried to convince him to leave quietly, by
the back door preferably, without being seen. He'd given
her a look and reminded her that the whole *point* was that
he should be seen. This was the perfect addition to the
story they were weaving for the press—and it seemed
important to remember that this morning. Otherwise, a
guy might start to get ideas.

Except there were no press waiting for him outside
the town house as he left—although he did bump into
Jacob Hunter on the stairs, which was more than a little
awkward.

His good mood lasted all through his walk home,
while he showered and dressed and loaded the car—
taking an extra coffee to keep himself awake on the
drive—and right up until he pulled his car into the driveway of Sorrelton House.

Christmas with the family. He'd wish he could have

just stayed with Celeste for the day, except then he'd have been spending Christmas with *her* family, which, after last night, he wasn't sure was demonstrably better.

Except he'd have been with Celeste. Touching her. Kissing her. As if they really *were* a couple, and not just pretend.

She'd been quick enough to denounce that anything had changed between them to her brother, but it *had* changed, hadn't it? Surely it had to, after a night like that?

The only question was, what had it changed into? He'd have to wait until he was back in London, back with Celeste, to answer that one.

He killed the engine, but stayed sitting in the car on the driveway for a moment, staring up at Sorrelton House. He wished Celeste could be with him again this time. For all his duty visits to his parents drained him, it had somehow seemed less awful when she was beside him. Not that he imagined she'd be volunteering for another visit any time soon. Just as he wouldn't be attending one of her father's lectures.

Different worlds.

But in some ways they intersected. She didn't laugh at his studies. He didn't tell her she should stick to academia, not TV. She made him think that maybe, just maybe, there really was something more to him than his name and his face, after all. And he hoped he'd shown her last night that he knew she was a hell of a lot more than just a brain and the ability to recite facts.

Although, to be honest, he could sit and listen to her recite facts all day. Because they weren't just facts, just history, when Celeste said them. They were stories, a new way of looking at the world. The way *she* saw the world. And he was a little bit worried that he'd never get enough of that.

Theo sighed, and hoped that her confidence in him might help him make it through Christmas Day with his parents, without him starting to believe everything they said about him again.

He didn't notice the unfamiliar car on the driveway until he'd already dragged his overnight bag and box of gifts up the front step to the main door. He frowned at the vehicle as he waited for the door to be answered; Christmas was, of course, a formal occasion, and he knew he wouldn't be forgiven for using the side entrance on such a day.

Who could possibly be here?

Other than his aunt Gladys, who always joined them for high days and holidays, and perhaps the widowed vicar from the church at the edge of the estate, he couldn't imagine *anyone* choosing to spend Christmas Day at Sorrelton House.

He got his answer quickly enough, however, as the door was yanked open, not by Jenkins, but by a vaguely familiar blonde in a green and red tartan dress. She was a good few years younger than him, as best he could guess, and Theo had the horrible feeling that he really should be able to place her. Especially if she was spending Christmas with his family.

He forced himself to smile instead of frown as he tried to buy time while he figured it out.

'Merry Christmas!' he said cheerfully. 'How are things going here this festive morning?'

The blonde smiled wanly at him. 'Happy Christmas, Theo. It's lovely to see you again.'

She pressed a dry kiss to his cheek, then moved aside to let him enter.

'Ah, the prodigal son returns, eh?'

That voice, Theo recognised. And the portly figure it belonged to, waddling into the hallway. Hugo Howard, his father's long-term friend and sometime business partner. Which meant the blonde had to be his daughter, Emmaline. Theo didn't think he'd seen her since she was about twelve, so he didn't feel quite so bad about not recognising her.

The family tableau was completed as Hugo's wife, Anna, a tall, thin woman who towered over her husband and glared at everything because she refused to wear her glasses and blamed poor inanimate objects for her not being able to see them, joined them.

'Hugo, Anna. Merry Christmas,' Theo repeated. 'Not that it's not lovely to see you all, but are my parents here too?'

Hugo laughed uproariously. 'You always were the funny one, Theo. Like your dad says, at least you found a way to make people laughing at you a good thing. They're through in the green sitting room. Come on, now.'

Theo shook off the only vaguely veiled insult without comment. But what did it say about his presence here that the unexpected Christmas guests were more likely to greet him at the door than his own parents?

'It's a good job I got to know you first, though. Because otherwise I might believe some of the things your parents said about you.'

Celeste's words, after their last visit. She knew him even better now, of course. But even then, even after only a few fake dates and an acquaintance of less than three weeks, she'd seen him more clearly than his own parents had. She'd understood him, in a way he knew now his own family never would. She made him see himself through her eyes—not the TV-viewing public's, or his father's critical gaze. But Celeste's clear, unwavering, uncompromisingly honest view.

And he saw her, too. She was becoming all he ever wanted to see.

He dumped his overnight bag at the foot of the grand staircase and fell into step beside Emmaline as they all headed for the sitting room.

'This is a surprise,' he said amiably. 'Is your joining us today a last-minute thing, or did my parents just forget to tell me again?'

'Fairly last minute, I think,' Emmaline said, with a smile that barely reached her lips, let alone her eyes. 'I think your father called mine last Sunday and asked us to join him. We were supposed to be going to my brother in Hampshire, but...' Shrugging, she trailed off.

Last Sunday. After he'd visited for lunch with Celeste, then. Suddenly, Theo was very suspicious about the presence of his unexpected guests.

'Didn't my mother tell me you were recently engaged?' He glanced down at her ring finger, and found it bare. Ah.

'It got called off.' No smile at all this time, understandably, just a tight, pinched look.

'I'm sorry.'

'No need to be sorry!' Hugo said, from in front of them. 'All for the best, I say. Plenty more fish in the sea, after all, right, Emmie?' He shot his daughter a significant look, then moved his gaze onto Theo.

Right. Of course.

The sequence of events was falling into place perfectly in his head now. He'd brought Celeste to lunch; his parents had been horrified. So, of course, they had to find someone more 'suitable' for him. And who could possibly be more suitable than the recently dumped daughter of his father's richer-than-sin best friend? The Howards had no title, or pretensions to one, but they had a lot of money. While Theo and his family had the cache of being on the fringe of the aristocracy.

He was sure his father would have preferred he marry someone with money *and* a title, but needs must. And they were obviously very set against Celeste.

It almost made him want her more.

But most of all, it made him want to take a stand against his parents. To step outside the toxic circle they surrounded him with whenever they were together. To tell them, finally, that enough was enough.

He was himself. *He* was enough. And he'd fall in love with whoever the hell he wanted, regardless of what they thought about it.

Not that he was in love with Celeste Hunter, of course. But the principle remained.

And for once, Theo didn't think his usual survival tactics of staying silent and trying not to care were going to get him through Christmas Day with the family. Because he saw things differently now. More clearly.

Thanks to Celeste.

'I really am sorry about this,' he murmured to Emmaline as they entered the sitting room.

She shrugged thin shoulders. 'Could be worse,' she said. 'My brother's wife has eight dogs, and only half of them are house-trained. At least I don't need to worry about that here.'

A ringing endorsement of their Christmas, Theo thought.

At least he wasn't standing in dog muck. Yay him.

It wasn't enough for him, any more. He was done being grateful to be part of the family, to have the name and the face that had put him where he was. He was worth more than that. He wasn't a disappointment—not to himself. At least, he *wouldn't* be, if he kept going after the things that mattered to him. He had more to give than just a charming smile and a posh accent. He could do more than marry money or fame.

And he had to tell his parents that. Today.

Celeste's parents were not, by nature, early risers. But since Damon and Rachel appeared to be fuelled solely by love that Christmas morning, by the time she'd shooed Theo out the front door and ventured into the kitchen in search of coffee, it seemed the whole house were up and ready for the day.

They were also all staring at her.

'What?' Did she have her dressing gown on inside out? Or were Theo's pants stuck to it, somehow? She'd thought this morning couldn't get more embarrassing, but she was willing to be proven wrong.

'I met your young man again on the stairs this morning,' her father said, over the rim of his coffee cup. 'He seemed to be leaving in a hurry.'

Celeste winced. 'Well, it's Christmas Day. He had to get back to his own family.' Poor sod. 'Did Damon and Rachel tell you their happy news?'

'They did.' Her mother poured her a cup of coffee—steaming hot and black, no sugar, the way they all took it. Damon joked it was the only thing all four of them actually had in common.

'Are you ready to reconsider the whole black for the maid of honour thing yet?' she asked Rachel. At least if her best friend was marrying in, she'd always have someone on her side in family debates.

Unless Rachel took Damon's side, of course. Hmm, maybe she hadn't thought this through well enough, when she'd encouraged Damon to follow his heart.

Rachel shook her head and turned her attention back to her coffee—milky white and loaded with sugar, just as she'd drunk it at university.

'Celeste, we're worried about you,' Damon said. Her parents nodded in agreement.

Wait. What?

'The three of you are worried about me?' She kind of needed the clarification. After all, she couldn't remember the last time it was Damon and her parents against her, instead of her and their parents against Damon, when it came to family disagreements.

She was the one who did everything her parents expected of her, followed the path they'd walked first, became what they'd hoped for in a child.

But apparently her sleeping with a TV star was where they all drew the line.

'Possibly for different reasons,' Damon said, giving her a look she knew all too well. It was his 'our parents are ridiculous' look. 'But all *four* of us are concerned.'

Oh, God, he was bringing Rachel into it now. He'd be talking about them as a pair *constantly* now, saying 'we think this' or 'we like to do it that way' as if they were so fused together it was impossible for them to have different thoughts or opinions on anything.

She hated it when people did that. She'd never imagined her brother would be one of *them*.

But then, she'd never imagined he'd agree with their parents about anything, but here they were.

'You too?' she asked her best friend.

Rachel gave her an apologetic smile and a small shrug. 'I don't want you to get hurt, that's all.'

Celeste raised her eyebrows. 'Seems to me I was saying the same thing to you not so long ago…'

'The point is, darling, that you need to think seriously

about how this looks.' Her mother rested her hands on the kitchen table and looked earnestly at Celeste.

'How it…looks?' Had she just not got enough sleep, or was this really as weird as it felt?

'For your career,' her father put in. 'How it looks to the university.'

'It's bad enough doing those puff pieces for those podcasts.' Diana shook her head at the very idea. 'But doing seasonal novelty television as well—and now cavorting around with that TV presenter, too!'

'Nobody is going to believe that you're serious about your research if you're peddling history-lite to the masses,' Jacob said firmly. 'And really, being seen with That Man is just another sign to everyone that you've made your choice—and it's not the right one.'

Celeste could feel strange emotions bubbling up inside her. Ones she wasn't used to feeling. This went beyond irritation or frustration. Yes, she snapped at people all the time when they interrupted her, and she got frustrated when people wouldn't just see that she was right. But those feelings were nothing like the anger that seared through her now.

'Let me get this straight,' she said, her voice clipped. 'Damon, you and Rachel are concerned because you think I'm going to get my heart broken by a TV heartthrob who is only dating me for the publicity, right?'

'Pretty much,' Damon replied.

'And Mum, Dad. You're worried that I'm sabotaging my academic career by taking on TV projects, and that associating with Theo will affect my position at the university.'

Jacob beamed. 'Exactly! See, Diana, I told you she'd understand.'

Celeste's smile felt wicked on her lips. 'Oh, I understand. I understand that you're all very, very wrong about me. And maybe I've been wrong about you, too.'

She spun towards Rachel and Damon. 'I appreciate your concern, guys, but, trust me, everything is fine. Theo and I have an understanding. This isn't like your festive fling, or whatever. That was always just a stupid excuse for you two to have sex without thinking about the consequences. Theo and I know exactly where we are—and it's not leading to flashy diamond rings on Christmas Eve. He's using me for the publicity, and I'm using him for that too—ready for the new TV show I've signed up to hopefully present next year.' Her mother gasped at that. Celeste didn't turn her head, but out of the corner of her eye she could see Diana resting her head dramatically against Jacob's chest. 'The sex,' she added, for impact, 'is just for fun. Nothing more.'

'Now hold on a moment. What is this about a TV show?' Jacob asked.

Celeste moved to face her parents now. 'And you two. You don't care at all that the guy I'm sleeping with is using me. You don't care about my heart, at all. You're just worried that I might show you guys up on the lecture circuit, that your colleagues will think you produced a lightweight, right?'

'Darling, *we* know you're a perfectly adequate historian,' Diana said.

Behind her, Celeste heard Damon smother a laugh.

Perfectly adequate. That wasn't, surprisingly, the part that got to her. It was the way they thought of her as a historian first. That really was all she was ever going to be to them, wasn't it? Or rather, she mattered more to them as an academic than as their daughter.

Suddenly, she had a feeling she knew how Damon had felt all these years.

She was more than just an academic or historian. She was a storyteller. She could bring history to life and share it with others, help other people to feel the same passion and enthusiasm she felt for the past. Show them how the present, the world they all lived in, was built on events that had happened decades or centuries before. How knowing the *truth* about the past made understanding the present—and the chance of change for the future—possible.

Why it mattered—not just to her, but to society.

Theo had shown her that.

'I don't want to talk about the TV show today,' she told them, calmly. 'We're not going to agree on it, I can see that. I believe that history belongs to everyone, and it's important to share it with anyone willing to learn it. I don't want to lock it up in academic texts—I want to live it, to show how it connects with the everyday.'

Her parents stared at her. They didn't get it. She'd known they wouldn't.

She took a deep breath. She'd said her piece about Theo. It was Christmas Day, and Damon and Rachel had just got engaged. And she needed to do a hell of a lot more thinking before she was sure what any of this meant for her future.

But she could see a conversation—no, an argument— with her parents in her future, about her career. And for the first time in her life, she realised that it didn't matter what they wanted or expected from her. She was never going to win their respect the way she'd always dreamt of.

But she could respect herself, and her own achievements. And maybe that would be enough.

'Come on,' she said. 'It's Christmas. Let's…let's just forget all this, just for today. Who wants a Bucks Fizz while we open presents?'

Damon squeezed her shoulder as she headed for the fridge to find the champagne and orange juice, and Rachel gave her a sympathetic smile.

But it didn't stop Celeste wishing that Theo were there, too.

Christmas Day seemed to go on for ever.

From the strategically placed mistletoe that somehow he and Emmaline kept being directed towards, to the barbed comments at dinner, and the discovery that the Howards would be staying until Boxing Day, Theo was exhausted by the time the clock chimed ten, and his mother yawned for the third time, and he figured he could reasonably excuse himself to bed.

To bed, but not to sleep. He had a call to make, first.

Celeste had never been far from his thoughts that day. In some ways, it had felt as if he were watching the whole scene through her eyes. He could hear her sharp comments and smart observations in the back of his mind, all day long.

Now he wanted to hear them for real.

He made it as far as the stairs before his father caught up to him—a surprise in itself. Normally he preferred to demand that people come to him.

'Theo. Son,' he said, and Theo turned, already on the fourth step, to face him.

'Yes?' Maybe this was a Christmas miracle, after all. Maybe his father was about to tell him he was proud of him—and even if it was all down to the whisky, Theo knew he'd take it.

But, no.

'I hope you appreciate the effort that everyone here has put in today to helping you,' his father said. 'And what you need to do next, in return.'

Theo blinked, slowly. 'I'm sorry?'

'I know you're not the smartest tool in the box but damn it, Theo, I thought even you'd be able to figure this one out.' Francis Montgomery's face grew redder with frustration, as well as alcohol. Theo just watched.

He felt strangely detached from the situation. He could see his mother coming up towards them now, carefully closing the door to the room where the rest of their party sat, to spare them hearing this, he supposed.

'Why don't you tell me, Dad?' His voice was calm, too. Calmer than he'd expected he'd manage. There was none of the energy he displayed on camera, and no smile, either. As if he felt nothing at all. 'What is it, exactly, that you're expecting me to do to win your favour?'

'As if you don't know!' Francis blustered, taking a step up the stairs. 'All you've ever needed to do was bring some sort of good to this family. We weren't expecting much from you, but really! Just marry a girl with money and save the family estate, how hard is that? We even *gave* you the girl today, gave you every opportunity, and you didn't make the smallest effort with her! If we have to sell this estate, it will all be your fault.'

Theo was glad of the calmness that flowed through him, wherever it came from. As his father grew angrier, the calmness only increased, letting him see the man before him more clearly than ever.

'No,' he said simply. 'It won't. *You* couldn't save it, Dad. *You* weren't good enough, not me.'

'Theo, don't you speak to your father that way! He's never said you're not good enough.' An outright lie from his mother. It didn't surprise him. She always liked to rewrite events to suit her own narrative.

But Theo was done believing it.

'I want you both to listen to me, for once,' he said. 'I

am not going to marry Emmaline, not least because she doesn't want us to get married any more than I do. In fact, I'm not going to marry anyone just because they have money, or because you approve of them. That's not the world we live in any more, in case you haven't noticed.'

His parents were uncharacteristically silent, so Theo carried on, amazed at how good it felt to say the words at last.

'If you want to save this house, save it. Don't expect me to do it for you. Because honestly? I'd rather you sell the place anyway.' His mother gasped at that, and his father's face turned an even more extreme shade of puce. But Theo didn't care. Because it was true. He didn't want Sorrelton House and all its memories—especially since so few of them were good ones.

He wanted his own life. His own decisions.

He wanted to find out for himself who he was and what he could achieve—not what his parents had always told him he couldn't.

'I don't need anything from you any more,' he said, feeling the truth of the words as he spoke them. 'Sell the house, do whatever you want with the money—I have my own. I have my own life, my own career, and you know what? I've worked damn hard to get where I am, and I'll keep working for the life that I want. Away from here.'

Then he spun round and jogged up the stairs, whistling a Christmas carol as he went.

He'd leave this place tomorrow, and he wasn't sure he'd ever come back. Wasn't sure he'd be welcome, even if he wanted to.

But that was okay.

He could find his own future now.

Theo changed out of the dinner jacket and bow tie he'd been expected to wear for Christmas evening at Sorrelton

House, and into a comfortable pair of sweatpants and a faded and worn T-shirt. Then, leaning back against the headboard of his bed, he relaxed his shoulders for the first time in hours, and called Celeste.

'Hey.'

'Hey. You in bed?' She picked up far too quickly to be in company. Or maybe he just liked the idea of her in bed. Preferably his.

'Yeah.' A rustle of sheets as she stretched out. He could imagine her there, in the bed they'd shared the night before. He liked that he could picture it perfectly. That he could see her in his mind, if not in reality.

Careful, Theo.

He was treading a line here, one he'd been teetering on for so long he'd almost stopped noticing it. It would be oh-so-easy to slide over to the other side.

Except he had a feeling that the line might actually be a cliff edge, and he didn't want to fall.

Theo pushed away the thought that it could already be too late.

'How was your Christmas Day?' he asked, settling himself down more comfortably against the pillows.

'It started with a family intervention about my sex life, but after the fourth Bucks Fizz things started to improve. How was yours?'

'My parents hustled me up a rich and recently dumped date for the occasion. She cried every time she saw the mistletoe they'd hung around the place.'

'Ouch.' He could picture her wincing, but also trying not to laugh. 'They hated me that much, huh?'

She was so quick, his Celeste. 'Apparently so.'

'Well, the good news is, my parents hate the idea of you just as much. Apparently, you're going to ruin my career prospects.'

'Probably true,' Theo admitted. 'You start hanging around with a lightweight like me for too long, they'll assume your brains have rotted out your ears.'

'Hey,' she said softly. It was a voice, a tone he'd not heard from her before. Gentle. Caring. 'Don't say that.'

He could get used to that voice.

'How are the happy couple?' he asked, shifting the conversation somewhere more comfortable. 'Did they at least get to celebrate in slightly more style than when they woke us up?'

'They're worried you're going to break my heart.' The mocking edge to her words told Theo exactly how ridiculous she thought that was. 'I reminded them that we had an agreement, and that this was all for show anyway.'

'Exactly,' Theo said, pushing away the part of his brain that had just been hoping for more. 'I mean, we could probably stop it now, if you wanted. Can't imagine anyone is going to be paying much attention to us over the festive period anyway, and we've kind of achieved what we set out to do.' Except then he'd never get to see her face as he told her how he'd stood up to his parents. Never get to see that small smile as she nodded and told him he'd done the right thing.

'The world no longer thinks you're a hideous, mansplaining arse-wipe,' Celeste said eloquently.

'And the TV-viewing public knows who you are, now,' he replied. 'So we're kind of done.'

'Yeah. I guess we are.'

The pause that followed was just about long enough to give him a tiny bit of hope back. Enough to say, 'Of course, if you wanted a last opportunity to laugh at me, I'm doing a freezing cold Boxing Day river swim in Henley tomorrow morning. I could pick you up on my way, if you wanted. Regale you with my Christmas Day recap—including a last-minute showdown with my father in which his face turned a shade of magenta not found in nature.'

It was, of course, completely out of his way, but he didn't feel like mentioning that.

'A wild swim?' Celeste laughed. 'Yeah, okay. I'd like to watch that. And hear about your showdown. Although I think nature really does have most shades of magenta, you know.'

He ignored that last bit, still smiling about the first. 'And then I'm supposed to be showing my face at some cocktails in igloos thing on Sunday,' he added.

'I've never had cocktails in an igloo before.'

'Apparently it's something everyone should try at least once in their lives.' Theo wondered if she knew how much he was making it up as he went along now. Talking absolute rubbish just for the excuse of seeing her again.

Probably. She was the smartest woman—smartest person—he'd ever met. She knew. And she was letting him get away with it. Why?

Maybe because she wants to spend more time with me, too. He hoped so anyway.

'Then how could I pass it up?' she said, laughing. 'Pick me up in the morning, and we can discuss whether swimming in the freezing cold Thames in December is better or worse than Christmas with our families.'

CHAPTER ELEVEN

IT WAS STILL dark when Theo picked her up from her parents' town house the next morning. They'd barely got off the phone six hours earlier, so she hadn't had time to go home to her flat for fresh clothes, but fortunately her personal uniform of black, black and more black made it easy enough for her to dress from the stash she'd left in her childhood bedroom when she moved out, and still not look out of place.

'Why are you doing this, again?' Celeste settled into the passenger seat of Theo's sports car, while he dumped her bag in the back.

'Same reason I end up doing most things that seem like a bad idea at the time,' he replied, starting the engine.

'Publicity,' they both said, at once.

'Are you comparing sleeping with me to swimming in the freezing-cold Thames?' She shifted sideways in her seat as he pulled away from the kerb. The position had two advantages: one, she could watch him better, and two, she could curl up here and get some more sleep while he drove.

'I'm comparing dating you in public to the Boxing Day Swim,' he corrected her. 'Sleeping with you was an added bonus.'

'I'm glad to hear it. And I want to hear about your showdown with your father, too.' Celeste yawned.

'Later,' Theo said. 'Get some more sleep for now.'

'Okay.' Her eyes fluttered shut as the motor purred, lulling her back to sleep.

When she awoke again, the built-up streets and buildings of London had given way to a gentler countryside—although Celeste knew they weren't far from the city centre, really.

Henley-on-Thames was only an hour's drive from London, and, given the early hour and the bank holiday emptiness of the roads in the pre-dawn, Celeste was pretty sure Theo had made it in considerably less. The Oxfordshire market town was famous for its Royal Regatta in the summer, which she could imagine Theo having to attend as part of his social obligations. It seemed *just* the sort of thing his parents would want to be seen at.

Somehow, a wild swim on a December morning seemed much more Theo-like, to her.

She hoped that his conversation with his parents would help him find more things that were more Theo-like, too. She liked Theo-like. And she was definitely still too tired to think properly if that was an actual sentence in her head.

Theo parked the car and they headed out together to find the other swimmers. There were more of them than Celeste had imagined would think this could possibly be a good idea, all lined up in swimsuits and blue-tinged skin.

'You don't even get to wear a wetsuit?' she asked Theo, incredulously.

'Apparently not.'

'There you are!' A young guy in a thick fleece coat hurried over to them, pushing through the crowd of warmly dressed bystanders who'd come to watch the spectacle. 'I was starting to think you weren't going to make it. Now, the camera crew is standing by to film the whole thing, but they'd like to get a quick chat with you before *and* after the swim, okay?'

Theo nodded. 'Fine. Remind me, how far am I swimming, Gaz?'

'Just seventy metres or so,' Gaz said. Celeste shivered in sympathy. 'From the hotel over there to some club down river, where they'll fish you out. The camera guys are going to follow you in the boat.'

'Great.' Theo looked as if he was starting to seriously reconsider his life choices. Celeste didn't blame him.

'I'll get you some coffee ready at the other end?' she suggested.

Gaz had other ideas. 'We definitely want to get some footage of you cheering on your man too, Celeste. And a kiss at the end would go down a treat, yeah?'

He turned away, heading back to where the camera guys were waiting, leaving Theo and Celeste alone for a moment, before the insanity of the Boxing Day swim started.

'Guess I'm still a publicity asset after all,' Celeste said, unable not to watch as Theo stripped down to his swimming shorts. *God, he looks cold.*

'Guess so.' He flashed her one of those TV smiles. How he could smile like that, half naked in the frost, she had no idea. Must be level one TV training, or something.

It occurred to her, not for the first time, that she might never actually know what Theo was thinking. He was so good at hiding it all behind that made-for-TV facade of his. She'd pegged him as a faker their first lunch together, but knowing he was faking was only part of it. Being completely certain when he *wasn't* was much harder.

How much of their fake relationship was really fake and how much was really real? And how could she ever be sure?

The dark thought clouded her tired brain, and she couldn't seem to shake it away. So she tried a little fakery of her own, instead.

'Well, I'll have your coffee *and* your kiss waiting for you, then,' she said brightly. Then, pressing a swift kiss to his cheek, she headed off down the bank to where the other spectators were gathering to watch the swimmers set off.

'I don't think I'm ever going to be properly warm again,' Theo lamented, several hours later, as they headed back towards London in his convertible, heating on full.

'Well, if you hadn't fallen back in, after you got out in the first place, you might have warmed up sooner,' Celeste said, unhelpfully.

He shot her a glare. 'If you hadn't been doubled over with laughter, you might have helped me out.'

'I'd have spilt the coffee,' she countered.

Theo shook his head. All he knew was that there were going to be photos of him floundering around in the water like a drunken duck, and his supposed girlfriend laughing uproariously at him, all over the Internet by teatime. So much for regaining his dignity yesterday, by finally standing up to his parents. At least he didn't have to deal with what his father might have to say about the whole debacle debasing the family name any more.

'Want me to see if the photos have hit the Internet yet?' Celeste asked, reading his mind, as always.

He sighed. 'Might as well, I suppose. I'm sure they've been on social media for ages. See if they've hit the news pages yet, though.'

Her winces as she scrolled through her phone told him everything he needed to know.

Well, so he looked like an idiot. Again. It was all people really expected of him anyway. He was that nice but dim TV presenter, the unthreatening boy next door, the safe crush for teenage girls and grandmas alike.

Pretending to date Celeste might have actually given him some intellectual and personal cache for once, but nobody expected it to last. Least of all him.

He knew his place in the world up to now. A rich kid without *quite* enough money, an aristocrat without *quite* enough connections, an average learner with a wasted education, one he couldn't even quite see through. The only thing that would impress his parents was if he married someone who'd bolster the family finances and/or social credibility—which he'd now told them he had no desire to do. And even if he had gone along with their plans, he was sure that within the year his mother would have been bemoaning the fact that he could have done better, and his father would be accusing him of not trying hard enough.

But where had trying hard ever got him, really?

It got you Celeste.

Not for long.

The victorious feeling he'd felt after standing up to his parents was already draining away like the freezing water he'd swum in. He'd closed one door, but had he really opened another? Yes, he wanted to go his own way, do his own thing. He just wasn't entirely sure what that way, or thing, was. Other than finishing his degree at last, and carrying on with work as always, what would really change?

'How bad is it?' Even humiliating photos had to be better than this train of thought. He could laugh them off, the same way he laughed off every insult and barb from his parents over the years, every time he was told he wasn't good enough. Every person who walked away when they realised that he wasn't quite enough of anything, after all.

'I mean… *I* think the way you're floundering around on the bank is quite endearing, really. Possibly.'

Theo smiled. From Celeste, that was positively a compliment. At least she was trying to make it less awful for him. She wouldn't have bothered to do that when they first met.

'So, hilariously humiliating, then?'

She nodded. 'Definitely going to be the funny story at the end of the news tonight, sorry.'

Theo sighed. He expected nothing less, really.

'Wait, though…'

He glanced across at Celeste and found her frowning at her phone. 'What?'

'There's a link to another article from this morning… Hang on…'

Maybe the bad feeling rising in his stomach had to do with how much of the River Thames he'd swallowed that morning.

But maybe not.

'What is it?' he asked, when she didn't say anything.

'Shhh. I'm reading.'

There was a junction coming up, and Theo took it, swinging off the motorway and into the forecourt of a service station. 'Show me,' he said, parking the car.

Silently, Celeste handed the phone over. Well, that wasn't good for a start. Celeste was seldom without something to say on a subject.

Theo scanned the article on her phone. Oh. Well, he didn't blame her.

'This was from when you took me to the Cressingham Arcade, before Christmas?' he guessed.

Celeste nodded. 'Must have been. Don't know why we didn't see it before now, but I suppose it's only been a few days.'

They'd been shopping for a present suitable for his mother, since he'd left it to the last minute as usual. Celeste had suggested the arcade where her brother and Rachel were working, so they'd popped there after one of their regular 'out to be seen' lunches together.

And apparently someone had snapped a photo of them supposedly looking at engagement rings at the grumpy old jeweller's shop.

Following the links in the article, he traced the story back to its original source—a tweet posted by a random member of the public, four days ago. 'Looks like it was just some normal person posting it, and they misspelt the hashtag, so it took a while for the gossip sites to pick it up.'

'So, the world thinks we're getting married? Our parents are going to hate that.'

Theo chuckled. 'They definitely are.'

'Good thing it's not true, then.'

And it was. A good thing. Because he wasn't looking to settle down and get married, not even just to prove a point to his parents. And if he were… He and Celeste were from different worlds, different expectations, and different ambitions. He was populist, she was highbrow. He was lightweight, she was a walking history textbook.

She'd be bored of him in no time, and he was sure he'd be a disappointment to her the same way he'd always been to his parents.

Except…if his parents were wrong, if he'd stepped out of that toxic family circle and accepted that maybe there was more to him than they saw...what if Celeste could see that too?

As he pulled back onto the motorway, he couldn't help but let a little hope bubble up inside him.

Theo dropped her back at her own flat, and for the first time since Christmas Eve Celeste finally had space to think. To figure out what the hell was going on in her head—and in her heart.

The rest of the journey back from Henley-on-Thames had been mostly silent. And knowing how badly Theo had needed a shower and a sleep, she hadn't even considered inviting him up to the flat with her.

But now she was there, alone with her thoughts, she almost wished she had. If nothing else, Theo was always a pleasant distraction.

Except he was so much more than that. That was the problem.

They needed to talk. They'd gone into this as a fun scheme, a trick to play on social media, almost. A way to rehabilitate Theo's reputation after Celeste's performance on the *Christmas Cracker Cranium Quiz*, and to raise her profile ahead of her potential TV show.

A TV show she'd heard nothing but warnings from her parents about all Christmas Day, even after she'd told them she didn't want to talk about it, to the point where she was starting to wonder if they might even be right. Oh, not about the need to share history with anyone willing to learn it; she still believed that. But was she really the right person to do it? Was she choosing a career in media as a mediocre historian over her academic focus? All her life, she'd followed the path laid out for her by her parents, but now she was standing at a fork in that road, and choosing the one they'd put 'do not cross' tape over.

And that led her right back to Theo.

She and her agent had pitched the show before she'd met Theo, of course, but back then it was just a concept, a possibility. Now, her agent was emailing daily with updates instead of monthly. Apparently, her raised media profile had everyone keen to get moving with the project, and it looked more like a sure thing every day. And while she'd planned to be mostly consulting and narrating, now they wanted her front and centre on camera.

They'd even changed the title of the show to include her name. Suddenly, it was more about her than the history, than the stories of ancient women she wanted to tell.

She wasn't an idiot. She knew all of that was because of Theo, not her. But what would happen when Theo wasn't part of her life—or her image—any more?

Because he wouldn't be.

They hadn't expressly discussed breaking up, but the plan had never been a long-term one. They lived in different worlds, for all that she might be inhabiting his for a little while. She had research to do, a book to finish, a name to make for herself in her chosen niche.

The TV show was one project, one year. What about the rest of her life?

Theo had talked about what might happen next for her over dinner one night, while they had both studiously avoiding looking at the guy seated at the next table taking their photo.

'You've got your foot in the door now, and that's all it takes,' he'd said, while feeding her one of the prawns from his starter. 'Radio appearances was one thing, but once you're on TV once, that's it. You'll be the channel's go-to expert on all things historical.'

'But I'm *not* an expert on all things historical,' she'd

pointed out. 'I have a speciality. *That's* what I'm an expert in.'

'You know more general history than almost everyone else in the population,' he'd countered. 'That's what matters. They'll rope you in for all sorts of historical programmes now—look at that guy who does all the science stuff. What's his name? He's a physicist, but he ends up on shows about all sorts.'

He was right, Celeste knew now. Her area of expertise was women's history, especially women in the ancient world. But already she'd found herself approached to talk on other topics. Topics that fascinated her, sure, but they weren't her niche. They weren't what she was supposed to be talking about.

Like the history of Christmas. She'd spent a week reading up on that before the quiz show, and look where that landed her. At dire risk of falling for a guy who was only in it for the publicity. And who would always belong to a world she wasn't sure she wanted to be a part of.

She pulled her phone back out to look again at the photo of her and Theo at the jeweller's shop. They hadn't been looking at rings, of course. But some strange emotion tugging at her heart kept whispering, *What if you had?*

Stop it. She wasn't going down that road.

She swiped out of the browser and checked her message and email notifications instead.

Eight messages. Two from Rachel, one linking her to the article about the jeweller's and asking if there was something she needed to tell her, and one with a link to a navy bridesmaid's dress with the word Compromise? underneath. One from Damon that was just a picture of Theo falling in the water at the wild swim and a lot of laughing emojis.

Two from her mother, obliquely mentioning Theo's existence and her disapproval of it, and another one from her father doing the same but without any of the subtlety.

One from her agent, with a thumbs-up emoji next to a photo of her and Theo, and a note about a meeting with the production company first thing in the new year.

And one from Theo, of course.

Igloo cocktails tomorrow. I'll pick you up at eight. x

CHAPTER TWELVE

Igloos on a roof terrace in a city centre, with integral champagne bars.

'Only in London,' Theo observed as they stood outside their own private igloo and took in the city skyline.

The igloos themselves had a large window built in—or left open, really—to enjoy the views, but since Theo had a feeling it would be even colder in there than outside, he was putting it off for the moment. He still hadn't fully warmed up since his dip in the Thames, and even the fake fur coats provided by the owners of the establishment weren't doing much except make him feel like an extra in *Game of Thrones*.

'Mmm,' Celeste agreed absently as she leaned against the railings to look out.

She'd seemed mostly absent since he picked her up. As if her body was present, but her mind had gone wandering. When he'd asked her about it, she'd muttered something about her book, and research, and thinking through ideas.

He was glad she was able to think about work. Because the only thing *he'd* been able to think about for days now was her.

Whatever this thing between them had morphed into, it wasn't what they'd agreed at the start. Which meant they had to talk about what happened next. And that meant talking about what had happened on Christmas Eve, too—and if she wanted it to happen again.

Theo had done a lot of thinking the day before, once he'd warmed up enough for proper thoughts, but he wasn't sure he'd come to any sensible conclusions. Despite it being Boxing Day, and a bank holiday, his agent Cerys had been on the phone the moment she'd seen the pictures of them at the jeweller's shop in the arcade, asking what was going on.

'I told you that you could call it off,' she'd said, sounding amused. 'Do I take this to mean you're heading in a rather different direction?'

'It wasn't what it looked like,' Theo had told her tiredly. 'But…but if it was, would it be so bad?'

Cerys had paused at that, and when she'd spoken again, he'd been able to hear the surprise in her voice. 'Well, I guess that depends on your perspective. I mean, getting married to anyone would kind of dampen your crush appeal a little bit, and I'm guessing you wouldn't want to court social media by appearing in public with up-and-coming celebrities on your arm any more, so there's that. But stars settle down and it doesn't ruin their careers or anything, if that's what you mean. But really, Theo…her? Are you sure? She decimated you on that quiz show. To be honest, I thought there was solid chance she'd do worse than throw coffee over you on that first date.'

'She doesn't like it when history doesn't tell the truth,' Theo had replied, automatically. 'And the answers on those cards were wrong. Well, incomplete, at least.'

Cerys had laughed at that. 'Well, that tells me everything I need to know. You've got it bad. Good luck with that, then.' And she'd hung up.

Theo had wanted to call back, to tell her that Celeste wasn't the person people seemed to think. That, maybe, neither was he.

Because when he was with Celeste, he believed that there was more to him than he'd ever been led to believe. More than just a rich kid with every advantage who still couldn't be anything more than a nice smile and a winning personality.

Something more than just the Montgomery name, as his parents believed, or his face, as the viewing public seemed to think.

The question was, did she feel the same way when she was with him? Or, as he feared, did she think he made her less?

Unfortunately, there was only one way to find out. And that meant having a conversation he wasn't at all sure he wanted to have.

The one about what happened next.

He waited until they both had fresh drinks, and had taken their icy seats inside the igloo. Celeste still seemed a little as if she were on another planet, but she smiled at least as he handed her an extra blanket, laying it out across both of them as they looked out of the cut-out window.

'If I interrupt your thinking will you throw a drink at me?' Theo figured it was best to start with the basics and work up.

Celeste turned to him with a smirk hovering around her lips. 'You're tempting fate just asking, you realise?'

'I know.'

She sipped at her drink. 'But luckily for you this cocktail is too delicious for me to waste it on you. And I'm being a terrible fake date, right? Sorry. Am I supposed to be fawning over you more?'

'No one is looking,' Theo said. It felt weirdly uncomfortable to hear her talk about them that way, after everything. 'And besides, I think we're past all that now, aren't we?'

'*Are* we?' Celeste asked. 'Have you seen the photos from the Boxing Day swim? Whoever is in charge of social media over at your channel has been having a grand old time showcasing our relationship right alongside the listings for your New Year's Eve show.'

'That's just coincidence. And that's not about us anyway.'

'Except it is, right?' Celeste pressed. 'I mean, right from the start that's exactly what we were about. Putting forward the right image for you—and for me too, I guess.'

He didn't like where this was going. Something was twisting in his gut, and he didn't think it was the cocktails.

'At the start, sure. But after Christmas Eve—'

She interrupted him with a laugh, high and tinkling, one that barely sounded like Celeste at all.

He was missing something here. She hadn't been like this at Henley, had she? What had changed since yesterday?

The photo of them at the jeweller's. Was that what was bothering her?

'Is this about the photos yesterday? The stories about us getting engaged?'

'Why would it be about them?' She looked down into her glass as she spoke, and Theo knew she was avoiding his gaze. He was right, even if she wasn't going to admit it. 'They were just stupid stories. We know it's not like that between us.'

'Right.' Except... 'Why isn't it?'

Her shocked gaze met his in an instant. 'What do you mean?'

Theo took a breath. This was it. His chance.

He wanted this feeling to last—the feeling he had when he was with Celeste. Which meant being honest with her. Being real. No TV charm and smile, no spin for social media. No faking.

Just him. And her.

'Why isn't it that way between us? I mean, not getting married exactly, but...we've had fun, right? Together? We could keep having fun, maybe?'

No.

She'd thought she could read him, but she'd never seen this coming. She'd known he was a faker, but she'd never though he'd take it this far.

She'd thought she'd known what she was doing, but now she was pretty sure she had no idea at all.

'I think we should break up. Fake break up. Send a press release, whatever it is we need to do to end this.' Celeste started to stand up, pushing the blanket away from her lap, before she realised she was about to bang her head on the rounded ceiling of the igloo, and sat back down.

She wanted to get away, but she didn't want an audience for this, either. So apparently, she was having the most important conversation of her life so far that didn't take place in front of an academic board in an igloo. Because that was the sort of thing that happened when a person hung around with Theo Montgomery for too long.

'You think... Why?' He shook his head as he looked at her. 'You can't tell me we're not good together. Christmas Eve—'

'Was lovely,' she interrupted him again. The only way

she was going to get through this was by not letting him talk too much. That silver tongue of his could probably talk her into anything; wasn't that how she'd ended up in this mess to begin with?

'So what's the problem here, exactly?' Theo asked.

'You and me…it's been fun,' she admitted. 'But it hasn't been real, we both know that. Hell, that was what we agreed! It was all for show. And yes, I'm attracted to you, yes, I had fun with you—'

'Then why—?'

'But that doesn't change the basic facts of this situation,' she shouted over him.

'And those facts are?' His voice was calmer than she thought she'd ever heard it before. He almost didn't sound like himself. Everything about him was always so alive, so full of fun and mischief. But right now he sounded as dry as her last boyfriend, the philosophy student.

As if this wasn't an act at all.

Don't think about that.

'We come from different worlds,' she said slowly. 'Yes, I'm dabbling in TV, but I've spent my whole life building up my academic career.'

'And you think that continuing to be seen with me would undermine your credentials. I'd make you look lightweight.'

'No! That wasn't what I—'

'Wasn't it?' His mouth twisted in an unfriendly smile. 'Or is it worse than that? You've had your fun with me, but I'm not an intellectual match for you, right? You were slumming it with the stupid TV star for a while, having fun looking at my little history essays for my meaningless bachelor's degree, but I'm never going to live up to those professors you meet at conferences, or whatever.'

'You're not stupid,' Celeste said quietly. 'I never said—or thought—you were stupid.'

'Didn't you?' Theo shook his head. 'Then you must have been the first. If you think I don't know what people say about me—' He broke off.

'Look, it's not you,' she said desperately. 'It's me. And, God, I know that's the most overused line in break-up history, but really. Think about it. I'm grumpy and hyper-focussed, I have no ability to connect with people, really. I can't help but tell them when they're wrong. Your parents hate me—'

'Yours hate me, too.'

'True. And maybe…maybe they're right.'

'To hate me?' Theo's eyebrows went up at that.

'No! They think…they think that your lifestyle, your fame, would distract me from my studies. It would lead me away from academia into the sort of history lite you see in bad documentaries on TV. Like you said, the producers don't care about my area of expertise—history is just history to them. I wouldn't be taken seriously as an academic any more.'

'You might have a lot more fun, though,' Theo pointed out quietly. 'You *love* history, Celeste. Not just certain parts of it—all of it. Is it really so important to you to be an expert in one thing, rather than good at lots of it? More than sharing it with the world?'

'Yes.' Because it always had been. That had been the message from her parents from her earliest days. Find what you're passionate about and pursue it with everything you have. Don't look left or right, don't get distracted. Find what matters to you and make yourself matter.

Damon had gone the other way entirely, but she…she'd embraced the philosophy. She'd gone after academia, a professorship, as her ultimate goal. Working to publish her academic tome on women in history, to prove her place in the canon. And if she gave it up now…what did that leave her?

She'd only ever been good at talking to other academics. If she tried to teach the Great British Public about history instead…would they even listen?

What if she was just wasting her time?

This wasn't one fun quiz show where she was a novelty, a festive amusement. And it wasn't being seen around town with Theo, a curiosity. This was trying to be the real thing, and make people listen to her—when the only person outside academia and Rachel who'd ever done that was Theo, and she didn't even know for sure that he wasn't just faking it.

The university was safer. She knew the rules there, had been training for it all her life.

Life with Theo was the opposite of safe. It was people watching her, commenting on her all the time. It was expanding her secure little bubble so much further outside the university than she'd planned.

This wasn't a one-off TV show. This was a career change—a life change—she wasn't sure she was ready for.

Theo's jaw was clenched, as if he was holding in all the words he wanted to say. He always did, she realised suddenly, surprised that she knew such a detail about him. But this was how he'd been at lunch with his parents, too. Biting his tongue, holding in everything he was thinking.

Was that just how he'd been brought up? Or was it part of who he was now? All the years smiling for the cameras, being the nice guy…hell, he'd only fake dated her in the first place to preserve that image.

But Celeste wanted to hear what he *really* thought, not what he believed he *should* think.

He'd said it to his parents on Christmas Day, by all accounts. How much had that taken out of him? To finally speak up to them?

It didn't look as if he was going to do the same for her, though.

He threw down the rest of his cocktail, swallowing it fast, and slamming his glass onto the ice table. Getting to his feet, his head still bowed to avoid hitting it on the ceiling, he gave her an awkward nod. 'Do you need me to take you home?'

'Theo...' She trailed off. What could she say? He'd asked for something she wasn't ready or able to give. How could she now ask him to stay?

She shook her head. 'I'm fine.'

'In that case... I'll see you around, Celeste.' He turned and walked out, leaving her alone in the icy shelter.

She wished her heart were as frozen as the igloo. Then maybe it wouldn't hurt so much.

'Are you sure you're okay to do this?' Cerys asked as Theo had his mic checked for what was hopefully the last time.

'Of course, I'm okay. Why wouldn't I be?' He wasn't even sure what his agent was *doing* here for the *New Year's Eve Spectacular*. She didn't normally come to his filming, but maybe she had nowhere else to be for the biggest party night of the calendar.

Although he supposed he was sort of *hosting* the biggest party on that biggest party night. Other people probably really wanted to be there. Even if he was wishing he were anywhere but.

'Because you've been—how can I put this?—not your charming self over the last few days.'

Days filled with last-minute meetings and planning, and absolutely no Celeste. Except for the photos of her, which were still all over social media, and people asking him about her.

There was even one photo of her leaving the igloo bar, after him. He'd been staring at it for days now trying to figure out if her eyes in it were red from crying or the cold.

Probably the cold. This was Celeste, after all.

As she'd told him, she didn't really *do* people. At least, not ones who weren't dead and were without an interesting backstory or place in history.

He'd known. He'd known from the start that he couldn't fit into her world, that she'd be another person he wasn't good enough for. And yet he'd let himself hope...

She was the one person who'd made him believe he was more than his name or his face, more than his TV-star status, and more than his parents told him he could be.

It just turned out *she* didn't believe it.

'And now you look like you're trying to burn down the Tower of London with lasers from your eyes,' Cerys went on. 'Is this about Celeste?'

He spun away from the Tower to face her. 'Why would it be about Celeste?' And who the hell decided to do the filming here, where he had to look at that place—the place he'd kissed her properly for the first time—all night long?

Probably him, in one of those meetings he hadn't been paying attention in.

'Because you haven't been seen with her in days, you haven't mentioned her name once until now, and you've

practically growled at anyone who mentions it to you.'
Cerys was not a touchy-feely, reassuring agent. The fact
that she felt the need to pat Theo's arm gently was a definite warning sign that he was losing it completely. 'What
happened, Theo?'

'We ended it,' he said, with a shrug.

*She ripped half my heart out with an ice pick, froze it
and used it to cool her cocktail.*

'It was all very mutual and friendly. After all, we
were never *really* together in the first place, remember.'

*Even if it felt like we were. Even if it felt like every-
thing.*

'Right.' Cerys did not look in any way convinced.
'Did you tell her?'

'Tell her what?' he asked, confused.

'That you're in love with her.'

He had enough practice at looking amused when he
wasn't from listening to the poor jokes told on various
shows he'd hosted, but it still took everything in his
power to laugh at Cerys's words, when what was left of
his heart felt as if it were trying to break out of his body.

'Why on earth would I tell her that?' he scoffed.

Cerys rolled her eyes and patted his arm again. 'Just
get through tonight, yeah? Then we can go get really
drunk and you can cry on my shoulder for a while, and in
the morning it'll be a brand-new year and you can move
on. Well, after the hangover subsides.'

He waited until she'd moved out of his line of sight to
let his amused smile drop.

Oh, God, he was in love with Celeste Hunter. How the
hell had that happened?

The worst part was, he knew *exactly* how and when
it had happened, and he hadn't done anything to stop it.

No. The worst part was that she didn't love him back.

But the *second*-to-worst part…he'd fallen for her the moment she'd scowled at him, maybe. Or when she'd thrown coffee over his lap. Or when she'd sat in a hot tub on a boat and looked so adorably baffled by the whole experience. Or when he'd kissed her on the ice rink across the river at the Tower. Or when she'd sat through a hideous dinner with his parents. Or when she'd talked to him about history and expected him to keep up. Or when she'd told him he was nothing like the man his parents thought he was. Or when she'd kissed him in the hallway and taken him to bed. Or when she'd pulled him out of the river, or when she'd sat with him in an igloo…

The truth was, he hadn't fallen for her once. It hadn't been love at first sight. It had been love, inch by inch. With every story about a ghost bear or the truth about Christmas trees. He'd been fascinated from the start, but the love…that had crept in, without him even knowing it was there.

Until it was so much a part of his heart he thought it might stop beating without it.

God, he was pathetic.

But he didn't have time to dwell on that right now. He had a show to present, and a cheery persona to find again. Cerys was right: he could mope once the work was done, and not before.

Turning his back firmly on the Tower of London, Theo took a deep breath, turned to the anxious-looking production assistant hovering nearby, and said, 'I'm ready.'

CHAPTER THIRTEEN

'WHERE HAVE YOU BEEN?' Rachel asked as Celeste eased her way through the crowds of people at the Cressingham Arcade, all there to celebrate her brother and best friend's engagement, and the new year, not necessarily in that order.

'Sorry, I got caught up writing, lost track of time,' Celeste lied. Well, sort of lied. The losing track of time part was real. The writing, less so.

Seemed as though ever since she'd let Theo walk away so she could focus on her academic writing, she'd written less than ever.

Rachel gave her the sort of look that told her she wasn't buying it at all, then led her over to where the bar was situated, at the back of the arcade. Right next to the jeweller's shop, where she'd been photographed with Theo.

That was the real reason she was late. She hadn't wanted to come. Damon had bought her a T-shirt with that on it one year: 'Sorry I'm late, I didn't want to come.' She should have worn it tonight.

She'd only been here with Theo for an hour or so, and yet it was already filled with memories of him. Her parents' house was unbearable, and she wasn't letting herself anywhere near the Tower of London.

She wanted to stay safe, locked away in her office, where there were no memories of Theo to distract her.

Rachel shoved a champagne flute into her hand. 'Okay, time to talk. What's going on? It's to do with Theo, I take it?'

Celeste looked at her best friend—newly engaged, madly in love, with newfound confidence at work and in herself—and burst into tears.

'Right. This way, then.' Rachel bundled her towards a door, hidden away in the wall between two tiled pillars, and pushed her through it. Together, they climbed a metal staircase to a balcony Celeste hadn't ever even noticed from the ground floor.

Sitting with their backs against the door, champagne glasses in hand, the two best friends looked up at the painted ceiling of the Victorian shopping arcade.

'What do you see?' Rachel asked.

Celeste blinked as the ceiling came into focus. 'Butterflies!'

Dozens of tiny painted butterflies, so realistic she almost thought one might flutter down and land on her outstretched finger.

'Damon brought me up here, the first time I visited the arcade,' Rachel said. 'He showed me so many secret things about the place. But that's not why I fell in love with him.'

'Why *did* you fall in love with him?' As much as Celeste loved her brother, she wasn't sure he was an automatic catch for any woman, and she still thought he'd probably got the far better end of the bargain in marrying Rachel.

'Because he showed me the secret places inside me, too,' Rachel said.

Celeste pulled a face. 'If this is a sex thing, I really

don't want to hear it. That's my brother, remember, and I'm having a hard enough time this week as it is.'

Rachel laughed, the sound ringing off the metal railings. 'That's not what I meant! I mean...he showed me who I could be, if I let myself. If I believed in myself, even—believed it was possible, and went after it.'

'And here I was thinking *you* were the one who showed him he could fall in love, and stop jumping from one thing to the next,' Celeste replied, bumping her shoulder against her best friend's.

'Maybe that's the point,' Rachel mused. 'We both changed—or rather, we both found the parts of ourselves we'd stopped believing in, over the years.'

'That sounds nice.'

'It is,' Rachel agreed. 'So, what did Theo teach *you* about yourself?'

'What do you mean?' Celeste started at the question, and Rachel rolled her eyes.

'Come on, it's obvious that you've fallen for him. You're madly in love and, to be honest, I think that was kind of inevitable from the start.'

'Coming from someone who tried to claim that she was having nothing but a "festive fling" and ended up engaged before Christmas morning,' Celeste grumbled.

'So I know what I'm talking about.' Sighing, Rachel rested her head against Celeste's shoulder. 'It's just me, Celeste. Tell me everything.'

Celeste took one last look up at the butterflies, free and wild and unreal on the ceiling, and started talking.

She told her about the kiss on the ice rink, about the way Theo actually listened when she talked about weird historical facts, and didn't mind—even liked it—when she corrected those things that everyone thought they knew. She talked about how his parents hated her, and hers hated him, and how she didn't care. Because her parents only cared about her career, and his parents only cared about their name and their money, so why should either of them care what they thought anyway? And she talked about Christmas Eve, and the wild swim and the jeweller's photos and then she talked about the igloos…

'Why?' Rachel asked. 'Why did you tell him that your academic career was more important than what's between you? I know you better than that, Celeste, even if he doesn't, yet. You're not your parents, even if you think you are. So why?'

'You're not your parents.'

She wasn't sure if she'd ever realised how much she needed someone to say those words to her.

'Because… I was scared.' Rachel would know how much it cost her to admit it. She'd always powered through life, pretending she didn't care when people laughed at her, or rolled their eyes and walked away when she corrected them. 'He's not like me, Rach. People *like* him. He's friendly and nice and gorgeous and popular and—'

'And you didn't think you could have that?'

'I didn't think I could keep it. I still don't. I'm not good at people—everyone knows that about me. So I pretended it was all about work, and my academic reputation, because I didn't want to admit the truth. I'm in love with him and it would hurt like hell when he walked away from me like every other guy in my life has, when they realise that this is just me. I can't not tell them when they're wrong. I can't play nice with their parents. And I'm going to forget about important dinners and stuff if I'm reading something interesting.'

'Or abandon your brother and best friend at a party while you escape to the library,' Rachel added, mildly.

Celeste rolled her eyes. 'It was nine years ago, Rachel. Are you two ever going to forgive me for that?'

She grinned. 'I think we probably will. And I think Theo would too, if you asked him to.'

'If I admitted I was wrong?' That…did not sound like the sort of thing she would do.

'Is he worth it?'

'Yes.' The word was out before she could even think about it. 'But he was talking about a casual thing. We never said anything about love. And I don't think I could take it if—'

'Give him a chance,' Rachel suggested. 'You never told him you loved him, either, right?'

'No.'

'So tell him. Tell him you were wrong and that you love him.'

'And what if he says he doesn't love me back?'

Rachel gave her a sympathetic smile. 'Then you're no worse off than you are now. And at least you'll know, yeah?'

'I suppose.' It still sounded like a risky deal to her.

'Just…trust me, okay?' Rachel said. 'The people we love are worth taking a chance on. Even if it means admitting we're wrong, sometimes.'

'Damon taught you that too?'

'And you.' Rachel flashed her a grin. 'After all, it's hard to be best friends with you for a decade without admitting you're wrong a couple of hundred times.'

'Very true.' Celeste got to her feet, saying a silent goodbye to the butterflies. 'So, this is your engagement party. I'm guessing a good maid of honour would stay until the end?'

'As long as you promise me you're going to find Theo and not run off to the library, I'll cover for you.'

Grinning, Celeste pressed a quick kiss to her best friend's cheek and raced down the stairs.

It was almost a new year. And she had to do something very important before the clock chimed midnight.

He could feel the Tower of London looming behind him, reminding him of everything he was leaving behind in the old year.

Even as midnight approached, and the crowd of revellers along the banks of the Thames grew louder, and more excitable, Theo couldn't get himself in the right mood. Oh, he pasted on the work smile and played the part, but inside, he was thinking. Hard.

While the band of the moment played their last song before the midnight countdown, he used the break to marshal his thoughts into an order—or rather a list.

New Year's Resolutions.
One: Finish my history degree.

He'd been working on it part-time for years now, and it was time to wrap it up. Not least because he knew, deep down, he'd only been putting it off because he still didn't feel he deserved it.

Well, sod that. He'd done the work—or most of it anyway. Even Celeste had said it was good. So he'd finish the rest. He'd earned it. It might not be an Oxbridge first, but it was something he'd worked for himself, without any extra credit for his name or his face, and that made it all the more valuable to Theo.

Two: Figure out what I want to do next.

He'd told his parents it wouldn't be what they wanted. Maybe he needed to say the same thing to the TV studios. Take a break, and figure out what it was that he wanted to achieve. To do something for himself, for a change. He'd made enough money from his TV career—probably even enough to save a money pit like the family home if he wanted to, which he didn't. He could afford to take a break, a step back at least, while he got his head straight.

His whole life, he'd tried to make nice, to keep everyone on side, to earn *someone's* approval at least. Hell, even fake dating Celeste had been about winning back public approval, to start with. And where had that desperate need to be liked got him?

Well, actually, it had got him pretty far in his career, he thought, looking out over the crowd cheering the band up on stage. But in his personal life?

He supposed it had brought him to Celeste, but it hadn't been enough to let him keep her. And it had also brought him to the place where his parents thought it was okay to try and arrange a marriage for him to further their own ambitions.

That was not okay. And he'd told them so. He wanted to keep that feeling of freedom he'd experienced when he'd done it.

New Year, new Theo.

They'd called—well, his mother had, merrily whitewashing the whole of Christmas Day as if it had never happened. And normally he'd let her get away with it.

Not this time.

He'd go and see them again, as they'd asked. But he was standing firm, now. He'd tell them that he had his own life, his own career. That he was happy and successful. That if he ever married it would be because he loved the person, and it wouldn't matter to him what they thought of his choice. Because they'd never really been particularly pleased that *he* was their son. Never said they were proud of him, or that they loved him. Only ever pointed out his faults.

And he had no intention of letting them do that to his wife, or any children that might be in his future.

He'd put up with it his whole life, but that was no reason anyone else had to.

What else could he put on his list for his best year ever?

Three: Fall in love.

Except he'd already done that, hadn't he?

He shook the thought away. The band were coming to the end of the song, and could feel the atmosphere rising around him as midnight drew closer.

This was why he loved his job; being around so many people at moments like this, connecting with them, helping them celebrate, feeling a part of it all.

He just wished Celeste were there to share it with him.

The last chord rang out across the crowd, rippling over the river, past the Tower of London behind him. The giant video screen they'd set up at the edge of the water switched from showing the band on stage, to showing him again—then split to show a live image of Big Ben, further down the river.

'It's nearly time, guys!' Theo yelled into his mic, earning a roar of excitement from the crowd in return. 'Are you ready to count down with me?' Another screaming affirmative.

He waited until he got the signal in his earpiece, pressing it into his ear and concentrating to make sure it didn't get lost in the noise of the party below.

'Ten!' he shouted, knowing from there on he was almost obsolete. He'd given them their starting line, and from here the crowd would take the momentum he'd built and run with it.

Except there was something happening, just below where he stood on the stage. Something distracting the crowd from the most important countdown of the year.

'Nine,' he yelled, almost a millisecond too late, as he frowned down at the scene. What was happening down there?

'Eight!' There was someone pushing through the crowds.

'Seven!' Someone with dark hair.

'Six!' And a familiar white coat.

'Five!' And bright red lips as she smiled up at him. *Celeste.*

He lost his place in the countdown for a second, as he tried to process the reality of her being there, now.

'Four!' he yelled, slightly behind the rest of the crowd. The people at the front of the crowd were helping her up onto the stage now. Everyone knew who she was, clearly. And who she was to him.

'Three!' She stood before him, eyes hopeful, biting her lip.

'I couldn't start the new year without you,' she shouted, the words hitting his heart.

'Two!' He hadn't moved. He needed to move, to respond, something.

Celeste took a step back, and he reached out to grab her hand and pull her close against his side, as the crowd screamed for them both.

'One!' He looked Celeste in the eye and hoped she could read in his face everything he couldn't say. At least, not without the crowd and millions of TV viewers hearing it too, through his microphone.

The confetti cannons went off, the balloons sailed down river, and Big Ben bonged to mark the end of one year and the start of another.

'Happy New Year!' Theo yelled, to the crowd, to the viewers, to Celeste and to himself.

And then he kissed her, in front of millions of people, and there wasn't anything fake about it at all.

Celeste fell into his kiss as if she'd been waiting aeons for it, not days. She didn't care who was watching, or what anybody thought. She just knew she was where she belonged. Standing in the shadow of the Tower of London, kissing the man she loved.

Oh. She should probably tell him that, shouldn't she?

'I love you,' she murmured between kisses.

'I love you, too,' he replied, just as an almighty crash tore through the air as the fireworks started. They turned to watch as the sky over the Tower was lit up with colours and patterns, and 'Auld Lang Syne' kicked in on the bagpipes over on the other stage.

'I'm sorry.' Now she was here, she felt the desperate need to tell him all the things she hadn't, that night in the igloo. 'I was a fool. I was scared.'

'Me, too,' Theo admitted. 'Think that maybe we could be scared together?'

She smiled up at him. 'If I'm with you, I don't think I'll have to be afraid.'

'Not ever,' he promised.

Celeste snuggled into his arms as the party continued below.

'How much longer are you hosting this shindig for?' she asked.

'We're live for another fifteen minutes. But after that… I'm all yours.'

'For ever?' It was a big ask. Too big. They still hadn't talked about all the reasons she'd pulled away, or why he'd let her. All the things that were holding them back from the lives they could be living, together.

'If you'll have me,' Theo replied, and she knew suddenly that none of it mattered.

Yes, they had plenty of stuff to work through, but it would all be easier with each other by their sides. They had a whole new year stretching out before them—a whole new life, even—in which to work out the details.

'Always,' she replied.

There was an anxious-looking production assistant waving at Theo from just off camera. Celeste waved back and pressed a quick kiss to Theo's cheek before starting to move away.

Theo grabbed her back and kissed her properly, on the lips. 'Don't go far.'

'Promise.'

She slid away, out of camera view, and watched as the live broadcast on the big screen lit up with Theo's face again. She hid her smile behind her hand as she realised he had her pillar-box red lipstick liberally smeared around his mouth. *Oops.*

'And that's it, folks!' Theo said finally, wrapping up the live broadcast. 'The old year has passed, the new one is here. No need to stop celebrating though! And I hope the rest of your night—the rest of your year, for that matter—is as incredible as I hope mine is going to be. Happy New Year, Britain!'

More cheering as the cameras panned out over the crowds, the river and the Tower of London again. Theo shook hands with a dozen or more people as he made his way towards her, but Celeste didn't mind the wait.

He was right. They had a whole year to make special—and, she hoped, a whole lifetime. Together.

Finally, he reached her side and took her hand in his. 'Ready?' he asked.

'For what?'

'Our future.'

Celeste smiled. 'Absolutely.' History was her first love, of course. But even it couldn't live up to the prospect of a future with the man she loved more than anything.

* * * * *

HER TEXAS
NEW YEAR'S WISH

MICHELLE MAJOR

To the Fortunes of Texas team—
thanks for making this journey so much fun.

Chapter One

"I wouldn't drink that if I were you."

Wiley Fortune plucked the glass from his sister's hand and placed it back on the polished mahogany bar.

Nicole gave him a funny look. "It's water, Wi. Roja is providing the food for this party. I may be a guest, but I'm also still on the clock."

"I know it's water." Wiley tugged on the end of Nicole's long blond hair, the way he used to do when they were kids. "That's my point."

Nicole, Ashley and Megan Fortune—the triplets—had been born seven years after Wiley, miracle babies in every sense of the word. Their parents, David and Marci, had married after a whirlwind courtship,

blending four sons from their respective first mar-
riages in a way that would have made Carol Brady's
head spin back in the day.

The boys had gotten off to a bit of a rocky start
as they attempted to figure out their roles in the new
family. Everything had changed when his mom gave
birth to Stephanie five years later. One thing all four
boys could agree on was how much they adored their
baby sister. Mom had hoped to add another sibling
to the mix right away, but she'd had trouble conceiv-
ing. Although she'd tried to hide her emotional pain
and physical exhaustion, Wiley knew that season of
loss had taken a toll on her.

Wiley loved every member of his family, but he'd
been a quiet, introverted kid and it was a lot to grow up
in such a big, boisterous family. Maybe that fact had
something to do with the distance that had seemed to
grow between him and the rest of his siblings.

He was the only one who hadn't migrated to the
quaint town of Rambling Rose, Texas, although they'd
convinced him to visit over Christmas and return for
his cousin Adam Fortune's son's first birthday party.

"What's wrong with the water in Rambling Rose?"
Nicole asked, scrunching her perfect nose.

"It's obviously tainted," Wiley said, keeping his
features neutral and using the same tone with her that
he did for contract negotiations in his law firm back
in Chicago. "Look around at all the nauseatingly
happy couples here tonight. Something happens

when a Fortune drinks the Rambling Rose water. They lose all sense and succumb to Cupid's arrow."

Nicole rolled her bright blue eyes toward the tile ceiling that had just been installed in the restaurant. "I guess that explains why you're on your second whiskey of the night."

He lifted the etched-glass tumbler in her direction. "Much safer. Can I buy you a drink?"

"I'm running the restaurant and bar tonight," Nicole said with a delicate sniff. "I don't need you to buy me a drink."

She swatted his arm, then grabbed the water and made a show of drinking down half of it in a few gulps. "Besides—" she delicately dabbed at the corner of her mouth with the flowing sleeve of her batik-print dress "—what's wrong with love?"

"It's a distraction," he answered without hesitation.

"That's cynical, Wiley, even for you." Nicole climbed onto the bar stool next to him and swiveled so that they were both facing out toward the crowd. "Look at how happy Callum and Dillon are."

She pointed toward their brothers, who stood near the front of the banquet room greeting guests. Dillon stood close to Hailey Miller, his fiancée, whom he'd met because she worked at the local spa the family had opened in town last year, while Callum and his wife, Becky, held hands. They'd met and quickly married after Callum moved to Rambling Rose and fell in love with the sweet nurse and her adorable twin toddlers, Sasha and Luna.

"It's the water," he repeated. "Or they've all been stricken by the Texas heat. Even Steven is all googly-eyed for his lady. I barely recognize my own brothers."

A second sister, Megan, let out a mild laugh as she approached from the other side of him and helped herself to a sip of his drink. "If you don't recognize your brothers, it's because you spend too much time on your own."

"I'm here now," Wiley muttered.

"Because Mom guilted you into it," Megan reminded him. She, Nicole and Ashley looked almost identical with their shiny hair and delicate features. They'd followed their brothers to Rambling Rose and opened a farm-to-table restaurant, Provisions, to a great deal of success. Megan was the most serious of the trio and handled the finances for both Provisions and Roja, located inside the Hotel Fortune, which was due to open in just over a month. Nicole was the more flamboyantly creative and was using her culinary skills to create an innovative menu for Roja as the restaurant's executive chef. Ashley took on the role of bossy micromanager in the best way possible, and as the general manager for Provisions.

"Wiley thinks Rambling Rose is a bad influence on all of us because the Fortunes are falling in love here."

"You could use some more love in your life."

Megan poked a finger into his biceps. "You work too much."

"How would you know? I live in Chicago. Don't tell me you're keeping tabs on my life from halfway across the country." Wiley felt heat prick the back of his neck as his sisters exchanged a knowing glance. He didn't think he'd sounded defensive, but this was the reason he skipped so many family gatherings. There was no privacy to be had once his brothers and sisters got involved.

"All you talk about is work," Megan answered, smoothing a hand over her cream-colored sweater.

"I like my job." Wiley took a long drink of whiskey, welcoming the burn of the liquor in his throat. "It's fascinating."

"Contract law isn't fascinating." Nicole laughed. "The restaurant business is fascinating. It's always evolving."

"Not to mention there's no shortage of yummy food to taste," Megan added.

"Being an attorney is fascinating to me," Wiley grumbled.

"Because you need more excitement in your life." Nicole turned to him. "Don't you long for a change, Wi? For years, you've been at the same firm in the same position—"

"And living in the same condo." Megan fist-bumped her sister.

"I'm stable and consistent," Wiley told them.

"Boring," Nicole countered.

"When was the last time you did something spontaneous?" Megan demanded, placing a hand on his knee and pinching like she used to when they were kids.

"What the hell?" Wiley squirmed and then shooed away her hand.

"You're still girl-crazy," Megan told him with a laugh. "You always have been."

"You just need to improve your taste," Nicole advised.

Megan nodded. "Maybe then it will last beyond a couple of months."

Wiley resisted the urge to growl or to stomp away the way he had when his baby sisters bothered him when they were younger. He pointed to their cousin, Kane, who'd joined Callum's construction company last year once Callum moved the operation to Rambling Rose. "Go bother Kane with your meddling," he said.

Nicole laughed. "What are we, the Scooby-Doo gang?"

"Those meddling sisters," Megan said, making her voice low like a cartoon villain's.

"You have so many choices of Fortunes to annoy here tonight."

"But you're our current favorite." Megan leaned in and placed a smacking kiss on Wiley's cheek.

"The rest of them aren't half as much fun now that they've found love," Nicole admitted, resting her head on his shoulder as her tone turned wistful. "They're all so blissed out from true love."

"You're still an easy target." Megan smiled at him, but it didn't quite reach her blue eyes.

"Why doesn't that sound like a compliment?"

"We want you to be happy," Megan told him, but Wiley wasn't sure if she was truly talking about him or thinking of herself. He wasn't about to point out that neither Nicole nor Megan had found love in Rambling Rose.

Nicole handed him her nearly empty glass of water. "You should have some of this. If there really is something in the water, it will be good for you."

"You know that was a joke." He took the water from her and finished it in one swallow. "First, I don't believe in true love. It isn't pragmatic, and the odds of it being successful are ridiculously bad. Besides, whatever my future holds, I'm pretty sure it doesn't include finding my perfect match in a town that's no more than a tiny speck on the Texas map. I'm here temporarily to support all of you. Nothing more."

"You have to keep your heart open," Megan told him. "You never know when love will find you." She gestured toward Callum, who lifted one of the twins into the air. "When Callum and Becky met, he wasn't looking for love."

"Now he'd tell you he couldn't imagine his life without Becky, Sasha and Luna."

Wiley sighed. His sisters were right about Callum.

It still felt strange that his brother had taken on the role of father figure to the pretty widow's daughters so seamlessly. Not that Callum wasn't great with kids. He'd had plenty of experience with Stephanie and the triplets. But up until he'd met Becky, Wiley had been certain Callum didn't want kids. The same went for Dillon and Steven. In fact, it had been the change in each of his brothers that made him feel like even more of an odd man out in his family.

He glanced between Nicole and Megan, at the similar wistful expressions as they surveyed the crowd. No way would he rain on their romantic parade, even if he knew their unwavering belief in true love might have more to do with youth and inexperience than anything else. Wiley had been around the dating block enough to know that some people weren't cut out for love. People like him.

His siblings had a lot to be proud of. They'd accomplished so much in their time in Rambling Rose. He'd watched from a distance with fascination over the past year and half as they'd transformed the sleepy community into a thriving small town.

Wiley smiled as Ashley, the third triplet, approached, wagging her finger. "You three need to mingle."

Ashley had always been the bossiest. Now that she was settled in Rambling Rose and happy with her fiancé, Rodrigo Mendoza, and the success of Provisions, she was even more confident in her ability to order her siblings around.

"We're doing important work here," Megan told Ashley with an arched brow. "Convincing Wiley to move to Rambling Rose."

"He's about to agree." Nicole nodded.

"That's wonderful." Ashley gave Wiley a tight hug.

"And a total lie." He extricated himself from her embrace and held up his empty glass toward the bartender, silently requesting a refill. He was staying out at the Fame and Fortune Ranch where several of his siblings lived, so Nicole had given him a ride to the hotel tonight. Might as well take advantage, especially with his sisters on a mission.

"Larkin is a cute baby," he said casually, then smiled to himself as the triplets began to talk over one another, extolling the virtues of the birthday boy.

Nothing distracted them like an adorable kid.

He thanked the bartender when the man brought him a fresh glass and took a step away from the triplets. Time to make a quick exit from that conversation.

Steven waved to him, and Wiley started in that direction, then paused when a flash of blue caught his attention. A beautiful woman wearing a tailored cerulean sheath dress.

The party was being held on the second floor of Roja, the signature restaurant that was part of the Hotel Fortune. The boutique hotel, with its Spanish architecture and Western decor that was a nod to the town's history, was the crowning achievement for his brothers. Callum, Dillon and Steven had successfully opened various businesses in town over the past year, from the medical clinic to a spa to several upscale retail shops. He knew they'd received the most push-back from the community about the initial plan for the hotel, and it had been Kane who'd smoothed over the waters in town, convincing Callum to rescale the project to be smaller and more intimate.

The Hotel Fortune was set to open in just over a month, and Wiley had no doubt it would be a huge success. His brothers and sisters wouldn't settle for anything less.

There were at least fifty people in attendance for Larkin's birthday. In addition to his parents, Adam and Laurel, and his immediate and extended family, the pri-vate banquet room on the restaurant's second floor was filled with friends and hotel employees. The commu-nity had banded together last year to support the baby when he needed a bone marrow transplant. Everyone was thrilled to celebrate the little boy who'd overcome so much. And to Wiley's surprise, based on how his siblings had talked about the celebration, all the differ-ent Fortune factions seemed to be getting along.

He turned toward the wall of windows and patio doors that had been opened for the evening. It was unseasonably warm for this time of year, even by Texas standards. In the center of the exterior wall was a stamped concrete balcony with wrought iron railings that overlooked the patio and pool below.

His gaze snagged on the same woman who'd caught his attention a few moments earlier. She had long, bourbon-colored hair, a slender build and creamy skin from what he could see of her arms in the sleeveless dress she wore. She spoke to Callum and Mariana, one of the town's most illustrious residents, who was working with Nicole as the sous chef in the Roja kitchen. For years, Mariana had run a successful outdoor market in downtown Rambling Rose, with vendors selling all kinds of food and wares. And her food stall had been one of the most—if not the most—popular stand of all. It was in no small part thanks to her influence with the local vendors that the Fortune family had been able to go ahead with some of their most successful new projects, all because Mariana understood that they would bring new life to her hometown.

Wiley didn't recognize the woman in blue, although he couldn't help but think they'd met before. There was nothing else that would explain the strange connection when he hadn't even fully seen her face.

Then she turned, and the breath whooshed out of him on a long exhale. It was like a piece of a puzzle snapping together with its perfect match. His heart seemed to skip a beat. No, that couldn't be right. The woman was a stranger. There was no question, because he would never forget his reaction to her.

She might be a stranger, but he had to meet her.

He made his way through the crowd. Mariana walked away, but Callum remained in conversation with the woman as Wiley stopped just behind his brother.

"Hey, Wi." Callum glanced over his shoulder. "Have you met Grace Williams? She's one of our management trainees. Grace, this is my brother Wiley. He's our big-shot family attorney visiting from Chicago."

Wiley barely registered the introduction as Grace smiled at him. Her eyes, the same bright blue of a clear summer sky, crinkled at the corners.

"Hi." He struggled to regain control over the rapid cadence of his breathing. If he didn't know better, Wiley would think he was having some sort of heart attack. There was no logical explanation for his reaction. He'd met countless beautiful women over the years and dated his fair share of them. But Grace Williams leveled him with just a smile.

Callum cleared his throat, and Wiley realized Grace had offered her hand to shake.

"It's nice to meet you," she said softly, a blush staining her cheeks.

He took her hand, almost expecting to feel the zap of an electric current when he touched her. No literal shock, which he realized was a ridiculous expectation in the first place.

"Hey, Wiley," Steven called from a few feet away. "Come over here for a second. I have a couple hotel employees I want you to meet."

Wiley had already met a dozen new people tonight, employees, local business owners and members of the extended Fortune family. He'd enjoyed the various introductions until this moment. Now he was done talking to people other than Grace.

"It's fine," Callum told him with a dismissive pat on the shoulder. "Grace and I are discussing some hotel business, anyway."

Wiley wanted to argue, but that would be rude. He looked toward Grace once more and her breath hitched.

"I'll be around all night," she told him, darting a quick glance toward Callum before her gaze returned to Wiley. "I hope we can chat some more."

"Definitely," he told her, the band around his heart loosening slightly. He had all night to talk to Grace.

That thought calmed Wiley enough so that he could shift his attention to Steven as he walked away. He wasn't about to lose his chance with Grace when they'd only just met.

Wiley Fortune was quite possibly the most handsome man Grace had ever seen. And in his family, that was saying something.

He shared the same tall, lean build as Steven and that innate Fortune spark, but Grace's reaction to Wiley had been unexpected. As he walked away, she worked to regain control. The last thing she needed was to make a spectacle of herself in front of Callum.

She did her best not to fidget as she gave an update on the water heater that had leaked in one of the hotel's main-floor utility rooms. She hated relaying anything that seemed like bad news, especially in the middle of a first birthday party, but hoped the fact that she had a solution for the potential dilemma would help.

"It sounds like you handled it perfectly," Callum told her, and she let out a small sigh of relief. "Just like tonight. Larkin's celebration has gone off without a hitch."

"I can't take all the credit," Grace admitted because that was her way. "The Roja staff has done an amazing job. Everyone's pitched in where they were supposed to. And a roomful of Fortunes isn't as intimidating as you led me to believe."

Callum grinned. "We're on our best behavior." He leaned closer. "It's a bit of a surprise, I'll admit. This night makes me feel like we're actually on track for the grand opening next month."

"Definitely," Grace agreed. "By then, all the details will be ironed out. Everyone in Rambling Rose is going to be talking about the Hotel Fortune."

"I hope you're right. This venture has definitely given us the most headaches, although it will all be worth it when we have a full slate of guests."

"You and your brothers and sisters have made sure every step of the redevelopment plan for the town has been thoughtfully crafted and executed. I'm honored to be a part of it." Grace inwardly cringed, hoping she didn't sound like a total suck-up, but Callum smiled.

"We're glad to have you on the team. I'm sorry things at Cowboy Country didn't work out, but their loss is our gain."

Grace forced a smile, although mention of her previous job had her stomach tightening painfully. She didn't think anyone in Rambling Rose knew the full truth of why she'd left the cowboy theme park run by another branch of the Fortune family in the town of Horseback Hollow. There was no way she was going to share her heartbreak and humiliation, not when her life was finally getting back on track.

"Take a break." Callum gestured to the row of food tables. "Have a piece of cake or a drink or just enjoy the beautiful night. You've earned it, Grace."

She nodded. "Thanks. I'll have a piece of birthday cake. I'm glad things are going so well and Larkin's enjoying the attention."

Someone called to Callum, and she turned for the cake table but first detoured toward the empty balcony overlooking the hotel's impeccably landscaped pool area. She needed to cool off as she could still feel her cheeks burning from the way Wiley had looked at her.

She wouldn't jeopardize her future for any man, no matter how attractive. In some ways, she still felt like pinching herself, because despite all the things that had gone wrong in her life, the three and half months she'd spent in the Hotel Fortune management training program seemed to make all the trouble worth it.

Yes, she'd had to drop out of college to help take care of her older brother after he'd been seriously injured in a car accident almost a decade earlier. Yes, she'd struggled to fit in when she'd finally returned to school, unable to enjoy life in the way regular college students did. She'd been too serious and too focused, determined to get her degree but always guilty that she was able to have a life Jake couldn't due to his recovery. After finally graduating with a degree in hospitality management, she'd landed a job in the Cowboy Country front office. At that point, Grace thought she was finally on her way. She'd had a good job, a handsome boyfriend and a fresh start in life.

Discovering that Craig had been cheating on her with a fellow employee—and that pretty much everyone at Cowboy Country knew it except Grace—had been a blow she hadn't expected. One that brought her to her knees, literally and figuratively.

But she was leaving the past behind for her new future with the Hotel Fortune. Although members of the family had been taking the lead on running things during construction, they planned to promote someone from within the training program to the role of general manager as part of the grand opening. There might be other employees vying for the coveted position, but Grace was determined to earn it.

She stepped to the edge of the balcony, running her palms across the smooth wrought iron railing. She couldn't remember ever feeling such a sense of anticipation as she did at this moment.

Drawing in a long pull of the fresh air from the open patio doors, she turned back toward the party. Pride swelled in her chest at the crowd of happy people. She'd had a lot to do with making this evening a success.

Her gaze snagged on Wiley once again as he moved away from the group where he stood. One corner of his full mouth tugged into a sexy smirk, like he could feel the way her body went on high alert from across the room. Grace felt like she was on a roller coaster, climbing the track of the first giant hill. Her heart raced as she thought about the free fall to come.

When he started toward her, she turned and leaned forward, gripping the railing with rigid fingers. It wasn't that she didn't want to meet him. In fact, her body practically yearned to get close to him.

But she'd given herself to a man once before with disastrous results. No way would she fall again.

A loud crack split the air, and she stumbled as the balcony pitched forward. Then she was falling so fast she didn't even have time to scream.

Chapter Two

"This doesn't make any sense." Callum dashed a hand through his hair as he paced the small waiting room in the Rambling Rose Medical Center emergency room. "In all my years of construction, I've never had something like that happen on one of our projects."

"We'll figure out what caused it," Wiley said from where he sat on a patterned chair situated against the far wall. "But first we need to make sure Grace is okay. She's the priority right now."

Callum nodded. "You're right. But what if it had been a hotel guest or one of the kids on that balcony when it collapsed? Can you imagine if there were people on the patio below?"

Wiley understood his brother's train of thought but felt oddly defensive at the subtle suggestion that the accident wasn't as catastrophic because a mere employee had been injured.

As if sensing his irritation, Callum held up a hand. He wore dark slacks and a button-down shirt that was covered with dust from the rubble of the mess that had been made when the balcony collapsed. "I'm not insinuating that Grace is disposable. I would never put her or any employee at risk. You know that, Wi."

"She was unconscious," Wiley muttered, his nerve endings pulling tight at the memory of the EMTs lifting her limp body onto a stretcher. "She could have died in that fall."

The thought of losing her before he got to know her felt like a punch to the gut.

"But she woke up in the ambulance." Callum continued to pace back and forth. "She was obviously in shock but seemed lucid. Her ankle was in bad shape, but I have to believe that's the worst of her injuries. We need to believe Grace will be okay."

Grace Williams.

Callum had shared the woman's name with the first responders when they arrived at the hotel mere minutes after Nicole made the 911 call.

In the chaos that ensued after the balcony's collapse, Callum had been designated to accompany Grace to the hospital while his brothers and sisters dealt with things on-site. Wiley couldn't explain why he'd stalked to his car and followed the emergency vehicle, but he couldn't seem to release the impulse to be near Grace, even if she didn't want or need him there.

"You better hope she's okay," Wiley muttered.

Callum stopped directly in front of him, his eyes narrowing. "What's that supposed to mean?"

Wiley drew in a breath. How was he supposed to explain the fierce protectiveness he felt toward a woman he'd only just met? He didn't understand it, so there was no way his brother would.

"The hotel bears a responsibility for the accident. If the construction was faulty or the building materials subpar—"

"Are you kidding?" Callum's jaw tightened. "You know I don't cut corners, Wiley. Everything I build is rock solid."

"Other than the balcony that just collapsed with a woman standing on it." Wiley rose from his chair to stand toe-to-toe with his brother.

"I'm going to assume you're playing devil's advocate because you're an attorney and concerned about the family's liability. I sure as hell hope you aren't suggesting that we didn't take all the necessary steps to ensure proper construction." Temper flared between them, and Wiley wanted to kick himself in the family jewels for goading his brother at a time like this. The thought of Grace's injuries made him want to lash out at anyone and everyone.

He gave a tight nod. "I'm sorry, Callum. You're right. I'm worried about your employee and I'm concerned about the hotel's responsibility and the potential negative press of this kind of accident. There's no doubt about the quality of the work you do. I don't want a single incident to tarnish your track record in town."

Callum eyed him for a moment longer, then stepped away and began to pace again. "We won't let it. Of course we'll take care of any medical bills that aren't covered by Grace's insurance and continue to pay her salary while she's recovering. Once she returns to work—"

"You don't even know the extent of her injuries," Wiley felt compelled to point out.

"I can help with that."

They both turned as a tall man in light blue scrubs entered the waiting room. Callum strode forward and shook the man's hand, reminding Wiley of his brother's ties to the town.

"Mark, how is she?"

The man threw a glance in Wiley's direction.

"This is my brother Wiley. He's in town for Larkin's party."

"Quite an event," the other man murmured, which to Wiley's mind was the understatement of the new year.

"Wiley, this is Dr. Mark Matthews." Callum gestured to the doctor. "Becky says he's one of the best emergency room physicians she knows." He turned his attention fully to Mark. "I'm glad you're on duty tonight. How is Grace?"

"Good, given what she's been through." The doctor looked past Callum and Wiley to the empty waiting room. "Have you called her family?"

Callum nodded. "Ashley tracked down her parents' number and spoke to her mom. They're on their way here."

"Can we see her?" Wiley demanded, crossing his arms over his chest when both men gave him a strange look.

"I suppose that would be all right," Mark agreed almost reluctantly. "We've moved her to a room on the third floor for the night."

"How bad are the injuries?" Callum asked as Dr. Matthews turned toward a bank of elevators.

"You're not family, so I can't share any details." Mark jabbed at the elevator's button. "Grace will decide what she wants to tell you. She was awake when I left, but if she's fallen back asleep I don't want you to wake her. She's in room three sixty-five. I need to check on another patient, and then I'll be up."

Callum nodded. "Thanks, Mark. We won't disturb her if she's resting."

The elevator doors swished open as the doctor turned away. Wiley followed his brother into the small space.

"I appreciate you being here," Callum said as he

pushed the button for the third floor. "But you don't have to go with me to see her."

Wiley kept his gaze on the carpeted floor. "I'll stay."

He could feel Callum studying him but didn't answer. Let his brother think that his interest in Grace Williams was due to concern over the hotel's liability for the accident.

It made sense, and not only because of Wiley's career as an attorney. He'd never gotten particularly involved in the details of the lives of his siblings, at least as much as he could help it. After years of being part of such a large family, his identity as a separate individual meant the world to him.

He couldn't figure out why Grace had changed that in a split second, and he wasn't ready to examine it now.

Grace glanced up at the soft knock on the hospital door. Her head felt heavy and somewhat muddled, but now that the pain medicine had kicked in, at least her entire body no longer throbbed in agony.

She expected to see her parents' familiar faces. Shock rippled through her as Callum Fortune entered. She couldn't imagine that the man responsible for the construction of most of the new buildings in Rambling Rose would be too happy that one of his employees had managed to get herself practically killed in the middle of an important family event.

"Hey there," Callum said gently as he came closer to the bed. "Are you up for a couple of visitors?"

Her gaze moved beyond his broad frame and shivers erupted along her skin as she met the intense gaze of the man who'd captured her attention just before the balcony collapsed. Grace stifled a giggle that she knew must be caused by the pain medicine at the thought that her body's overwhelming reaction to Wiley might have caused the earth to move under her feet.

"Grace?" Callum gave her a strange look, and for an instant she worried she'd been singing the words to the classic tune out loud.

She swallowed and tried to pull together her tangled musings. "Thanks for stopping by," she said, and immediately thought she sounded ridiculous. As if Callum Fortune had come to her hospital room for some kind of social call. "I'm sorry I broke your balcony." Her voice sounded strange to her ears, thick and garbled.

Callum shook his head. "You didn't do anything wrong," he assured her. "There's no reason to be sorry. I'm the one who owes you an apology, Grace. I don't understand how or why that balcony collapsed. The county building inspector was out before the holidays and we passed everything."

Wiley stepped forward, clearing his throat. "We're glad you're okay."

The gentle gleam in Wiley's brown eyes made her

stomach flutter once again. When they'd been introduced, his eyes had appeared regular brown, but as he approached the bed she could see flecks of gold in their depths. His lashes were also outrageously long for a man. Cosmetics companies could build entire ad campaigns around the promise of achieving lashes like his.

She blinked and tried to focus, realizing she was staring at him like some cow-eyed teenager. "Hi," she breathed, unable to form a more coherent greeting.

"Hello, Grace," he said, lifting her hand and squeezing her fingers with what felt like something close to admiration.

She'd always hated her plain, one-syllable name, but on Wiley's lips it sounded like a poem.

"Hi," she repeated and felt color heating her cheeks. Too bad she couldn't blame the pain medicine for her reaction to him.

"How are you?" he asked, like he truly cared about her answer and not just her physical injuries.

"Did you two know each other before the party?" Callum interrupted before she could answer, sounding both confused and irritated.

Oh, I know this man, Grace thought to herself. At least she wanted to know him.

Wiley abruptly released Grace's hand. Immediately she wanted to reach for him again. Something flashed in his eyes, and she had the thought that he might feel the same as her.

He broke eye contact with her to glance at his brother. "No. You introduced us."

"That's what I thought," Callum said, his voice flat.

Grace forced herself to focus on Callum. "I know the accident wasn't your fault, Callum. I—"

"Someone is sure as hell to blame."

She winced and brought a hand to her head at her brother's overly loud words. Jake and her parents hurried into the room, crowding around her bedside as the Fortune brothers stepped back.

Grace closed her eyes and wished for everyone to disappear other than Wiley. She wanted him to hold her hand again and ask how she was. She wanted to tell him she felt better when he was with her, even though that didn't make any sense. Still, it felt totally justifiable to her heart.

"Jake, this isn't the time." Grace opened her eyes as her mother placed a gentle hand on her brother's arm. "Our focus right now is Grace."

Her brother, older by two years, crossed his arms over his chest. "We can all agree that she wouldn't be fighting for her life in this hospital bed if it weren't for the shoddy construction at the hotel."

"I'm not fighting for my life," Grace said, lifting a hand to cover her mouth when another bubble of laughter threatened to escape. Her brother had always had a quick temper, but she sobered as she noted the look of consternation that crossed Callum's features.

"Oh, sweetheart." Her mother let out a soft sob, and regret pricked at the hazy fog filling Grace's mind. The last thing she wanted was to upset her mother. "We were so worried when that Fortune woman called."

Grace searched her brain for the details the doctor had shared about the extent of her injuries. "I'm okay, Mom. I broke my ankle and have a minor concussion."

Barbara Williams gasped. "A head injury?"

"Minor," Grace assured her, remembering the weeks after Jake's car accident when he'd lain in a medically induced coma while they waited for the brain swelling to subside. "Plus a few bruises and scrapes. Everything else came back clear."

"Are you sure?" her father asked, his tone gruff. Grace knew that rough exterior hid the heart of a teddy bear.

Her parents turned as Dr. Matthews entered the room. "She's sure. Grace was incredibly lucky that her injuries weren't worse. We're going to keep her overnight for observation due to the concussion, but we anticipate a straightforward recovery."

"Thank God." Her mother leaned forward to brush a kiss across Grace's forehead. "My sweet baby."

"I'm not a baby," Grace muttered. Even the cloud of fogginess from the pain medicine couldn't dull the annoyance at her mother's pronouncement, especially in front of Callum and Wiley.

Despite the caregiver role Grace had taken on during Jake's convalescence and the fact that she'd been managing her own life for years, her mom and dad continued to treat her like a dependent little girl. She tried to be patient with them, because she knew how much Jake's accident had made them aware of the mortality of their children.

Things had only been exacerbated when Grace moved back to Rambling Rose after the debacle at Cowboy Country. But her duties at the hotel gave her a sense of purpose and a feeling of independence once again. Now it felt like everything was in jeopardy.

Dr. Matthews frowned as she swiped a hand across her cheek, obviously misinterpreting the reason for her unwelcome tears. Grace didn't care what had caused the balcony's collapse, assuming nothing like that happened again. She did worry about what her recovery might mean for her future.

"That doesn't change the fact that someone is responsible for my sister being hurt." Jake shifted his glare between Callum and Wiley.

Callum's mouth thinned. "The hotel will take care of any medical expenses not covered by insurance.

Our priority is that she feels better as quickly as possible."

"To cover your assets," Jake muttered.

"Not at all," Callum countered.

"Do you really need to have this discussion in front of Grace?" the doctor asked impatiently.

"Or at all?" Grace added. She sent a beseeching glance toward her brother, silently pleading with him to give it a rest, but Jake only shook his head.

"You want to step out into the hall for a moment?" he asked Callum.

"Good idea," Callum agreed, and turned for the door.

Grace reached for her father's hand. "Don't let Jake be rude, Dad. This wasn't Callum's fault. The Fortunes aren't to blame. I know it."

A muscle ticked in Mike Williams's bearded jaw. Her father retained the stocky build he'd had as younger man, and added a few inches of girth around the waist. "I'll try to keep him calm." He patted the top of Grace's hand. "We're glad you're okay, baby girl."

Her stomach knotted as she watched her father follow the two younger men out into the hall.

Dr. Matthews gave her an encouraging smile. "You doing okay?"

"Fine," she murmured.

Her mom began to pepper the doctor with a litany of questions about her injuries and a recovery plan. Grace hated that she was causing her family this kind of worry or that she could be seen as a burden to the hotel.

"That 'fine' didn't seem convincing," Wiley said as he lowered himself into the chair next to her bed and scooted closer. "You're going to be okay, Grace. I promise."

She automatically smoothed a hand over her hair as if she had a reason to worry about looking pretty for Wiley Fortune. He was so close she could reach out and touch him. The urge was both overwhelming and nonsensical.

"You don't owe me any promises," she said instead, working to keep her wits about her despite the pounding of her heart and the effects of the pain medicine.

"I get that." He offered a tentative smile. "I can't seem to help myself."

She blinked and then looked away, wondering if he was truly as sincere as he seemed. Her mother was still talking with the doctor, nodding furiously and taking notes on a small pad of paper she'd pulled from her purse as he spoke in hushed tones. Her father had closed the door behind him when he'd ventured into the hallway. Grace had a feeling Jake was giving Callum all kinds of trouble, and she wished she could make it stop.

"My brother is protective," she told Wiley. "I'm

sure he'll realize that the balcony collapse was an unfortunate accident. Not anyone's fault."

"It's good that you have people to look out for you," he said.

"I guess you're right." She ran a finger along the edge of the thin blanket that covered her. "Although at the moment, I wish Jake would back off. I do want you to know that his accusations aren't personal. He doesn't have it in for your family or anything like that."

"Good to know." Wiley studied her for a long moment and then lifted his hand like he might touch her. With a shake of his head he drew it back again, and disappointment pounded through Grace.

"Do you have any other brothers or sisters?" he asked.

She got the impression he was trying to distract her from worrying about what kind of scene might be unfolding in the hall.

"No." She flashed a smile. "We're a small family compared to yours."

"Nothing wrong with that." He returned her smile. "What about a boyfriend?"

She felt her mouth drop open, and he immediately rose from the chair. He scrubbed a hand over his jaw, looking uncomfortable. "I'm sorry. Forget I asked that. It's none of my business."

"No boyfriend," she told him quietly, feeling heat rise to her cheeks. "My focus right now is the training program at the hotel." She wiggled her toes, which stuck out of the cast on her left leg that stopped just below her knee. "This couldn't have come at a worse time."

"Is there ever a good time to be standing on a balcony when it collapses?" Wiley asked, smiling again. Teasing her. Possibly even flirting with her?

Before Grace had a chance to process that, her father and Callum reentered the room.

Her mother took a step away from the doctor and frowned. "Where's Jake?"

"I sent him home," Grace's father said with a small shake of his head.

Callum's cheeks were flushed, his jaw taut. He motioned to Wiley. "We should go."

Grace sat up straighter on the bed. She wanted to protest Wiley leaving, but that would be stupid.

"Thank you for being here with me." She looked to Callum first before turning her attention to Wiley. "It helped a lot."

"I'm glad," he said, and the intensity in his gaze made it feel like they were the only two people in the room.

"Grace, I can't tell you how sorry we are that you were hurt tonight." Callum's commanding tone forced her to return her gaze to him. "Like I said earlier, anything you need, our family will take care of it. Just focus on getting well again."

"And back to work," she added quickly. "I want

to get back to work as soon as possible. Please let everyone know that."

Callum smiled tightly. "Of course."

"Work is the last thing you need to be concerned with right now," her father said with a sniff. He gave Callum a sidelong glass. "I want confirmation that your hotel is safe before I let my little girl go back there."

Grace bit back a frustrated groan. Was her father trying to make the Fortunes angry? Her potential future at the hotel meant everything. She wouldn't let anything—not even a collapsing balcony—jeopardize that.

"I understand, sir," Callum answered, but she could see by the set of his shoulders that it bothered him to have his workmanship called into question.

"It's fine." Wiley said, moving close to her again. His fingers brushed the top of her cast and despite the layers of plaster, she felt the touch like he was caressing her skin. "Callum understands that your family is upset. I'll talk to him."

"Thank you," she whispered, and bit down on the inside of her cheek to stem her tears. She didn't want to start sobbing in front of the two Fortunes on top of everything else.

Wiley thanked the doctor and offered a heartfelt reassurance to her parents, then followed Callum out of the room.

"I'll give you all a few minutes," Dr. Matthews said, "and then we can talk about next steps."

When the door closed behind the doctor, Grace let the tears flow.

"Oh, sweetie." Barbara was at her bedside in an instant. "You must have been terrified."

Grace took the tissue her mother handed her and blew her nose. "It happened so fast I barely had time to be scared."

"The point is it never should have happened in the first place," her father said, crossing his arms over his meaty chest. "What the hell kind of karma are we saddled with, Gracie, that we almost lose your brother and now you?"

"You didn't almost lose me, Dad."

"A second-floor balcony collapsed with you standing on it," Mike reminded her—as if she needed reminding. "You're very lucky."

"I know." Grace crumpled the tissue. "My injuries aren't anywhere near what Jake went through. I don't want either of you to worry about my recovery process. I'm going to get back to normal sooner than later."

"You can't rush it," her mother said, smoothing the hair from her forehead. "Let me get you a mirror and a wet towel. I'm sure you want to fix your face a bit."

Grace lifted a hand to her cheek. Fix her face? What was wrong with her face?

"You'll move home, of course." Her father's tone brooked no argument.

Grace argued, anyway. "I love my apartment, Dad. I can recover there just as easily." In truth, she didn't exactly love the cramped walk-up she'd rented when she returned to Rambling Rose, but it was better than moving back in with her parents.

Her father snorted. "You live on the second floor of a building with a staircase so narrow I can't believe it's even up to code. No way can you manage that with a cast."

"I could try," she insisted, even though she knew her dad was right.

"Grace Elizabeth."

She resisted the urge to roll her eyes but knew she had little chance of winning an argument when he used her middle name, as well.

"I appreciate the offer," she said instead. "It would make things easier until I'm out of the cast." Her parents lived in a quiet section of Rambling Rose in the same house Grace had grown up in. The house, a rancher, wasn't big, but it did have plenty of space for her.

"We'll take care of packing your things," her mother said, returning from the bathroom with a small handheld mirror and a stack of wet paper towels. "All you need to focus on is resting."

And returning to work, Grace thought to herself.

No point in saying the words out loud and engaging in another argument with her parents.

She took the mirror and a paper towel from her mom. "Oh, no." She glanced up and met her mother's concerned gaze. "Why didn't you tell me?"

"You'll clean up in a jiffy," Barbara said brightly.

All Grace could think about was Wiley seeing her like this. The cast was one thing, but her face was a mess. It wasn't injured—for that she was grateful—but she looked like she'd been on a three-day bender. Her hair hung limp around her shoulders and stuck to her head in several places. Her skin was pasty and pale, and the mascara she'd carefully applied before the event was puddled under her eyes.

If she had any question as to whether Wiley Fortune had been interested in her or simply concerned about her being injured at his family's hotel, she was fairly certain her appearance answered it.

Her ruined makeup and the ruined evening seemed to be par for the course in Grace's life. Finally things had been turning around for her, and then something had to happen to send her veering off her chosen path once again.

She began to wipe her face as she listened to her parents make plans for her unexpected homecoming. Grace couldn't help but wonder if she'd ever truly attain the future she wanted so badly.

Chapter Three

"That was sure as hell a shock."

Wiley turned as Steven approached from one of the hotel's patio doors. His brother kicked a small piece of terra-cotta-colored stone as he walked toward Wiley.

It was nearly nine on the morning after the party. Wiley wanted to survey the balcony rubble in the daylight and had held out an odd kind of hope that things wouldn't seem as bad in the aftermath of the accident.

Instead, they were worse.

The balcony's deck had ripped off the exterior wall, sending thousands of pounds of concrete and metal plummeting to the ground. Grace had fallen a good twenty-five feet, and it was truly a miracle she hadn't been hurt worse.

He said as much to his brother, who nodded. "Callum said she was in good spirits at the hospital. You were there with him, right?"

Wiley nodded. "She was also doped up on painkillers," he muttered. "I'm not sure we should judge her feelings about the accident based on last night, especially not if her family has any influence on her opinion."

Steven nodded. The two of them had an unspoken language. Wiley had been a toddler when their mother married David Fortune, who'd quickly adopted both of his new wife's young sons and given them his name. Wiley was close to all of his siblings, but he and Steven had a special bond.

Steven had been a committed bachelor until he'd met and fallen for Ellie Hernandez, the mayor of Rambling Rose. Things had started off rocky between them, but they'd quickly fallen deeply in love. Another Fortune who found his perfect future in this small Texas town. "That's to be expected, but we're all committed to doing the right thing by Grace. She's been a huge asset to the hotel. I know Nicole and Mariana feel the same."

"She's special," Wiley said as his gaze zeroed in on a flash of silver under a pile of debris.

"That's an odd description coming from you. I

didn't realize you and Grace had met before last night."

He could feel Steven studying him but didn't meet his brother's gaze. "We hadn't." Wiley walked forward, carefully picking his way through the mess.

He wore dark jeans and a cotton sweater plus the cowboy boots the triplets had given him for Christmas. As a confirmed city slicker, Wiley felt a little strange sporting boots, but they seemed to be expected in Texas.

He bent down and pulled a high heel from the rubble. Clearly one of Grace's shoes. The image of her unconscious on the ground flashed in his mind again, and his chest clenched in response.

"What's the deal?" Steven asked, sounding both curious and concerned. "You went to the hospital with Callum, and he said you were acting strange. Now you look like you've seen a ghost. If you and Grace don't know each other, why are you—"

"She could have died," Wiley blurted out, then rolled his lips inward. He needed to get a handle on his emotions when it came to Grace Williams. He couldn't explain to his brother the connection he felt with her. It had been immediate and intense, like a bolt of lightning slamming through him. "She was injured in a fall at our family's hotel. The hotel that Fortune Brothers Construction built. We're responsible for her, Steven."

His brother's thick brows drew together. "Are you

thinking about our potential liability in the accident? Is Wiley the attorney making sure we cover our—"

They both turned when a feminine throat cleared. "Sorry to bother you, Steven." A woman walked toward them from the far side of the pool. She looked to be in her midtwenties and wore a pencil skirt and a silk blouse that made her seem a bit overdressed for a casual Sunday. "There's a reporter in the lobby asking to speak to the hotel manager." She tucked a perfect blond curl behind one ear. "If you'd like I can talk to him?"

Wiley frowned at the gleam in the woman's gaze. "Who are you?" he demanded, not bothering to gentle his tone. In the same way that he'd felt an immediate connection with Grace, he had an instant dislike of this woman.

She swallowed visibly, her gaze darting from Wiley to Steven, who'd pulled out his phone and was typing in a message.

"Jillian Steward," she said, clearing her throat. "I'm one of the management program trainees at the hotel. I have a background in public relations as well as hospitality at my last position, so I'm more than equipped to deal with the press. That's part of the role of whoever is promoted to the GM position."

Grace had mentioned something about the trainee program last night. She'd seemed worried about her job given the extent of her injuries. Did she suspect one of her coworkers was going to take advantage of her absence? Wiley didn't like the thought of that.

Steven nodded absently. "I texted Callum and Nicole, but if you want to—"

"I'll talk to the reporter," Wiley interrupted.

Jillian's lips tightened. "I don't mind."

"Someone in the family should handle the media," he said. "As hotel counsel, it makes sense that I act as spokesperson."

"Hotel counsel?" Steven whistled under his breath. "Another new development."

Wiley nodded and focused his attention on Jillian. "Would you please tell the reporter I'll be with him in a minute?"

"Sure." The woman flashed a cheery smile. "We won't let Grace's absence hold us back. If you need anything else—"

"We don't," Wiley told her.

"She's just doing her job," Steven said as Jillian disappeared into the hotel.

"It sounded to me like she was trying to encroach on Grace's role." Wiley drew in a calming breath. "I don't like the thought of someone taking advantage of the accident."

"It sounds to me like you have a lot of thoughts where Grace is concerned."

"I'm doing my job," Wiley shot back.

"As far as you being the hotel's counsel, obviously I'm all for it. You know we'd like you to stick around Rambling Rose longer. In fact, weren't you scheduled to fly back to Chicago this afternoon?"

"I changed my ticket."

"Seriously?"

"Stop studying me like I'm some puzzle to figure out," Wiley grumbled. He didn't want to think that his brother could read the feelings he was trying to hide.

He'd texted his secretary early this morning asking her to change his airline reservation to give him a few extra days in Texas, mainly because he wanted to see for himself that Grace was doing okay. He wanted more than he cared to admit to see her again. No point in sharing those details with his brother. "The Hotel Fortune is a huge deal for the rest of you. That makes it a huge deal for me."

Steven's shoulders relaxed ever so slightly. "Thanks, Wi." He clapped Wiley on the back. "Appreciate you stepping in, even if it's temporary. I know that small-town life isn't your deal."

"Yeah." Wiley massaged a hand over the back of his neck. He would have agreed 100 percent with Steven's assessment before last night. Now he couldn't say for sure how he felt. "I'm going to go deal with this reporter. He won't be the only one interested in the accident. Let's plan to meet with everyone out at the ranch later and come up with some talking points going forward."

He nodded at his brother and then headed for the

front of the hotel, his mind wandering to Grace and when he might see her again.

Grace tossed her cell phone down on the hospital bed with more force than necessary. "You can't avoid me forever," she muttered, then glared at her cast leg.

She knew that everyone at the hotel was busy with preparations for the grand opening, but she'd called and texted Jillian Steward, her counterpart in the management program, a half dozen times and had yet to receive a response.

Grace and Jillian weren't the only two trainees, but they were the pair that had been singled out by the Fortunes to be considered for the promotion at the end of the six-month program. That meant Jillian was the competition, and Grace knew the woman would use every advantage she could to make herself seem more deserving of the general manger position.

And Grace was stuck in a hospital bed.

She'd received calls from a range of Fortunes since the accident, all of them conciliatory and thoughtful.

The family had sent an enormous bouquet of flowers. Grace appreciated the gesture, but when she'd asked about joining the regular Monday staff meeting by phone, Callum had told her that her only focus at the moment needed to be healing. She wondered if her mom had gotten to him.

"Who's avoiding you?"

Her gaze darted to the open door to find Wiley Fortune standing there, looking just as handsome as he had Saturday night. He wore dark jeans and a gray sweater that somehow made his brown eyes look even darker.

"No one important," she said, and offered him a weak smile, once again aware of the disparity in their appearances. She wore an old flannel shirt over her hospital gown. Although she'd managed a shower earlier with her mom's help, Grace hadn't bothered to apply makeup or do anything with her hair. She tucked a thick strand behind one ear, wishing she'd considered the possibility of a visitor she might want to impress.

"Are you up for some company?" he asked, almost hesitantly.

It was strange to see a man like Wiley appear anything but totally confident.

"I'd like that," she said, and he approached the bed. He'd been holding one hand behind his back and pulled it out to reveal an exquisite bouquet of flowers arranged in a beautiful cut-glass vase.

"These are for you." He gave a soft laugh. "Obviously."

"Thank you." She gestured him closer and sat up in the bed. "They're beautiful. Calla lilies are my favorite."

His smile widened. "You're just saying that to be nice."

"It's true," she assured him. "They remind me of summer."

"They reminded me of you," he told her. Something in the low rumble of his voice made goose bumps erupt along her skin.

She breathed in the sweet floral scent as he held the bouquet close to her. "Mine seem a bit small in comparison." He touched a finger to the enormous arrangement on her bedside table as he placed his vase next to it.

"The hotel sent those," she said. "Along with a fruit basket."

"Thoughtful," he murmured. "Everyone is relieved that you weren't hurt worse." His gaze clouded over as it roamed over the cast. "It could have been really bad."

"If I spent my time worried about things that could have happened, I'd never have the strength to get out of bed in the morning." She squeezed her hands together and focused on staying calm. "I would have given up a long time ago."

He sat down in the chair her mother had situated next to the bed. "You can't ever give up, Grace."

"I'll keep that in mind if I can convince my parents to stop coddling me." She didn't want to sound bitter but couldn't help her frustration. "I know I'm lucky, but what good does that do me if I lose my job at the hotel?"

Wiley frowned. "You aren't going to lose your job. They'll give you time to heal. Healing is your priority."

She let out a groan of frustration. "I'm so sick of hearing that," she all but shouted, then realized how she must sound when Wiley's eyes widened in shock.

"Are you sure we hadn't met before yesterday?" She shook her head. "Because I don't normally vent to people who are practically complete strangers."

"The first time I saw you was at the party," he said, his tone gentle. "That brief introduction wasn't enough, but I thought we'd have all night to talk. Then you walked out onto the balcony and…" He ran a hand through his hair and looked away. "I wish I wouldn't have left your side."

"You couldn't have known what would happen." She reached out and covered his hand with hers before thinking about what she was doing. For several seconds, they both stared at the place where they touched. Hers was paler and looked small against his larger, golden-hued skin.

"I still regret not being able to protect you."

"But if you'd been on the balcony we both would have been hurt." Her heart beat against her rib cage, and she drew back her hand. She liked touching Wiley way too much. "I don't need to be protected and am doing my best to convince my parents of that."

"Parents worry. It's part of the job description."

Something in his tone made her wonder what he wasn't saying. "Do you…um…have kids?"

"God, no." He held up his hands in protest, like she'd just asked if he had cooties. "No wife or girlfriend, either, for the record."

She laughed softly. "Thanks for sharing."

"I'm more the uncle versus father type. Some people just aren't cut out to be a parent, you know?"

"Some aren't cut out for monogamy, either," she countered. "Unfortunately, my last boyfriend was one of those."

Wiley cringed. "Sorry."

"Me, too."

He tapped a finger on the chair's wooden armrest. "People should know their limits. If a guy can't be committed, he shouldn't commit."

Grace wasn't sure how they'd gone down this path of conversation. But it was par for the course that she was harboring an unexpected attraction for a man who just admitted to basically being allergic to relationships.

"That's why my focus is my career," Grace said, then cleared her throat. Could she really claim a career after three months in a management training program? "My job at the hotel and the possible promotion after the grand opening. It's everything to me."

"That's right," Wiley said with a nod. "They're going to hire a general manager locally. I met someone else today who's part of the training program. Jillian something or other."

"Steward." Frustration balled in Grace's stomach. "Jillian Steward. She also wants the GM role, and I'm sure she's going to take advantage of me being on leave to ingratiate herself to everyone." She groaned out loud when Wiley shifted in his chair. "I'm sorry. I don't know why I'm sharing so many of my personal struggles with you. Jillian is a qualified candidate. Not more qualified than me, of course. Your brothers and sisters can make whatever decision they want about the promotion. I just hope I'm cleared to return to work sooner rather than later."

"My brothers and sisters think highly of you," he said with a sincere smile. "Missing a few weeks from work won't change that."

"Weeks?" She shook her head. "There's no way I'm waiting weeks. The hotel will practically be open by then. There's way too much to do and—" She paused, narrowed her eyes at Wiley. "Is that why you're here? Did they send you to tell me I can't come back until I'm done with the blasted cast? I know that's what my mom wants, but she's—"

Grace's mother entered the room, closing the door harder than she needed to. "Your mother has your well-being at the forefront of her mind. I'm sure Mr. Fortune would agree that your recovery is most important."

Wiley quickly stood and took a step away from

the bed. "Most important," he repeated, and Grace felt her lips twitch at how discombobulated he looked facing down her mother.

Barbara Williams was a petite woman, several inches shorter than Grace, with a delicate frame that belied her inner strength. She worked part-time at the high school library and had since Grace and Jake went to school there. Their mother claimed it kept her busy and out of her husband's hair. Unfortunately, when she arrived at the hospital this morning, she'd also announced she was taking a few weeks of unpaid leave until Grace was up and around.

Except Grace wasn't sure how that was supposed to happen while living under her mom's overprotective thumb.

"I assume that's why you're here," Barbara said to Wiley, her tone cool. "To assure Grace she has no worries about her position since she was injured on the job."

"I stopped by to…" Wiley scrubbed a hand over his jaw, the slight scratching sound doing funny things to Grace's insides. "That is to say I'm…"

"Why are you here?" Grace frowned at how flustered Wiley seemed. She certainly hoped that didn't mean his plan had actually been to give her some bad news about her job. When he'd walked in, she'd been so darn happy to see him that she hadn't bothered to question his appearance.

She couldn't deny the connection she'd felt with

him from the moment they locked eyes across the Roja banquet room. Given the invisible thread that apparently linked them together, it had seemed appropriate for him to visit her.

But her mother's skeptical gaze made Grace doubt what she felt.

If doubts were dollar bills, she'd be a millionaire.

"Your job is secure," he said, sounding less like the flirting man who'd entered her room and more like a stuffy attorney. The type of professional she'd come to distrust during her brother's fight to ensure that insurance paid his medical bills after the car accident.

Somehow those words did little to relieve her anxiety.

"Thanks for relaying that message," her mother said. "I'm sure the Fortunes who were responsible for the construction are far too busy trying to determine what went wrong to bother stopping by."

"Mom, stop. Callum called earlier and both Steven and Dillon as well as Nicole and Megan have texted. It's fine."

Her mother sniffed, then sent another glare in Wiley's direction.

"I should go," he said, offering Grace a wan smile. "I'm glad you're doing well, Grace, and hope you'll be out of the hospital soon."

"The doctor wants another round of concussion

testing before she's released." Barbara flung the words at Wiley like they were a personal accusation.

"Do they suspect things are worse?"

Grace wasn't sure what to make of the concern in his gaze, but it warmed her heart. Of course, it could just be that he didn't want his family on the hook for additional medical expenses. That's what her brother would say. Somehow, she didn't believe it.

"She's fine," her mother said before Grace could answer. "But this is really a situation for the people close to her to handle. Her family."

"I understand," Wiley said with a pinched smile. "Please let me know if there's anything I…any of us at the hotel can do to help."

His gaze darted to Grace and then back to her mother before he left the room.

As soon as he disappeared, Barbara began to flit about the room, clearly filled with agitation.

"Mom, you were so rude to him." Grace wanted to go after Wiley, but she couldn't do anything stuck in this bed. The crutches a nurse had brought in rested against the wall, but it would take far too much time to manage them.

"Why was he here, Gracie?" her mother demanded, clasping her hands tight in front of her like she had to hold them together to keep in her nervous energy.

"To check on me."

"That doesn't make sense. He barely knows you."

Grace had to agree that in theory it didn't make

sense, but her heart told her it was perfectly reasonable for Wiley to be at her side.

"He's being nice," she said, because explaining the feeling of connection she had with him would be a losing argument.

"Covering his family's assets is more like it."

"You sound like Jake." Her brother had visited earlier, railing about the hotel and rumors of shoddy construction he'd heard from friends around town after reports of the balcony collapse got out. Since Rambling Rose was such a tight-knit community, word spread fast. "What happened at the hotel was a freak accident. The Fortunes are good people, Mom. They've already done so much for the town."

Barbara's mouth thinned, but she nodded. "I agree, but buildings don't just fall apart for no reason. Jake feels that there's something suspicious about the balcony collapsing the way it did."

"Jake needs more hobbies," Grace grumbled. "Or to watch less true-crime television."

Her mother's features gentled. "You have a point, but the Fortunes have had problems in the past. I remember hearing about some crazy ex-wife causing all sorts of trouble for the family. There was even talk about a kidnapping."

"Those aren't the same Fortunes." Grace closed her eyes and silently counted to ten, hoping for patience. "It was Jerome Fortune—the tech giant who reinvented himself as Gerald Robinson—whose family had those issues. He eventually found happiness, though, with his first love. And Wiley's father, David, wasn't involved in any of that. The difficulties haven't followed the Fortunes to Rambling Rose as far as I've heard."

She wanted to strangle her brother for putting these doubts into her mother's head. Barbara had always been protective, but she'd become even more of a worrier after Jake's accident. The severity of his injuries and the fear of losing him had rocked their small family to its core. Grace knew her mother's fear had seeped into her consciousness, as well. It had made Grace hesitant about taking chances, and now that she was finally getting a shot at a real career at the Hotel Fortune, she wasn't going to let unfounded rumors derail her.

"I thought they were all related in some way."

Grace opened her eyes to see her mother studying Wiley's bouquet.

"Distantly," she agreed. "But Callum and his siblings weren't close to their cousins growing up. From everything I've learned working for the hotel, they moved here from Florida with the intent to establish themselves without significant ties to the rest of the Fortune family. No one is out to get them. Why would they be?"

"These are pretty," her mother said absently. "Calla lilies are your favorite."

"I know." Warmth infused Grace's chest once more as she thought about the fact that Wiley had somehow known her preference in flowers. "Mom, tell me you believe what I'm saying. I'm not in danger working at the hotel."

"I believe the Fortunes mean well," her mother conceded. "At first, I was skeptical of the scope of their plan for the town. It felt like a bit of an invasion to those of us who grew up here and were happy with things the way they were."

"The town was dying, Mom."

"That's going a little far."

"But it's true. The Fortunes have attracted new residents and visitors from all over Texas and the surrounding states. Already-established local businesses have benefited, as well. Even the mayor agrees." Ellie Fortune Hernandez, the town's popular young mayor, had expressed doubts about Callum's plan at the start but had quickly come to be one of the Fortune family's staunchest supporters, in no small part thanks to falling in love with and ultimately marrying Steven. "And Mariana is helping with the hotel's signature restaurant. Everyone in town loves her for all those years she ran her famous market. If she's behind the project, we know it's in the town's best interest."

Her mother held up her hands, palms out. "Okay, Gracie. No need to take out a billboard to advertise all of the wonderful things the Fortunes have done in

Rambling Rose. I'm glad for the town to benefit from their efforts, but my main concern is you. It's all well and good for some new-to-town family to have success, but not if my baby is at risk because of it."

Grace blew out a frustrated breath. "I'm not at risk. And I'm going back to work as soon as the doctor tells me I can. This injury won't jeopardize my future."

"I heard Wiley say your position is secure."

"My current position," Grace clarified. "He has no control over the GM role, and he already hinted that Jillian was making a play for it. If she takes over my responsibilities while I'm out as well as handling her own, she could make a strong case for why she's the best candidate."

"There are plenty of places to work that don't involve the Fortunes," her mother said, even though they both knew that wasn't true. At least not places in Rambling Rose that offered Grace the opportunities she craved.

"Mom, I'm happy to be back here." She loved Rambling Rose but hated that she'd returned on the heels of her life imploding. It was why she was so determined to earn the GM position. "But I can only stay if I can make a future for myself. I feel like the Hotel Fortune is my best chance for that. My only chance right now. I need you to support me and to make sure Dad and Jake do, too."

Her mother sniffed. "Good luck with that."

"That's what I'm afraid of." Grace leaned forward and touched her cast, blinking away tears. "Please, Mom. I know you're worried, but this is important to me. After I found out about Craig cheating and resigned from Cowboy Country, it felt like I'd never have another chance to prove myself. I don't regret coming home from college after Jake's accident, but my life veered off path after that. I want a course correction. I need it."

"Oh, Gracie." Her mother lowered herself to the edge of the bed and put her arms around Grace's shoulders. "You know I support you. Your dad and your brother, too, in their own way. We all just want what's best for you."

Sloppy tears flowed down Grace's cheeks, and she didn't try to stop them. She'd tried for the past twenty-four hours to put on a brave face, but so much felt out of her control.

After a minute, she pulled back. She hated that her mother was crying, as well. There had been so many tears during Jake's recovery. Grace didn't want to be the cause of any more. "I don't know what's best," she admitted. "But I do know what feels right, and the hotel is a big part of that for me." She wiped the cuff of her flannel shirt across her mom's cheeks, earning a watery smile. "I trust the Fortunes, especially Wiley. I can't explain it, but there's something about him."

"Well, he's quite handsome." Barbara skimmed

her thumbs over Grace's cheeks. "He has a very cute butt."

"Mom." Grace laughed. "That's pretty bold."

"I might be middle-aged, but I'm not dead."

Grace hugged her mom again, then blew out a shuddery breath. "It's more than how he looks. It's how he looks at me. Like I'm special."

"You are special. But—"

"I know nothing will come of it," Grace said quickly, embarrassed that she admitted so much to her mom. "He was only in town for the birthday party, and I understand he's checking on me because he's an attorney and he's worried about the family's liability. That's how lawyers are."

A part of her hoped her mother would argue, but Barbara nodded. "Smart girl. Keep your wits about you when it comes to men who seem too good to be true. I remember how fast you fell for Craig."

Grace frowned, not sure how to explain that her connection to Wiley felt different from anything she'd experienced before. Why bother? Chances were she'd never see him again, anyway. She pressed her fingers to her chest and tried to rub away the sudden pinch.

"Will you help me convince Dad and Jake not to make trouble with the Fortunes?"

Barbara looked away for a long moment but finally nodded. "I'm not quite convinced, but you deserve happiness. As long as you follow the doctor's orders and don't push yourself too much, I'll support you."

Grace smiled. "Thank you, Mom. I promise I'll take care."

Chapter Four

Wiley sat at the empty Roja bar the following evening, sipping a scotch as he stared out the patio doors to the rubble of the collapsed balcony. Callum's crew would begin cleanup and new construction tomorrow morning. Although the mess was both an eyesore and, more importantly, a reminder of the accident, they'd had to wait until the insurance adjuster and building inspector gave them the go-ahead.

Unfortunately, the inspector's report had been both better and worse than any of them could have imagined. Better because the man verified that the accident hadn't been a result of shoddy workmanship. Worse because his finding indicated that the support beams had possibly been tampered with, rendering them structurally unsafe and likely the cause of the collapse.

"Mind if I join you?" Nicole asked as she approached from the restaurant's kitchen. She wore a white chef's coat and dark pants, her mass of thick hair pulled back into a tight bun. The restaurant had been open on select weekends but wouldn't expand its hours until the following month when the hotel officially opened. Nicole spent as much time on-site as their brothers, working on Roja's menu and training the staff. Sometimes it still shocked Wiley to see his baby sisters functioning as capable adults. He'd left for college when the triplets were still in middle school. While he'd been home for vacations and holidays, he hadn't paid much attention to the fact that Nicole, Ashley and Megan had grown up while he was away living his life.

"It's your liquor," he told her, gesturing to the bottle.

She scrunched up her nose. "I'm going to have a glass of wine."

"I'll take a glass of what Wiley's offering." Callum appeared in the doorway, his brows drawn together and stress lines bracketing either side of his mouth.

Wiley imagined he looked just as tense. Nicole did, as well. They hadn't shared the news of potential sabotage with anyone outside the family yet, but it was only a matter of time until the information leaked. Wiley wasn't sure what made him angrier, the idea that Grace had been hurt by some unknown adversary or that other employees at the hotel might still be at risk.

"We don't have enemies," Callum said as if reading Wiley's thoughts. He took a seat on the plush leather bar stool next to Wiley, and Nicole handed him a glass. "I know the deputy raised questions based on the report, but it isn't true."

He poured himself a generous amount of scotch, then refilled Wiley's glass.

"Are you sure?" Wiley demanded.

"What other explanation could there be?" Nicole added as she came around the bar and sat on Wiley's other side.

"I don't know," Callum admitted. Wiley understood how much it took for his capable brother to say those words out loud.

"You told me that people around here weren't thrilled with your plans for the hotel." Wiley sipped the scotch, the dark liquor doing very little to warm him.

"We handled it." Callum nodded like he was trying to convince all of them. "Kane was instrumental in helping smooth things over. We got input from a whole cross section of the community and implemented their ideas into the design. As far as we've heard since then, everyone is behind the project. People understand that the hotel will benefit local businesses across the board, not just the ones we own."

Nicole twirled her wineglass between two fingers. "Do either of you think it was strange that the officer asked about the situation with Gerald Robinson and his ex-wife?"

"The evil ex-wife," Callum muttered.

"Charlotte," Wiley said. "I didn't know the details, so I did a little digging this afternoon and called Dad to see what he remembered about her case."

"Dad and I were together at the wedding when Charlotte tried to kidnap one of the guests." Callum drew in a deep breath. "That woman was definitely trouble."

Wiley wiped a droplet of condensation from the rim of his glass. "It wasn't just the attempted kidnapping. Charlotte burned down Gerald's house and caused all kinds of trouble. She was off the rails."

"But she's in a psychiatric hospital now," Callum said.

"And why would she want to harm any of us?" Nicole asked. "Dad isn't even close to his half brothers, and we have very little contact with that branch of the family. The Austin Fortunes I've met are nice, but it's a stretch to think anyone from their world has a grudge against us."

Wiley nodded. "I agree, but it would be nice if discovering the culprit could be cut-and-dried or if we could say for certain that whatever happened with the beams was a onetime accident. At this point, the idea that someone wants to sabotage us and not knowing who or why isn't doing much for my peace of mind."

"Imagine how the rest of us feel," Callum said. "You're upset, and you don't have anything at stake in this venture. If we don't get a handle on what might be happening, I could lose everything."

Wiley's blood pressure spiked at his brother's words. He knew Callum was right in a business sense, but Wiley did have something to lose. Someone, anyway.

He'd heard that Grace had been discharged yesterday after his visit. While he was happy to know she was well enough to go home, he didn't know what to do with his strong desire to see her again. He couldn't very well just show up at her parents' house without a good reason.

He also couldn't seem to stop thinking about her. No point in explaining the attraction to his brother when Wiley still didn't understand it himself.

"We're going to make sure that doesn't happen," he promised.

Callum gave him a curious look. "What are you planning to do from Chicago?"

"I'm actually thinking of staying on in Rambling Rose until the hotel opens next month." He said the words calmly, hoping neither of his siblings would question him.

"Wi, that would be amazing." Nicole set her

wineglass on the glossy bar top and threw her arms around him. "It will be like old times with all of us together. You're the last holdout, you know."

Callum clasped his shoulder. "Are you sure?"

"I talked to the senior partner today and confirmed that I can work remotely for a few weeks. I'll still have to give time to my clients. We're working on closing a huge deal with a manufacturing company, but I should be able to manage it. That way I can also help with whatever needs to be done around here." Thinking about having a purpose made him feel calmer. "I'd like to review the employment contracts and insurance policies for the various ventures in town to make sure everything is in good shape."

"Sounds great," Callum told him.

"I'd also like to talk to some of the employees," Wiley said.

Nicole gasped softly. "You aren't suggesting that someone who works for us was involved with the balcony?" She shook her head. "This is a tight community, Wiley. It's not like the big city where people are out for themselves. Like Callum said, we got people to support the hotel. I don't want to even consider that anyone would want to do us harm."

"I hope you're right." Wiley drained his glass and then stood. "But one of your employees was injured in that balcony collapse. Grace could have died."

His sister's blue eyes filled with tears, and she glanced away. "I know."

"Don't get upset." Wiley wanted to kick himself and even more so when Callum's fingers tightened around his scotch glass. The last thing he should be doing was making his siblings feel bad. They had the best intentions when it came to their plan for Rambling Rose. He knew that.

"I don't believe for a minute that anyone working for the hotel was involved," Callum said. "Fortune Brothers Construction has never dealt with sabotage, but I know of contractors who've had their sites vandalized and projects derailed. Sometimes the motivation is as simple as someone looking for attention."

Wiley nodded. "The reporter I talked to yesterday was from the local paper, but that doesn't mean the story won't be picked up by news outlets in bigger cities around Texas if it's a slow news cycle."

"I hate having our business out there for public consumption." A muscle ticked in Callum's jaw. Wiley could feel the anger and frustration radiating from both his brother and sister. He wanted to find a way to ease their anxiety, however he could manage it.

"The paper here comes out weekly, right?"

Nicole nodded.

"Hopefully," Wiley said, clasping his hands together in front of his chest, "this incident will have blown over by the time the story runs. We should come up with an event to bring some positive publicity to the hotel before the grand opening. Show the town that the Fortunes are here for the long haul and dedicated to doing what's right for Rambling Rose."

Callum and Nicole both expressed their agreement with his idea. Nicole pulled out her phone. "Grace would have been our go-to for a community event. She has a way with people."

The understatement of the century, as far as Wiley was concerned.

"We'll have to ask Jillian to take the lead. I can text her tonight and then schedule a meeting with her and the other trainees tomorrow for—"

"No." Wiley stepped forward quickly and held up a hand. "We should let Grace handle this if she's up for it."

He kept his features neutral as his brother and sister stared at him in disbelief.

"You must be joking," Callum said finally. "She was the one hurt in the accident. Why would we ask her to coordinate a publicity event in response?"

"She called earlier today," Nicole added, "and said that she's staying with her parents while her leg heals. They're encouraging her to rest and recuperate for at least a few weeks. Of course I told her that she can take all the time she needs, so I can't very well turn around and push her to return to work right away."

"I know what her parents want," Wiley said, thinking of Grace's distress in the hospital. "But do you think she agrees? When I talked to her, she was eager to return to work."

"When did you talk to her?" Callum's tone was suddenly suspicious.

"In the hospital," Wiley said with a wave of his hand. "You know that." He hadn't told anyone about his visit to her the previous day.

"She was loopy on pain medicine." Callum shook his head. "We can't trust anything she said that night."

"We should at least ask her." Wiley pointed at Callum. "As for why, the reason should be obvious." And it had nothing to do with Wiley's desire to spend more time with her, or at least that's what he wanted to believe. "If the employee who was injured is the one representing the hotel, that shows her faith in the family and the Hotel Fortune. You can't buy that kind of press."

"Good point," Callum agreed.

Nicole didn't look convinced, but she nodded. "I don't want to bother her at night. I'll call her in the morning and ask, but I won't pressure her."

"Let me talk to her," Wiley offered with what he hoped was a reassuring smile. "Since she was such an integral part of the team before the accident, I'd love to ask if she noticed anything suspicious before Larkin's birthday. I can mention the idea of an event and see what she thinks."

"I'm not sure," Nicole said, her tone hesitant. "She barely knows you."

Exactly, Wiley thought to himself. He needed an excuse to spend time with her. Maybe that would quench the thirst he had deep in his soul when it came to Grace. "She won't think I have an ulterior motive with regards to her job security."

Callum barked out a rough laugh. "You're an attorney. She'll think you have an ulterior motive. Your profession isn't known for rampant altruism."

"Thanks for the vote of confidence," Wiley grumbled. "Come on, Callum. I want to help while I'm here, and I'm here until all of this gets settled." He turned his attention to his sister. "I promise I'll be nice to Grace and make sure she knows her healing is our top priority. At least let me start the conversation with her. If it doesn't go well, you can take over."

Nicole looked like she wanted to argue, then glanced at Callum. "We're overextended as it is. If Wiley wants to talk to Grace, I guess that would be okay. But being nice is no joke."

"Nicole is right." Callum leveled him with a steely stare. "Don't go corporate attorney and terrify her or offend her family. The whole point of the hotel's training program is to generate goodwill within the community by offering opportunities to Rambling Rose locals, and now one of them has been hurt on the job. Any way you look at it, the situation is a PR nightmare. We have to keep Grace happy."

Wiley wasn't about to go into all the ways he wanted to keep Grace happy. "I understand," he said, hoping his expression didn't give away the anticipation building inside him now that he had a reason to visit her. "Nicole, would you text me her parents' address? I'll stop by tomorrow and then check in with you both and let you know how it went."

He said goodbye and headed for his car. All he could think about was the impending visit to Grace's house and how he couldn't wait to be near her again.

Grace sat on the overstuffed couch in her parents' cozy family room the following morning, staring at the book in her hand and realizing she'd read the same page three times. With a groan, she flung the paperback across the room. It slammed into the wall and dropped with a thud to the floor just as her mother appeared in the doorway.

"I guess you're not a fan of romance novels," Barbara said with a shake of her head. "Grace, if you're done with the outburst, you have a visitor."

"Sorry," Grace muttered. "I just hate lying around like this. I feel so useless." She raised a brow when she finally met her mother's gentle gaze. Barbara's cheeks were flushed, and she worried her hands in front of her. "What is it? Who's here, Mom?"

Her mother glanced over her shoulder in the direction of the front hall and gestured the visitor forward. "It's…um…"

"Hello, Grace." Wiley came to stand next to her mom. "I apologize for not calling first. It actually didn't cross my mind until your mom answered the door. If this isn't a good time…"

"It's… No…this is…great…fine… I'm happy to… It's fine…" She started to straighten, nervous energy scrambling her brain cells. Wiley Fortune, the man who had consumed her thoughts since he'd walked out of her hospital room two days earlier, had come to see her. He was standing in her parents' modest house, staring at her like—well, like she was someone special.

"Grace appreciates you stopping by," her mother said, the corner of her mouth twitching.

Realizing she wasn't going anywhere gracefully with the cast, Grace settled back onto the cushions and offered Wiley a friendly smile. She hoped it came off as friendly and not deranged, although he made her feel just a touch unbalanced. "What she said," Grace muttered.

Barbara picked up the book Grace had thrown against the wall and handed it to Wiley. "Have a seat," she told him. "I'll check on the two of you in a bit. Would you like a glass of iced tea, Wiley?"

"Yes, ma'am. Thank you."

Color crept up Barbara's cheeks as Wiley focused his attention on her. *See, Mom*, Grace thought. *You can be suspicious all you want, but a man that handsome is hard to resist.*

When her mother disappeared toward the kitchen, Wiley took another step into the room, glancing down at the book he held.

"Don't you dare make fun," Grace said, tugging on the hem of the Rambling Rose High School sweatshirt she wore. She hadn't dressed expecting visitors. Her parents had grabbed a random assortment of clothes from her apartment, so this morning Grace had thrown on an old high school sweatshirt and a pair of baggy sweatpants after cutting off one leg at the knee. Now she wished she'd thought to dab on a bit of lip gloss or at least a spritz of perfume.

"I wouldn't dream of it," Wiley promised. "I assume the duke mentioned in the title would be the brawny man on the cover."

"You'd assume correctly."

"I never imagined old-time aristocrats to be gym rats—" He held up the book and tapped a finger on one of the duke's broad shoulders "—but this one is quite the impressive physical specimen."

"He fences and boxes," Grace said, hiding her smile.

"Ah." Wiley placed the book on the coffee table. "That explains it. Although not why I heard the book crashing against the wall when I arrived. Too much throwing punches and not enough wooing for your taste?"

"Plenty of wooing," she confirmed. "But I'm already sick of sitting around." She reached out a hand

and brushed an invisible crumb off the cast. "I'm going to go crazy by the time my ankle heals."

Wiley offered her a smile so sweet it made her knees go weak. "We'll make sure that doesn't happen," he promised.

Grace desperately wanted to believe Wiley. Still her family's warnings ricocheted through her brain, and she told herself not to be taken in by his charm. Was that even possible? "Shouldn't you be back in Chicago?"

He lowered himself into the chair beside the couch, and she tried to see her parents' house through his eyes. It looked much the same as it had when she'd been a kid, with wood-paneled walls, bookshelves filled with family photos and her father's collection of historical nonfiction books.

"I've decided to stay in Rambling Rose until the hotel opens."

She tried to keep her features neutral even as excitement spiraled through her. Did that mean he wanted to see her more over the next few weeks? She should know better than to read too much into the way he looked at her, but she couldn't seem to stop her body's reaction to the intensity of his gaze.

"I'm sure that makes your brothers and sisters happy."

"For now." He laughed softly. "I'm going to make sure everything is in order with employment agreements and contracts for the various businesses they've gotten involved in. They'll be happy to have me here unless it makes more work for them."

"I doubt that. I can tell from seeing them interact at the hotel that your family is really close."

"They are," he murmured.

"Why doesn't it sound like you include yourself in that 'they'?"

He shrugged. "I've always been a sort of odd man out when it comes to our branch of the Fortune family. For me, it was important to feel like I'm making my own way, which is why I left Florida for college and didn't return even after law school. I wanted my life to be my own."

"I know how that feels." She swallowed back the emotion that clogged her throat. "You're lucky you've been able to accomplish it."

"Lucky," he repeated, then frowned. "I suppose you're right."

A few seconds of silence descended between them, and although it was weighted, the quiet didn't feel uncomfortable. In fact, Grace's chest loosened as she drew in air laced with Wiley's spicy scent.

She snapped back to attention at the sound of a bag crinkling. Her eyes had zeroed in on his handsome face, and she hadn't even seen the sack he held.

"I didn't come here to bore you with my family dynamics." Wiley flashed a self-deprecating smile. "I'm here to deliver a get-well care package."

"You've already brought me flowers."

One thick brow arched. "Is there a limit on the number of gifts I'm allowed to bring you?"

She wanted to laugh at the absurdity of that question. "I'm not going to put one on you." She reached for the bag he now held out. "I'm just not used to being on the receiving end of so much generosity." She inwardly cringed, embarrassed to admit she was comparing Wiley to her ex-boyfriend. Craig had been steady and reliable—or so she'd thought—but never the romantic type.

Grace had convinced herself she didn't care. She thought it was important to have a man she could build a life with, not someone who lavished her with gifts and romantic gestures. She got enough of that vicariously through books and movies.

As she peeked in the brown paper bag with the Hotel Fortune logo stamped on the outside, she tried to remember that Wiley was just being nice because she was a hotel employee. His brothers and sisters were all busy with preparations for the opening and taking care of their other businesses in town. Chances were good that they'd designated him as the family liaison for the injured employee. At least that's what Grace's brother would tell her.

She put aside thoughts of her ankle and her brother as she pulled out a stack of puzzles, a candle and a box of chocolates. "How thoughtful. I love all of it. You didn't have to…" She glanced up at him as she continued to remove items from the seemingly bottomless bag. "Did you buy one of everything in the hotel gift shop?"

Wiley scrubbed a hand over the back of his neck. "Just about. I didn't know what type of games you might like, so I got word searches, sudoku and crossword puzzles."

"I like word searches," she told him with a smile.

He nodded. "They had both dark chocolate and milk, and I can tell you my sisters are very specific with their chocolate, so I got a box of each."

"I like both." She held up two candles.

"They both smelled good," he said, sounding almost embarrassed that he'd packed so much into the bag. "But not as good as you. You smell like a spring rain shower." He gave her a sheepish smile. "Do I sound like a sad imitation of your romance duke?"

"No, but for the record I smell like water," she said with a laugh, then reached out and patted Wiley's leg when he frowned. "I'm joking. The lotion I use is actually named Rainforest Mist so you're right on the money with that."

Wiley's eyes darkened even more and the space between them seemed to shift—growing thick with a yearning that Grace didn't understand, although it sent shivers rippling along her skin.

"Thank you," she managed after a weighted moment. "I appreciate all of this and you coming to see me. I haven't reached out to many friends because I don't want to talk about the accident. People are so curious, and I just want to forget."

There was an immediate shift in Wiley, as if she'd just doused him with a bucket of icy water. "I figured people would be talking to you about the incident. In fact, a reporter came by the hotel on Sunday. The local paper is doing an article on the circumstances of the accident."

The thought of having her name associated with the event that was bringing the hotel bad publicity made Grace's stomach clench, but she nodded. "He reached out to me, as well. He wants to interview me for the story."

"Are you going to talk to him?"

She shrugged. "I guess I should, but I'm not ready yet. Don't worry, though. I'll be sure to make it clear that the hotel had nothing to do with the balcony's collapse."

"You don't have to do that. We appreciate your loyalty, Grace, but you can speak freely."

"I know," she whispered, distressed by the formality that had seeped into his tone. "But it's true. Obviously, I wish it wouldn't have happened, but the hotel isn't responsible."

His opened his mouth as if to deny her claim, then closed it again. "Speaking of the hotel..." He flashed a smile that was different from the one he'd given her before. It didn't reach his eyes. "I do have a speck of official business to discuss with you."

"Sure." Grace ignored her disappointment and reminded herself that she could read whatever she wanted into the way Wiley looked at her. That didn't make the promise in his gaze something real.

"Callum, Nicole and I talked about coordinating a small community event before the official grand opening. Nothing elaborate or time-consuming for the staff, but something that would…"

"Make people forget that I could have died in the balcony collapse?"

He blew out a shaky breath. "Yes."

She nodded, appreciating that he didn't try to sugarcoat the motivation. There was nothing wrong with what the hotel wanted to do. The Fortunes were running a business, and they needed positive PR. They couldn't run a successful hotel without paying customers. If the hotel didn't make money, Grace wouldn't have to worry whether her injury would prevent her from earning the promotion. There would be no promotion to be had.

"It's a great idea." She sat forward on the sofa, lifting her cast leg and placing her foot on the floor. The doctor had told her it was important to elevate the leg, but somehow she felt too much like a blushing maiden from one of her historical romances sprawled out on her parents' sofa as she and Wiley discussed actual business. Grace was thrilled to talk about something other than the accident, even if she wasn't officially on the clock. "I'd actually recommend focusing on other local business owners. We should also involve the spa and Provisions. Nicole and Roja can provide the food—samplings from the regular menu. I bet even the vet clinic could set up a booth in conjunction with a local animal rescue. It's important to remind the community leaders how much your family has already contributed to the town and give a glimpse of how good it's going to be. A Rambling Rose partnership would benefit everyone."

"Those are great suggestions."

Grace held up a hand. "I'm not done." She shifted again, wishing she could get up and pace as she worked through the possibilities in her head. Her crutches rested against the stone fireplace on the wall across from the seating arrangement, but she didn't want to bother with hopping over to retrieve them. Plus, she'd look like a complete fool trying to pace using crutches. For what felt like the millionth time since Saturday night, she cursed that blasted fall.

"Tell me more." Wiley reached out and squeezed her hand, as if he could sense her frustration. His touch had the immediate effect of calming her, and she drew in a breath before continuing.

"We want Rambling Rose businesess to feel connected to the hotel. Do you think your brothers and sisters would consider offering a 'locals' weekend'?"

"Um…probably."

She clapped her hands together. "I should have thought of that even before the accident. The hotel can give a discounted rate for a particular weekend, one during a slow season where occupancy would naturally be down. They'd get the great deal if they booked during the reception, and we could do a raffle for a free dinner for two at Roja." She paused and scrunched up her nose. "I keep saying 'we,' but I mean 'you' obviously. The Fortunes and the employees who are actually working. I'm sure other people will have ideas, as well." Jillian, Grace thought inwardly, would have plenty.

"Are you interested in the 'we' part?" Wiley asked and, once more, Grace's brain seemed to short-circuit. All she could think about was a "we" that involved her and Wiley. She was interested like nobody's business.

"Yes," she managed, hoping he assumed she was talking about being engaged on a professional level.

"There's no pressure, of course." He smiled at her again, encouraging and warm, and she felt it all the way to her toes. "I'm being nice, right?"

She frowned. "Is that a trick question?"

"Nicole warned me I had to be nice," he said with another laugh. "Callum told me not to act like an attorney."

"I actually haven't been thinking about you being an attorney during this visit," she admitted. "If that helps."

"Good." He nodded. "If you think you're up for it, we'd like you to handle the reception. You can take care of a lot of the planning from here. Whatever works best for your recovery. Obviously, you're qualified based on the rush of ideas you just offered. Getting more buy-in from local business owners makes sense to me, although you'll have to run that focus by my siblings. Again, only if you feel like it wouldn't be too much."

"No." She tried to breathe around the knot that had formed in her chest. This was her dream come true as far as the scenario for the weeks of her recovery.

"No, you're not up for it?" His brows drew together.

"No, it's not too much. I'd love to be involved in any capacity. If you feel like I can handle it, then absolutely yes. I'd love it."

"Absolutely not."

At the sound of the booming male voice, Grace glanced at the door to find her father standing next to her mother, his arms crossed over his chest in a stance Grace knew all too well. Barbara held a tray with iced tea glasses and a bowl of pretzels. The look she threw Grace was both resigned and apologetic.

This would be a battle, and it was one she didn't intend to lose.

Chapter Five

Wiley stood as Grace's father entered the room. "Hello, sir. Grace and I were just discussing—"

"She's not going back." Mike narrowed his eyes at Wiley, then switched his glare to Grace. "You aren't going back."

"Dad, I'm a grown woman." She made to stand, but her cast hit the edge of the coffee table, and she sat back down, wincing as pain radiated up her leg.

Her mother let out a gasp, and Wiley reached for her.

"Don't touch my daughter." Her father's voice seemed to reverberate through the room.

Grace felt her face color with humiliation as Wiley drew back his hand and took a step away from her. Barbara put the tray of drinks and snacks on a side table and moved closer to her husband. Grace wasn't sure if it was to lend silent support to Mike or to protect Wiley from him.

"I'm sorry, Mr. Williams. I just wanted to help."

"By putting her at risk again? Not going to happen."

"I want to work." She lifted her hands, palms up. "I can't sit around here for the next month. I'll go stir-crazy." She bit down on the inside of her cheek when her voice caught. No way was she going to start crying in front of Wiley.

"Did he tell you that someone's out to get the Fortunes?" Mike asked Grace the question but looked at Wiley as he spat out the words.

"What are you talking about?"

"Sabotage." Mike said the word like it was poison on his tongue.

"We don't know that yet," Wiley argued, then turned to Grace. "The building inspector said it's possible someone tampered with the balcony's support beams. The investigation is ongoing, but that could have contributed to the collapse."

"Definitely is more like it," her father said. "Why is someone messing with the hotel construction?" he demanded of Wiley.

"We don't know, sir." Wiley scrubbed a hand over his jaw. "But I promise you we'll get to the bottom of it."

"Not by making my daughter a potential target."

"I promise I would never—" Wiley cleared his throat. "I won't let anything happen to Grace. I'll keep her safe. You have my word." He turned to her fully, and her breath caught in her throat at the ferocity in his gaze. "I'll keep you safe."

"I know," she said softly. Somehow she had no doubt that Wiley, a man she barely knew, would do everything in his power to ensure her safety. It baffled her why she felt so confident in that, but her heart remained certain.

"He's using you," her father said through clenched teeth.

"Mike, don't." To Grace's surprise, her mother stepped forward and placed a hand on her husband's arm. "What happened to Grace was an accident. The Fortunes didn't intentionally put her in danger. I agree that she should take it easy." Barbara glanced at Grace. "You need to rest so that your recovery isn't impacted."

Grace opened her mouth to argue, but her mother held up a hand.

"I also understand that you're accustomed to being busy, and your job means a lot to you." She squeezed Mike's arm. "She's an adult capable of making her own decisions."

"I know what I'm doing," Grace said, looking between her parents. "Going back to work will actually be helpful to my recovery." She ignored her dad's snort of disbelief. "I mean it. I can't do nothing for a month. If the Fortunes are willing to let me make my own hours and work remotely when possible—"

"We are." Wiley nodded. "Whatever you need."

"I want to try." She got to her feet again, this time careful about her leg, and hopped the short distance to where her parents stood. "I understand you're worried, and I have no idea who would want to sabotage the hotel or why. But it has nothing to do with me."

"You've got a cast on your leg that tells a different story," Mike said, but his voice had gentled. Grace knew he wasn't going to fight her on this any longer.

"I'll be careful."

Mike turned to Wiley. "My daughter is old enough and smart enough to make her own decisions. But I'm holding you to the promise to keep her safe. I understand you don't have skin in the game in Rambling Rose the way some of your brothers and sisters do, but consider my girl your number one priority while you're in town."

"Dad, that's ridiculous." Grace cringed even as longing threaded through her like a needle binding two pieces of fabric. What would it feel like to be a priority for Wiley? "Wiley has plenty of other—"

"Done," Wiley said, and held out a hand to Grace's father. They shook and suddenly Grace felt like some sort of Victorian spinster who'd just been promised to the roguish hero. She needed to lay off the historical romances for a while.

"Can Wiley and I have a few minutes alone?" she asked her parents. "To go over next steps."

Mike looked as though he didn't want to leave them, but Barbara tugged him toward the hall. "Let us know if you need anything. It was nice to see you again, Wiley."

"You as well, Mrs. Williams. Thank you."

When her parents were gone, Grace turned to Wiley, ready to give him a litany of excuses for her father's behavior. Instead an enormous yawn stretched her lips and exhaustion made her limbs grow heavy.

"This is too much," Wiley said without hesitation. "I promise that wasn't my intention, Grace. Or to upset your father."

She waved away his concern. "I'll be fine," she told him with a wobbly smile. "I probably need a tiny nap first. My dad's worry has more to do with what happened to my brother than this situation. Although I wish you would have told me about the possibility of the beams being tampered with."

"I'm sorry." He squeezed her fingers. "I should have brought it up right away but didn't want to upset or worry you. I meant what I said about protecting you, Grace."

"Thank you," she managed, even though her throat had gone dry. It was difficult to remember that her relationship with Wiley was only professional when he touched her with such exquisite sweetness and looked at her as though he wanted to kiss her. It had to be the exhaustion making her imagine that. "I appreciate the opportunity to coordinate an event for the hotel. I'm going to take a short rest, and then I'll put together my ideas and email them to Callum and Nicole. We can schedule a call to discuss their thoughts and go from there."

"All business," Wiley murmured, dropping his hand. If Grace didn't know better, she would have sworn she heard disappointment in his tone.

"Not all." She flashed a smile and gestured to the pile of puzzle books on the table. "You've given me a lot to keep myself busy. I appreciate it." She covered her mouth when another yawn escaped.

"We'll talk soon." Wiley stepped away from her. "Enjoy your nap, Grace. Sweet dreams."

Butterflies fluttered across her stomach as he walked away. If Wiley Fortune was a part of her dreams, they'd be sweet indeed.

"I'm still not sure why we couldn't have taken one of the ATVs," Wiley grumbled the following night as he tugged on the reins of his horse when the animal once again veered off the path to munch on a nearby bush.

"We wanted to give you the full Texas experience," Megan said, glancing over her shoulder with a wink.

"Besides, your boots are too shiny." Their cousin

Kane rode up next to him on his chestnut mare. "You need some more dust to make you look like a legit cowboy."

Wiley barked out a laugh at the absurdity of that statement. "I'm nowhere near a cowboy. Attorneys aren't cowboys. It's mutually exclusive."

"Not in Texas," Megan told him. Her horse came to a stop at the edge of a low rise, the surrounding property spread out in front of them like a postcard.

"How much of this do we own?" Wiley asked, somewhat overwhelmed by the wide-open space and big sky. He knew this part of Texas was expansive, especially compared to the crowded high-rises of downtown Chicago.

"As far as the eye can see," Megan told him softly. There was something about the moment and the vista that called for quiet. Wiley suddenly understood what had drawn his siblings to this part of the country. Maybe it was something in the Fortune DNA that made Texas appeal to so many of them.

He thought Callum had lost his mind when he'd moved to Rambling Rose over a year ago and then convinced Dillon, Steven and Stephanie to go with him. By the previous spring, the triplets had joined them. Wiley had stayed in the Midwest, telling himself he was content with his big-city life far away from his family. He loved each one of them, but growing up in a house with so many kids had made him savor his independence and stake it out with all the dedication of a dogged adventurer. His career and his life belonged solely to him, and that seemed like enough.

But spending time with his siblings and the cousins he was enjoying getting to know planted tiny seeds of doubt in his mind. Although he was keeping up on his regular workload remotely, he didn't miss the bustle of the city and his busy professional life the way he assumed he would. He'd been going on full tilt for as long as he could remember, never pausing to reflect whether the path he was so intent on taking was the right one.

Of course it was right. He'd chosen it. He couldn't let a few weeks of fresh air and the sweet smile of a woman derail him. Yes, it was fun to be involved in the family business, but that didn't mean it would be better to return to the life he knew.

"I'm happy for you guys." Wiley leaned forward and patted the horse's strong neck. "You all seem to have found your place here."

"It's an easy town to call home," Megan said, a trace of wistfulness in her voice. "Also easy for some people to find love, apparently."

Kane snorted, adjusting the brim of his hat. "You don't need love to be happy."

Wiley nodded. "Amen, cousin."

"You are two peas in a pod." Megan wrinkled her nose. "What do you have against falling in love?"

"Not a thing." Kane shrugged a big shoulder. "It's just not for me."

"Me, neither, yet," Megan conceded, "but I'm not opposed to Mr. Right walking into my life. The hotel is going to open right around Valentine's Day. Wouldn't it be nice to have a romantic date with the perfect girl to share it with?"

An image of Grace popped into Wiley's brain, and he shifted in the saddle. "I think we need to keep our focus on making sure the grand opening goes off without any more problems. That's way more important than romance."

Kane nodded, a muscle ticking in his jaw. "I'd feel a lot more confident if we could get to the bottom of whether or not someone tampered with the balcony's support beams."

"I want to believe there's some explanation for the collapse." Megan blew out a frustrated sigh. "It's too scary to think that someone has it out for us or that we might be putting our employees or potential customers in danger." She adjusted one of her stirrups and glanced between Wiley and Kane. "Everything is going so well with the businesses, especially Provisions. The reservation book is filled almost every night, and the online reviews are excellent. I know Roja will be just as much of a success, assuming nothing else happens."

"It won't," Kane promised. Their cousin was taking the lead on hotel security, and Wiley had been impressed with his attention to detail.

"How do you know?"

"I met with a security company earlier today," Kane confided. "Another firm is coming in to look over the property tomorrow. I'm going to fast-track the process of getting bids so that we can have an updated system installed by the grand opening. There won't be any loose ends."

"I've started meeting with employees," Wiley said. "Everyone seems positive so far. No hint of discontent, which is good. It could be that the balcony was just a fluke or someone looking for attention."

"I hope you're right." Megan gave her horse a soft kiss, and the animal turned toward the path again. She met Wiley's gaze as she passed him, and he hated the anxiety in her cornflower blue eyes. All the brothers were protective of the triplets. He wanted his sisters to be able to focus on the positive aspects of their new business ventures without worrying about potential sabotage.

Wiley brought his horse abreast of hers. "It's going to be okay, Meggie."

"You make me believe that." She gave him a warm smile. "It's your commanding attorney presence. I was on the call with Grace this morning. We video-conferenced, and it was the first time I'd seen her since the accident. She looked good."

"What did you expect?"

"I'm not sure," she admitted. "I thought maybe she'd seem bitter or angry that she was dealing with a broken ankle."

"Grace has always struck me as a practical girl," Kane called from behind them. "All of the trainees are great, but she shines under pressure."

"Pressure is one thing," Megan answered. "Falling from the second story of the hotel is quite another."

"True," Kane admitted tightly. Wiley knew the accident weighed heavily on everyone's mind.

"How did the call go?" he asked, trying to sound casual. "I felt bad that I couldn't be a part of it, but a client meeting came up that my assistant wasn't able to reschedule."

"It's fine," Megan told him. "We appreciate you pitching in here while managing your regular life at the same time. No doubt you'll be glad when the hotel opens, and you can be rid of us and our troubles for a while."

"You aren't a trouble," he told her.

"That's nice." She laughed. "But you aren't fooling me, Wi. I remember how crazy our full house drove you when we were younger. You'd hide in the basement with the water heater just to get a little privacy."

"Nothing wrong with a teenage boy wanting privacy," he muttered, earning a loud chuckle from his cousin. He leveled a stare at Kane over his shoulder. "Not for the reasons you're thinking."

"Gross." Megan snorted. "Enough about teenage boys and privacy. The call went well. Grace put together a really comprehensive time frame and plan for a preopening reception aimed at local business leaders. We're going to suggest a Rambling Rose partnership, where restaurants, shops and other local businesses actively work to promote each other. It's a short turnaround, with her idea to put the event on the calendar for the last week of January, but it will be a perfect lead-up to the grand opening."

"Her parents are worried that she's going to do too much and compromise her recovery." A knot formed in his stomach as he recalled the look her father had given him, like Wiley was the lowest form of scum he could imagine. Wiley prided himself on his moral compass but should probably to do a little more research into the accident Grace's brother had a few years ago.

He could tell by the comments Grace made that Jake's situation had impacted everyone in the Williams family, and he wanted to understand how traumatic it had been for them.

"We won't let that happen," Megan said as the horses approached the barn at the ranch. "You won't let that happen."

He arched a brow and kept his features bland, hoping to hide the thrill of anticipation that pulsed inside him. Keeping an eye on Grace was the easiest assignment he could imagine.

"I mean it, Wiley." The three of them dismounted, and Megan wagged a finger at him. "We're counting on you to take care of her."

"Not exactly a chore," Kane said as he took the reins of Wiley's horse and started toward the barn. "Grace is fantastic."

Wiley didn't like the bolt of jealousy that zipped through him at his cousin's words. He had no reason to believe Kane had designs on Grace. They worked together, just like she and Wiley did. Ugh. That thought didn't make him feel any better.

"I'll make sure she's taken care of," he told his sister as they followed Kane into the barn, reminding himself to keep his attraction to her under control. It would be best for everyone involved—but more difficult for him than anyone would imagine.

Chapter Six

Grace sat on the porch swing looking out over her parents' front yard the next day. Her leg was elevated and her other foot bare as she swung gently in the cool afternoon air.

She'd had to put on a heavy jacket, but it was worth it to escape her mother's fussing, her father's silent admonishment and her brother's outright agitation at the fact that she was already back to work less than a week after the accident.

The doctor had told her to take recovery at her own pace, she'd reminded them, and she was being careful not to spend too much time on the phone or at the computer. She'd even napped for an hour after lunch, even though it frustrated her how weak she still felt compared to her normal energy level. Grace liked moving and working. From the time she'd gotten her first babysitting job as a teenager, the ability to make her own money and her way in the world had always appealed to her. Her parents had provided a great life for Jake and her, but finances had always been tight. As a girl, she remembered hearing her parents argue about the monthly budget. Her father had a tendency to spend beyond their means, a constant source of worry for Grace's mom.

Grace had grown up with the deep desire to never be a burden on anyone. She knew Jake felt the same, and that was part of the reason why his accident had been so difficult. His recovery had taken months and had been a challenge for every member of their close-knit family.

That didn't make it any easier to hear him degrade Wiley and the Fortunes. The hotel was one of the best things that had happened to Rambling Rose, and certainly for Grace, so she was already tired of having to defend her employer.

She blew out a breath and hit Send on the email she'd just written to Nicole, making suggestions of potential offerings for the business reception that would showcase Roja's planned menu. The Fortune triplets certainly had a way with food, and Grace envied their confidence and the bond they obviously shared. She'd met their other sister, Stephanie, as well, and although she wasn't involved in the hospitality industry, she was helping to coordinate a booth for the local vet clinic where she worked.

Grace waved as Collin Waldon walked across her lawn from his father's house next door.

"Tell me you're not posting cast selfies on social media," he called to her.

Collin was as close as Grace got to having a second brother. They had been tight friends since she could remember. Her mother loved to trot out photos of Grace and Collin playing together in the plastic baby pool in their diapers, and Grace knew that her parents and Collin's father, Sam, still held a secret hope that the two of them would eventually end up together.

The idea of a match between them was comical. It would be like dating her brother, although she couldn't deny that Collin had grown into an insanely handsome man. He was tall with a lean build, dark hair and coppery eyes with gorgeous light brown skin. As a captain in the army, he was currently stationed in Germany. His years in the military had honed his body into a network of hard planes and muscles.

"I'm working," she told him, then glanced toward the house. "As well as getting a much-needed break from my family."

"Jake said you weren't going back to the hotel." Collin climbed the porch steps two at a time.

Grace growled and made a face. "Jake is even

worse than Dad right now. He's not the boss of me, and it's high time he figures that out."

"Aw, Gracie, he means well."

"Don't even go there, Collin." She wagged a finger in his direction. "You're my friend, so you have to be on my side."

"Always." He rested a hip against the porch railing. "But you can't believe that your parents and Jake aren't on your side. They love you."

"I know." She blew out a frustrated breath. As aggravated as she was by her family's fussing, she knew everything they did was motivated by love. "But I want to work, and I love my job at the hotel. I'd love it even more if they made me general manager when the hotel opens. I've worked so hard, Collin. I need a chance to prove myself."

"Even if the hotel is being targeted?" He raised a challenging brow.

"Jake needs to stop spreading rumors," she muttered.

"You could have died, Grace."

"Why does everyone keep reminding me of that?" She slammed her laptop closed, once again cursing the cast and her limited mobility. There was no way she could stomp off the way she wanted. As soon as the blasted cast was off, Grace would never take walking freely for granted again.

That thought took the wind out of her sails of righteous anger in an instant. Of course Jake and her

parents were extra worried and overprotective. He'd
battled back after the accident, working with physical therapists and doctors and on his own for months
in order to walk again. Yes, Grace had left college
and come home to help, but no one could understand what Jake had been through during that time
other than him. She had no doubt the accident and
the ensuing long, painful recovery and legal fight
over responsibility had changed her once happy-go-
lucky brother.

Now she was annoyed by not being able to walk
across the front porch without her crutches. She
rubbed a hand over the top of her leg and nodded
at Collin. "I understand how bad the accident could
have been, and I appreciate my family. But I told myself when I came back to Rambling Rose that I was
going to find a way to have the life I wanted, to go
after my dreams and not let anyone stand in my way."

Collin frowned. "Are you talking about your jerk-
wad ex-boyfriend?"

"Maybe," Grace admitted. "We both worked at
Cowboy Country, but I did my job and helped him
with his. Did I tell you he got a promotion based off
a marketing plan I basically wrote for him?"

"Five minutes alone in a room with him," Collin
said with a dark laugh. "That's all I need."

"You sound like my brother," she told him, shaking her head.

"Great minds."

"I'm happy to be back to work, and I can't wait until I feel strong enough to go into the hotel and have my social life back, too." She held up a hand when her friend would have argued. "I'll be safe there, Collin."

He shifted to sit more fully on the porch rail. "How do you know?"

Wiley's handsome face appeared in her mind. "I just do. You should come by and check it out. The restaurant is going to be fantastic. I know you appreciate a good kitchen."

"Yeah." He nodded. "My dad doesn't exactly have gourmet tastes."

"How's he doing?" Grace knew it hadn't been Collin's plan to return to their small hometown, but when his father had taken a turn for the worse after Collin's stepmother passed away, he'd come back. Although not officially related, Grace and Collin had the family-duty gene in common.

"He seems okay since I've been here, but I've don't have a lot of leave time. I'm still worried about how out of sorts he's been since my stepmom died."

"He loved Sharon very much," Grace said gently. "I'm sure having you here on leave helps him feel better. I only wish you could stay longer."

They both glanced toward the street as a sleek black sedan pulled up to the curb. Grace's heart fluttered against her ribs when Wiley climbed out of the vehicle. He wore a crisp white button-down shirt and dark pants with aviator sunglasses covering his brown eyes.

"What were you saying about a social life, Gracie?" Collin lifted a brow. "Because you're blushing at the stranger in the fancy clothes."

"Shut up, Collin." Grace returned the wave Wiley gave her as he approached the house. "He's not a stranger. He's a Fortune."

Collin elbowed her. "Well, isn't that interesting."

"Not to you," she muttered.

"Hello, Grace." Wiley glanced between her and Collin. "You look well."

It was kind of crazy how two words—*hello, Grace*—could cause a riot of sensation to pulse through her body every time he said them.

"I'm working." She held up her laptop. "On plans for the reception. It's coming along really well. I'm well, too, of course. Just like you said."

Collin straightened from the porch rail and leaned in. "You're babbling."

"Go away, Collin."

He threw back his head and laughed. As much as he was annoying her in this moment, it was good to hear him laugh. He'd done far too little of it since returning home.

Collin gave the swing a little push, then turned to Wiley. "Collin Waldon," he said, holding out his hand. "I'm a good friend of Grace's."

Wiley's chest expanded as he nodded. "I'm Wiley Fortune. Grace and I—"

"Are working together on the hotel event," Grace said, planting her foot on the wood porch to stop the swing. "In fact, we're discussing plans this afternoon. Collin was just leaving."

Her childhood friend grinned at her over his shoulder. "I'll talk to you later, Gracie."

She shifted on the porch swing as Collin headed back to his father's house, moving her cast leg to the ground.

"Would you like to sit down?" She patted the cushion next to her and offered a smile.

"Does he live next door?" Wiley asked as he moved toward her.

A shallow line of tension had appeared between his brows.

"Since we were babies," she confirmed. "We grew up together—best friends for as long as I can remember. Collin's in town on leave to visit his dad. He's been in the army for years."

Wiley took a seat next to her. "And now you're staying with your parents. How convenient for catching up."

She glanced at him from the corner of her eye. If Grace didn't know better, she'd think Wiley sounded jealous of Collin. A thrill passed through her at the thought of that. She really didn't want the attraction she felt for the handsome attorney to be completely one-sided.

"Collin's a good guy," she said, and maybe she kept her phrasing slightly cryptic just to gauge Wiley's reaction.

She wasn't disappointed. His jaw tightened for several seconds before he finally turned to her with a smile that was patently forced. "It's important to have good friends in your life."

"Yeah." She tried to keep her mouth from twitching in amusement, but Wiley's gaze narrowed on her.

"What's funny?"

"Nothing. I'm just happy to see you."

He visibly relaxed at her words. "I didn't really come here to discuss the hotel event. Although I'm happy to talk about it if you want. Nicole and Megan said you're doing an amazing job already."

Pride blossomed in her chest at the praise. "We're just getting started, and I still wish I was coordinating everything on-site. I hope by next week I'll feel strong enough to come to work at the hotel."

"That's great." A breeze blew a few curls across Grace's face and before she could push them away, Wiley reached out and with a gentle touch, tucked her hair behind one ear. "You have the most beautiful hair."

She swallowed back a nervous giggle. "I used to hate having wavy hair. When I was growing up, the popular style was sleek and straight. No matter how much product I used, mine would never behave. But I've gotten used to it, although it's a rat's nest when I wake up." She raised a hand to her mouth when she realized she was babbling again, but Wiley didn't seem to notice.

"I'm sure it's beautiful in the morning, too."

The rough timbre of his voice tickled her skin as she thought about waking up with a man like him next to her. Good Lord, that would be something special.

She cleared her throat and gave herself a mental "down, girl" command. "If you aren't here to talk about the event, is there something else? Do you have more information on who was behind the balcony collapse?"

"I wish I could say I did. Not yet, though. I stopped by to… I wanted to see you."

Oh.

Grace felt heat flame her cheeks. Wiley Fortune wanted to see her. She could definitely get used to that.

A tapping sound came from the house, and she turned to see her mother standing at the living room window looking out at them. Grace suddenly felt like she was a teenager again with her nosy parents trying to insert themselves into her business. Wiley waved at her mother, who returned the wave and gave him a beaming smile. At least her mother was being friendly. Grace didn't want to think about what would happen when her dad realized Wiley was here.

"Would you like to go for a drive?" She stood as she asked the question.

"Sure," he answered, quickly straightening to join her. "If you have time?"

She hopped toward the front door, laptop tucked under her arm. "All the time in the world. Just give me a minute to tell Mom I'm leaving and grab my shoes and crutches." She didn't really like using them, so she typically hopped around her parents' house.

"I'll be here."

Great. Wiley would be waiting for her.

Her mother opened the door as she reached for the handle. "Wiley is here," she stage-whispered.

"Yes, I saw you watching us from the window."

Barbara winced. "Sorry. That was too much."

"It's fine. We're going for a drive." Grace made her way past her mom and gently closed the door. "Can you grab my crutches from the family room?"

"Where are you driving to?" Her mother placed a hand on her arm. "Do you need something, sweetie? Your dad is in the garage. He'd be happy to get you—"

"Wiley came to see me." Grace covered her mother's hand with her own. "Not to talk about work or the balcony. To see me."

Her mother's mouth formed into a small O.

"Exactly." Grace bit down on her lower lip. "We're going for a drive. I don't know where." She checked her watch. "Maybe out for dinner. Maybe…it's a date."

"I'll get the crutches," her mother said with an enthusiastic nod. She gently pinched Grace's cheeks and smoothed a hand over her hair. "There now. You look so pretty with a little color in your face."

"Mom, have you become a Fortune fan?" Grace asked as she bent to retrieve her shoes—or shoe—from under the front table.

"I'm a fan of seeing my daughter happy," Barbara said. "You look happy for the first time in a while, sweetie."

"Thanks, Mom."

With a nod, her mother headed down the hall while Grace sat on the chair in the foyer and tied the laces of her sneaker. They weren't the most exciting choice in footwear, but she was still getting used to the crutches. Better to be practical than wind up on her back end in front of Wiley.

She glanced at the front door while she waited for her mom. It was probably rude to leave him standing out there, but Grace had needed a minute to compose herself. He'd said he wanted to see her. It wasn't some grand profession of devotion, despite the way her heart reacted. Other than his family, he probably didn't have many friends in town. Maybe he was just bored, and she was a distraction.

A short-term distraction, she reminded herself, even though her body ignored the warning. Her mother was right. Grace hadn't felt this excited in a long time.

Her mother returned with the crutches. "Have a good time on the drive or dinner or whatever you do."

Whatever. Grace couldn't even entertain the possibilities of "whatever." Not with her leg in a cast and her mother standing next to her. She grabbed the crutches and smiled. "I appreciate that," she told her mom, then scrunched up her nose. "I'd also appreciate if you not mention it to Dad or Jake—"

"Go have fun with your friend." Barbara reached around her to open the door. "Your dad and brother don't need any details."

Wiley turned as Grace hopped out and closed the door behind her. She arranged the crutches under her arms and started forward. "Sorry about the wait."

"No problem." He glanced between her and the porch steps. "But speaking of problems…"

"I can manage." She gave him a bright smile. Okay, so she hadn't actually dealt with steps other than when she'd returned from the hospital, but she would make it work. "I appreciate you taking me out for a bit." She got to the top step and handed him the crutches. "Could you hold these for a moment?"

"Of course. Are you sure you can manage it?"

No. "Yes."

"I could help you…"

"I've got it." Grace was probably a fool for refusing an excuse to get close to Wiley, but she wanted to prove to herself that she could handle a flight of stairs on her own—even if it was just five wooden porch steps. If she was going to head back to work the following week, she'd need to get a lot more proficient at moving around on her own.

She grabbed hold of the railing for support and hopped down each step, proud when she didn't once lose her balance. "I didn't fall," she announced with a wide smile as he returned the crutches.

"You did great." He looked at her with a huge smile.

"That was silly," she said as they started down the walk toward his car. "Maneuvering down a few steps isn't a big deal, but this is the farthest I've gone on my own since the accident. If my parents had their way, they'd encase me in Bubble Wrap for the rest of my life to make sure I stayed safe."

"It's an understandable sentiment from people who care about you."

"But not what I want."

He opened the car door for her, and she gave him the crutches to stow in the back seat. The whole process was slow and awkward. By the time Grace was buckled in next to Wiley, sweat dripped between her shoulder blades, and she felt like she'd run a marathon. How could less than a week of inactivity make her feel like such an invalid?

As if sensing her frustration, Wiley placed a gentle hand on her arm. "You've been through a lot, Grace. Your ankle and the cast are the biggest outward signs of the accident, but you fell from the second story."

She offered a wan smile. "I have the bruises to prove it."

"Give yourself a bit of...well, grace."

"I never thought of attorneys as naturally comforting people," she admitted. "But you're good at giving support."

"It's a hidden skill." He released her hand and pulled away from the curb. "We lawyers don't like to let anyone know about our human side. It ruins the reputation of being coldhearted, and then people aren't afraid of us."

"You're the opposite of scary."

"Where are we headed?" he asked when he got to the stop sign at the end of the block.

"The highway," she said without hesitation. "As much as I love Rambling Rose, I need a break. Let's get out of this town, Wiley."

Chapter Seven

Wiley sensed the change in Grace as they cruised down the open road. She'd given him directions to the highway, and they were headed west out of Rambling Rose, destination unknown—at least to Wiley. He liked giving control to Grace. Wiley's life was normally a rigid list of schedules and meetings, so the idea of not having to worry about anything for an evening was strangely liberating.

The sun was just beginning to set, and fluffy clouds filled the sky overhead, swaths of cotton candy against the blue of the sky.

He couldn't explain how right it felt to have Grace next to him, to finally be alone with her, even on a drive to nowhere special. He wanted to make whatever time they spent together special. She deserved that, and he had a primal urge to be the man to give it to her.

Tiny remnants of jealousy still quivered in his stomach, out of character for him. Even when he dated, Wiley had never been the jealous type, but seeing Collin Waldon lean close to Grace had made him want to lose his mind. She'd described him as a friend, but their connection was obvious. What man in his right mind wouldn't want more from Grace?

Wiley certainly did.

"I love this time of day," she murmured, splaying her hand against the passenger window. "It's amazing how we take for granted the little things in the hustle and hurry of regular life. I never thought about it being a treat to leave the house whenever I wanted."

"I'm honored to be the one to help you escape," he told her with a wink. Open pastures and fields filled with herds of cattle glided by on either side of the highway. Similar to the trail ride with Megan and Kane, this drive gave him another glimpse into the Texas landscape, and the sheer scope and size of it gave him an unexpected sense of peace. How was it that a self-described city slicker could feel such a connection with wide-open spaces?

"You're being nice again," she said, a teasing lilt

to her voice. "While I appreciate it, I'm sure you have better things you could be doing tonight than this."

"Nope." He shook his head. "Driving down the highway with you tops my list." He made the comment casually, because he didn't exactly want to share how much this moment meant to him.

"If that's the case, I bet you're champing at the bit to get back to your regular life."

"I'm enjoying the break."

"Really?" She shifted in her seat to look at him more fully. "Tell me about Chicago. The city must be so exciting. I've always wanted to visit."

"The pace is definitely different than you have around here, but not necessarily better. Just different."

"What would you be doing on a normal weekday night if you were in the city?"

He glanced at the clock on the dashboard. "Most likely I'd still be at the office."

"Describe it," she said. "Did you decorate it yourself?"

He chuckled at her attention to detail. "Not really, although I worked with the firm's interior designer to choose paint colors and a few pieces of generic art. If my diploma weren't hanging on the wall, the space could belong to anyone."

"But you spend a lot of time there. Are you part of a big firm?"

He nodded and explained how he'd interviewed

with several law firms during his final semester at law school and chosen this one because of its size and the variety of clients. At the time, Wiley had been captivated by the thought of working in an office with a dozen other associates. He'd assumed he'd have the chance to work with myriad different types of clients, although in reality the work was more monotonous than varied.

As Grace peppered him with questions about his coworkers, his hobbies and his friends, he realized how one-dimensional he'd allowed his life to become. Much like a robot, he functioned on autopilot. Not that daily life in Rambling Rose was a roller coaster of excitement, but observing his siblings for the past week, he realized that they'd managed to create rich, layered lives filled with friends, new ventures and sometimes love.

He had very little to share that made his life sound fun. Hell, he'd even gotten into the habit of ordering the same rotation of meals from the carryout restaurant around the corner from his condo. He had all the freedom in the world, he realized, but took advantage of none of it.

As quickly as possible, he turned the conversation toward Grace's life. She recounted in more detail the aftermath of her brother's car accident and what it had meant for her. She didn't complain about having to leave college to help with Jake's recovery, and he admired her dedication to her family and her positive attitude.

He wanted to ask more about her time at the cowboy-themed amusement park his relatives ran in the small town of Horseback Hollow, but she suddenly sat forward in the seat. "Get off here," she told him, and he veered onto the exit ramp, although he hadn't even noticed a sign for services along the empty stretch of ranch land.

"We came here when I was a kid," she told him, looking around with a sentimental gleam in her eye.

"Where exactly is here?"

"Turn right off the exit." She pulled her phone from the purse she'd looped around her shoulder. "Shoot. I don't have service, but I'm pretty sure there's a restaurant about a mile down the road."

"In the middle of nowhere?" He grinned at her. "Should I be concerned about what they might be serving on the menu?"

"It's part of the adventure," she told him. "Let yourself go crazy, Counselor."

"So long as crazy doesn't end up with either of us hugging the porcelain throne later tonight."

She laughed at that, and the sound reverberated through him like music. He still couldn't tell what it was about Grace, but Wiley felt completely at ease with her.

The road wound in a gentle curve, grand oak trees flanking it. He liked the differences in the north

Texas landscape. The way the scenery could change from wide-open fields to rows of trees standing sentry, their bare branches reaching toward the heavens.

Suddenly, a small house—or inn—appeared in a clearing. The decades-old structure was painted deep purple with a yard filled with whirligigs and metal lawn art out front.

"That's it." Grace clasped her hands together. "I remember the sculptures. I was fascinated with watching them move when we came here."

He pulled into the gravel parking lot, which was half-filled with cars. "I can't believe you found this place," he said, grinning at the happiness in Grace's blue eyes. She looked like a kid about to enter her favorite candy store.

"I can't believe it, either." She reached out and squeezed his hand. "It must be a sign."

He lifted a brow. "Of what?"

"This is the moment my luck changes. No more cheating boyfriends or accidents or dead-end jobs. This place shows that I can find something great if I trust my instincts."

Wiley turned over his hand so their palms touched, once more amazed at how soft her skin felt against his. He wasn't certain he believed in luck or signs, but he knew enough to savor this moment and his time with Grace.

"Then let's go try your luck with the Oak Tree Inn."

By the time he pulled her crutches from the back seat and made his way around the car, Grace had climbed out, gazing at the inn's clapboard front like it was the entrance to Shangri-la.

She adjusted the crutches under her arm and started toward the building, stumbling slightly when the bottom of a crutch slipped on a large rock.

"I've got it," she said before he could offer assistance.

Her quiet independence was a new experience for Wiley. Although he kept his romantic life casual, he definitely had a type. Gorgeous, young and happy to have him take care of everything from planning dates to choosing menu items and definitely setting limits on how close he would get. He tended to go out with women whom his sisters liked to describe as damsels in distress. It wasn't as if he purposely sought out the role of "knight in shining Italian loafers" but that was often the position he found himself in.

He expected things to be the same with Grace, especially given what she'd been through. Her injuries were the perfect excuse to sit back and let him pamper her, which he would be happy to do.

But the more time he spent with her, the more he understood that making her own way was important to Grace. She didn't want to be handled or coddled, despite all the stumbling blocks life had put in her way. Her determination captivated him. Maybe that's why he found himself becoming more and more fascinated by her with every passing minute.

Grace couldn't remember a night when she'd had more fun than she had spending the evening with Wiley.

They sat near the firepit on the back deck of the cozy inn, the only two people who'd ventured out from the dining room. Dinner had been even yummier than she imagined, with the chef offering simple dishes with an Italian flair.

Her frustrations and struggles with work and her family seemed a million miles away. To her great relief, Wiley appeared just as relaxed as she felt. The inn's owner had given them a couple of thick fleece blankets to take out with them, and they sat close together on an outdoor love seat.

"This is how I want people to feel when they stay at the Hotel Fortune," she murmured, her breath catching as Wiley shifted so that their thighs pressed against each other.

"Blissed out on good food?" he asked with a wink.

"Happy," she answered simply.

Her response seemed to catch him off guard, and he gazed into the fire for several long seconds before speaking.

"I feel it, too." His voice was a quiet rumble and did funny things to Grace's insides. "Happy."

He bent forward to place his wineglass on the stamped concrete patio.

"But I think my happiness has more to do with you than this place." He gestured to the building behind him. "Or the food and drinks, although everything was fantastic."

Pleasure swirled through her at his words, because she felt the exact same way. Grace reminded herself that she not only didn't believe in love at first sight, but she wasn't interested in anything that would take her focus from her position at the hotel and the potential of earning the coveted general manager promotion.

"But if we can offer our guests—both local and out-of-town visitors—an experience that lets them forget the troubles of regular life so quickly, they'll definitely come back over and over."

Her lips tingled when he placed a gentle finger against them. "I thought we agreed no work talk tonight."

She gave a shaky nod, then wrapped her fingers around his. "Yes, but you know I'm right."

He chuckled. "You're right," he conceded without hesitation. "This night is special."

Then he leaned close and brushed his mouth over hers. It was a tentative kiss, a question of sorts. Grace couldn't tell which one of them he expected to answer. Her body had no doubt, however, and she reached up and wound her hands around his neck, needing to be close to him.

A low groan escaped Wiley's lips, and it felt like a gift that she could affect a man like him. He cupped her face between his big hands, angling her head and deepening the kiss. Their tongues met and melded, making heat shoot through Grace's body in a way that shocked and thrilled her. No simple kiss had ever stirred her in this way.

Normally, she would wait for a man to push for more, but Wiley seemed content to savor her and the moment like they had all the time in the world to discover each other. Within moments, Grace lost herself in the sensation.

After what felt like hours but was probably only minutes, Wiley pulled away. He stared into her eyes without speaking, but his gaze told her everything she needed to know. "Wow," he murmured, one side of his mouth curving.

"Exactly what I was thinking." She went to shift closer and banged her foot on the edge of the love seat, and muffled a yelp of pain. Nothing like the reminder of her injury to put a damper on the most romantic interlude she'd had in forever.

"Are you okay?" Wiley's hand immediately went to her leg, and Grace lost all ability to think coherently.

"Fine," she managed, trying not to wheeze. "But maybe you should kiss me again and make it better."

He flashed a wolfish grin and claimed her mouth again.

Grace jerked back when she heard the sound of voices headed in their direction. Two older couples were walking toward the firepit from the restaurant.

"We should probably go," Grace said, although she didn't want the moment to end. She didn't want anything about this night to end.

"Will your parents be worried?"

She shook her head. "I texted my mom while you were in the restroom so she doesn't worry. It's weird to be an adult and still check in, but she appreciates it." She stifled a yawn. "I wish I had my normal energy."

"You're overdoing it." Wiley immediately shrugged off the blanket, stood and then scooped her into his arms.

Grace sputtered out a shocked protest. "I'm not that tired."

"Could you hand me those crutches?" Wiley asked one of the men from the group that circled the other side of the firepit.

The stranger did as he was asked while the two women looked on with similar expressions of fascination. "That's so sweet," one of them told the other.

Color rushed to Grace's cheeks. "You can put me down," she said into Wiley's ear.

"Young love," the second woman responded. "If

Carl tried to pick me up like that, he'd pull out his back."

The women laughed as Wiley started down the back steps and around the side of the inn. They'd already paid their bill so didn't need to return inside.

"Wiley." Grace squeezed his shoulder. "You don't need to carry me."

He paused and kissed her again. "I know you're more than capable on your own, Grace. But please let me hold you for a few minutes."

Well, when he put it like that, how could she refuse?

Reassured that he wasn't taking pity on her, she settled into his embrace for the short walk to the parking lot. He was warm and strong, and she couldn't resist tracing one finger along the strong column of his neck. His Adam's apple bobbed as he swallowed.

"You're going to cause me to stumble, and we'll both hit the ground," he said with a gruff laugh.

"I trust you."

His arms tightened around her for a few blissful seconds, and then they were at the car. He deposited her on the ground and rested her crutches against the back door.

"Thank you," he said, and pressed a gentle kiss to her forehead.

"I think I should be thanking you." She grinned.

"As should those two women at the firepit. From the sound of it, you made their night with your heroics."

His gaze darkened. "I'm not a hero. I just wanted an excuse to wrap my arms around you."

"Do you need an excuse?"

He turned his head, as if he needed to look away in order to gather his thoughts. "I like you, Grace. A lot. From the moment I saw you at the birthday party, there was something…"

"I know," she said, lifting a hand to his jaw. "I felt the same thing."

He met her gaze once again. "I don't want to take advantage of you."

Please, her body screamed silently. *Take advantage*.

"I'm a big girl, Wiley."

"I'm only in town until the hotel's grand opening," he reminded her, as if she could forget.

"That gives us a few more weeks."

One side of his mouth twitched. "What exactly did you have in mind during that time?"

Heat pooled low in her belly, but there was no way she could articulate all the things she had in mind for Wiley. Her uninjured leg began to ache, an outward sign of her current limitations. The cast was going to make anything physical between them awkward at best.

Then she realized that as much as she desired the man standing in front of her, she liked talking to him and just being around him as much if not more. He made her feel smart and capable. Right now she wanted—needed—more of that in her life.

"We could hang out," she suggested. "Like tonight."

"Tonight was a date."

The words sent pleasure spiraling through her. "Then we could date more."

His thick brows drew together. "Until the opening?"

She nodded. "You're returning to Chicago, and I'm focused on my career. Neither of us has time for anything serious, but we have fun together. Right?"

"So much fun," he murmured, still teasing.

"It's a mutually beneficial arrangement." Grace held her breath as she waited for his response. In truth she barely recognized herself, suggesting a short-term fling with a man like Wiley. The brother of her bosses at the hotel.

There were so many reasons it might be a bad idea, not the least of which was the way he made her heart stutter and her body ache when he looked at her. And when he kissed her...

She couldn't focus on the risks. Grace had spent so long playing it safe. Her vow when she'd returned to Rambling Rose had been to live life to the fullest, to push herself out of her comfort zone. This was definitely ticking off those boxes.

Wiley's dark gaze searched her face for several

seconds, and then he nodded. "This is the start of a few weeks of as much mutually beneficial fun as we can manage."

Chapter Eight

Wiley followed the sound of construction toward the hotel's back patio two days later. He'd spent most of the previous day holed up in his bedroom suite at the ranch, on a never-ending stream of calls and videoconferences. Working remotely was turning out to be more of a challenge than he'd expected, but the thought of returning to Chicago held little appeal, especially when staying in Texas meant spending time with Grace.

He'd walked her to her parents' front door after their dinner together, and the urge to kiss her again had been difficult to resist. At least until her father opened the door as they climbed the porch steps, giving Wiley a look that clearly communicated Mike's disapproval.

After taking the crutches from him with a sigh, Grace had balanced herself on her uninjured leg and leaned in for a quick peck on his cheek and a murmured thank-you before disappearing into the house.

Her father had slammed the door in Wiley's face before he'd even had a chance to say goodbye. He'd climbed in his car and started toward home, pressing two fingers to the place her lips had touched, feeling like a lovesick teenager for wanting to vow not to wash that side of his face again.

Although Grace's mother seemed to approve of their friendship, it bothered Wiley that her dad and brother clearly wanted no part of him in Grace's life. He didn't date seriously, but Wiley had met his share of parents over the years, and all of them seemed inclined to support their daughters getting serious with an attorney, especially one who came from a well-to-do family. Wiley's stepfather, David, had made a fortune in the video game industry. He and his siblings were intent on carving their own path, yet there was no doubt in anyone's mind that they came from a good family.

Wiley would have thought the Fortune name garnered extra approval in Texas, where the expanded family had such a long and illustrious history. He knew better than to take Mike's and Jake's animosity personally. The idea that someone might have sabotaged the balcony's structural beams worried him, especially given what could have happened to Grace in the fall. But he was determined to prove that he only had Grace's best interests in mind.

Callum waved to him as he stepped out into the bright sunlight of the mid-January day. Wiley glanced at the workers on ladders affixing new lumber to the hotel's exterior. Once local law enforcement and the insurance company finished their investigations, the crew had wasted no time in cleaning up the fallen balcony and starting to rebuild.

"You're making great progress," he said as he joined Callum.

His brother gave a tight nod. "We need to have the balcony reconstructed completely before the opening. I want this place to look like an accident never happened."

Wiley drew in a deep breath. Callum was right, of course. It wouldn't do them any good for the hotel's reputation to be tainted even before they had their first paying guest. Hell, that was the whole point of the event Grace was coordinating. But it bothered him that they had no idea what or who had caused the problems with the beams. Their insurance company and the police might suspect sabotage, but they couldn't prove it.

Plans for the opening were moving ahead despite the shadow of potential foul play hanging over them. The fact that Kane had already begun the process of upgrading the property's security system gave Wiley a measure of comfort. Kane was also recommending that they take increased precautions at the other businesses in town, although no one wanted to believe the balcony collapse had been personal.

"I'm not saying I want to ignore what happened to Grace," Callum said, hands on his hips. "The safety of our employees and potential guests is the first priority."

"I know," Wiley agreed. "But I don't like loose ends. If we knew for certain what had caused the accident—either way—I'd feel better."

"I feel the same, but we can't let that derail us from our goal."

They both turned as a feminine voice called a greeting. Mariana approached from the far side of the pool, her bleached blond hair pulled into a loose ponytail and reading glasses resting on top of her head. Her smile faltered slightly as she glanced up to the second floor, but it was bright once more when she returned her gaze to the brothers.

"Good morning, Fortunes," she said, holding up several brown paper bags. "I've brought lunch for your crew."

There was a resounding cheer from the men, who'd all turned to watch Mariana. The woman truly was a force of nature and well-loved in the Rambling Rose community.

"That's the best thing I've heard all day," Callum

said, returning her grin as he took one of the bags. "To what do we owe the pleasure?"

She placed a bejeweled hand on his shoulder. "Ah, Callum. I'm here spreading sunshine and light in the form of my famous empanadas."

Wiley chuckled. "Food that makes everything better. That could be your new tagline." And he had no doubt it was true. Mariana had run her popular food truck for years at Mariana's Marketplace, Rambling Rose's busy flea market. Last year, she took an active role in the town's future businesses and even discovered a connection to the Fortunes through the town's old Foundling Hospital.

His brothers and sisters had been wise to involve Mariana in the hotel's development. She helped Nicole run the Roja kitchen and brought her usual enthusiasm and style to that role. Everyone on staff seemed to love her, and Wiley felt like she might give additional credibility to the venture. Not many people in town would go up against the formidable Mariana.

"How is Grace Williams?" she asked Callum.

Wiley forced himself not to answer, although his brother sent him a curious look. On the way home from dinner, Grace had told him she wanted to keep anything other than friendship strictly between them. He rubbed the heel of his hand against his chest to ease the ache that suddenly appeared there. It made no sense that he felt disappointed at the thought of not being able to publicly claim Grace as his, even temporarily.

He understood the rationale, given her position in the training program and the impending announcement about the general manager promotion. Although he would never try to influence his brothers or sisters based on his personal feelings, there was no need to in this case. After spending more time with the other trainees, particularly Jillian Steward, Wiley felt even more certain that Grace should earn the new role. Jillian rubbed him the wrong way, always trying to make it seem like she was in charge. He liked one of the other trainees, an easygoing man named Jay Cross, well enough, but Jay seemed more interested in filling in wherever needed than adept at running the entire hotel.

"From what she tells us, she's doing better." Callum nodded. "The event she's putting together is going to be a huge success. We had a phone meeting yesterday, and she's gotten the whole thing coordinated in less than a week."

"She was always such a hard worker," Mariana murmured thoughtfully. "I hope she's not overdoing it."

"Me, too."

Wiley could feel Callum's gaze on him but ignored it.

"She did look a little worn down on the call," Callum continued, turning to Mariana.

Wiley sucked in a breath. Worn down? He hadn't seen Grace since their date, but they'd been texting regularly, and he was supposed to pick her up for dinner after work tonight.

"The accident could have been so much worse," Mariana said. "She needs to make rest a priority."

Callum nodded. "Agreed, although it's hard to convince her of that. I'm going to ask Nicole or Megan to reach out, as well. We scheduled a physical therapist to work with her on any lingering soreness or potential back issues. The ankle is the most obvious injury, but she mentioned the doctor was worried about mobility and her range of motion."

"She told you that?" Wiley ran a hand through his hair and tried to mask his reaction. Grace hadn't talked to him about other injuries.

"Yeah," his brother answered. "But she hasn't returned the PT's calls. Knowing Grace, she feels like she's taking advantage since she knows we're paying for it."

"The money doesn't matter," Wiley said, realizing the harshness of his tone when both Callum and Mariana startled.

"I understand," Callum told him. "We all do. Someone just needs to convince Grace of that. I'm sure one of the triplets can—"

"I'll handle it," Wiley said.

Mariana shook her head. "Grace has always been determined to make her own way. She'd probably respond better to one of your sisters since she knows them."

"She knows me," Wiley said, making his voice gentle. "We're friends."

"Friends?" Mariana murmured while Callum shook his head.

"You don't have friends," his brother said. "You have us, coworkers and the arm candy you date."

"Wow. That's a real shot in the arm. Trust me. Grace and I are friends, and I'll convince her to work with the physical therapist." He looked between the two of them. "For the record, she's not the delicate flower that everyone around here assumes her to be. She's strong and capable, and it's about time people stop underestimating her."

When both Callum and Mariana appeared to be shocked into silence, Wiley turned and stalked away.

"You saw Wiley a couple of nights ago. I thought we were going to hang out tonight."

Grace paused in the act of applying mascara and looked at her brother in the mirror that hung above the dresser in her childhood bedroom. It still amazed her that their parents hadn't changed either her bedroom or Jake's since they'd moved out. She vaguely remembered that her mother had been planning on a whole house clean-out just before Jake's accident. Everything had been put on hold in the months after

that as they all rallied around him to support his recovery.

"I know you have something better to do than
watch movies with your little sister." She pointed the
mascara wand at Jake. "I heard you were becoming
pretty chummy with Melissa Wagner."

Jake made a face. "Shouldn't you be busy resting
and getting better? Why do you have time for petty
gossip about my love life?"

"Because I've been doing very little other than
resting." She placed the mascara tube on the glass
charger that held her simple supply of cosmetics and
turned. "I need to get out more."

"That's not true." Jake adjusted the pillow he'd
propped behind his head as he sprawled across her
comforter. "Mom and Dad are already worried about
how much time you're devoting to this hotel event,
and it's not good for anyone—especially you—to be
spending time with some big-city attorney."

"We're friends." Grace hopped over to the closet
to pull out a jacket, not wanting her brother to wit-
ness the heat she could feel crawling up her cheeks
at the thought of Wiley. They'd agreed to keep their
relationship secret, so she couldn't give her feelings
away to her brother. Feelings that were probably not
wise, given that Wiley was leaving town after the
grand opening.

She might have suggested a short-term arrangement with her mind dizzy from his kisses, but in the

past couple days she'd realized that wouldn't stop her heart from wanting more.

Jake gestured to the arrangement of flowers that sat on the taller dresser. "Why does a friend send you flowers? And cheesecake?" He snorted. "Who sends a woman cheesecake?"

"Um…you better not complain after I saw you scarf down a huge slice when Mom told you about it."

"Well, I love cheesecake."

"Me, too." Grace pulled on her jacket. "I happened to mention it to Wiley, and he told me about some bakery in New York City that makes the best."

"And then had it sent to you? Classic rich-boy move."

"Don't be a jerk, Jake. This whole business with the accident has been hard. I hate having people look at me with pity or reminding me that I'm lucky to be alive."

"Trust me, I get that."

She heard the bitterness in her brother's tone and immediately regretted her comment. "I know you do. So I hope you can also understand that I like Wiley. He's nice, and he doesn't treat me like I'm weak. He helps take my mind off of what happened."

"I get it." Jake sat up straighter with a sigh. "But that's what I'm worried about, Gracie. I don't trust the Fortunes, and especially not the attorney. Don't you think it's a little too convenient that he just happened to decide to stay in Rambling Rose after the balcony collapsed?"

"He wants to make sure everything goes smoothly with plans for the opening. He's supporting his family." She drew in a deep breath and added, "He's supporting me."

Jake studied her for several moments, and Grace decided she wasn't going to hide her emotions from her brother. She was a grown woman and could make her own choices about who she spent her time with.

"Don't let him take advantage of you," he warned, his gentle tone almost harder to handle than the snarky remarks he'd made earlier.

"I trust him," she said, because that was the only truth that mattered to her at the moment.

The sound of the doorbell had her turning for the hallway. "Come back tomorrow night, Jake. I'll kick your butt in Scrabble."

"You wish." He climbed off her bed and followed her out of the room. "I don't suppose you want me to greet the Fortune with you?"

"Can you be nice?" she asked over her shoulder.

He pounded a fist to his chest like she'd wounded him. "Of course I can. I just prefer not to."

She smiled despite her annoyance and made her way down the hall. Once again, she'd left her crutches in the front entry. Although she didn't enjoy hopping around her parents' house, the hallway was narrow, and the rooms were filled with furniture that made it difficult to maneuver with crutches.

Her parents were in the backyard discussing plans for a garden bed her mom wanted in the spring. She desperately needed to get to the door and away from the house before they realized Wiley had arrived to pick her up. She knew her mom would be nice but couldn't say the same for her dad. He was almost as bad as Jake as far as doubting Wiley's motives. She could only imagine what they would think if they knew she was dating the handsome Fortune.

She opened the door and smiled at him, anticipation curling in her belly as she waited for his greeting.

"Hello, Grace," he said in that smooth tone, and she felt her grin widen. Did he even realize what those two words did to her?

"Hi." She groaned in frustration when one of the crutches slipped from her hand and clattered to the floor. "I swear I'm going to get better with these before I get to the hotel."

Wiley bent and retrieved the crutch, handing it to her. "I have a better idea." He reached to one side of the door and pulled a black scooter into view. It had foam handles and a wide pad clearly meant for her injured leg. "I brought you a gift."

Grace's mouth dropped open. "Oh, my gosh. My own set of wheels?"

Wiley nodded. "I called a doctor friend, and he

suggested it. Apparently, it's a lot easier to maneuver and can help with your mobility. Not that you aren't doing great with the crutches."

"I hate the crutches." She put her hands on the scooter's handle and then lifted her leg onto the long black cushion. It was so easy to push herself to the far side of the porch and then turn the scooter to head back toward Wiley. "I'm a natural on this."

When she got close to the door, she called for her brother. It didn't matter what Jake thought about Wiley. He had to see her scooter.

He appeared in the doorway a moment later. "Wow. That's cool, Gracie. Where'd you get the spankin' new ride?"

"Wiley brought it for me. It's amazing, right?"

"Yeah." Jake crossed his muscled arms over his chest as he glanced at Wiley. "Nice work, Fortune."

"Thanks," Wiley muttered.

Grace laughed at the two men, who looked equally uncomfortable exchanging even the most basic pleasantries.

"Tell Mom and Dad not to wait up," she said to her brother. "Now that I actually get around, who knows what fun we can find."

"It's Rambling Rose," Jake said with a wry laugh. "We all know there are limits to the fun you can have in this town."

"I don't know about that." Wiley lifted the scooter when Grace took hold of the staircase railing.

Grace was glad she had her back to her brother, because she couldn't prevent the wide grin at the thought of all the fun she and Wiley could have together.

Chapter Nine

"I'm not sure this is such a good idea." Grace leaned forward to look at the entrance of Provisions, the farm-to-table restaurant Wiley's sisters ran in town, along with Ashley's fiancé, Rodrigo Mendoza. "I thought we agreed to keep our relationship between us."

"We're friends," Wiley assured her. "Everyone in my family likes you, and they don't need to know more than I'm helping you out with a ride. I haven't had a chance to do more than stop by the restaurant. Ashley won't quit giving me grief." He flashed what he hoped amounted to a convincing smile. "You'd be doing me a huge favor."

"I guess," she relented after a few seconds of chewing on her bottom lip. "I've wanted to eat here since they opened Provisions last year. Plus, I need to be familiar with other restaurants in town so I can make recommendations to hotel guests. Right?"

"Exactly. This is a perfect excuse for that. But if you aren't comfortable with it, we can drive out of town and—"

"Let's eat here." She reached out and squeezed his arm. "But no kissing."

He chuckled. "That's a bummer. Can we find some place to park after dinner so we can make out in my car like a couple of teenagers?"

"You joke, but I'm serious. I don't want anyone in your family to know we're dating."

"Our secret is safe with me." Wiley kept his smile on his face as he climbed out the car, ignoring the pang of disappointment that stabbed his gut knowing that Grace wanted to keep what was between them hidden. Her insistence on secrecy was an unwelcome reminder that their relationship was temporary. Of course, he knew it. After all, he'd be returning to Chicago in a matter of weeks, and Grace would be busy with the hotel. He should be feeling relief. Normally, he was the one placing parameters on his dating life about what he was and wasn't willing to offer. A few weeks was plenty of time to get a woman out of his system, but somehow Wiley knew Grace wasn't like other women.

He thought back to that moment he'd spotted her across the Roja banquet room and the word that had whispered inside him like trace of a melody he couldn't quite place. *Mine.* The idea was ridiculous, and he knew it. Grace didn't belong to anyone but herself. That didn't stop Wiley from wanting her. From wanting more.

As he retrieved the scooter from the trunk, he tried to shake off his disturbing train of thought. Obviously, he was just reacting to being away from his regular life. He didn't have his work and his hectic schedule to keep him busy, so he had too much time to think about Grace. Once he returned to Chicago, things would get back to normal. No way was he falling under the spell of this sleepy Texas town the way his siblings had.

Grace was already standing next to the car, using the open passenger door for balance, when he got there.

She smiled up at him, a teasing light in her eyes. "You might have all the willpower, but it's going to be hard for me not to kiss you."

Just like that, every last one of Wiley's rationales about remaining distant or getting her out of his system disappeared like a puff of smoke in a brisk wind.

"Later," he promised, brushing his hand against hers. "Save that thought for later."

"Who was the first girl you kissed?" Grace asked

as they made their way toward the restaurant's entrance.

"Jessica Meyer in seventh grade. We were in the same math class, and she was way smarter than me."

"You were a late bloomer," Grace said, clearly delighted. "I kissed Miles Spicaro on the playground in second grade."

"Not Collin?" Wiley asked, then regretted the question. He felt like a fool revealing how much her friendship with the boy—now man—next door bothered him.

She gave him a funny look. "Not Collin. And Miles ended up being a onetime interlude. Too much pressure for elementary school. What about this Jessica? Was it first love?"

Wiley opened the heavy wood door to Provisions and gestured Grace forward. "I've never had a first love."

"Oh." That one syllable conveyed so much about what she thought of his confession, and once more, he wished he would have kept his personal business to himself. It wasn't like him to share details about his feelings or really anything with the women he dated. He hadn't planned on not falling in love, of course. He wasn't completely coldhearted.

But love meant compromise, and Wiley valued his independence too much to give it up on any meaningful level. At least that's what he told himself.

"Hi, guys." Ashley met them at the hostess stand

when they entered the restaurant. She gave Grace a one-armed hug and touched a finger to the scab that had almost completely healed on Grace's forehead. "You look amazing, and I love that scooter. How are you feeling?"

"Thank you," Grace answered almost shyly. "I'm doing better every day and looking forward to getting back to work. Wiley found the scooter, and it's a huge improvement over the crutches. I could never quite find my balance with them."

"Nice work, Wi." Ashley turned to hug him. "Did you just eat a lemon?"

He frowned at the question. "No, why?"

"Your face is all puckered. Is something wrong?"

He shook his head, willing some random alien ship to appear and beam his sister up into its depths. Grace was looking at him oddly now that Ashley had pointed out his lemon face. Even though he was certain he didn't have any kind of furrowed expression. He simply didn't want to think about what he couldn't give to a woman like Grace.

"Everything is great. We're excited for dinner." He gestured to the dining room. "You have quite a crowd."

Ashley followed his gaze to the open-concept restaurant, situated with tables filled with customers. "I hope the hotel does as well as we are. It's beyond my wildest dreams."

"We're going to make sure the hotel is a huge success," Grace offered. "Your brothers and sisters have been working so hard to get things ready."

"With your help," Ashley answered. "From what Nicole says, they miss having you at work. Not that the other trainees aren't doing a great job, but…"

Grace nodded, color blooming on her cheeks. "I can't wait to be back."

"You all need to stop pressuring her," Wiley grumbled, hating that he sounded like some kind of overprotective grandpa. But he couldn't stop himself. After speaking to Callum and Mariana about Grace not following up on the PT appointments, he wondered if anxiety about returning to work was making her sacrifice her recovery.

Were her parents actually right?

"No pressure," Ashley promised as she led them through the dining room. "You getting well is the top priority."

"I'm really feeling much better," Grace assured her, darting a quelling glance at Wiley over her shoulder.

Ashley opened the door to a private room on one side of the restaurant. "I hope it's okay with both of you, but we prepared a special tasting menu for tonight." She grinned at Wiley. "I want a chance to impress my big brother and figured you might enjoy a bit of privacy." She gave Grace a sympathetic nod. "It feels like everyone is still talking about the accident, you know?"

"I do," Grace agreed with a grateful smile. "I hate being a topic of conversation. Thank you for your thoughtfulness, Ashley. I really appreciate it."

As his sister closed the door to the private dining area, Wiley glanced around the space, pleased at how things had turned out. He'd suggested to Ashley that Grace didn't like the attention she was receiving for her injury, feeling like that was a plausible reason to request a space of their own.

The room retained the character of the grain silo that had once occupied the space, with high ceilings and painted shiplap on the walls. A white cloth covered an impeccably set table in the middle of the room. Grace wheeled the scooter slowly toward the table, taking in the flowers and candles on the sideboard. He wondered what would happen if he told her how he was truly coming to feel about her—the way his heart stammered every time he looked at her and the anticipation of seeing one of her sweet smiles. Would she admit to the same level of connection, or would he scare her away by deviating from the path they'd agreed to?

Was he brave enough to risk finding out?

Just as he was about to speak, she turned to him, and the anger flashing in her blue eyes took him by surprise.

"Do you think I need to be coddled in the same way my parents do?" she whispered, the pain in her voice cutting off all thoughts of a revelation about his feelings. Confusion filled him, and he wanted a do-over on the past few minutes. Apparently, Wiley had misjudged her reaction to his plan for a private dinner in a monumental way.

Grace regretted the words as soon as they left her mouth. She looked away from Wiley's shocked expression and took in the beauty of the room. From the soft lighting punctuated with flickering candles to the scent of flowers perfuming the air, she couldn't have asked for a more romantic setup. Calla lilies took center stage in the flower arrangements, not a surprise since Wiley knew they were her favorite.

She had no doubt he'd orchestrated this room and the mood it set. She didn't want to consider what the attention to detail that had gone into it might reveal to the Provisions staff—and more importantly to his sister—about the nature of their relationship. She'd expect nothing less of her big-city attorney. From food to the little gifts and flowers he'd brought her, it was clear he was a master of thoughtful gestures.

As much as she appreciated being spoiled in this way, what Grace liked best about Wiley was that he'd seemed to believe in her. He hadn't treated her like a child the way her parents tended to. Despite her struggles, he never gave any indication that he thought her incapable of dealing with challenges or making her own decisions.

Until tonight.

"I don't know what you're talking about." He shook his head. "I'm not trying to coddle you, Grace."

"Then why mention to your sister how I need to make recovering my priority as if I'm not already doing that?" She moved closer to the table. "You sound like my dad or Jake. I thought you believed I could manage my own life?"

"I do."

"That's not what it sounded like." She dashed a hand across her cheek, cursing the tears that gathered in her eyes. She didn't want to cry but was working so hard to prove that she could handle everything. The truth was, sometimes she doubted herself. She felt tired and achy and like she wanted to crawl into bed, but she kept going. She wouldn't have the opportunity for the promotion at the hotel taken from her because she wasn't up to the task of it.

"Grace." He stepped closer, and she wanted to back away, but that wasn't so easy to manage with the scooter. "I know how determined you are to return to the hotel, even though you're practically managing as much as two people working remotely. But I'd be lying if I told you I wasn't worried about you."

Betrayal ripped through her, but he held up a hand before she could speak. "Tell me why you haven't contacted the physical therapist my family arranged."

"How do you know about that?" she demanded instead of answering, hating to be put on the spot in this way.

"Callum mentioned it," he said gently. "You understand that people realize how serious the fall could have been? More serious than it was." He paused, looked away for moment before his gaze returned to hers. "Deadly."

"Of course I do." She squeezed her eyes shut. "And I hate it. I hate that people are talking about me or feeling sorry for me." She slapped her hand against the scooter's metal frame. "I hate that the cast is a visible reminder of the accident. I'm forever going to be associated with this black spot that I'm sure everyone at the Hotel Fortune would like to erase."

"They don't want to erase you, sweetheart." He took her hand and lifted it to his lips, placing a kiss on each one of her knuckles.

"No kissing," she reminded him, but didn't pull away.

"You're too hard to resist." He inclined his head. "Will you make an appointment with the PT? I know how strong you are. And brave. I know that you'll work through almost anything, but that doesn't mean I don't worry." He leaned in, his forehead pressing against hers in a way that felt strangely intimate. "Not like your parents, Grace. I worry like a man who cares about a woman. The fact that I want you to take care of yourself doesn't mean I don't believe in you."

"Okay," she answered, unsure that her jumbled

brain was capable of saying anything more. He cared about her. What did that mean?

Because she knew what it meant for her. It meant that her heart was happy when Wiley was around and that the depth of feeling she already had for him scared her to her core. She knew what it was like to have her heart broken, and here she was risking it with a man who'd just blithely told her he'd never been in love.

It wasn't as if she thought he was going to change for her, despite how much she might want him to try.

Yet she had to admit he was right about pushing herself. "I don't want the Fortunes to think I'm trying to take advantage of them or that I think they're responsible for me being hurt. It felt like if I worked with a physical therapist on the injuries I have unrelated to my ankle, I'd be admitting that I was hurt more seriously than people thought." She placed a finger to his lips when he would have spoken. "Which I'm not, although my back is stiff, and I probably rely on over-the-counter anti-inflammatories more often than I should."

Wiley gave a sharp shake of his head. "That's it. I'm making sure the therapist is at your house first thing Monday morning."

Grace smiled. "I'm coming into the hotel next week for a meeting about the preopening event."

"No."

She rolled her eyes at him. "Wiley."

"Grace, you just admitted you're in pain. I hate the thought of you in pain."

She leaned in and kissed him, unable to stop herself. "I appreciate that and the fact that you're concerned and not overprotective. I'll call the PT and schedule a session for Monday afternoon, but no more talk about my injuries, especially with your siblings."

He looked like he wanted to argue, so she kissed him again.

"You can't resist me, either," he said with a sexy smirk as she pulled back.

"I guess you're right." Her heart hammered in her chest at the thought of how much she was already coming to care for him. A part of her wanted to tell him, but she was too afraid of scaring him off. Instead, she moved aside the scooter and eased herself into the chair. "Let's leave talk of the hotel behind tonight. I want to enjoy every moment of this friendly dinner."

To her great relief, he nodded and sat next to her. A discreet knock sounded on the door, and the server entered, carrying a tray filled with an assortment of appetizers that both smelled and looked divine.

Yes, Grace liked Wiley for the man he'd shown himself to be and the way he made her feel. She also appreciated that he wanted what was best for her, and tonight she was content to let herself be treated like someone special. She couldn't deny that she wanted more from him. Tomorrow she'd remind herself that her priority was proving herself at the hotel and winning the promotion. Tonight she'd let her heart lead the way.

Chapter Ten

"Are you sure you don't want me to help you in?" her mother asked as they rounded the corner toward the Hotel Fortune.

Grace blew out a huff of nervous laughter. "Mom, this isn't the first day of kindergarten."

"I get it," Barbara said with a chuckle. "I know you're a capable adult, Gracie. Your father and I are proud of how you've dealt with everything life has thrown your way. A lesser woman would have let it ruin them."

"I learned my strength from you," Grace said quietly.

It was true. After Jake's car accident, her mother

had never wavered in her outward confidence that her son would fully recover, despite the grueling process and all the setbacks they faced. Grace wanted to find a way to have that kind of faith in herself.

Her mother pulled to a stop at the curb in front of the hotel's main entrance. Grace smiled as she saw Jay Cross heading toward her.

"I've got this," Grace said as she opened her door, not sure who she was trying to convince.

"I love you, sweetie," Barbara said as she pushed the button to open the sedan's trunk. "I'd tell you to break a leg, but I'm afraid you might take me literally."

Grace turned to her mother with a smile. "I'll text you in a bit to let you know I'm fine."

A look of obvious relief crossed her mom's face, but she shook her head. "You don't have to, but I'd appreciate the update."

Jay had the scooter out of the trunk when Grace climbed out of the car. "Look at you, Ms. Overachiever," he said in his country drawl as she placed her purse and files in the scooter's wire basket and positioned her cast on the pad. "Are you trying to make the rest of us look like slackers?"

Excitement flooded through her as she looked at the hotel's stucco exterior. She tipped her head to the sky and said a silent thank-you for the ability to return to work and the beautiful day for it. "I'm a twenty-eight-year-old woman getting dropped off at work by my mom." She lifted a brow. "She even offered to pack lunch for me, which is sweet but also humiliating in a humbling way."

"I'll take your mom's lunch," Jay answered with a laugh, running a hand through his cropped hair.

"You'll take free food from anyone." Grace started for the hotel. "And we both know you aren't a slacker. You're just strangely tranquil."

Jay looked startled for a brief moment before his features shifted back to self-possessed. He was her favorite person in the trainee program. His easygoing attitude and willingness to pitch in made everything more fun. He definitely cared about the hotel and he worked hard, but didn't seem to have the same drive as Jillian and Grace.

"Someone needs to be tranquil with Jillian taking the lead in your absence."

Grace let out a small groan. "I was afraid of that."

"I don't think anyone is buying her 'I'm the second coming of Conrad Hilton' routine," Jay confided. "But that isn't stopping her from trying to convince them. It's like she's on a mission to suck up to every Fortune in this town."

His derision was clear, and Grace appreciated that he felt the same as she did about Jillian's attempts to cast herself in the starring role for the hotel. But she wondered if the Fortunes saw it that way.

Jillian had positive qualities. She was organized and detail-oriented, but Grace had worked in hospitality long enough to know that Jillian's snobby attitude would be a turnoff to certain guests. One of the cardinal rules about the hospitality industry was a focus on service, and in Grace's opinion, her rival still had a ways to go in learning to put the guests above her own ambition.

"I'm back," Grace murmured, unsure whether she was trying to reassure Jay or herself. "At least for a few hours every morning."

"How are you really feeling?" Jay asked, and she appreciated the concern in his voice.

"Other than the cast, I'm doing okay." She didn't bother mentioning the aches and pains she still had every morning. True to her word to Callum, she'd left a message for the physical therapist. She hadn't expected to hear back until today, but the woman had returned her call almost immediately. So fast, in fact, that Grace wondered if the PT had been instructed to respond as soon as Grace reached out. Either way, she was coming to the house for an initial consultation that afternoon. Although she'd been assured the hotel's insurance would cover all of the expenses related to her accident, Grace still didn't feel comfortable letting the Fortunes pay for the sessions, but she'd work that part out later.

Jay opened one of the hotel's large iron doors. She wheeled through and then gasped at the crowd of her coworkers congregating in front of the reservation desk. Everyone clapped for her arrival and several people—Nicole and Ashley included—held up signs welcoming her back.

Tears sprang to Grace's eyes, and she quickly tried to blink them away. Callum stood at the back of the crowd. He gave a slow nod as their gazes met. She'd wondered if anyone would even notice her absence, but this reception made her feel like the people at the hotel were truly a part of her family.

"I wasn't the only one who missed you," Jay said as he came to stand next to her.

"Welcome back, Grace." Callum stepped forward. "It's great to have you here again."

"Thank you," Grace answered, swallowing around the emotion clogging her throat. "A lot of people would be happy for an excuse to spend a few weeks binge-watching television, but it's a testament to all of you and how amazing this hotel is going to be that I just can't stay away. The Hotel Fortune will be the crowning jewel of this town, and I'm grateful to be even a small part of our success."

Another round of applause greeted her words, and Callum's grin broadened. He was such a serious man, focused and driven, so Grace felt particularly grateful that he seemed satisfied with her impromptu speech.

"We're the ones who are grateful to you," he told her, and then stepped aside so that other employees could greet her. It was almost fifteen minutes later before Grace was alone in the lobby with just Jillian and Jay. She stifled a yawn, wondering if her mom had been right and she was taking on too much.

How could talking make her so tired? She blamed it on the emotions of the morning, from returning to the hotel to the warm welcome she received and then being asked to recount the accident for her curious coworkers.

"You're like the mayor of this hotel," Jay said with a laugh as she turned to him and Jillian.

That comment earned a scowl from Jillian. "We have a meeting with Nicole to discuss restaurant logistics for the grand opening." She eyed Grace's leg. "I'm sure it will take a while for you to get up to speed. So much has happened since you've been on vacation."

"I wouldn't call it a vacation," Grace said, forcing her tone to remain steady.

Jillian waved a hand in front of her face. "Whatever. You practically just admitted that you've been doing nothing but watching television."

"And planning the preopening event," Jay added quietly.

"Busywork," Jillian muttered.

Grace smiled. Kill them with kindness, she thought. "I appreciate the two of you taking care of things while I was recovering. If there's anything you need me to pitch in on now that I'm back—"

"Part-time." Jillian sniffed. "No, I've got it handled. In fact, our meeting with Nicole is about to start." She gave Grace a condescending smile. "I scheduled us to meet in the banquet room upstairs. You probably don't want to deal with all those steps. They're doing maintenance on the elevators today, so they aren't an option."

Grace's heart sank as she glanced over to the bank of windows that overlooked the lobby from Roja's private room. The staircase was just off the entrance to the restaurant and would indeed be difficult for her to manage.

"How about if we switch the meeting to the first floor?" Jay glanced between the two women.

"There are things we need to discuss about seating arrangements upstairs," Jillian insisted. "Grace can check the hotel's email inbox while we're doing the important stuff. Of course, every little detail is important. You know what I mean."

Grace resisted the urge to grit her teeth. As difficult as she sometimes found it to stick up for herself, she had to start acting like a manager if that's what she wanted to be. "Jillian, I want to be part of the meeting. I'm sure Nicole will understand if we change the location."

At that moment, Nicole appeared at the Roja entrance situated off the lobby. She punched something into her cell phone, then shoved it into the back pocket of the stylish trousers she wore. "Did I hear you talking about a venue change?" she asked the three of them.

"Yes." Grace spoke before Jillian had a chance to. "Would it be okay if we met down here so that I don't have to contend with the stairs? I have some ideas I think you'll want to hear."

"Great idea," Nicole said easily. "I want everyone to contribute."

Jillian's face went blank. "But we have seating charts to discuss so we should be upstairs if—"

"We'll manage. We can review the charts on the digital floor plan." Nicole gave a pointed look to the tablet Jillian carried. "Grace, I can't wait to hear your thoughts on plans for the grand opening. You've done such an amazing job so far with the pre-event."

"Thanks," Grace whispered. Clearly annoyed and just as clearly trying to hide it, Jillian followed Nicole into the restaurant. Jay held open the door for Grace, who wheeled forward, proud of her tiny victory in derailing Jillian's attempt at undermining her. Grace was no longer going to fade into the background for anyone.

"Thank you for the ride," Grace said later that afternoon as Wiley pulled out of the hotel's parking lot. "My mom or Jake could have picked me up."

"It's not a problem," he told her. "I'm heading back to the Fame and Fortune anyway to work on some contracts that came in for review earlier."

She rolled her head on the seat back to look at him. "It must be difficult to balance everything you've taken on at the hotel with the work from your regular job."

He shrugged. "I don't mind."

"Because it's temporary?" She couldn't help but ask, needing the reminder not to get used to Wiley's presence in her life, no matter how much she wanted to.

"Because I like the work I do at the law firm, and I enjoy helping my family."

His magnanimous answer made her feel petty and small. There was no reason to goad Wiley, especially when he'd been so kind and helpful.

"That's nice," she said when her exhausted brain couldn't come up with anything better.

"Are you okay?" He reached across the console and placed a warm hand on the top of her thigh. "Did you have a good morning at the hotel?"

She nodded. "Yes. I liked feeling productive, and it was so nice of everyone on staff to welcome me back." She stifled a yawn. "But it makes me mad to get so tired after only working a few hours. I'm used to being able to go all day and still have energy left over. Now I feel like I just ran a marathon."

"It will get better. Your body is still healing."

"I hate it," she grumbled, then blew out a breath. "I'm sorry. I know I'm not the best company right now. And the physical therapist is supposed to be at the house in an hour. All I actually want to do is take a nap and then watch movies in bed for the rest of the night." She tapped a finger to the top of Wiley's hand. "I think I might need to reschedule the PT appointment."

"Nope." He shook his head. "It's set."

"I can call her back."

"But you won't," he insisted. "The only way to get stronger is to work at it."

She folded her arms across her middle, irritation crawling through her like an army of spiders. Wiley was right, of course, but that didn't mean Grace wanted to hear it. "I think I liked you better when you were bringing me flowers and being all sweet and romantic."

"We're saving sweet and romantic for after the therapy session," he promised. "Right now, I'm being your friend."

She opened her mouth, then shut it again, his words wiping away the irritation. As much as she enjoyed the kisses they shared, the thought of being Wiley's friend was just as appealing. "Friend or drill sergeant?" she asked, not bothering to hide the sarcasm from her voice. Sarcasm was an easy mask to hide behind.

"A little of both, actually." He pulled onto her parents' street. "Text me after the PT leaves, and I'm happy to come over or pick you up." He stopped at the curb. "Or if you just want a night alone with Netflix, I understand."

She snorted softly. "If it weren't for this stupid cast, I'd be all about the Netflix and chill with you."

He laughed. "We're in no hurry."

Those words splashed cold water on the flame that ignited inside her every time she thought about being with Wiley in an intimate way. Maybe there was no hurry, but they did have a built-in end date, and she'd do well to remember that.

"Sure," she whispered.

"Grace." He took her hand, and just that gentle touch sent shivers across her skin. "I mean it. No pressure."

Oh, heavens. He thought she was upset because he might be pushing her for something she wasn't ready to handle. What would he think if he knew that without the cast, she'd be tempted to crawl over the console and attach herself to him like a barnacle? Maybe not the most romantic image, but that's how she felt.

"I appreciate it," she answered, and placed her hand on the door handle. The thought of attaching any part of herself to Wiley had her feeling a bit unhinged. She was tired. And frustrated. And she wanted him more than she cared to admit. "I should go."

Wiley looked past her out the passenger window and gave a little wave. "Your mom is coming."

All thoughts of desire vanished into thin air. Grace sighed as her mother headed down the front walk toward them. She opened her door and called out a greeting as Wiley went around to the trunk of the car to retrieve her scooter.

"How was your day?" her mother asked as Grace climbed out.

"I texted you, Mom." She tried to keep the impatience out of her voice. "It was fine."

"You look tired."

"I'm fine."

"She's tired," Wiley confirmed. "After the physical therapy appointment, she should rest. If there's anything she needs—"

"I'll ask for it," Grace said through clenched teeth. She knew he was trying to be nice and she didn't want to take his generosity for granted, but being smothered with caring chafed at her, even if it was done with the best intentions.

Barbara bestowed a beaming smile on Wiley. "I appreciate you looking out for her. It makes me feel better about her going back to work before she's fully healed."

"It's my pleasure," Wiley answered. "Everyone at the hotel was happy to see her return."

"The photos you sent were adorable," her mother told him, reaching out to pat his arm.

Grace blinked. "Wait." She looked from her mom to Wiley. "You sent photos? You're texting my mother?"

"I asked him to, sweetheart," her mom explained. "I didn't want to bother you."

"So you bothered him instead?" Grace snapped, shaking her head.

"It was my pleasure," Wiley assured her.

"Not the point." Grace placed her purse and files into the scooter's basket with more force than was probably necessary. "I'm going into the house. Thank you for the ride, Wiley. I think after my appointment, I'll rest for the night after all."

His gaze clouded. "Whatever you want."

"Other than managing my own business," she muttered, and scooted toward the house as fast as she could manage.

"Gracie, don't be mad." Her mother caught up with her in a couple of quick steps. "Wiley was only doing what I asked. I know your father and I are overprotective, but you're our daughter. Please."

The catch in her mother's voice wound its way around Grace's heart. Of course she understood why her parents worried so much, even if she didn't like it. "I know, Mom," she said softly, pausing just before the front porch. "Give me a minute out here, okay?"

Barbara nodded and waved to Wiley before heading back into the house.

Grace turned the scooter, not a graceful move by any stretch of the imagination. As always, her breath caught at Wiley's pure physical perfection. She liked that he always dressed a touch more formally than his brothers, retaining his city polish even in Rambling Rose.

"You sent photos to my mom," she said, more a statement and less an accusation this time.

He took a step toward her and nodded.

She appreciated that he didn't try to make excuses or mansplain his behavior.

"I appreciate you looking out for me," she said quietly, looking down to the end of the block when the intensity of his gaze was too much. "But it's important to me that you understand I can take care of myself."

He moved closer slowly, as if approaching some feral creature. In truth, that's how Grace felt on the inside. Frustration and fatigue combined to sharpen her edges.

"I understand," he said. "You've proven yourself to be one of the most competent women I've ever known. You don't need my help, because you can handle anything."

"Right now it doesn't feel that way," she admitted. "It hasn't for a while. I let my prior relationship, and before that my family, dictate what I did in life. People around me were my priority, and I thought I had to put the needs of others before my own. I'm trying to change that." She reached down and massaged a hand along the top of her thigh. "Current circumstances aren't making it easy."

"I want to make it easier, Grace."

She studied him for a moment, the sophisticated attorney who seemed intent on making her feel special. It still boggled her mind that Wiley would be interested in a woman like her. In truth, that's part of why she resisted his involvement. She didn't want him to see her as a charity case.

"I don't mean to sound ungrateful." She crooked a finger, beckoning him closer. "I'm grateful for your help at the hotel. I'm grateful for you." When her voice threatened to crack, she swallowed back anything else she might say to him. Her feelings were too raw, too new at this point.

He laced their fingers together. "That goes both ways."

She felt a smile tug one corner of her mouth as butterflies fluttered across her stomach. "I want to kiss you right now, but we're standing on my parents' front lawn."

"Rain check?" he asked, leaning in close.

As an answer she brushed her lips over his, unable to resist. She drew back quickly, still cognizant of being on display for half the neighborhood. "I'll text you after my PT appointment."

The look of relief that filled his bourbon-hued gaze surprised her. It was as if he actually worried she might push him away. That he truly cared about her feelings.

He carried the scooter up the steps to the porch, and it was difficult to watch him walk toward his car again. Grace could imagine how much good it would do her exhausted spirit to spend an hour napping in Wiley's arms. But that certainly wasn't an option living with her parents.

It might be time for a change.

Chapter Eleven

Are you free for dinner?

Wiley blew out a relieved breath when Grace's simple text appeared on his phone screen the following afternoon. He'd gotten stuck on a series of conference calls with his Chicago colleagues that morning and then had a meeting at the county building inspector's office, so he didn't arrive at the hotel until after lunch. Grace had already left for home.

He couldn't tell why not seeing her for twenty-four hours made him feel anxious. Normally, Wiley set strict limits on his relationships so that the women he dated didn't get the wrong impression about his level of commitment.

Grace had practically accused him of trying to run her life yesterday, a clear sign that he was in too deep with her. He never got involved with women at that level. Flowers and other gifts—like the ones he'd given her after the accident—were…well, Wiley wouldn't describe them as meaningless. But they were superficial in a way that felt comfortable. He liked boundaries and limits. He liked control, especially after feeling he had so little of it as a kid in his overlarge blended family.

But the tiny town of Rambling Rose, and Grace in particular, made him want more.

He replied to the text that he'd pick her up at her parents' around six and received an immediate response with an unfamiliar address along with a message to come hungry for pizza.

The rest of the afternoon seemed to tick by in slow motion. He resisted the urge to google the address she'd sent him to see if they were meeting at a restaurant or something that would clue him in to her plan for the night. It occurred to Wiley that he might have a bit of an issue with control if he couldn't relinquish it long enough to allow Grace to surprise him with plans for the evening.

He left the hotel after checking progress on the balcony reconstruction. The painter had put the finishing touches on it, and the structure looked as good as new. Part of why Wiley had gone to the inspector's office was to discuss the possibility of sabotage in more detail. The man had assured him that they couldn't make a definite determination on what had caused the collapse. For now they believed the accident to be just that—an accident.

Wiley breathed a little easier at that news, although the cynic in him had a hard time totally trusting it. He would reserve judgment until the hotel opened without incident. But the relief on the faces of his brothers and sisters when he'd shared the news that the balcony may not have been tampered with made him want to believe. There was enough stress in putting the finishing touches on the hotel to have it ready for opening in less than a month. The idea that right now they wouldn't have to worry about sabotage on top of everything else clearly helped everyone. He also knew that the security system Kane had installed was top-notch. Nothing was going to get past them.

Anticipation continued to build in him as he drove to the ranch to change out of his suit and then headed back to town, following his car's GPS to the address Grace had given him. He parked in front of a nondescript brick fourplex in a residential neighborhood that he'd never been to before. Why would Grace have sent him there?

Frowning as he surveyed the block, Wiley was about to pull out his phone to text her when she called his name. He glanced toward the house to see Grace waving at him from a second-floor window.

"Come on up," she shouted. "I'll text you the code for the front door."

"How'd you get up there?" he asked as he approached the house.

She grinned, looking more relaxed than he'd seen her since that first night. "It's amazing what a girl can manage with the right motivation."

He entered the building, using the code that appeared on his phone. The converted house had two apartments on the first floor. The staircase that led to the second floor was narrow, and he couldn't imagine how Grace would have climbed the stairs. Obviously she'd made it to the second floor somehow.

She stood in the doorway of one of the upstairs apartments, looking more beautiful than ever in a simple sweater and a pair of loose sweatpants with the right leg cut off at the knee. Her hair was down around her shoulders, and although he'd seen her almost every day for the past week, there was something different about her tonight—a light in her eye that hadn't been there before.

"Welcome to my apartment," she said, backing up the scooter to give him room to enter. "It's not fancy, but guess what?" She took his hand as he entered and drew him close for a lingering kiss. "We're alone."

The thought sent a sensation surging through

him. He gave his body a silent command to settle down. Being alone with Grace didn't change anything. They were dating or friends or friends who were dating, depending on how he felt at any given moment.

"Why the change in location? Is everything okay with your family?" He squeezed her fingers. "I hope I didn't cause lingering problems between you and your mom because of updating her. Like I said—".

"Wiley, stop." She looked at him strangely, and he realized he was blathering. He wasn't a man who spoke compulsively or without prior thought. He chose his words deliberately, took action with purposeful thought. Wiley valued control above almost everything else, and suddenly one soft-spoken woman had turned everything he knew about himself on its side. "Everything is fine with my family." She shut the door behind him and released her hold on his hand, moving across the hardwood floor on the scooter toward the small kitchen positioned at the other end of the open space.

"Then why are you here?" He looked around the apartment and saw Grace's personality reflected in almost every part of it. It wasn't fancy, but from the row of bookshelves to the framed botanical posters above the slipcovered sofa, he could imagine her choosing every item with care. A complete contrast to his apartment in a sleek complex in downtown Chicago. He'd lived in his place for nearly seven years and had yet to hang a single piece of art on the walls.

The more time he spent in Rambling Rose, the more obvious it became that he was living life but hadn't created a home.

"I actually have you to thank once again," she said, grinning at him over her shoulder. "Thanks to your bullying, I didn't cancel the PT appointment yesterday."

"*Bullying* is such a harsh word," he told her with a grimace. "Can we use *support* or *encouragement*?"

"Bullying in the best way possible." She turned to him. "I needed it. You were right. Avoiding therapy wasn't going to help me heal faster or make anyone forget about the injury. The cast is kind of a give-away, you know?"

"That doesn't explain you moving back to a second-floor apartment."

"The therapist was wonderful. She gave me some exercises to help strengthen my leg muscles for the time I'm still in the cast. I explained to her how much trouble I'd been having with the crutches. She helped me learn to use them more effectively."

Grace pointed to the metal crutches that rested against the wall. "We even did some work on get-ting up and down stairs. Once I felt more confident, I knew I could move back here. I don't have to stay with my parents anymore."

"That's great." The radiant smile she gave him

did funny things to his heart. "And your folks are okay with it?"

Her smile dimmed slightly. "They aren't thrilled," she admitted, "but it's not their choice. My dad picked me up from work and drove me here this afternoon while Mom did some grocery shopping, so I won't starve." She opened the refrigerator to reveal the fully stocked shelves. "Once they saw that I could manage the stairs, it made them feel better about things. I need this so badly. I need to feel like I can make it on my own."

"Of course you can," he said because even though he didn't like to think of her struggling, he knew her independence was important to who she was, and he'd never take that from her. "You know I'll help with anything you need."

"Yeah," she whispered, biting down on her lower lip. "And I do have a few places that are achy."

He immediately took a step closer. "Have you been overdoing it at the hotel?"

She chuckled and tapped a finger to her mouth. "I hurt right here," she told him with a wink. "Any chance you'll kiss it and make it better?"

Every feeling of desire Wiley had locked down came roaring back to the surface. They were alone in her apartment. The thought of what it might mean made his body grow heavy with need.

Just as he reached her, the landline phone on the counter rang.

"Hold that thought." Grace pointed at him. "I think the pizza just arrived."

Food was the last thing Wiley cared about at the moment, but he opened the door for the delivery guy after Grace buzzed him into the building. To his surprise, she'd already paid over the phone, so all that was left for Wiley to do was hand the kid a couple of dollars as a tip.

"You don't have to buy me dinner," he told her as he carried the box to the two-seater kitchen table positioned in front of a window. "I'm the man. I should pay."

He wanted to slap himself as soon as the words left his mouth, and she flat out laughed at that statement. "You need to update your thoughts about relationships," she told him as she pulled two plates from the cupboard. "As much as I appreciate your gentlemanly tendencies, I'm a modern woman."

"I'm an ass," he muttered. "My mom and my sisters would kill me if they overheard that."

"Your intentions are noble."

"That's something, I guess. Are you sure you want to put up with me?"

She laughed again. "It's only for a couple—" He watched as she closed her eyes and drew in a deep breath. There was the reminder of his dwindling time in Texas, which was beginning to feel like a specter haunting the moments he shared with Grace.

So many things would be easier once he returned

to Chicago. Although Wiley was keeping up with his client load, working remotely meant everything seemed to take longer than it would if he were handling it at the main office. Despite that, he found he didn't want to think about leaving Rambling Rose or Grace. Especially Grace.

"Would you like a beer?" she asked when she met his gaze again, her eyes almost aggressively bright. "I had my mom pick up the same brand you ordered at dinner the other night."

"You're wining and dining me." He took the plates from her hand and leaned forward to kiss her neck, needing the sweet scent of her to ground him in the moment and help him forget the inevitable end to their time together. "I should push you out of your comfort zone more often."

Her shoulders relaxed, as though she appreciated his attempt to lighten the mood. "Be careful, Counselor," she warned, "or this modern woman might push your comfort zone right back."

Grace couldn't remember the last time she'd felt so content. It was nearly ten and she sat cradled in the crook of Wiley's arm as the final scene of an old sci-fi movie played on her small TV.

He was the first man she'd had in her apartment, and nerves had plagued her after she'd texted him the invitation earlier. She knew her place wasn't anything special, especially for a man who was probably used to living the high life in the city. Most of her furniture consisted of hand-me-downs from her parents or thrift-store finds. She'd shared a duplex apartment with her ex-boyfriend in Horseback Hollow and after discovering the depth of his betrayal, she'd been so intent on getting out of town, she'd simply left behind everything that wouldn't fit in her car.

It had only been a year since she'd returned to Rambling Rose, but her relationship with Craig seemed like a lifetime ago. It still amazed her how deeply she'd come to care for Wiley in such a short time. Maybe it was due to growing close to him in the aftermath of her accident, but Grace couldn't help but believe there was more to their connection.

If only she didn't keep getting the unwanted reminders that he'd be leaving sooner than later. She snuggled against him, reminding herself to stay in the moment instead of worrying about things she had no control over. That plan seemed to be serving her well as far as her job. Even though Jillian had found ways to remind Grace every day since her return about all the ways she wasn't contributing to progress toward the grand opening, Grace stayed focused on the pieces she could do. She'd invited owners of various local businesses, and plans for the Rambling Rose partnership reception were almost complete.

When the movie's credits rolled, Wiley dropped a gentle kiss on the top of her forehead. "This is nice," he said, one hand tracing lazy circles on her arm. The featherlight touch did funny things to her insides, her pulse thrumming at the thought of being truly alone with this irresistible man. Up until now, the only moments they'd had to themselves had been in his car, and there was only so much that could happen with a console separating them.

Not that a lot more could happen with her leg in the cast, but Grace tipped up her chin and trailed kisses along Wiley's strong jaw. His arms tightened around her, and he claimed her mouth, their tongues meeting as the kiss deepened. She wound her arms around his neck, reveling in the heat that surrounded her.

It felt like she could kiss him forever and never tire of it. Her body grew heavy with need and she shifted, wanting to get closer but not quite able to manage it with the cast hindering her.

"Are you okay?" he asked her when a frustrated sigh escaped her lips. "Am I hurting you? Is it your leg?"

She pulled back to gaze into his dark eyes. "I want more," she whispered. "What would the physical therapist think of me if I asked her how to manage…" She broke off and wrinkled her nose. "Being with you despite my cast."

One side of his mouth twitched. "I'm not sure, but I like the way your mind works." He smoothed a stray lock of hair from her face. "I like everything about you, Grace. So much so that I don't want to rush this."

As much as her brain appreciated his chivalry, Grace's body wasn't cooperating. "Will you stay with me tonight?" she asked, then felt heat rise to her cheeks at her own bluntness. Grace wasn't the type of woman to ask for what she wanted or take the lead in the bedroom. But it was different somehow with Wiley.

A thought wiggled its way into her mind. Maybe Wiley was being a gentleman because he didn't feel the same way about her. Although even her dad seemed to be warming to him, her brother still had suspicions about his motives. Jake still seemed to believe Wiley was protecting his family by getting close to her and sent her at least one text a day with some sort of veiled warning about not opening her heart to the Fortune attorney.

Grace didn't bother to tell Jake it was way too late for that. Her heart was already well in the mix.

She held her breath as she waited for Wiley's response. She could feel his heart beating a rapid-fire pace against his chest. "No pressure," she added when he didn't respond. "I'm not expecting anything to happen. Sleeping, of course. But otherwise—"

"Yes." He said the word with a level of reverence that sent shivers across her skin, then kissed her again.

By the time he finally pulled away, Grace felt dizzy with need.

"Don't ever doubt that I want you," he told her. "I do, Grace. So badly." He reached out and placed a hand on her leg just above the cast. "But not until you're healed totally. What I have planned for the two of us is going to be worth the wait. I promise."

"Okay," she said, her voice a squeak. How else could she answer?

She pushed away from him, needing a little bit of distance because she felt like she was in danger of spontaneously combusting. "I'm going to change into my pajamas and…" She covered her face with her hands. "This is weird, right? We're two adults—who are dating—and we're having a platonic sleepover. You must think I'm the biggest dork you've ever met."

"I think you're amazing," he assured her. He rose from the sofa, grabbed the remote to turn off the television and then extended his hands toward her.

She allowed him to pull her to standing but shook her head when he bent as if to pick her up. "I can make it to the bedroom on my own."

"Amazing," he repeated.

She laughed at that. "It's not far."

"I'm going to text Callum," Wiley said, "and tell them not to expect me home tonight."

She made a face. "Is that going to be weird?"

"I'm a grown man," he reminded her. "They might give me a little grief, but no one will be shocked."

As she made her way to the bedroom, Grace wasn't sure whether to be comforted or terrified by Wiley's comment. Did he make a habit of spending the night away from the ranch in beds that didn't belong to him?

No reason to go looking for trouble when it had a way of finding Grace without any prompting on her part. It only took a few minutes to change into her pj's and finish her nighttime routine.

Wiley was sitting on the edge of the bed when she came out of the bathroom. He'd taken off his sweatshirt and socks and shoes but still had on a T-shirt and jeans.

Somehow the sight of his bare feet on her rug made Grace's toes curl.

"Are you planning to sleep in your clothes?" she asked, trying for a light tone.

He shrugged. "I don't want to make you uncomfortable."

She kicked out her injured leg. "The cast beat you to it. It's okay, Wiley. I know nothing is going to happen between us, but I want you to get a decent night's sleep, as well."

He rose and approached her, running his hands up and down her arms. "Even if I don't sleep a wink, it will be worth it to spend the night holding you."

Damn, the guy knew what he was doing with the smooth talk.

She reached for his belt, slowly unbuckling it as she felt him watching her. "I'm glad to hear you say that. But drop trou, Mr. Fortune. I'm ready for bed."

He grinned at her teasing, and Grace felt her heart tug once more. She liked who she was with Wiley. He seemed willing to let her be who she was in a way that most people didn't appreciate, and that gave her the confidence to explore her inner strength.

Too bad she couldn't spend the whole night exploring him.

She climbed into bed and watched him undress, forcing herself not to whimper as he tugged off his T-shirt to reveal the most perfect physique she'd ever seen in person. He was lean and muscled, hard planes and angles on display in a way that reminded her of an actual sculpture. A smattering of dark hair covered his chest.

And he was going to spend the night with her.

He joined her under the covers, and she flipped off the light, then sighed with pleasure as he pulled her close. As much as she wanted him, there was something about the comfort of his arms around her that made the fatigue she tried to keep at bay rise up like a wave inside her.

"You can sleep, Grace," he said against her hair, as if he could sense her struggle to remain awake. "I'm not going anywhere."

She loved the sound of that, although she told herself not to forget that he meant he was with her for now. So for now she cuddled up against him and drifted off to sleep.

Chapter Twelve

The next week went by more quickly than Grace could have imagined. Between work at the hotel in the mornings and working at home on the business leaders' event during the afternoon hours, plus the physical therapy sessions and her time with Wiley, it felt like every minute was filled with something.

She'd never been happier.

It was strange that falling off the balcony seemed to be a catalyst for her newfound sense of confidence. Yet there was nothing like knowing she could have died to make her realize she needed to be willing to take more chances in life.

Grace had started to speak up more in meetings

and insert her ideas, not only for the opening, but for how she thought things would work best in the daily running of the hotel once they were filled with guests. To her surprise, the Fortunes seemed happy to let her take the lead, and she realized that the point of the training program might have been more than simply familiarizing locals with the business model. Because they were committed to hiring most of the hotel staff locally, the Fortune family needed a way to make sure whoever they chose was going to be up for the job.

Grace and Jillian had similar backgrounds and experience in hospitality, but they had very different methods for how to deal with guests and the hotel's overall ambiance. Jillian clearly felt as though it should be an exclusive oasis that would cater to big-city guests from Houston or other parts of the state who wanted to get away from the pressures of city life but still retain the trappings of privilege. Grace saw the value in that, but because she'd grown up in Rambling Rose, she also understood what the town had to offer. Her idea was to capitalize on the community feel. Yes, the hotel was an escape but one that guests would choose in part because of the charm of the surrounding area.

It's why her Rambling Rose partnership reception felt so important. She wanted local business owners to buy in on the hotel so that when it opened and guests came to town, the community would welcome

them in a way that would make people want to return over and over.

"Am I interrupting?"

The soft knock on the office door had her glancing
up from her laptop. She grinned as Wiley entered,
looking handsome as ever in his dark suit and crisp
white tailored shirt.

"You're never an interruption," she told him, feeling the familiar rush of heat that rose to her cheeks
whenever Wiley spoke to her. Since she moved back
to her apartment, he'd been over almost every evening for dinner. He didn't always spend the night but
stayed long enough to kiss and caress her until her
body was on fire with wanting more.

"You have the office to yourself this morning?"
He gestured toward the other workstations situated
around the perimeter of the room. All of the employees involved with the trainee program shared this
space, which would be the official management office once the hotel opened.

"Jillian and Jay are in a meeting upstairs to finalize the choice for bed linens for the guest rooms."
She shrugged. "I had a call with Hailey at the spa
about the giveaways for the preopening event. I figured they could handle it without me."

"Look at you delegating like you've already earned
the promotion." He bent down and gave her a swift
kiss. "I like watching you take control."

As much as she wanted to draw him in, Grace

gave him a playful nudge instead. "You can't kiss me at work," she admonished. "People will talk."

"There's no one here."

"Still." She held up a hand. "And I'm not delegating. We're dividing and conquering."

He lifted a brow. "Own it, Grace. You want that promotion, and you're going after it."

"Yeah," she whispered, delighted that she didn't have to hide her ambition from Wiley. Her ex hadn't liked it when she tried to better herself, at least if it made her seem like she was trying to surpass him in any way. Maybe it was because Wiley was already so successful and sure of himself, but he seemed to be attracted to her even more when she stood up for herself or went after what she wanted.

It was a heady vote of confidence.

"Saturday's event is going to be great." She grinned and pushed away from her computer. "Do you know what's going to make it even better?"

Wiley tapped a finger against his chin. "The fact that every time we make eye contact you'll know that I'm thinking about kissing you senseless?"

She laughed. "No, but I'll keep that in mind. I get the cast off Friday afternoon."

His mouth dropped open and something flashed in his eyes that she didn't understand—it looked almost like dismay. "I thought you had a full month in the cast?"

"Me, too. But I saw Dr. Matthews early this morning. My mom took me in before work. He did more scans and said the fracture is healing faster than expected. The plan was to make an appointment for next week to get it off, but when I explained about the event on Saturday, he agreed to see me Friday afternoon. I'll still have to be in a walking boot for another few weeks, but…" She threw up her hands. "Walking, Wiley. Without crutches or the scooter. I'm going to almost be a normal person again."

"That's fantastic news." He continued to look shocked and definitely not thrilled the way she expected. "Are you sure you aren't pushing the recovery? What does the PT say?"

"Wow, that's not exactly the reaction I'd hoped for," Grace told him with a frown. "The doctor is okay with it, so I don't think I'm pushing anything. We already have physical therapy sessions set up for next week to start working on strengthening my ankle." She didn't bother to keep the frustration out of her voice. "This is a huge step forward—literally and figuratively—and comes at the best possible time. Not just because of work." She swallowed. "I mean you and I can…well, we'll be free to take the next step in our relationship."

He sucked in a sharp breath. "Yes. That's amazing." He waved a hand in the air, looking so discombobulated she almost felt sorry for him. "Every part of it is amazing, Grace. I'm really so happy for you. It's just a shock, you know? Because the plan changed and all."

"For the better," she reminded him.

"Of course."

Jillian entered the office in her usual flourish, then stopped when she realized Wiley was standing next to Grace's chair. "Thank God I was at that meeting."

He took a step back and ran a hand through his hair.

"Nice work with arranging the spa gift certificate," he told Grace with a perfunctory nod.

She gave him a wan smile, hoping that Jillian was fooled by his somewhat lame attempt to offer a reason for being in here with her. She wished they didn't have to keep their relationship secret, but until the promotion was announced, she wouldn't take any chances on her coworkers thinking she would be given preferential treatment during the assessment process.

Even being with him in secret felt risky, but she also couldn't imagine not taking advantage of their time together.

"Nice to see you, Jillian," Wiley said, and for a moment Grace hoped Wiley wasn't a poker player, because the man's inability to display a convincing game face was comical.

He exited the office as Jillian took a seat at her desk.

"The linen meeting went well?" Grace asked, knowing that the other woman loved to talk about herself and hoping she'd be easily distracted from Wiley's presence in the office.

"If it weren't for me, our guests would have been sleeping on discount sheets and scratchy comforters." Jillian opened her laptop. "The bedding company sales guy was definitely trying to pull something over on us."

"What did Jay think?" Grace valued his practical opinion to balance out Jillian's tendency toward drama.

"He actually agreed with me." Jillian sounded as shocked as Grace felt. "I would not have expected Jay to be the type of man who understood the value of Egyptian cotton or a high thread count. He seems like a guy who'd change his sheets once a month and only because he got sick of crumbs in the bed."

"Yuck." Grace shook her head. "You're selling him a little short."

"He's just so regular," Jillian said with a sniff. "Nice enough but definitely not someone with my level of ambition."

Grace inclined her head. "I hate to ask where I rate on your ambition scale, but I'm curious."

Jillian steepled her hands together as she turned her chair fully to face Grace. "Well, you take it to a whole new level."

That didn't sound like a compliment, so Grace offered her best placating smile. As much as she wanted to earn the promotion, there was no doubt that Jillian would be an asset to the hotel staff in some capacity, so Grace didn't want to be the woman's sworn enemy. "You do a great job as well," she said.

"But I don't do the boss's brother," Jillian said with a smirk. "I earn my accolades with hard work and talent."

Anger and alarm rose in Grace like two waves crashing in on each other. This was exactly why she'd been leery of dating Wiley before the grand opening. The fact that Jillian could even hint—let alone nearly accuse—Grace of being given some kind of preferential treatment pained her to the core.

"I don't know what you're talking about," she said, making sure not one bit of emotion seeped into her voice. "Wiley and I are friends. He was kind after the accident."

"I assume you repaid that kindness on your back?" Jillian asked, almost conversationally.

Grace gasped. "That's a horrible thing to say."

"But is it true?"

"No, it's not. I don't appreciate the insinuation about my character. I've earned my place at the Hotel Fortune."

"He's only friendly to you because they're afraid you're going to sue for damages or try to get some kind of settlement from the hotel."

"That's not true," Grace whispered even as her

brother's words played over in her head like an annoying refrain. She reminded herself that Jillian wanted to get under her skin, and Grace had to keep it together. She knew Wiley truly cared about her. He told her as much—maybe not in so many words, but the way he held her communicated everything she needed to know.

"I overheard him talking to Callum and Nicole right after the accident." Jillian stood and moved closer to Grace's workstation. "He told them that he'd 'handle you.' We all know what that means when an attorney says those words."

"You're lying."

"I'm not. Ask him if you want. But men like Wiley Fortune don't fall for small-town girls like you, Grace. He's not even staying in Rambling Rose, so if you can't see that you're just an easy distraction with the added benefit that he protects his family, then you're even stupider than I suspected." She pressed her glossy lips together. "I feel sorry for you, actually. I have a friend who works at Cowboy Country and she told me how you were publicly humiliated by your boyfriend up there. Some people can't ever learn the lesson."

Without waiting for a response, Jillian turned and left the room.

Grace stared blankly at her computer screen as her body began to tremble. Was it possible Jillian had told her the truth? The woman was conniving and egotistical, but Grace had never once heard her lie in the months they'd worked together.

She hadn't understood Wiley's reaction to her news about the cast coming off early. Maybe he liked having an excuse not to be intimate with her. He'd given her too many reasons to believe he was a gentleman for her to doubt him on that front. It would then make sense if he was really stringing her along or getting close to her to make sure she didn't go after his family for the accident that he wouldn't want things to go too far.

As many times as Grace had warned herself not to let her feelings for him get out of control, that's exactly what had happened. She was falling for Wiley Fortune—falling in love with him. And now she feared she might end up with a broken heart and a betrayal that would hurt far worse than Craig's. If Wiley was the man Jillian claimed him to be, Grace wasn't sure if she'd ever recover.

The following morning Wiley walked toward a popular barbecue joint in downtown Austin where he was meeting his cousin Gavin for lunch. Gavin was the youngest son of Kenneth, the half brother of Wiley's dad. Similar to Wiley's branch of the clan, Gavin's was a big family who hadn't known about their connection to the famous Texas Fortunes until the past few years. Gavin and his siblings had grown up in Texas. Like Wiley, Gavin was an attorney and specialized in corporate law.

They hadn't met, but Wiley knew his cousin worked for a prominent firm out of Austin. It was Wiley's understanding that Gavin had transferred there from Denver when he decided to return permanently to Texas.

After the conversation with Grace yesterday, Wiley had reached out and asked to meet Gavin to discuss possible opportunities within his firm.

The news that Grace was getting her cast off early had been a shock, and he knew he hadn't handled it well. But that wasn't due to the reasons Grace might suspect. In truth, the thought of making love to her appealed to him more than he could say. He wanted to learn every inch of her body and how she liked to be touched, what he could do to bring her pleasure. He'd forced himself to put fantasies about the two of them to the side out of respect for her recovery. It had been an exquisite torture to kiss her and hold her in his arms each night when he stayed at her apartment and know that they couldn't go any further.

But a part of him, a tiny rational sliver of his brain, appreciated having the cast as an excuse not to take things further. Grace was different from any other woman he'd dated. He suspected that being with her intimately, instead of quenching his thirst, would only make him want her more.

The thought of taking that step and then walking

away after the hotel's grand opening made a sharp ache slice across his chest. The alternative—a long-distance relationship—held no appeal, either. Because of that, Wiley had decided to think about his future in a new way.

He immediately spotted Gavin as he entered the restaurant since he'd read his cousin's bio on the firm's website. Gavin was tall and good-looking, with dark blond hair and air of confidence about him. He waved and then gave Wiley's hand a firm shake when he got to the table.

"I'm glad you called," his cousin said, and Wiley appreciated the open expression on the other man's face.

"Thanks for being willing to meet me so quickly." He took a seat, and a waitress put a glass of water and a menu in front of him. "It's strange to think our fathers are brothers but we're virtual strangers."

Gavin nodded. "My dad had a bit of struggle getting used to being part of the Fortune clan."

"I know how that goes," Wiley said with a laugh. His father had actively discouraged Callum and the rest of the siblings from getting close to their new-found relatives. "But it's a hard family to resist."

"How do you like Rambling Rose?" Gavin asked. "From everything I hear, your siblings are making quite the mark on that little town."

"It's growing on me," Wiley admitted, glancing at the menu. "Which I didn't expect."

The waitress returned to take their orders. After she'd gone, Gavin sat back in his seat with a contented sigh. "I'm familiar with that, as well. I certainly hadn't planned to end up in Texas when I came for my sister's wedding. Denver had been my home since I graduated from law school."

"So what changed?" Wiley leaned in, curious to get the insight of a man who on the surface appeared so like him. "Did the wide-open spaces of Texas call you home again?"

"Not exactly. There's plenty of space in Colorado, although it's certainly not the same. The truth is, I met a woman. It's as simple as that."

Wiley chuckled. "In my experience, women are never simple."

"The way I felt about Christine is." Gavin inclined his head. "Although it took me a bit of time to figure it out. I might be great with contract law, but I wasn't exactly a quick study when it came to love. Luckily, my firm had a Austin office, so it was easy to transfer without missing a beat. Best decision I ever made."

"I don't have your luck," Wiley told the other man, still reeling at the fact that Gavin seemed to be acting like it had been no big deal to make that kind of a move for a relationship. "How long have you and Christine been together?"

"Two years this month," Gavin told him with a

smile. "Smartest thing I ever did was make her my wife. We'll be adding to our family this spring."

"Congratulations." Wiley rubbed two fingers against his chest, wondering if the emotion there that felt like jealousy could actually be that base. It wasn't as if he'd completely rejected the idea of someday getting married and having a family of his own. But having his own space and independence had always been more of a priority. As much as he appreciated the sacrifices his mom and stepdad had made, he didn't know if he was capable of being that selfless.

"It's incredible. Christine is incredible. I really am the luckiest damn man alive."

The waitress brought their food at that moment— brisket for Wiley and a pulled pork sandwich for Gavin. As they ate, Gavin asked Wiley about his work in Chicago and how he was able to balance everything remotely from Rambling Rose. They discussed Gavin's transition to Texas and what that had meant for his career and his standing in the firm.

Before this month, Wiley had never considered that he might want a change from the firm where he was on the fast track to partner. He'd made a life in Chicago that suited him, although he was quickly coming to realize his desire to stay in Rambling Rose was more than just a need for a break from the pace of city life.

He wanted a change.

As if reading his thoughts, Gavin gave him a knowing look across the table. "You've told me everything I need to know about your focus as an attorney," his distant cousin said. "Obviously you've had a lot of success in your career and from the sound of it, you have a great life in Chicago. Yet you called to discuss opportunities with my firm in Austin?"

As ridiculous as it seemed, Wiley's first instinct was to deny it. No point, since that's exactly why he had called Gavin, but saying the words out loud felt monumental, like he'd be making a huge shift from the path that had always seemed solid in front of him.

"I think it might be time to consider other opportunities," he answered slowly. "I've enjoyed reconnecting with my brothers and sisters. Somehow being part of a big family doesn't quite feel as stifling as it once did. Now it's more of a comfort, and I like the idea of being able to help out legally with what they're doing in Rambling Rose. But I'm not ready to give up corporate law. I'd like to find a way to do both."

Gavin studied him for several long beats. "You want to move to Texas permanently to be closer to your family?"

"Yes."

"That's the only reason?" Gavin prompted.

"I'm ready for a new challenge." Wiley kept his features neutral. He could tell the other man wanted something more, a revelation about love or a woman.

But Wiley wasn't ready for that. The idea of taking his relationship with Grace to the next level had certainly contributed to his desire to explore new opportunities in Texas. She wasn't the type of woman he would expect to have a casual relationship.

Yes, they'd agreed to date temporarily while he was in town, but that arrangement had been made while she was at the beginning of her recovery. He hadn't expected his feelings for her to grow so deep in such a short time. The idea of making love to her and then walking away after the grand opening held no appeal. Even if he wasn't ready to talk to her yet about his emotions, he needed to be moving forward. The thought of living permanently in Texas helped him to retain some level of control.

"I'd like to set up a meeting with you and one of the senior partners," Gavin told him. "Our Austin office is continuing to expand, and it would be a huge win to attract an associate with your level of experience." He leaned forward. "Are you thinking of living in Austin, or do you want to stay close to your family in Rambling Rose?"

"Rambling Rose," Wiley said without hesitation. He knew what working at the hotel meant to Grace. Although Austin wasn't far, he'd grown accustomed to being able to see her every night. He liked having dinner with her and hearing about her day and sharing the details of his. He'd always been serious and analytical, comfortable with seeing the world through his view alone. Her mind worked in a different way than his did, and it fascinated him.

"Okay, then." Gavin nodded. "Let's see what we can do to make this happen."

Wiley released a breath he hadn't realized he was holding. Moving forward with a potential relocation to Texas permanently made him feel like he could take the next step with Grace with no reservations. And his body and his heart wanted that next step in equal measure.

Chapter Thirteen

Grace stared at her left ankle as if she'd never seen it before. The feeling of air on her skin after so long was both strange and exhilarating. Although her un-injured leg hadn't gotten any exposure to the winter sun, the skin on her newly exposed leg looked par-ticularly sallow and a bit pinched. It felt odd to be able to move her foot. Her entire body felt lighter without the weight of the cast.

"You're sure it's time?"

The orthopedic surgeon chuckled. "Normally my patients don't second-guess me when I remove a cast. They're too busy thanking me."

She placed a hand over her face and gave him an

embarrassed smile. "I'm sorry, Doctor. Of course I trust you. You're the expert. It's just such a surprise to have it happening earlier than I expected. Now I just need a shower and to shave my legs."

"You're young and healthy," he said with a chuckle. "The body is a miraculous healer, and yours did an amazing job at it. Let's not get ahead of ourselves. You'll still need to wear the walking boot for another month. Physical therapy is going to be critical to strengthen the ankle. I know you've gone back to work, which is fine, but I don't want you to overdo it."

"I won't," she promised. "I'll be careful. I'm just so excited to not have to use the crutches or the scooter."

"I'm happy to be able to help you."

"What about driving?" Grace said, still marveling at the thrill of being able to return to a somewhat normal life.

"I would say take it slow." The doctor typed in a few notes on his laptop as he spoke. "And no standard transmission. The boot and a clutch aren't going to be a good mix. But if the car is an automatic, then I see no issue."

"I get my life back," Grace said on a happy sigh.

"Listen to your body," he advised. "If you need to rest, do that. I mean it, Grace. I know that you're driven and motivated. We want to see the progress you've made so far continue."

"Got it. Thank you so much."

They finished up the appointment, and she scheduled a follow-up with the desk. The boot was awkward, but not nearly as cumbersome as the cast had been. Grace smiled as she walked out to the reception area where her mother and brother were waiting.

"No more cast," her mother said and enveloped Grace in a tight hug. "This is fantastic, Gracie."

Jake playfully ruffled her hair. "I was getting ready to put a bell on your scooter. It slowed you down at bit."

"No more time for slow," she said, then glanced over her shoulder. She didn't need the doctor to overhear her. Of course, she wasn't going to push it, but Grace felt more than ready to get back to regular life. Especially when that involved taking her relationship with Wiley to the next level. "I even get to drive."

"You behind the wheel is scary on a good day," Jake said with a chuckle.

Grace narrowed her eyes. "Not helpful."

They walked out into the medical center parking lot. "I need to stop at the grocery store on the way home," Barbara said, turning to Grace. "Do you want to go with me? Or Jake can give you a ride to your apartment."

"I'd like to get back," Grace said. "Wiley is coming for dinner so—"

"Seriously?" Jake bit back a groan. "Isn't it time to

cut the cord with that guy? You're basically healed. You don't need him keeping tabs on you anymore."

"Jake, be nice," their mother said gently.

"Or just be quiet," Grace added.

"I still don't trust him." Jake lowered his mirrored sunglasses to look at Grace. "I'm sure he'll be doing a happy dance now that you don't seem to have any long-term, potentially expensive injuries for his family to take care of."

"Wiley has been kind to your sister." Barbara smiled. "He's a good friend."

Jake sniffed but Grace held up a hand when he would have argued with their mother. "It's my life, Jake. I get to live it how I see fit. Maybe I'll go to the grocery store with Mom just so I don't have to listen to you."

"Come on, Gracie." He looped an arm around her shoulder. "Let me drive you home. I won't talk any more about the Fortunes."

"Call if you need anything," her mother said. "I expect you both at the house for Sunday supper." She patted Grace's arm. "Bring your Wiley if you'd like, sweetie. We can all get to know each other better."

"Thanks, Mom. Love you." Grace gave her mother a final hug, then followed Jake to his truck. She didn't like the tense silence that had fallen between them. She and Jake had always been close, even more so when she returned home to help after his car accident.

"Will you give Wiley a chance?" she asked softly

as her brother pulled out of the medical center parking lot.

"Is it actually serious between the two of you?"

She bit down on the inside of her cheek, unsure how to answer that question. From the standpoint of her heart, it certainly felt serious. Although it had only been a few weeks since they'd met, she could hardly imagine her life before Wiley or how she'd kept herself occupied. At the same time, she knew he was leaving, so it wouldn't make sense to become too attached. The sharp ache in her heart told her it might be too late for that.

"I like him," she said, because that was the truth without revealing too much. "I'm not expecting whatever is going on between us to continue after he leaves, although I wouldn't be opposed to a long-distance relationship."

"Really?" Jake's fingers tightened on the steering wheel. "I know I'm rough on him, Grace, but it's because I don't want to see you get hurt." He glanced over at her. "You didn't talk much about the breakup with Craig, but it obviously was hard on you."

She ran a finger along the seam of her jeans. "The hardest thing about Craig was that he cheated on me and humiliated me in front of everyone we worked with at Cowboy Country."

"Snake," Jake muttered. "I still wish you would have let me pay him a visit."

"Stop trying to sound like you're auditioning

for a gangster movie," she said with an affectionate chuckle. Although she and Jake might argue, there was no doubt her brother would do anything to protect her, and she appreciated his unwavering loyalty. "Wiley isn't like Craig."

"He's an attorney," Jake said with a derisive smirk. "If you look up the word in the dictionary, there might be a picture of a snake next to the definition."

"You have to trust me. Wiley isn't like that. He's honorable. I might not be able to adequately explain our connection or how instantaneous it was, but I know it doesn't have anything to do with my injury." Her gut tightened as she remembered Jillian's nasty comments about Wiley's motivations for being with Grace. She tried to put her rival's suspicions out of her head, chalking them up to jealousy or Jillian's attempts to undermine Grace's confidence.

"I do trust you. But the verdict's still out on the Fortune."

"Jake." As he pulled in front of her apartment building, Grace reached across the console and flicked his arm the way she used to do when they were kids. "Come on. Even Dad had a civil conversation with him a few days ago."

"I'm glad you're happy, Gracie." Her brother shrugged. "Can that be enough for now?"

"For now." She opened the car door and climbed out.

"I'd ask if you need help, but I already know the answer. Call or text if that changes."

"I will." Grace turned. "You're going to come to my event tomorrow, right?"

"The one where Fortunes will be crawling all over the place?" Jake grimaced.

"The one where you'll be supporting your favorite sister," Grace countered.

Jake gave a mock shudder but nodded. "I'll be there."

Grace waved as he pulled away, then headed upstairs. She wasn't going to win any sprinting contests with the boot, but it was a lot easier to manage the staircase without crutches. She checked her watch as she let herself into her apartment. The doctor's appointment had taken longer than she expected, so she only had an hour until Wiley was scheduled to arrive.

Her plan to go to the grocery store on her own for the first time since the accident so she could make him a proper home-cooked dinner would have to be saved for another night. Once again, she put aside thoughts of how few nights they might have left together. What would Wiley think if she proposed attempting to continue their relationship across the miles?

She got undressed, undid the Velcro straps on the walking boot and climbed into the shower as she considered that option. For her, a long-distance romance wouldn't be enough, but she'd be willing to try. Anything so that Wiley could remain a part of her life. He seemed to truly enjoy Rambling Rose, and she knew he loved spending more time with his siblings, so maybe he'd be in favor of visiting Texas on a more regular basis.

Hope and trepidation battled silently inside her at the thought of what their future might hold.

Her phone pinged as she came out of the bathroom, a series of texts from Callum with a minor crisis regarding the setup for tomorrow's event. Grace didn't hesitate to begin making calls and sending off messages from her laptop to mitigate any potential issues. A few months ago, she wasn't sure she would have had the confidence to take charge without an internal panic attack plaguing her. Her time in the training program and working toward the goal of the manager promotion had taught her a lot about herself and what she was capable of handling.

Unfortunately, when the knock sounded on her apartment door, Grace realized she'd lost track of time. Instead of putting on a nice outfit and hoping to impress Wiley before a potential next step in their relationship, she made her way to the door in a fuzzy polka-dot robe with her still-damp hair loose around her shoulders. She didn't even bother to put on a dab of lip gloss. What was the point? She'd messed up this night before it even started.

* * *

Wiley sucked in a breath and tried to control his rapidly beating heart when Grace smiled at him as she opened the door to her apartment.

He wasn't sure what he'd expected, but Grace in a soft bathrobe—and possibly nothing more—with her damp hair cascading over her shoulders and a pink glow tingeing her cheeks definitely was more than he bargained for.

"Sorry," she said immediately, taking a step back to let him enter. "I had to take care of something for tomorrow and lost track of—"

She let out a small yelp when he scooped her into his arms, kicking shut the door with one foot. He claimed her mouth with an urgency he hadn't realized he felt until that moment. The entire drive back from Austin, Wiley had been weighing in his mind the pros and cons of making a permanent move to Texas.

Was it too much? Too soon? Would he lose the independence and autonomy he'd carved out in his life like he was sculpting it from precious marble if he gave up his life in Chicago?

But seeing Grace made him understand in an instant that he wouldn't be giving up anything. In fact, it felt like he'd be moving toward something, claiming a future he hadn't imagined for himself. One that now felt like it was his destiny.

He wondered if the woman in his arms might be his destiny.

"You are beautiful," he told her as he trailed kisses along her neck. She smelled clean, like soap and lemons, a combination that had his senses reeling.

"I didn't even do my hair," she said with a laugh that quickly turned into a moan as he nipped at the sensitive place under her earlobe.

"Your hair is perfect," he said, sifting his fingers through the silky strands. "Tell me you aren't wearing anything under this robe."

He felt more than heard the hitch in her breath. "Nothing."

"Thank God," he murmured, then forced himself to pause. She wasn't trying to seduce him, he knew, or be purposely tempting the way some women would. Wiley wanted her all the more because of it.

But he also wanted to respect a pace that made her comfortable. Until he talked to his boss back in Chicago and the senior partners from Gavin's firm in Austin, he wasn't ready to discuss a potential move with her. He had to make sure everything was going to work out before he made any commitments or promises to Grace.

A little voice niggled at the corner of his mind, one that warned him love wasn't something he could control or put in a neat little box the way Wiley liked to do with the pieces of his life. But he shoved that warning into a dark corner. This was new territory for him, even being willing to consider a change in his life for another person. He wasn't quite ready to make the jump without knowing he had a solid place to land on the other side.

He would give her at least that same consideration. "Do you want to talk about the issue for tomorrow?" he asked as he put her down, then gripped her arms and shifted her away from him. The robe had loosened as they'd embraced, and he tried not to look at the expanse of soft skin he could see in the deep vee where it gaped.

She gave him a strange look, although her eyes were still cloudy with desire. "I handled it."

"Of course," he agreed. "How is your ankle?" He leaned down to take in the black walking boot that covered her leg from midcalf to foot. "Your text said the doctor thinks everything is healing properly?"

"Properly," she repeated, and he heard something in her tone that sounded like amusement. He couldn't figure out what was funny about the struggle to be a gentleman instead of continuing to ravish her the way he wanted to.

"Are you hungry?" He glanced over her shoulder toward the kitchen. She'd mentioned making dinner, but by the looks of the clean counters it seemed as though they might be going out. That was fine. He could wait to kiss her—and more. He could wait as long as needed.

"Wiley." She reached out and cupped his cheek

in her palm. He leaned in, soothed as always by her touch. "Did you hear the part where I said I'm naked under my robe?"

He swallowed and locked his knees as his legs suddenly went weak. "Yes."

"And your reaction is that you want to talk about the hotel event or my ankle or dinner?"

"I want to not take advantage of…" He licked his lips. "You lost track of time. The part about the robe…and you being…" Words abandoned him for a few moments as he struggled to retain control. "I don't want to rush you, Grace."

The corner of her mouth twitched, and he would have given anything to read her thoughts at the moment.

"I don't want to rush, either."

He felt his eyes go wide as she hooked her thumb in the robe's thick sash and undid it.

"In fact…" Her smile widened. "I hope that what comes next takes us all night." Then she pushed the robe off her shoulders.

Grace waited for Wiley's reaction to her bold move with her heart practically beating out of her chest. She wasn't normally one to make the first move—or any move—and certainly not to be assertive when it came to intimacy.

Her ex-boyfriend had been her first and only partner, and their intimacy had always been more about his pleasure than hers. She figured that was simply how it worked for a woman like her. As Craig had told her when she confronted him about his cheating, there were women men dated because they made good girlfriends and women men wanted because they were desirable.

He'd left no question that Grace fell into the former category.

But she wanted more from Wiley—with Wiley. She wanted more from herself and was quickly learning that the best way to achieve what she wanted was to take risks.

Standing naked in front of a man who looked like he belonged in some sort of catalog for genetic lottery winners, the lower part of one leg still encased in an orthopedic boot, definitely felt like a risk.

One she realized was worth it when Wiley's dark gaze traveled over her body, and his chest began to rise and fall in ragged breaths.

"I never expected..." He broke off, gave a small shake of his head and reached for her.

"Me, neither," she said against his mouth as he drew her close, his warm hands splayed across her bare back and bottom.

He muttered a curse low in his throat as he lifted her into his arms. "I can't wait," he said. "I want you so badly, Grace. I've wanted you since that first moment I saw you at the hotel."

She wrapped her arms tight around his neck, inhaling his scent as sensation swirled through her. She should feel vulnerable. After all, she was completely exposed while he remained fully dressed. But instead, she felt powerful in a way she didn't recognize. Like she was finally claiming a part of herself that had been waiting for her to realize it was important.

Wiley gave her the confidence to step into the woman she was meant to be.

He paused when he came to the door of her bedroom.

"I want you, too," she told him, brushing a kiss over his lips. "No more waiting, Wiley. We're in this together."

"Together," he repeated on a rush of air.

He pulled down the covers and placed her on the bed with exquisite care.

But when he reached for the strap of her boot, she placed her hand over his.

"You have too many clothes on," she told him with a smile.

"Easily remedied." He stood without hesitation, loosened his tie and then unbuttoned his shirt, pausing halfway through. "My fingers are shaking," he told her with an almost shy smile. "That's what you do to me."

Heat infused every part of her body at the thought of having an effect on this man.

Then her chest tightened as he continued to divest himself of his clothes, and Grace realized that they were truly taking the next step in their relationship. Sex meant something to her, and a moment of panic broke through the desire filling her brain, at the realization that she was embarking on this act with a man who might willingly walk away from her.

As he sat on the edge of the bed and placed a gentle hand on her booted leg, she realized it didn't matter. She might want more than they'd agreed to at the beginning of their time together, but she had to believe that he wanted it, too.

There might not be words yet, but the tenderness of his touch and the intensity of his gaze on hers were enough to make her trust that she was choosing the right path.

He undid the straps of the boot and slipped it off her leg. "Is this okay?" he asked softly, then bent to place a soft kiss on the top of her knee. "I don't want to hurt you, Grace. I'd never purposely hurt you."

"It's fine," she said, surprised when emotion clogged her throat. She didn't want to read more into his words. She knew he wouldn't hurt her deliberately, but she also understood that didn't mean she wouldn't end up with a broken heart.

But as his hand moved across her skin and he kissed a path up her body, nothing else mattered. He lavished attention on all the most sensitive parts of her, like he wanted to memorize her with his tongue and fingers.

"Stay still, sweetheart," he whispered against her. "We're going to be gentle with your ankle."

Gentle was the last thing on Grace's mind, but she did her best not to writhe under his kisses. It felt as though he was undoing her, desire thrumming through her like the crest of a wave. The pressure built inside her as he continued to explore her body, and minutes—or hours—later he drove her to the edge and over, and a cry broke from her lips.

Still it wasn't enough. As mind-blowing as her release had been, she wanted more. She wanted all of him. It might only be for now, the time he was in town, but Grace wouldn't consider that. All she knew was at this moment, they were meant to be together.

"Now, Wiley," she said. "I need you now."

"I'm here," he told her, and captured her mouth.

"More."

He pulled away and reached for his wallet on her nightstand and pulled out a condom. A few moments later he was poised between her legs, and Grace had never wanted anything more than she wanted this man inside her.

His hands were braced on either side of her head and he entered her in one long stroke. She breathed him in and then lifted her head to kiss him, needing to be joined with him as much as she could manage.

Her eyes drifted closed as the rhythm of their kiss synced with the motion of their bodies. They moved together like they were built for each other, and in some ways Grace wondered if that were the truth. Had she been made for this man? Had everything that had come before led to the moment when their eyes met across that crowded party?

Because she'd never been certain what her place in the world was, but there was no doubt she'd found where she belonged in Wiley Fortune's arms.

He whispered little nothings into her ear between kisses, his hands holding her like she was the most precious thing in the world to him. Passion skyrocketed inside her until it felt like electricity coursed through her veins. She wasn't certain how much more pleasure she could take. The depth of it was like nothing she'd ever experienced.

And then she fell over the cliff she'd been racing toward, her body dissolving as if it were made of champagne bubbles fizzing into the air. Her body tightened around Wiley and a few seconds later, he cried out her name.

It was the most amazing thing she'd ever heard. They might not have made promises to each other with words, but Grace had no doubt that his body had just pledged something to her that guaranteed she would never be the same.

Chapter Fourteen

"The timing couldn't be worse," Wiley muttered as he packed his suitcase the following morning.

Megan flopped onto his bed in the suite where he was staying at the ranch. He'd been as skeptical about the property as he had about his siblings settling in Rambling Rose when he'd first come to Texas. The idea of his brothers and sisters living together seemed like a recipe for disaster to Wiley, who had far too many memories of their bustling house growing up and never being able to get a moment's peace.

But the arrangement worked—surprisingly—in large part because the setup of the house allowed whoever was living there to have their own private space while still being under the same roof. He'd enjoyed reconnecting with his siblings on a daily basis, sharing coffee in the morning and whatever was on the menu for dinner.

The ranch employed a caretaker, who took care of most things, including meals, although Nicole and Megan took their turns in the kitchen because they found great pleasure in feeding the people they loved.

Wiley wondered if his memories of childhood weren't exactly accurate. Had he been the only one to feel stifled by their crowded, sometimes overbearing family? Or had he just been so committed to finding his own way and establishing an identity away from his successful stepfather and the rest of the family that he'd gone too far in the other direction?

"You'll be back for the grand opening though?" she asked, her tone sympathetic.

"Yes." He zipped shut the suitcase. "Well before that, I hope. I'm not sure exactly how the other associate botched the contract negotiations so badly. I'd given him everything he needed. Landing this client should have been a slam dunk."

"Obviously, your coworker doesn't have your level of skill," Megan said without a trace of sarcasm or irony. That was the other nice thing about family—even if they argued and teased, when the chips were down they had his back without question.

Right now he needed all the support he could get. He'd set his phone to silent when he and Grace went to bed last night and had woken this morning to a barrage of angry texts and messages from the firm's senior partner. Wiley had been leading a team over the last six months to land one of the biggest clients in their history. His extended stay in Texas had complicated the process, but he'd been diligent about conveying information to the associate who was the local point of contact in Chicago with their potential client. Much of Wiley's remote working had centered on this deal, which was set to close in two days. For some reason the client had pulled out without warning and no one at the firm could get a straight answer as to why.

He'd tried to convince his boss that he could handle the emergency from Texas, but the man gave him no choice. Hence, he was booked on a flight leaving early that afternoon.

Leaving today meant he'd miss Grace's preopening event, and he wanted to be there to watch her shine.

There had barely been time to say goodbye to her before he'd had to bolt from her apartment that morning, leaving her sleepy and rumpled in the bed. He couldn't believe how amazing it felt to finally make love to her, and he would have been happy to spend all weekend with her.

Wiley almost never spent extended periods of time with the women he dated, but as with everything, Grace broke the rules he'd set for relationships. He wanted her more for it.

He hadn't known when he'd left her that the work emergency was so dire that he'd be flying back to Chicago, and he wished he'd had time to call and explain it to her.

"I appreciate your vote of confidence," he said to his sister. "Just make sure to give my note to Grace, okay? I'm sure I'll talk to her before the reception, but I want her to have it."

Megan sat up on the bed and plucked the thin envelope from the nightstand. "I'd ask if you were with Grace last night, but she's staying at her parents', and I figure you've outgrown sneaking out of your girlfriends' windows so angry dads don't catch you."

He snorted. "Grace moved back to her apartment."

"Ah." Megan gave him a knowing smile.

"There's no 'ah,'" he muttered. "But I have to go. Just give her the note."

"I'll walk you out."

"No need."

"Sure there is." She followed him out of the room toward the front of the house. Everyone else was going about their daily business, so at least Wiley only had one sister to deal with. But one was more than enough. "You like Grace."

He tried to ignore the way his heart began to beat a staccato rhythm in his chest, telling him in no uncertain terms that he more than liked Grace.

"Everyone likes Grace. Don't you have somewhere to be?"

"Not at the moment. It's okay to fall for a woman, Wiley. Especially one as sweet as Grace Williams. You were bound to find the right one at some point. I think it's wonderful that you've found her in Rambling Rose."

He'd just gotten to the front door but paused with his hand on the knob. "It's not wonderful. I'm leaving before her big event today, and I'm going back to Chicago for good once the hotel opens." He wasn't ready to reveal his meeting with Gavin. What if things didn't work out and he disappointed his siblings as well as Grace? He looked toward his sister, figuring her pained expression mirrored his. "Tell me how that's anything but the opposite of wonderful."

"Oh, Wi."

"Why?" he repeated, purposely misinterpreting her shortening of his name. "That's exactly what I'm wondering at the moment."

"You know Chicago isn't the only city that employs attorneys," Megan told him, her voice gentle. "Even towns like Rambling Rose have need of them. You've done so much to help at the hotel so—"

"My time here is temporary." He walked out of the house and squinted against the bright light of morning. "Grace and I both know it. Hell, it's what we agreed to in the first place. I'm not even sure she'd want me for longer."

"Don't be ridiculous. Women fall all over themselves for you. They always have."

He hit the button on the key fob to open the trunk. "Grace doesn't." He couldn't help the smile that tugged at his lips thinking about the way she didn't let him off the hook about anything. "She's stronger than people give her credit for," he said as he stowed the suitcase. It was the same thing he'd told Callum and Nicole, but he'd never get sick of saying it. "Independent, too. She's already told me she wants to focus on her career."

"Here's a pro tip." Megan placed a hand on his arm. "Women can have careers and successful relationships. Look at Stephanie and Ashley. Don't sell Grace short."

"I'm not." He opened the door to the car. "I just told you I thought she was strong."

"And don't use her strength and independence as an excuse."

Wiley shook his head. "Since when did my baby sisters grow up and get so smart?"

"We've always been smart." Megan rolled her eyes. "Me in particular."

"I've got to go. Give Grace the note and please tell her I'll be thinking of her. I'll call as soon as I can."

"Have a safe trip." She blew him a kiss. "We'll expect you back here as soon as you can make it."

* * *

Grace smiled as another coworker came up and congratulated her on the success of the local business owners' reception. There was no doubt she'd exceeded everyone's expectations. She gave partial credit to the beautiful weekend weather. It was unseasonably warm for the last weekend of January, even by Texas standards, with temperatures hovering in the low seventies and a cloudless blue sky above them. Although the trees planted around the hotel's pool held no leaves, they'd been strung with party lights, giving the impression of stars twinkling when they caught the sunlight.

The other businesses owned by the Fortunes had come out in force, from Stephanie giving information on local rescue animals to the spa staff doing five-minute chair massages and offering samples of the products they used with their clients.

There had been a steady stream of local business owners who'd meandered through the booths and demonstration tents that she'd had set up along the patio's perimeter. Jillian and Jay had done a great job with the photos of the hotel's interior they'd displayed on easels. According to Jay, they'd taken over two dozen reservations for the special local employee weekend Grace had arranged, and even more people had filled out tickets for the raffle to win a romantic dinner for two at Roja. Every business owner she'd invited had agreed to be part of their local partnership.

Grace had no doubt this gesture of good will would go a long way to encouraging Rambling Rose business owners to feel a sense of pride in the hotel once it opened, which would be key to making sure that out-of-town guests had an unforgettable experience during their stay in town.

She was also happy that no one had asked her specifically about the rumor of sabotage that had initially swirled around the balcony collapse. Grace did her best to reassure people that the accident hadn't been as bad as some wanted to believe and that she'd healed without any lingering issues.

The only thing that marred her happiness was that Wiley wasn't there with her. She'd received a voice message and text from him earlier explaining that the work emergency that had forced him to rush from her apartment early this morning had turned into something even bigger and he had to return to Chicago for a few days.

The timing couldn't have been worse, and not just because it meant he was missing today's preopening reception. Last night had been one of the most amazing in Grace's life. She'd felt so close to Wiley, like their connection would last beyond his stay in town. For him to leave the way he did... Well, she didn't want to read anything into it but couldn't seem to stop herself.

He'd seemed to enjoy himself as much as she had, but in truth Grace didn't really have the experience to judge that. Was their night together a onetime thing of finally being able to scratch an itch that had plagued them both? Or could it be more? Was it the start to the next step in their relationship that she desperately wanted?

"You don't look like someone who is basking in the glow of her success."

Grace turned to find her friend Collin standing next to her. "You came," she said, and reached out to hug him. "What do you think?"

He glanced around, lifting his sunglasses from his nose so she could see his dark gaze. "I think the Fortunes are lucky to have you working for them," he said. "Everyone I've talked to is suddenly huge fans of the hotel."

"Were people not fans before today?" The suggestion genuinely confused Grace. She thought the locals had overcome their concerns about the hotel when the Fortunes had changed plans based on community feedback.

"No one was talking too publicly about your accident," he said gently. "But it's a small town. People were still talking. I get the sense that the local business leaders now see that the hotel won't just be good for the Fortunes. The fact that you're here looking happy and toeing the Fortune line gives them a lot more confidence that everything's well with the construction."

"It is," she assured him. "They still don't exactly

know why the balcony collapsed. But from now on, it's going to be all good news coming from the hotel."

"Like you earning the general manager position," Collin said with a wink. "No one can hold a candle to the partnerships you're creating here, Grace."

Pride bloomed in her chest at her old friend's compliment. "Do you think so?" she asked, biting down on her lower lip. "I really want that job."

"You're going to get it." He nudged her shoulder. "I have a feeling about it."

She laughed. "Then I'm going to trust your feeling. We'll have to celebrate when you come back to town."

He crossed his arms over his broad chest. "I'm not sure your special Fortune friend would want you and me celebrating together. I could tell Wiley wasn't a fan of our friendship."

"That's not true," she argued, although she remembered Wiley's reaction to finding Collin sitting with her on her parents' porch. At the time, she'd been charmed by the fact that he might be jealous of her childhood friend. She'd wanted to believe it meant he didn't like the thought of her dating other men. Not that she and Collin were dating, but that wasn't outside the realm of possibility.

"So where is your new man?" Collin made a show of glancing around. "It seems like I can't trip without falling over a Fortune at this event, but I haven't seen Wiley."

"He's not my man," Grace clarified. "We're friends."

Collin lifted a brow. "Like you and I are friends?"

"Not exactly." She did her best not to squirm. "But he's not here. He had to fly back to Chicago for work."

"With no warning?"

"It was an emergency."

"Must have been important if he took off the morning of your moment in the spotlight."

"This partnership plan isn't about me," Grace said, forcing a neutral tone. She wasn't about to let anyone know that it hurt that Wiley wasn't here. "The point was to draw positive attention to the hotel. We did that. Joint effort."

"Grace." Collin gave her a gentle elbow jab. "We've been friends for a long time. You don't have to pretend with me."

She waved to Mariana and Jay, who were standing with Callum on the far side of the pool, then blew out a breath and turned to face Collin. "I'm upset that he had to leave, okay? Does that make you happy?"

"You know it doesn't."

"I'm sure it really was an emergency," she said, as much to convince herself as Collin. "He seemed worried about whatever was going on with his firm."

"But he didn't share details with you?"

"No," she admitted. "He called as he was getting on the airplane, but I missed it. His message didn't tell me much." She glanced up at the blue sky overhead, then checked her watch. "He's probably in the air right now."

"I hope he gets it worked out quickly. If not and he hurts you, I'll kick his butt."

"You'll have to get in line behind Jake," she said. "Please don't mention this to him. He still doesn't trust Wiley or the Fortunes, and I don't want to give him any more reason to be a jerk."

"Your brother isn't a jerk," Collin reminded her. "He cares about you. Just like I do."

"I know." Grace gave Collin a hug before he walked away.

She turned back to the crowd to see Nicole, Ashley and Megan watching her. Ashley and Megan waved, but Nicole's attention seemed to be focused on Collin's retreating back. Strange, Grace thought. She didn't think her friend knew the Fortune sisters, but she figured there were plenty of things going on that she wasn't aware of thanks to her own busy schedule.

Just as she was about to turn away, Megan called her name.

"Hey, Grace," the slender blonde said as she approached. "You've done such an amazing job today. Everyone's talking about the hotel but also about the spa and Provisions. It's like the other business owners finally see we want to work with them and they're willing to give us more of chance to prove it."

"That's great." Grace smiled again but this time

noticed how the muscles in her face were beginning to feel sore. Her leg ached, and her lower back was stiff from standing for so long today. She wondered if she'd feel so tired if she had Wiley at her side, then chided herself for even feeling a hint of depending on him. She'd learned that lesson with Craig. Grace knew she could only depend on herself. She had to be her own number one priority, not expect any man to make her his.

Even if Wiley had given every impression that he was doing exactly that.

"Are you okay?" Megan asked, concern obvious in her tone.

"Of course. I'm happy today has gone so well. I know the grand opening is going to be a huge success. Every business we invited today has agreed to be part of the downtown partnership so that should garner even more positive word of mouth for the hotel. You and your siblings have done so much for Rambling Rose. I'm honored to be a part of it."

"I know we're all glad to have you on the team." Megan pulled a thin envelope out of her purse. "I'm sorry but with all the excitement today, I forgot to give this to you." She handed the envelope to Grace, who was surprised to see her name scrawled across the front.

"It's from Wiley," Megan explained. "He felt bad about having to take off this morning. I know he wanted to be here for you today."

"Oh." Grace took the envelope and held it between two fingers. The urge to tear it open was strong, but she didn't want to read the note in front of Wiley's sister. Her emotions were jumbled at the moment, and she might reveal too much about her feelings for the missing Fortune.

"Don't worry." Megan patted Grace's arm. "I told him he has to come back to help with the last-minute grand opening preparations. He's not getting off easy with us. He can go back to his fancy big-city life when the work here is done."

Grace smiled, because that's what the other woman obviously expected, but inside her heart cracked. Megan had given her exactly the reminder she needed that even if Wiley returned, his time in Rambling Rose—and with Grace—was coming to an end.

And so were Grace's secret dreams for any possible future between them.

Chapter Fifteen

Two days later, Wiley popped the last bite of a stale turkey sandwich into his mouth and washed it down with a swig of cold coffee.

He glanced at the clock on his phone, not surprised to find that it was nearing midnight. He'd been working around-the-clock since he'd landed in Chicago on Saturday afternoon.

In almost a decade of practicing law, there had never been a deal that had gone so far south so quickly. The associate who was supposed to be managing the client while Wiley handled the bigger contract stipulations had wound up getting himself and their potential client's twenty-one-year-old son arrested in a gentleman's club Friday night. It had been a stupid, thoughtless rookie mistake, especially considering Ron Burnett, the company's CEO, had built his business on a motto of "family values." Now the entire deal was in jeopardy.

To make matters worse for Wiley, his boss had fired the associate, Jon Kirchman, after threatening to have him disbarred, and the young associate had taken every paper file he had regarding the contract with him and deleted all of the electronic correspondence and documents.

Wiley had spent the past twenty-four hours in constant contact with the firm's technology specialist in an attempt to recover the data. He'd reached out to Jon, hoping to convince him to turn over his files, but there had been no response yet.

Although no one specifically blamed Wiley for the crisis, he couldn't help but think that things wouldn't have gone so far off the rails if he hadn't been trying to manage the project remotely.

He'd never given less than 110 percent to his career but had to admit now that he'd returned to the office that the past few weeks in Rambling Rose had put that dedication to the test.

"Burning the late-night oil, I see."

Wiley stifled a yawn as Derek Curtis entered his office. Derek was a year older than Wiley, and they'd been hired with the firm at approximately the same time. Wiley respected the other man's instincts for negotiating contract transactions, although Derek had a tendency to start each week a bit slow on the uptake, often coming off a weekend of partying.

"We have a meeting with Ron Burnett and his board tomorrow. They're going to make the final vote on new corporate counsel." Wiley tapped a finger on one of the stacks of files that he and the paralegal staff had compiled. "I'm trying to make up a lot of ground from the hole Jon left us in."

"I still can't believe the guy just took off when he got fired. Who does that?"

Wiley shook his head. "Someone who isn't planning to have a law career in Chicago anytime soon."

"You need any help?" Derek lowered himself into the chair on the other side of Wiley's desk.

"I think I've done everything I can. I hope it's enough."

"This isn't your fault," Derek reminded him.

"Why does it feel that way? If I'd been here to head up the deal instead of trying to manage it from Texas…"

"Tell me about Texas." Derek sat forward. "You never explained exactly why you extended your stay. When we talked before you headed down there, you were planning on doing the family duty stuff, then heading back as soon as possible."

"It ended up being important for me to help with a few things at my family's hotel."

"A few things? Legal issues?"

Wiley shrugged. He didn't really want to share details of his life in Texas. It felt so separate from his life in the city, and he had no doubt his coworker and sometime-friend wouldn't understand the appeal. "A construction accident."

"Was anyone hurt?"

"One of the employees broke her ankle."

"Ouch." Derek whistled under his breath. "Sounds like a workers' comp lawsuit waiting to happen. You're making sure to cover your a—"

"Grace isn't going to sue the hotel," he said through clenched teeth.

"How do you know?" Derek shook his head. "I once saw a guy trip over his own two feet on a building site and then sue for six figures."

"I know her," Wiley said, then immediately regretted the words based on the smile Derek gave him.

"Is that so? Smart move, Counselor."

"It's not like that. We're friends."

Derek chuckled. "I get it."

"No, you don't." Wiley couldn't decide whether the exhaustion of working so many hours or the stress of the deal or simply missing Grace so badly was making him want to stand up and punch his colleague in the face. Maybe a combination of all those things.

"Come on, don't get bent out of shape," Derek said. "I've heard how you talk about your family, even if you don't see them a lot. We both know you're going to protect blood over some piece of—"

"Stop talking." Wiley pushed back from his desk. "Grace isn't going to come after the hotel, and I'm not friends with her for any other reason than I like spending time with her."

"But it's not serious, right?" Derek leaned back in his chair, and Wiley had the secret wish that he'd topple backward. "I know you, Wiley. You don't do serious. We're the same. Relationships are a distraction and never worth the trouble. You know that."

Wiley stared at the other attorney.

Derek gestured to the papers piled all over the desk. "If nothing else, the situation you're in now proves it. The reason you stayed in Texas was a chick, and look at what it's led to. You could lose everything you've worked for over one deal that wasn't managed right."

"I'm not going to lose anything," Wiley said, although he knew Derek was right. Wiley had taken his eye off the ball, and now he was struggling to make sure he kept it in the air.

"Let me know if you need help," Derek offered again as he rose from the chair. "My focus is right where it needs to be. Always."

"Thanks," Wiley muttered, then sank back down in his chair as the other man disappeared into the hall. He shut down his computer and began to pack up his briefcase. The rest of what needed to be reviewed before tomorrow could be handled in the morning. Right now, he needed a few hours of rest to get his head on straight again.

He didn't want to admit that Grace had been the reason he'd prolonged his stay in Rambling Rose or that his preoccupation with her had affected his work. He'd continued to manage his clients and his job from the tiny Texas town. More importantly, he'd been able to reconnect with his brothers and sisters. That was worth more than anything else.

Although perhaps not more than the career he'd dedicated the last ten years of his life to.

He had to keep focused now. Get through tomorrow and land the client, then he could think about what came next. He was supposed to meet with the senior partners at his cousin's firm in Austin in a couple of days, but Wiley wasn't even sure what he wanted now. Could he really close the biggest deal of his life and then walk away to start over halfway across the country?

His brother and sisters had made it work, but he'd always been different. The odd Fortune out, so to speak. What would happen if he tried to start over?

What would happen if he told Grace the truth about his feelings for her?

As he flipped off the light to his office, his phone buzzed with an incoming text. A message from Grace. Simple, to the point, and the words utterly gutted him.

I miss you.

How could one simple sentence possibly convey so much?

His heart seemed to skip a beat as he ran a thumb over the smooth screen, as if he could somehow reach out and touch her across the miles.

He gave his head a hard shake and pocketed the phone. As much as he wanted to respond or to call her, he'd promised himself that his focus would remain on work until he salvaged the deal with Ron and his company. The firm was counting on him, and he already felt as if he'd let them down.

Grace knew how he felt about her. She would wait. He had to take care of his current life if he was going to truly choose a future with her.

"I think we're nearly there," Nicole announced as she placed plates filled with roasted chicken and Brie over pasta on the table in front of Grace, Jillian and Jay.

"Everything we make is delicious," Mariana said with a genuine smile as she poured sparkling lemonade into their glasses.

"Some of the best food I've ever eaten." Jay scooped another huge bite of chicken into his mouth. "Seriously the best."

"Not that you probably have much to compare it

to," Jillian said with a delicate sniff. "I've actually traveled to both London and Paris."

Jay gave a haughty sniff. "Well, la-di-da then," he said, his Southern accent especially thick.

Grace pressed a napkin to her mouth to hide her giggle. "I'm certain Jay has a very discriminating palate," she said, wanting to be loyal to her friend in the face of Jillian's snobbery.

"Very," he agreed with mock severity, then winked at Grace.

She grinned and took a bite of the pasta, which truly was delicious. Mariana and Nicole discussed the dish as a potential winter season special while the three trainees enjoyed their lunch.

Nicole was continuing to refine the Roja menu with the grand opening around the corner. Her attention to detail and understanding of how to meld flavors together to showcase a variety of refined but still comforting foods amazed Grace. She had no doubt that the restaurant was going to be a huge success and bolster the hotel's reputation.

Jillian and Jay continued to banter back and forth. It amused Grace to no end how much Jay seemed to enjoy irritating their uptight coworker. He might joke about his country roots while Jillian took great pleasure in giving him grief over his lack of worldliness, but there was something more to Jay Cross. Beyond his easygoing manner, Grace sensed a depth of experience he didn't want to share, so she never pushed him to reveal what had led him to Rambling Rose in the first place.

She understood the desire to make a fresh start without the past coloring every step.

Something caught her attention, and she turned in her seat to see Wiley entering the restaurant. He'd been gone almost a week. In that short time her emotions had run the gamut from disappointment to anger to heartbreak to resignation. Grace wanted to believe she'd settled on acceptance, especially when they'd barely spoken on the phone and he'd only sent a few short texts that told her no details of the emergency that forced him to leave so suddenly and when he would return.

Her brain might have taken the hint about him walking—or literally running—away the morning after making love to her, but her body hadn't gotten the message. Not when he looked as handsome as ever in a dark sweater and jeans with cowboy boots that finally appeared to be broken in. Like he belonged in Texas and in her world, although his absence this week had told her that wasn't true.

Grace had been thrown back into the same emotional turmoil she'd felt after her breakup with Craig. Of course it was different with Wiley, because he hadn't cheated on her or made her any promises about the future. Somehow that only made her heart hurt more.

She'd told herself after returning to town that she

was going to focus on herself and not let anything distract her from her goals. Instead, she'd spent the past few days making excuses to go to the bathroom at the hotel and fight back tears. Everything about her daily life reminded her of Wiley. The way she'd looked forward to seeing him in the hall, to stealing kisses in the office and to spending her evenings in his arms.

The Hotel Fortune had been her chance at a brand-new life, but she couldn't even walk into the lobby without thinking of Wiley. It had gotten so bad that she'd actually considered quitting her job and leaving Rambling Rose to reinvent herself again in a place that held no emotional pull for her.

It had been Collin who'd talked her off that ledge, reminding her that this was her home and she belonged here as much as any member of the Fortune family. Everything had made sense when Wiley wasn't nearby, but watching him walk toward the table, his gaze intense on her, her thoughts and feelings scattered like dandelion fluff in a strong wind.

"You're back," Nicole called to her brother as she turned.

Grace hated the jealousy that stabbed at her heart when Nicole gave him a huge hug. Grace yearned to touch him, but she had no right. They'd agreed to date secretly—her plan—but it hadn't been nearly enough. She wanted more. More than she should and likely more than Wiley was capable of giving her. It was time to remember that.

"Something smells amazing," he said.

"Your sister has outdone herself with this dish." Mariana came to stand next to Jay's chair. "We have three discerning customers right here." She patted Jay's shoulder. "If an empty plate is any indication, Roja is ready for business."

"I have no doubt," Wiley said, offering his sister a proud smile. "Any chance you have leftovers? I haven't had a decent meal in what feels like days. I've been living off takeout the entire trip."

Grace tamped down her sympathy. Now that she looked at him more closely, she could see the lines of exhaustion fanning out from his dark eyes and bracketing his mouth. It only made her want to pull him to her and offer whatever comfort she could.

Stupid, she reminded herself. She wasn't a love-sick schoolgirl anymore. The man had made it clear where his priorities were, and she needed to do the same.

As if reading her thoughts, Nicole pushed away and wagged a finger in front of Wiley. "I shouldn't give you even a bite. I forgot that I'm mad at you. You practically ghosted us this week. We didn't even know if you were coming back before the opening."

"Of course I was coming back." He looked genuinely surprised. "I told you I'd be here to help."

"Give your brother a break," Mariana said with a

gentle tsk. "He's here now." Her knowing gaze met Grace's across the table. "When the three of you are finished here, I'd love to get your thoughts on some of the grand opening events."

Grace pushed back from the table. "I actually have a meeting scheduled with Ellie to finalize plans to put a link for the hotel on the town's website."

"Smart plan." Nicole gave her an enthusiastic thumbs-up.

Jillian's lips pursed but she didn't say anything or try to one-up Grace, which made Grace suspicious. "Jay and I can take care of whatever Mariana needs," Jillian offered, then rolled her eyes when Grace gave her a shocked look.

Grace could feel Wiley's gaze on her but purposely didn't make eye contact with him. If Jillian was being nice enough to give her an out, Grace must not be doing as good a job at hiding her feelings as she hoped.

She thanked Nicole and Mariana for lunch, then hurried from the restaurant and out the hotel's front entrance, not even bothering to grab her purse from the office. She needed fresh air and a few minutes to gather her thoughts.

Wiley was back. She shouldn't be surprised. He had told her—and clearly his siblings—that he planned to return before the opening.

She just wished she could turn off her feelings for him as easily as he seemed to be able to manage it.

The afternoon was cloudy, and a brisk breeze whipped down the town's main street, making her regret the choice to rush out without a jacket. At least the cool air felt good on her heated skin.

"Grace."

Her stomach pitched and tumbled at the sound of Wiley's voice behind her. She turned, forcing a bland smile on her face as he jogged toward her.

"Hi," he said, and lifted his hand as if to reach for her but then lowered it again. He searched her face as if he couldn't quite understand why she wasn't greeting him with more enthusiasm, but Grace had finally gotten her body and heart under control, even though it felt like it was shattering inside her chest.

"How was your trip home?" She crossed her arms over her chest.

"Home," he repeated with a frown. "You mean back to Chicago?"

"Your home," she said, nodding. "I hope it was productive."

"We closed the deal. The firm is now the counsel for the largest plexiglass manufacturer in the US."

"Congratulations." Grace made a show of checking her watch. "I need to go. I don't want to be late for my appointment with Ellie."

"I'll walk with you," he offered.

"No."

His frown deepened. "What's wrong, Grace? Is

it your leg? Are you doing too much? If you need a break, I can talk to—"

She held up a hand, hating that her body responded to his offer of support. Hating that she didn't trust that he wasn't being kind to make certain she didn't cause trouble for his family. As much as she wanted to deny Jake's suspicions about Wiley's motives, his lack of communication had made her doubt everything she felt for him.

"I don't need you to talk to anyone on my behalf. I can manage my life and my career on my own, Wiley. I've been handling things just fine without you here."

"I know you can manage on your own," he said gently. "But I want to help, Grace. I care about you."

"Right." She bit off the word and forced her voice not to tremble. "We're friends."

"More than friends."

"Friends," she repeated, because if she allowed herself to entertain the thought of more, she'd be a goner for sure. "That's all."

"I don't understand. I missed you, Grace. Every moment away from you was—"

"Don't." *Don't say sweet things. Don't look at me with confusion and pain in your eyes.*

She swallowed, knowing she needed to be able to mutter more than one-syllable words at him. She needed to end this. The torture of being so close and yet feeling so far away from what she wanted her life to be. "I had some time to think about the future while you were gone, Wiley. I wasn't distracted by—" she waved a hand in his general direction "—by anything. The truth is we agreed what was between us would be temporary, and it's better that it end sooner rather than later."

A muscle jumped in jaw. "Better for whom?"

"Me," she whispered. "Both of us, I'm guessing, but I have to think about myself and my future. I can't... I won't put you ahead of me. Do you understand that?"

He shook his head. "I don't understand anything apparently."

"We're friends," she repeated. "That's all we were ever meant to be."

He stared at her long and hard like he wanted to argue. A piece of her wanted him to argue. She wanted him to fight for her, but she should have known better. Grace wasn't the type of woman that men fought for. She was a woman who fit herself into the compartment the people in her life needed her to be in.

But no more.

"Welcome back, Wiley. I'm sure your brothers and sisters will be thrilled to have you here again."

Without waiting for his response, she turned and walked away.

Chapter Sixteen

"I'm mad at you."

Wiley continued to stare at the basketball game playing on the television of the sitting room in his suite at the ranch, ignoring his sister's arrival.

"Really mad," Nicole said, walking into the room and picking up the remote from the side table. She pushed a button, and the TV went dark.

"Big brothers are supposed to make sisters mad," Wiley said. "It's part of the job description."

"Do you want to know why?" She sat on the chair next to the sofa.

"Not really." He took a long pull on the beer he'd been nursing for the past hour. "You know I was watching that game?"

"What was the score?" she demanded.

He shrugged. "One of the teams was winning."

Nicole's mouth curved into a smile. "Yeah, you were real invested in the game, Wi. Seriously, we need to talk."

"Not in the mood," he told her. Since Grace had basically broken off their temporary relationship in the middle of the street two days ago, Wiley hadn't been in the mood for anything. He'd kept himself busy and tried not to think about Grace, which was virtually impossible, especially when she seemed to be involved in almost every last-minute detail of the hotel's grand opening.

He'd found himself following her scent through an upstairs hallway yesterday until he'd heard her voice in one of the guest rooms, discussing something with Jillian and Jay. Wiley had ducked into a housekeeping closet when they came out to avoid being spotted. As he stared at shelves filled with crisp white linens and tiny bottles of toiletries, he'd realized how bad off he was with missing her.

Unlike him, Grace didn't seem the least bit affected by their breakup, if that's what he could call it. She appeared completely focused on making sure the grand opening went off without a hitch. Despite his heartache, he was so proud of her for the leadership role she'd taken on and the way her confidence had bloomed. He only wished he could share in the success with her.

"What did you do to Grace?"

Wiley sucked in a breath as he straightened. "Nothing. Not one damn thing, Nicole."

"It's obvious she's hurting."

"Not to me," he countered.

"Then you're a bigger fool than I suspected. Even Jillian is being nice, so you know Grace must be really upset. I thought you liked her."

"I did. I do."

"Then why dump her, Wiley? Especially right before the opening. I understand that commitment isn't your thing and being back in Chicago probably had you missing the city, but—"

"You have it wrong." He pointed the tip of his bottle toward his sister. "I was the dumpee in this situation. Grace broke up with me."

"Impossible," Nicole said immediately. "Women don't break up with you."

"I guess there's a first time for everything."

"What did you do?"

He placed the beer bottle on the coffee table with distinct thud. "Nothing."

His sister's blue eyes narrowed. "Are you sure?"

"How could I have done anything?" He lifted his hands, palms up, and didn't bother to hide his frustration. "I was working around-the-clock in Chicago to salvage the deal. There was no time for anything, not that I would have wanted it, anyway. I missed her."

"Did you tell her that?"

He nodded. "Right in front of the hotel when I got back. Just before she cut me off at the knees."

"And she gave no indication of being unhappy while you were away?"

"I don't know, Nicole. I was away. Maybe her brother convinced her not to trust me. Maybe she realized she doesn't want to deal with the complications of our family."

"Grace isn't the type to shy away from things that are hard," Nicole reminded him. "In fact, we all keep forgetting she's wearing the boot, because she doesn't let it slow her down one bit."

"She's amazing," he murmured. "Probably too smart to want something long-term with me."

"I don't believe that." Nicole tapped a finger against her chin. "You two were the worst-kept secret in town. Everyone could see she was crazy about you. Did she say anything when you talked to her during your trip that would give you a clue—"

"We didn't talk while I was gone."

Nicole's mouth dropped open. "You were in Chicago for nearly a week."

"I'm aware."

"How could you not talk to her?"

He shrugged. "It wasn't purposeful. I was busy."

"Not an excuse."

Agitation rolled through Wiley like a tidal wave. He didn't want to think that he was at fault. How could that be? No, he hadn't told Grace how he felt before he left. But she had to know, or at least have an idea. He'd never devoted so much of himself to a woman before. In fact, it had scared the hell out of him, especially when he returned to Chicago and saw the mess his firm had almost ended up in because he'd been distracted by his family and Grace while in Texas. Guilt had eaten at him, which was part of the reason he hadn't done the best job of communicating while he was away. But still…

He stood from the sofa and paced to the edge of the room. No way would he believe that he was the reason she'd broken things off. That simply couldn't be the case.

"I did call, Nicole. Or I tried." He heard the edge in his voice but regaining control was the last thing on his mind. He had to understand why she'd ended things between them. He had to know if there was a chance at winning her back. "We had trouble connecting because of how much I was at the office. It wasn't like I slept with her and then took off without a backward glance." He cringed when Nicole sucked in a harsh gasp, realizing exactly what he'd just blurted. Wiley would give anything if he could take the last ten seconds back.

"You slept with her?" Nicole moved to the edge of the seat, looking like their mother used to when she wanted to throttle one of the boys for making a stupid mistake.

"Forget I said anything." He shook his head. "I'm not thinking clearly, obviously. I shouldn't have—"

"She's our employee," Nicole reminded him through clenched teeth.

"Yours," Wiley countered. "Not mine. My relationship with her has nothing to do with the hotel."

"Does she know that?"

He opened his mouth to answer then shut it again.

Nicole's eyes widened. "Did she tell you about her ex-boyfriend?"

"The one who cheated on her?" Wiley nodded. "That has nothing to do with me, either."

"How much did she share about their breakup?"

"She didn't need to explain much. He cheated. End of story."

"Wiley."

"Stop sounding like Mom," he told her. "Your tone is freaking me out."

"I did Grace's reference check at Cowboy Country," Nicole said quietly. "The story she gave me about how things ended there was a little convoluted. I spoke with her boss in Horseback Hollow. Grace was an exemplary employee, just like she is for us. But when she discovered that her boyfriend was cheating on her with another coworker, there was a bit of a scene."

"What kind of a scene?" Wiley asked, even though he wasn't sure he wanted to know the answer.

"I only heard the details because the amusement

park manager felt bad for Grace and wanted her to get the position in the training program. Apparently, the whole thing blew up at an employee picnic. The ex very loudly blamed Grace. He made it known that he was cheating because Grace lacked—" she made a face "—spark in the bedroom."

Wiley breathed out a string of curses that would have horrified his mother. "She doesn't lack spark. Grace is the sparkliest damn woman I've ever known."

"Too much information." Nicole stood, making a show of covering her ears. "I don't want to talk about you and Grace and sparks. But think of the timing, Wi. The two of you…" She shrugged. "Took things to the next level and then you left town and didn't call her."

"I called. We just didn't get to talk." He cursed again because he hated knowing that he'd made Grace doubt anything about herself. Making love to her had been the most wonderful time of his life. Not that he had any intention of discussing details with his sister.

"Maybe you should try talking to her again," Nicole suggested gently. "If you really care about her."

"I care." He ran a hand through his hair. "I more than care about her."

"You can say the word." Nicole crossed to him and patted his arm. "It won't burn your tongue to speak it out loud."

"It might," he muttered, then sighed. "I love her, Nicole. I'm *in* love with her. I didn't expect it, and I'm not sure I want it."

His sister squealed with delight. "I knew it. We all knew it. Ashley, Megan and I knew it before you did. We're so much smarter than you."

He pulled away, although he couldn't help the way his mouth curved. "Why do you all have to keep pointing it out? I should mention it's annoying. If you're finished gloating, can we talk about how I'm going to fix this?"

"Do you *want* to fix it?"

He thought about it for a long moment. Although he expected panic to rise up inside him, instead he felt a sense of peace settle in his chest. "Yes."

She inclined her head. "Why do I think there's a 'but' coming?"

"More like an 'and,'" he admitted. "I need to figure some things out. I haven't done a great job of making her feel like she's a priority for me, and Grace deserves that. I want to give her that, Nic. I don't want to mess it up."

"What if Grace says no? Will you go back to Chicago?"

He shook his head. "My time in the city is finished. No matter what happens with Grace, I'm moving to Texas. Our big, crazy family used to feel like something I needed to escape. It didn't feel like I could have my own life when I was just one of the Fortune brothers."

"You've always been more than that," his sister said quietly.

"Took me a bit of time to realize it." He grinned at her. "It really grates on my nerves that my baby sisters are so smart, but you're right. I've had a great life in Chicago, but it's never been home. Home is where family is, and I want to put down roots in Texas. I want this place to be my home."

Grace climbed the stairs leading to Roja's banquet room on Tuesday morning, trying hard to control the nerves fluttering through her chest.

Callum had texted her last night, asking her to arrive at the hotel early the following morning for a private meeting. With less than a week until the grand opening, she couldn't imagine why the head of Fortune Brothers Construction would want to take time out of his busy schedule to meet with her, unless he'd found out about her relationship with Wiley.

After their breakup, Grace had done her best to go back to business as usual at work. It wasn't easy, because her body and her heart seemed tuned in to his presence like a radio dial. If he was anywhere nearby, awareness shivered across her skin, and it was difficult to draw a steady breath.

Yesterday she'd overheard Nicole tell Mariana that Wiley had gone to Austin for business. Of course, it was silly for Grace to be disappointed that he hadn't said goodbye to her. She'd told him she just wanted to be friends, but they both knew they couldn't go back to simple friendship after what they'd shared.

She'd walked away before she was tempted to ask Nicole how long he'd be gone and what his plans for the future were. Anything Grace heard was bound to hurt, since she understood his future wouldn't involve her.

The timing of this meeting seemed a bit of a coincidence, and part of her feared that the Fortunes would blame her for Wiley leaving again. She knew he would never try to put her in a bad position or do anything that might jeopardize her job, but after the way things ended in Horseback Hollow, it was difficult for her to trust that. She'd thought her future at Cowboy Country was secure until Craig had publicly humiliated her.

Her anxiety went into overdrive when she turned to find Callum seated at a banquet table along with Nicole and Kane. It felt like Grace was facing the Fortune tribunal.

"Good morning," she said, clearing her throat when the words came out sounding like a croak.

"Hey, Grace." Callum and his cousin stood as she approached. "How are you doing?" Callum glanced at her leg. "Damn, I'm sorry. I figured there'd be more privacy up here, but we probably should have met downstairs. I keep forgetting about your injury."

"It's fine," Grace assured him. "The walking boot makes it relatively easy to get around, and I'm slow on steps, but I can manage."

"Of course you can," Kane agreed with a chuckle. "These past few weeks have proven that you can manage just about anything."

Except holding on to Wiley, she thought to herself. "Thanks," she answered Kane. "What can I do for all of you today?"

Nicole offered a kind smile and gestured to the seat across from them. "Let's talk for a few minutes."

Grace's heart sank, and she wanted to run in the other direction. That's exactly how the conversation with her bosses at the amusement park had begun, during which it had become painfully obvious that the best course of action for everyone would be her resignation.

She did not want to give up her future at the hotel. An image of Wiley flashed in her mind. Would she walk away from the Fortunes if it meant another chance with him? Probably, although that might make her a fool. She'd never felt anything like she did when she was with Wiley. Regret made her chest pinch, and she wondered for the millionth time if she'd given up on him too easily.

Slipping into the chair, she kept her hands clasped tightly in front of her. "Is there a problem with last-minute details for the opening?"

Nicole shook her head. "Everything is right on

schedule. You, Jillian and Jay have done an incredible job."

"Far surpassed our expectations," Callum added.

"I'm glad." Grace forced a smile. "So what I am doing here?"

"The plan had been to choose the employee who would be promoted to the general manager position after the grand opening," Nicole explained. "It made sense to get through this last push and then focus on the future."

Grace nodded.

"But recent events have made us rethink the timing of our announcement." Callum inclined his head. "We want to show stability, to make sure that people understand we have things well under control at the Hotel Fortune."

"We're moving forward and expecting nothing but good things." Kane glanced behind him at the doors that led to the balcony.

The balcony that had collapsed with Grace on it.

"Okay." Grace's cheeks started to throb as she tried to keep her smile in place. Recent events? They had to be talking about her accident, and it felt as though her fall from the second floor was a metaphor for her life. Just when she thought she had time to pause and enjoy the view, she went tumbling off the edge. She should have known this would happen. Of course they wouldn't choose her for the general manager position. She was the physical representation of a public relations nightmare. The Fortunes would be smart to promote someone who was untarnished by any scandal. Jillian fit that bill without—

"What do you think, Grace?"

She blinked as Callum leaned forward, giving her an odd look, and she tried to catch up with the thread of the conversation.

"I think it's a wise decision."

His mouth twitched. "Then you're accepting the position?"

She blinked. "I think I missed something."

Nicole laughed. "He just offered you the general manager job."

"Oh." Grace sucked in a shallow breath. "I thought you were telling me I wasn't a fit because of the accident. I'm bad PR."

"On the contrary," Callum told her. "You've done more to bolster the hotel's image in town than we could have imagined. The partnership with the local businesses is going to be integral to our reputation as we open."

"Thank you," she whispered. "I'd be honored to accept the promotion. But…" She bit down on the inside of her cheek as she tried to determine the best way to share this next bit.

Kane sighed. "I hate a 'but.'"

"What is it?" Nicole asked gently, placing her hand on her cousin's beefy arm.

"I'm in love with your brother," she said, and Kane choked on the sip of water he'd just taken.

"Which one?"

"She's talking about our brother," Nicole clarified. "Wiley. You love Wiley."

"Yes." Grace nodded. "But we broke up."

Callum's mouth dropped open. "You were dating Wiley?"

"Get with the program," Nicole said, swatting his arm.

"What did he do?" Kane demanded. "Do I need to kill him?"

Grace almost laughed at the absurdity of that statement. "No, of course not. He didn't do anything. I just chose… My priority is the hotel. I want you to know that. I don't want there to be any doubts."

"You can have both," Callum said, as if it were the simplest thing in the world.

Grace squeezed her eyes shut for a moment, then opened them again. She could be the biggest idiot in the world for revealing all of this in a meeting where she was being offered her dream job. "That hasn't worked so well for me in the past."

"Wiley isn't him," Nicole told her with so much understanding that it felt like Grace's heart might break all over again.

"Who?" Kane and Callum asked in unison.

"I know." Grace kept her gaze focused on Wiley's sister. "I just wanted you to know where things stood.

It's meant a lot to Wiley to reconnect with all of you. As much as I'm looking forward to a long career at the hotel, it won't be at the expense of his relationship with his family."

Nicole leaned forward. "Are you saying you'd give up the promotion if he wasn't comfortable with you working here?"

Was that what Grace was telling them? How was that possible? The general manager job was everything she'd wanted for her life and a vindication of what she'd been through in Horseback Hollow. Wiley hadn't given her the impression that he wanted her to forgo her dream for him. Not once. He'd only been supportive and proud as she dedicated herself to her job.

But she knew how important his family was and understood the toll that feeling distanced from them had taken on him. She wouldn't be a part of that.

"Yes." The pain she expected at saying the word didn't materialize. Instead, she felt as if her world had stopped spinning and righted itself in a way that put her exactly where she wanted to be.

"That's ridiculous." Callum shook his head. "Wiley is a grown damn man. You're important to the hotel. To our family. He'll deal."

"But if not—"

"Thank you, Grace," Nicole said. "You've proven even more why you're the right person for this job.

We appreciate your loyalty and look forward to many years of you being part of Team Fortune."

"Really?" Grace swallowed. "I mean, that's what I want, as well." She pushed back from the table. "Just know that I have the best interests of the hotel at the forefront of my mind. Always."

"We know." Nicole stood and then came around the table to hug her. "And we appreciate it. We'll talk to Jillian and Jay as well and then plan to make the big announcement to the staff. Congratulations."

Chapter Seventeen

"Oh, hell, no."

"Hi, Jake." Wiley stepped out onto the path in front of Grace's brother, ignoring his less-than-cordial greeting. "Mind if I join you?"

Jake didn't break stride as he ran past Wiley on the dirt trail that wound through one of the local parks. "If you can keep up, Wyatt."

Wiley also didn't correct the mistake of his name. He simply ran alongside the other man, grateful for his almost-daily runs along Lake Michigan when he'd lived in Chicago. Jake set one hell of a pace.

They did a fast loop around the park's perimeter, passing a few families and slower joggers. The exercise actually helped to clear Wiley's jumbled thoughts. He was clear about what he wanted, but how to convince Grace's recalcitrant brother that his intentions were honorable was another story.

"We need to talk about your sister," Wiley said, huffing for breath, as they approached the parking lot where the trail ended.

"You hurt her," Jake said, and then bent at the waist. At least Wiley wasn't the only one sucking wind, a small consolation when it felt as though his lungs were on fire.

"I want to make it right. I love her."

Jake glanced up at him, a sneer curling one side of his mouth. "You don't have to say that. She's not going to come after your precious family and the hotel. Even if they wouldn't have handed her the promotion she—"

"Grace earning the general manager position had nothing to do with her injury." Wiley placed his hands on his hips and drew in big gulps of air, struggling to keep the temper out of his voice. He was here to win Jake over to his side, not to antagonize him further. But Wiley couldn't tolerate the suggestion that Grace had been offered the manager role at the hotel for any other reason than she deserved it.

"I know she's qualified," her brother conceded. "But even you have to admit—"

"I don't have to admit anything. Grace worked her butt off, both before and after the accident. She's a huge asset to the hotel, and everyone in my family sees that. We're not the ones selling her short."

Jake straightened. "What's that supposed to mean?"

"Why are you so hell-bent on convincing her that she can't make it on her own?"

"I'm not—"

"How do you think it makes her feel when her family is constantly telling her that the reason she's being recognized has more to do with her injury than her talent and skills?" For the moment, Wiley put aside trying to smooth the waters with Grace's brother. He couldn't stand to listen to one more suggestion that she was anything less than fully capable on her own.

"We don't do that."

"Are you sure? Because that's how it sounds to me. I fell in love with your sister and not because I was trying to protect my family or any other sort of cheap attorney tricks you might want to accuse me of. The fact is she's the most amazing woman I know. She's smart, strong and creative. She doesn't give up or give in, and we both know how big her heart is. She'd do anything for the people she loves."

Jake stared at him for several long moments, then looked away. "Did your brother or sister mention that Grace told them she wouldn't take the promotion if it upset you to have her at the hotel?"

"Yeah." Wiley kicked a small rock with the toe of

one sneaker, sending it skittering across the grass. "I would never let that happen, and neither would they. I want another chance with Grace, but it's her choice. If she's truly moved on from me, I'll respect the decision. Her place at the hotel is secure, and my brothers and sisters would never treat her unfairly."

"I know."

"In fact—" Wiley broke off as he tried to digest those two words coming from Jake. He was ready to argue as long as he needed to in order to convince her brother that his family had Grace's interests at heart. "You know what?"

"I'm not fully sold on the Fortunes," Jake said, wiping a sleeve across his forehead. "Trusting people outside my close circle of friends and family...well, it's been a struggle since the accident. Grace gave up a lot to come home and help during my recovery."

"She told me about that time," Wiley said. "I know she was happy to have the chance to pitch in and remains grateful that everything turned out okay for you."

"She's the best." Jake flashed a rueful smile. "We can agree on that."

"Yeah."

"And even though you aren't the man I'd choose for her, you're the one she's chosen."

Wiley mulled that over for a few seconds, then chuckled. "I can't decide if that's a compliment or an insult."

Jake's grin widened. "We'll call it a compliment. My sister deserves to be happy more than any person I know. If you make her happy, that's good enough for me."

"I appreciate that, Jake." Wiley held out a hand, and the other man shook it. "Family is important to Grace and to me. I want us to get along. You can believe me when I tell you I'll do my best to make her happy every day if she gives me another chance."

"I believe you, Fortune." Jake nodded. "You should know that if you ever hurt her, I'll be there."

Wiley shook his head. "Don't worry about that. You'll have to get in line behind most of my siblings. But all of this is moot if I can't convince her to try again. To be honest, I've never had to work very hard with women. That's another thing I love about your sister. She makes me want to try."

"What you need is a plan," Jake said, clapping Wiley on the shoulder as they headed toward their cars. "Grace is used to being the one to put in the effort. I think your willingness to try will go a long way."

"I hope it goes far enough," Wiley murmured, then stopped walking as an idea popped into his head. He turned to face Grace's brother, an unexpected ally but the perfect one for what Wiley wanted to accomplish. "And I hope that you'll help me make sure it does."

* * *

"Jake, are you sure we can't just get him something from the hardware store in town?" Grace drummed her fingers against her jeans and tried not to sound as impatient as she felt. Her brother had asked her to drive with him to pick up a gift for their dad's upcoming birthday.

Even though Grace had what felt like a never-ending to-do list with the opening in a few days, she'd agreed to accompany Jake on his errand. She and her brother hadn't been on the best terms lately, and she didn't want any more animosity between them.

Unfortunately, Jake hadn't mentioned that the place he was picking up some vintage baseball glove for Dad was a good half hour out of town. He'd been in a strange mood since picking her up at her apartment, uncharacteristically peppy one minute and then anxious the next.

"It's important, Gracie," he said, and gave her a bright smile. Way too bright for her to believe it was sincere. "This is going to be the best surprise ever."

"You're acting weird," she said as she looked out the window of his truck. The last time she'd driven this stretch of highway had been with Wiley on their first date.

A dull ache filled her chest at the thought of Wiley Fortune. The past few days without him had been awful. Grace missed him like crazy, even though she saw him around the hotel almost every day. But it wasn't the same.

Jillian and Jay had taken her out for a drink to celebrate her promotion. It astounded Grace that Jillian seemed to accept the decision the Fortunes had made without complaint. Grace realized that she had Jillian to thank, in part, for the opportunity. Their rivalry had pushed Grace outside her comfort zone and motivated her to go the extra mile with every task she was assigned.

Obviously, it had paid off, but the price for her success was steep. Grace wondered if she should have given Wiley more of a chance after he returned from Chicago. She'd been hurt and felt rejected because he hadn't called while away, but part of her knew she was transferring her emotions about her last relationship onto this one. Her ex's betrayal made her so sensitive to any slight. She'd built giant walls around her heart because that had seemed like the best way to protect it.

She was coming to understand that keeping potential hurt out almost meant that the love she had to give someone was trapped inside her. Yet as much as she wanted to risk her heart for Wiley, it was difficult to imagine how much it might shatter if he didn't want to try again.

She'd told herself she would wait until after the grand opening celebration and then reach out to him.

That way she'd have the time to fall apart in a way she didn't at the moment.

"You're so quiet," Jake said as he pulled into the right-hand lane of the highway and turned on his signal to exit. "Are you tired?"

"I'm fine." She leaned forward in her seat. "Where are you going? Why are you getting off here?"

"It's our exit." He gave her a sidelong glance. "What's wrong?"

"Nothing," she lied. It was the exit for the Oak Tree Inn. As Jake turned at the end of the ramp, she realized they were going to drive right past the converted farmhouse on the way to wherever this special baseball glove was located. It shouldn't bother her to see the place that she and Wiley had shared their first kiss. She'd handled much more challenging situations than a simple driveway. So why was her heart practically beating out of her chest?

"I want you to be happy, Grace." Jake's voice held a note of tenderness she wasn't used to hearing from her tough brother. "You deserve that."

"We both do," she answered.

"Wiley made you happy."

Her mouth dropped open at those words. "I don't want another lecture about the Fortunes, especially Wiley."

"It was an observation," he countered. "Not a lecture."

She smiled despite the sadness coursing through her. "I figured the lecture was coming next."

"You have no idea what's coming next," Jake said softly, and then shocked Grace by pulling into the parking lot of the Oak Tree Inn.

"Jake…"

"Happiness," he repeated. "You're a big girl, Gracie, and it's about time we all start treating you like one. I have a feeling I could learn something from Wiley Fortune in that regard. It's not up to me to determine what makes you happy. That's your decision. Now you just have to be brave enough to make it."

Her breath was coming out in shallow puffs. "What are you doing, Jake?"

After pulling to a stop in front of the inn, he reached over and opened the passenger-side door. "Hopefully giving you a little nudge in the right direction."

Too shocked to argue, Grace stepped out of the car. She'd barely closed the door when Jake took off, leaving her standing in the middle of nowhere in a cloud of dust.

"That wasn't exactly how he and I planned it."

She whirled around to the inn's front door to see Wiley walking toward her.

"You planned this?" Her brain felt like it was full of cotton, and her knees had gone weak. The thought that she could actually use her scooter or the crutches to help her balance almost made her smile. Almost.

"Jake agreed to bring you out here," Wiley said, his tone tentative. "I thought he was going to stay until we had a chance to talk."

"What if I don't want to talk?" she demanded, because it irritated her how good it felt to see him. She didn't want it to feel good. She wanted to stay strong and focused on the grand opening. That was her plan.

Wiley reached into the pocket of his dark jeans and pulled out a set of keys. "Take my car."

She narrowed her eyes. "So you had my brother drop me here, but you don't expect me to stay? I get that I'm tired, but I really don't understand what's going on right now."

"I should have asked Nicole or Megan for help," Wiley muttered, running an agitated hand through his hair. "They would have come up with a better plan. I'm sorry, Grace. I wanted tonight to be perfect. I thought if we were at a place that held good memories…" He gestured to the inn. "That first night we had dinner was one of the best nights of my life."

"Me, too," she whispered, suddenly nostalgic for the night when things had seemed so simple. He took a step forward, then stopped again.

"I asked your brother to help me win you back."

Grace choked back a snort. "And he agreed?"

Wiley shrugged. "He brought you to me, right?"

"I suppose he did." She glanced behind her, half expecting to see Jake come tearing back into the parking lot. "Wait." She turned back to Wiley. "You want to win me back?"

"More than anything," he confessed. "The fact is I'm miserable without you. It's like you brought the color to my life and now I'm stuck with boring black and white. I miss the color, Grace. I miss you."

She swallowed as emotion welled up in her throat. "It felt like you walked away without looking back," she told him. "You left for Chicago. You left me behind like I was nothing."

"I'm sorry." He moved closer until she could look up into his handsome face and see the golden flecks in his eyes. Heat radiated from him, and she had to force herself not to reach for him. She needed to stay strong. "I thought about you all the time. I hated being away from you."

"Why didn't you call?"

"I'm an idiot," he said with a harsh laugh. "I felt guilty that things had gone to hell back in Chicago while I was here with you. I told myself that I needed to make it right for the firm before I left the city. I thought you knew how I felt, Grace."

She shook her head.

"I love you," he whispered. "I think I fell a little bit in love that first night. Then I almost lost you before we ever had a chance."

Hope unfurled in her chest like a flower after a rainstorm. "What do you mean left the city?" As much as Grace loved hearing those three words from him, she was having trouble following this conversation. Did Wiley really—

"I quit my job," he said. "I'm going to join a firm out of Austin. Most of the work I do will be from Rambling Rose. I want to be here with you...for you."

He held up a hand when she would have spoken, and thank heaven for that because she had no idea how to respond. "But I'm staying no matter what you decide, Grace. I love you. That won't change. But even more, I respect you. I respect your strength and your integrity and the way you never give up. I don't want to give up on us, but the choice is yours."

Hers. He was giving her the power to decide her own fate, although Grace now realized she'd had it all along. She'd just been too scared to truly claim the life she wanted. Wiley had helped her see that she deserved to do just that.

Unable to resist one more moment, she threw her arms around him and pressed her mouth to his. "I love you, Wiley," she said against his lips. "I love the man you are and the way you believe in me. I love how you make me feel like I can do anything."

"You can, sweetheart." His arms tightened around her, and she could feel his heart thumping in his chest. "You can do anything, and I'm so damn grateful that you're choosing me. I will love you for always, Grace. I'm going to spend the rest of our lives proving that I'm the man who deserves you."

"You don't have to prove anything to me." She nuzzled her face into the crook of his neck, feeling like she'd finally come home. "I love you just the way you are."

He claimed her mouth again, kissing her until they were both breathless.

"Would you like to go upstairs?" he asked as he pulled away with a sexy grin.

"Did you get us a room here?" She grinned.

"I rented out the entire inn," he told her with a wink. "The whole place is ours for the night."

"And you're mine forever," she said. Joy exploded through her entire body, and she kissed him again.

* * * * *

MILLS & BOON

Coming next month

ITALIAN ESCAPE WITH THE CEO
Nina Milne

'What's wrong?'

'Nothing. Just keep talking. But I think we've been spotted.' Out of the corner of her peripheral vision, she saw someone point at their pod, camera in hand. 'We *have* been spotted.' Her mind went into overdrive, on automatic she appraised the scene. Champagne, private pod, the whole thing shrieked of date night. This was the perfect set up for a launch of their relationship, discovered by accident, it would reek of authenticity.

Instinct took over; and leaning over she kissed him; her intent had been a simple quick featherlight brush of the lips but she hadn't bargained for her body's reaction. Or his. Because it wasn't enough, the sheer giddy sensation whirled her head. After a first startled second where he froze, he turned his body, raised his hands and cupped her face in his hands, the firm cool grasp made her catch her breath.

Then he deepened the kiss, slowly languorously as if they had all the time in the world and Ava forgot where she was; forgot everything except this heady moment in time where nothing mattered except the sweet sensations that glided through her whole body. Then all too soon it was over, the wheel literally stopped turning and Ava realised they were near the top.

As she pulled away she caught sight of his expression, knew it mirrored her own. Shell shock, surprise. All wrong screamed the one bit of her brain that was still in gear. Pull this together. Seamlessly she pulled a smile to her lips and whispered. 'Don't look surprised.' Knew that a photo like that splashed on social media would give away too much.

To her relief Liam got it instantly, leant forward to hide his expression, looked as though he were whispering sweet nothings in her ear and then he moved away to pick up the champagne bottle to top up their glasses, a smile of sorts on his lips.

Ava focused on breathing, sipped the champagne, wished it were the bubbles that were swirling her head rather than the aftermath of the kiss. 'Sorry. I reacted on instinct – I saw an opportunity to make this look real and I took it without thinking.'

'There's no need to apologise – you took me by surprise that's all.' With an obvious effort he cleared his throat, brought his voice to a normal tone. 'What do you think will happen now?'

Continue reading
ITALIAN ESCAPE WITH THE CEO
Nina Milne

Available next month
www.millsandboon.co.uk

COMING SOON!

We really hope you enjoyed reading this book. If you're looking for more romance, be sure to head to the shops when new books are available on

Thursday 7th January

LET'S TALK
Romance

For exclusive extracts, competitions
and special offers, find us online:

JOIN US ON SOCIAL MEDIA!

Stay up to date with our latest releases, author news and gossip, special offers and discounts, and all the behind-the-scenes action from Mills & Boon...

 millsandboon

 millsandboonuk

 millsandboon

It might just be true love...

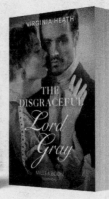

MILLS & BOON
MEDICAL
Pulse-Racing Passion

Set your pulse racing with dedicated, delectable doctors in the high-pressure world of medicine, where emotions run high and passion, comfort and love are the best medicine.